# THE RIVER OF TEARS

MARCUS LEE

# THE RIVER OF TEARS

THE CHOSEN BOOK III

Paperback ISBN: 9798371331151
Hardback ISBN: 9798378025787

For more information visit: www.marcusleebooks.com

First paperback edition Feb 2023
First eBook edition Feb 2023

**BY THE SAME AUTHOR**

***

**THE CHOSEN TRILOGY**

Book 1 - THE MOUNTAIN OF SOULS

Book 2 - THE LAST HOPE

Book 3 - THE RIVER OF TEARS

***

**THE GIFTED AND THE CURSED TRILOGY**

Book 1 - KINGS AND DAEMONS

Book 2 - TRISTAN'S FOLLY

Book 3 - THE END OF DREAMS

***

Follow the author at:

www.marcusleebooks.com
Twitter: marcusleebooks
Facebook: marcusleebooks
Bookbub: marcus-lee
Instagram: marcusleebooks

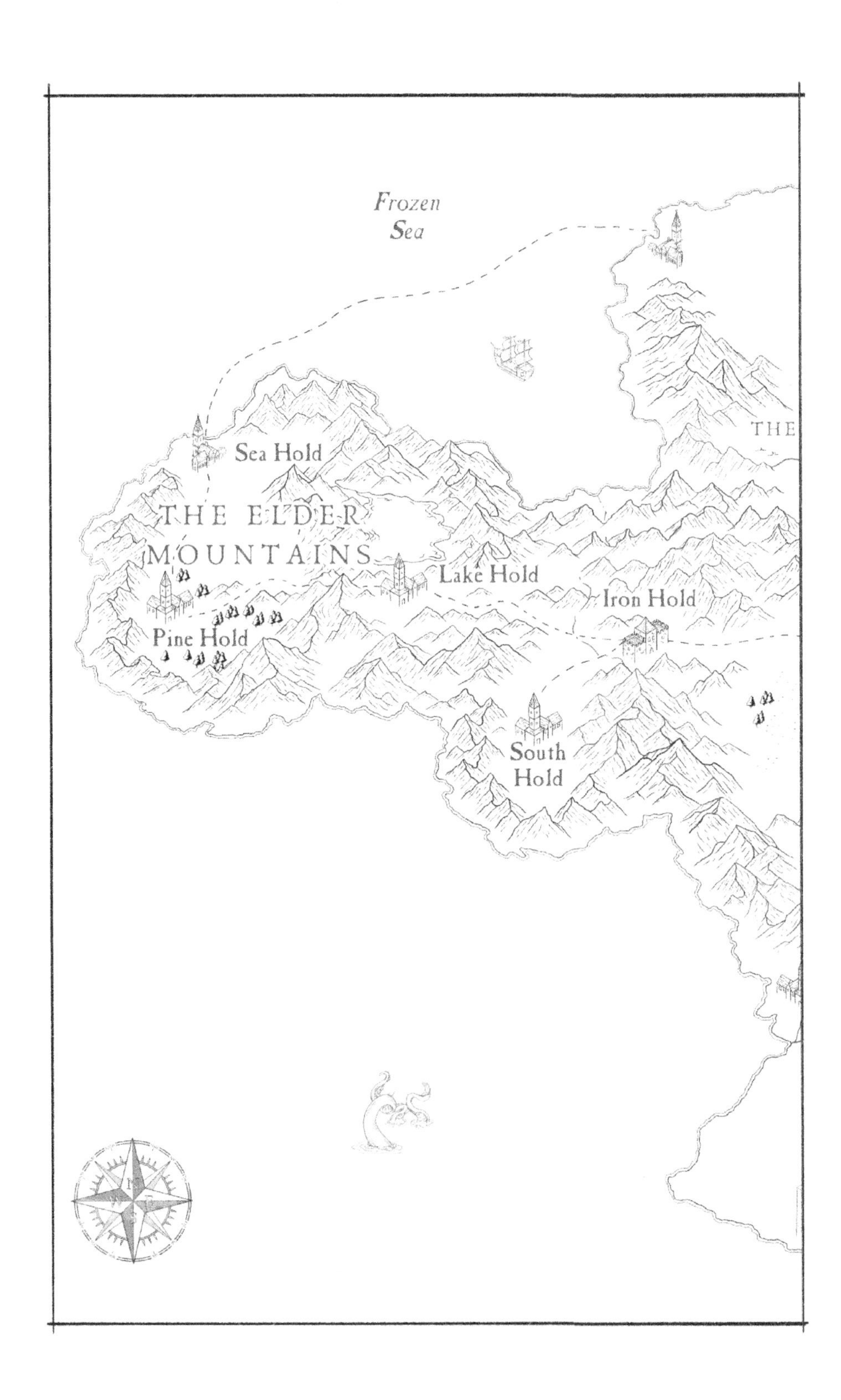

Frozen Sea
Sea Hold
THE ELDER MOUNTAINS
Lake Hold
Iron Hold
Pine Hold
South Hold
THE

Frozen Sea
Ice Hold
ICELANDIA
FIELDS OF GRASS
Highnor
Ast
ASTORIA
Eastnor
SURIA
Midnor
DELNOR
ROLANTRIA
High Delnor
Southnor
HASTIA
Isle of Sins
TARS
Lizard's Reach
THE SEA OF SAND
SSYTHLA

# CHAPTER I

Darkness.

For almost everyone, it's not the peaceful kind, the kind that holds you in its soft, warm embrace. A blanket of security as you dream, sweet, sweet dreams. No. It's the kind that's full of terror, gut-wrenching, bowel-loosening, monsters in the dark terror.

There's no doubt in anyone's mind that monsters are all too real and lurk in the darkness.

If only this was a tale to scare children to sleep at night. But no, this is our world, where going to sleep can mean death, for who knows when the monsters might come out to feast. Ogres, hags, and ssythlans, to name but a few, and now, human monsters as well.

During the night, those who disappear leave only a lingering scream and blood behind to tell of their passing. During the day, hundreds are escorted from the tunnels by armed ogres or ssythlans to begin their long journey west.

It's hard to believe that what humanity is experiencing now has happened repeatedly throughout the ages. How often has the history of the fey invasion been meticulously erased? When was the first time, and will there ever be a last?

Such are my thoughts as I open my eyes.

For me, there's no darkness. Changing into a fey certainly has benefits, for everything is revealed as if I were soulless again. I smile grimly, ensuring my senses are attuned to the surroundings before creeping from my sleeping niche.

The slumbering forms of injured soldiers lie everywhere, and I tread unsteadily around them. There might be no black in this world for me any longer, but there's red; so much red.

As I gaze upon them, I see glowing, pumping red hearts and the blood being pushed around their veins like lava. The hunger this evokes sickens me. I'm now part of this world's problem. Yet I won't give in to my fey desires, at least not on the innocent, especially when it can be at the expense of the unworthy.

The chamber exit beckons, and I leave temptation behind as I familiarise myself with the network of tunnels stretching out before me like strands of a spider's web. There's no rush, and I take my time, always conscious of the way back to safety if the need arises.

Whichever turn I take, the tunnel floors are lined with the huddled forms of men, women, and children. Some are awake, eyes wide, staring blankly into the darkness, unable to see their hands in front of their faces. Others clutch one another, hands clamped over mouths, trying to remain silent lest a whimper brings about their doom.

The air everywhere is thick with the stench of human misery, and it's almost overwhelming. The foulness of human excrement, rotting wounds, vomit, sweat, blood and tears, a cocktail of defeat and despair. It reminds me of when I was first Chosen. The seemingly endless journey in the ship's hold, the room with the bottomless pit, the fights for survival ... and death. I breathe deeply, a warped sense of nostalgia washing over me. For me, this almost feels like home.

A distant, flickering light catches my attention.

I advance, pausing to let a wave of dizziness pass, then continue, avoiding the humanity at my feet that remains unaware of my passing, drawing closer to the source, a flaming torch.

Light in the darkness should represent hope, dispel fears, and symbolise good and righteousness.

Sadly, the scene it illuminates is sickening, not that this broken world surprises me anymore.

Anger gives me strength as I approach the edge of the illuminated chamber.

Before me, the bodies of a man, a woman and a little girl are on the ground. They didn't have a chance against the five-strong gang armed with knives standing over them. I can tell the man tried to fight against his assailants from the defensive gashes on his arms and hands. How sad that this family had survived the fey invasion only to end their days here.

When I consider their demise and the woman's half-naked corpse, I struggle to see how the fey are worse than these scum.

My injuries are excruciating, and every breath has me swallow back a groan. The wounds in my side, back, and shoulder are festering, while my forehead burns with fever. I'm hardly fit to stand, let alone fight. Yet, what's about to occur, is part of my healing process, something I'd realised having survived the mortal wounds I'd suffered on the battlefield.

The life force in the dying ogre's blood as it spurted across my face and into my mouth had kept me alive. Barely. I can still recall its sweet taste ...

*Focus, Malina!*

Being physically weak, my magic answers reluctantly, yet it's enough.

The single torch lighting this tragic scene flickers and dies, extinguished by the gust of wind that certainly has no place in a tunnel this far below the earth.

'What the hell?' the skinny man holding the torch moans, and he starts patting himself down for a sparking stone.

I walk right up to him, his face pulsing red with blood. The dead torch in his hand glows with residual heat.

'You bloody idiot,' growls a brute of a man. 'What the hell did you do?'

'It doesn't matter as long as he sparks it up again. Now hush!' hisses a curly-haired woman.

Her authoritative voice shows she's the leader of this small gang.

I blow softly into the skinny man's face.

'Did you feel that?' he whispers, shaking uncontrollably.

'You'll feel my foot up your arse if you don't get that torch lit right away,' snarls a pock-faced thug.

Few like the dark. Even these, whose souls are black as night.

I circle the group, hissing softly. It's unnecessary, foolhardy even to let them know of my presence. But I want them to feel the same dreadful fear of death that their victims had experienced in the last moments of life.

'Something's bloody in here with us,' mewls another woman, sobbing.

They all draw daggers. Unfortunately, it seems the fey weren't too bothered in searching the civilians they incarcerated here. By comparison, anyone who'd fought on the battlefield had been left with only their clothes.

I grimace, feeling faint. Summoning that wind has brought me close to my limits.

It's time.

Reaching out, I swiftly grab the chin and the back of the skinny man's head and twist savagely. The snap of his neck echoes around the chamber. I grab the heavy torch from his lifeless grasp as he collapses. Frustratingly, the dagger escapes my clutches and clatters on the stone, but I sweep it up, cursing silently.

'Lester. Are you alright?' asks the leader.

'Yeah, I'm fine,' grumbles the brute. He slowly kneels, questing with his empty hand until he encounters the warm body. 'Festerlo is dead,' he whispers.

Those are the last words to leave his lips as I viciously swing the heavy torch into his head. He drops with a heavy thud on top of his erstwhile comrade.

'Oh, gods!' cries the younger woman.

I move behind her, giving her a shove into *pock-face.*

As she collides with him, they panic, stabbing each other in a frenzy. Against the backdrop of greys, the fountains of bright red droplets are mesmerising as they spurt from terrible wounds. Even as they collapse, screaming to the ground, they stab wildly until their last breath.

The gang leader backpedals, never realising that I'm already behind her.

The blinding pulse of her frantically bleeding heart is mesmerising, and an irresistible need overwhelms me. With trembling hands, I tuck the dagger into my waistband and quietly place the torch on the ground.

Grabbing her knife hand, I pull her against me, holding tight.

I want to tell her how she's brought this on herself, how this is retribution for her evil deeds. There are so many things I want to say, but I can't because my teeth are already deep in her neck, and the taste of her blood is as sweet as the golden elixir of life.

I close my eyes and drink.

***

I'm certain my absence has gone unnoticed because there's no light in these tunnels at night. The moon globes go out, people try to snatch some sleep, and torches are generally too valuable to leave burning.

As I lie on the cold stone floor, tucked behind two large crates, my thoughts drift as I rest, eyes closed, strength returning.

After my hunt, there's no denying that I'm one of this world's monsters. I'd purposely sought another human's blood to extend my life.

Even worse, I realise it wasn't the first time.

There was the brute who'd followed me into the marsh as I journeyed to Iron Hold with the Last Hope, and the soldier who'd supposedly run away as we fled back to High Delnor. Then, the thin man who'd followed me into the industrial district with murder and worse on his mind.

Through some kind of protective amnesia, my human side had hidden these memories. Now my fey side relishes in their return.

When had I started to become this monster?

When I'd joined with Nogoth, and he'd bitten me? I'd changed dramatically since then, but perhaps it was way before.

Yes.

It had started back at the Mountain of Souls. The stripping away of my innocence, losing the ability to feel guilt and empathy at a human level. We might have been left with love, but that's because it was the ultimate way to bind and control us all. To love Nogoth, our missions, where we lived, even one another. All part of a process that had been honed to perfection over millennia.

Yes, that's when my change started.

Is there any part of me left that's human?

I open my eyes as a moon globe brightens, bringing a faint light to the darkness, the only sign that a new day is dawning above ground. Groans, whispered curses, and other sounds of suffering begin to replace the silence.

Footsteps approach. They're laboured, heavy with the weight of defeat. A shadow falls across me.

'How are you today?'

I prop myself up, wincing.

'Like a bloody ogre stuck me with a dagger, and another shoved a spear through me! What about you, Dimitar?'

The Major's face creases at my using his first name, but only partially. The left side is a frozen mess. One eye is bloodied and glazed, never to see again, and everything else a mass of bruises.

'Just a small headache. Nothing to complain about!'

We've been exchanging this greeting for a few days, and it still elicits a smile.

Let me check your wounds.' His voice brooks no disagreement as he takes a torch from its wall bracket. 'Care to do the honours?'

A touch of my finger and it blazes into life.

With a grimace, I pull back my filthy shirt. It's covered in dried, black blood, mostly ogre, but a lot is mine. Kneeling down, Dimitar carefully removes a dressing to inspect the dagger wound in my shoulder and sniffs my skin. Since being stabbed, it's been releasing a torrent of pus and is a serious cause for worry. With a non-committal grunt, he tosses the dressing aside and lifts up my shirt. After unwrapping my bandaged torso, he examines the spear wound, front and back.

He shakes his head in disbelief and casts the fouled fabric aside.

'Still bad?'

'Hah,' he scoffs softly. 'If I wasn't seeing it, I wouldn't believe it. The corruption in your wounds was terrible yesterday, but it's entirely disappeared. They've healed a week's worth in the last day. I don't think you need checking on anymore. You should have been dead, Malina. I've seen enough injuries in my lifetime to know that.'

'I still hurt like hell,' I grumble.

'Who doesn't?'

He's right. There are thousands, maybe tens of thousands, here in the tunnels beneath High Delnor, and everyone is suffering, civilian or soldier alike. It isn't just injuries sustained in combat, although there are plenty of those. It's the pain of losing fathers and mothers, brothers and sisters, sons and daughters. It's a soul-deep pain that feeds on the absence of hope, an uncertain future, and not knowing when death might come to claim you ... just like that poor family last night.

Dimitar slowly climbs to his feet, using a crate of supplies to help him balance. His movements are slow, a sure sign of his head injury. Reaching down with his stone hand, he holds mine and pulls me upright.

'To think we considered these tunnels to be part of our salvation, and instead, they helped seal our doom,' he mutters to no one in particular as he turns away.

'No one could have known they were made by the fey.' I console him.

Yet that's not true. If only I'd seen them before the battle, I'd have been able to tell.

The tunnels are smooth, the work of ssythlan magic, not hands. They remind me of the Mountain of Souls, only these are much larger because they serve a dual purpose. First, to allow a sizeable attacking force to come up under the citadel unseen, and second, to imprison the survivors once the battle was over.

However, Nogoth and his fey don't want us to die here. Well, at least not in the thousands.

Unsurprisingly, all weapon crates, spare armour and crafting implements have been removed, but perhaps a quarter of the original supplies remain. There's dried food, fresh water, medical supplies, and of course, frozen fish. Who knows how long it will need to last? But Dimitar has already implemented strict rationing, and it's being felt by everyone.

'Major.'

The salutation is uttered a hundred times as we check on the wounded soldiers while walking around the large supply chamber we've commandeered. A week ago, these people were part of elite fighting forces, irrespective of which kingdom they fought for. Now they resemble little more than a group of battered people desperately clinging to survival.

However, routines are being re-established. Almost every soldier has rudimentary training in healing, and I briefly watch a bedraggled but still beautiful Tarsian sergeant breaking fast with a mixed group of lightly injured. They all bear satchels full of bandages and salves and will soon head out into the tunnels to administer aid to those within reach.

Another group is charged with food distribution and ensuring everyone in the chamber is fed before the tunnel dwellers come for theirs.

As we approach the still form of a lightly bandaged woman, it's evident from her pallor that she'll never wake up again. A few more steps and another ghostly corpse. When there's nothing good left to look forward to, even non-lethal wounds can be deadly when the will to live is absent.

'I need four volunteers,' Dimitar calls.

He could order these men and women, but believes he no longer has the right. He's told me, tears in his eyes, of how he feels the heavy guilt of failure.

Neither he nor Farsil foresaw the attack through the tunnels or from the sea. It doesn't matter that the rest of us didn't either. It was their responsibility, and they were blind to it. Now, as the highest-ranking survivor, he feels the blame for High Delnor's loss squarely on his shoulders.

Three lightly injured women and a man step forward, nodding respectfully.

'Please bring them,' Dimitar says, indicating the corpses.

He leans on me a little as we head toward the rear of the storage chamber. The air cools as we near the back, and our breath clouds.

We pass through a narrow entrance ahead of the others into the ice chamber. The light here is dim but steady, a moon globe hanging from the centre of the ceiling.

'Over there.' Dimitar gestures.

The corpse bearers dutifully lay the deceased down and leave.

I stand quietly while Dimitar murmurs a silent prayer. I'd given up on the gods long ago, although I occasionally use their names in vain.

More than fifty bodies are piled against the back wall, most already encased in ice. The frozen faces stare back, distorted, a hideous reflection of their former selves. On the other side of the chamber are hundreds of barrels of frozen fish, drinking water ... and one other thing.

I've only been here a minute, and I can detect my magic struggling to keep me warm. It's as weak as I am, and I don't want to linger more than I have to, yet I can't leave, not quite yet, not without trying.

'Come on, Kral. Even for you, it's too cold,' I call as I walk over, 'You were black and blue yesterday, and now you're just blue.'

My joke falls on deaf ears, so I put my arm around his shoulders. He might actually be warmer than me because he's encased in bandages, with only his face visible. He looks terrible and stares at the bodies in the ice while clutching a half-empty bottle of medical alcohol. There's a sizeable pile of discarded and broken ones behind him.

Does he see the face of his dead brother staring back at him? I'm not sure if he sees anything other than that final battle. Knowing Kral, he's replaying it a thousand times in his head, wondering how he could have done better ... how he could have won.

The thing is, he had won. He'd beaten a warrior-king who'd honed his skills for hundreds of years. The blow Kral had struck should have sent Nogoth to whatever hell awaited him, but it hadn't.

'You need food to keep up your strength, not alcohol!' Dimitar admonishes him softly, picking up a plate of untouched food from the ground and putting it on Kralgen's lap. 'We need you, Kral!'

Dimitar tries to gently pry the bottle from Kral's hand without success.

Kralgen manages a wan smile.

'Only the strong survive. Perhaps humankind doesn't deserve to. I know I don't.'

His words are slurred, his eyes slightly glazed, the harsh smell of neat spirit on his breath.

I kneel before him, and where Dimitar failed, I succeed and place the bottle on the floor.

'You beat him, Kral. In his entire life, I doubt Nogoth has ever been beaten.'

'Yet here we are!' Kral replies, dull eyes looking around. 'Food for the fey!'

I feel like slapping him, shouting at him. To witness his self-pitying drunkenness fills me with disgust. But I know that's due to my training, and everyone takes defeat differently. He isn't alone, far from it. Just outside the chamber, hundreds of soldiers and civilians barely eat or drink, perhaps hoping to simply slip away before the true horror begins.

I just don't want Kral to join them.

'What would Alyssa want you to do? Do you think she'd want you to give up, to drown yourself in alcohol?' It's a low blow meant to shock him. Kral's eyes narrow for a moment, but the anger they contain dies away before it takes hold.

'Maybe I'll go and ask her.' His voice breaks a little. 'I miss her, and she'll be waiting.'

Dimitar shakes his head subtly at me, but I push a little more.

'She died so you would live, Kral,' I say softly, kissing his forehead. 'It isn't your time to die ... not until we've avenged her death. You found a way to defeat Nogoth in your fight. Now I need something else from you. I need you to find a way to kill him.'

Kralgen looks up at me, and I sense the depth of his remorse. Like Dimitar, he feels the weight of defeat for thousands, especially his beloved Icelandian warriors who had so readily accepted him as their king, so few of whom had survived.

'I'm thinking of little else,' he sighs, voice trembling, verging on a sob. 'But every time I do, my thoughts return to one thing.'

'What's that, Kral?. Tell me,' I urge, trying through sheer force of will to reignite the fire that used to burn so brightly within him.

He grimaces, and to my surprise, leans forward to kiss my forehead.

'It's you, Malina. I'll never be able to kill him, not now I've just got the one hand.' He holds up his bloodied stump, swathed in bandages.

Kral's torment is so apparent that I think he'd have been happier had Nogoth taken his head.

'But you, you're the King Slayer.' He laughs bitterly, then continues. 'So it's your mission to find a way to slay that bastard! As for me, it's time for another drink.'

He turns his back and picks up a bottle, shoulders shaking as he hides his tears.

***

Another morning, and I'm much better. Rest and feeding on the gang leader have helped replenish most of my physical and magical strength and healed my wounds.

So why does my soul still feel weak?

Being defeated is hard to overcome, yet it's more than that.

I never thought I could miss the sun, the rain, the night stars or the moons so much. Simple things that gifted me their beauty, which I took for granted until they were denied me. I'm certain everyone else feels the same.

I munch my way happily through four dried siege biscuits, then reluctantly choke down a frozen fish. If only there was something other than water or alcohol to take away the taste. Incredible how the taste of blood is now so sweet, maybe ...

Damn.

I curse my train of thought.

Shouts and crying echo into the chamber from far away, accompanied by bestial roars and coarse ogre voices. The first time this had happened, we'd thought the end had come, but the ogres are here to shepherd, not kill. Accompanied by ssythlan mages, they create entrances on the tunnel walls at two different points and corral the unfortunates in between to the surface, either as food or more likely to begin the long journey back to the fey world.

The more seriously wounded are left behind to heal further. Understanding this, gang members have turned to wearing bloodied bandages stolen from the genuinely injured. It's a despicable strategy that ensures the thugs escape judgement day at the hands of the fey for a little longer.

What will I do on the day the fey come for me?

Capitulate and go quietly or fight and die, taking a few with me before I'm overwhelmed?

I smile because now that I'm recovering, there's a third option.

It's time to plan an escape.

Killing Nogoth will have to wait. Perhaps others will fare better.

Physical exertion always helps me concentrate, so I rise smoothly to my feet. My lower back has a slight twinge, but my shoulder is no longer stiff. I have a little space behind the empty crates I'd positioned to give me some privacy, so I stretch and gently exercise, testing my body alongside this new train of thought.

When I finish, it's to find Dimitar sitting a respectful distance away. However, the embarrassed look when I meet his eye suggests he's been watching a while.

'The strength and resilience of youth,' he says, limping over.

It pains me to see him so afflicted. I'm sure he'll recover his strength, even if not his vision in time. But in time for what?

To be eaten or sent to another world.

'Let's visit Kral,' I suggest. 'I want to share some ideas.'

'He's drinking already and not the most talkative at the moment, but sure, let's try.' Dimitar wrinkles his nose. 'I can't believe no latrine barrels were positioned in the tunnels and chambers. This stench is awful. People will get sick if they just relieve themselves everywhere.'

I can only agree. The air is rank, and every breath tastes foul.

'You seem to forget that Syrila was charged with preparing these tunnels. Their absence isn't an oversight. If people are desperate to get out of here, they're less likely to resist when they're taken.'

Dimitar nods.

'It's just another bloody thing to take care of.'

I sigh. He's right because nothing is ever easy. Yet on the flip side, these challenges keep everyone busy, which is a boon. Idle hands and minds are no one's friend in this environment.

'At least we can do something about it,' I say, looking around. 'We have empty crates for refuse, soiled clothes, bandages, fish bones and the like. Then, there are the fish barrels. When defrosted, there's always unusable saltwater in the bottom. They can be used for latrines.'

Dimitar points toward some carts that had helped bring everything down in the first place.

'Those can be used to move everything around. Give me a moment.'

He steps aside to talk with a group of lightly injured who appear happy as he instructs them on what to do. Dimitar might not want to give orders and couches everything as a request, but there's no denying the quiet aura of authority that has people do as he asks.

We enter the ice chamber, making way for a couple of soldiers rolling out a barrel of frozen fish.

Kral looks over, and I'm sad to see another untouched platter beside him.

He's sitting on a crate, bluer than ever. It must be his magic sustaining him in the cold, for however robust he is, I can't see how else he'd survive in such an environment. However, alcohol is probably helping.

'Why do you like it in here so much, Kral? It's freezing. It would be far more agreeable if you joined us in the other chamber,' Dimitar complains.

Kralgen gestures at two crates in front of him.

'I prefer the isolation.'

He pauses but continues when neither Dimitar nor I say anything. 'Ice-olation. It's cold, and I prefer to be alone!' He laughs somewhat darkly and points. 'The way out is that way.'

Dimitar chooses to ignore the insinuation and chuckles instead.

'That's truly awful.'

A hint of a twinkle appears in Kral's eyes, and my heart leaps.

'So, what's on your mind, King Slayer?' He punctuates the question by taking an overly long swig of spirit, and my brief moment of excitement fades.

I take a deep breath. I don't like what I'm going to propose, and they'll like it even less. Yet there's no turning back now. What I have to say needs to be said.

'We think the mission to kill Nogoth is everything, and nothing else matters. We're sitting here defeated because we think we lost the war, but we didn't. We lost a battle. Admittedly, it was a big one, but it won't be humanity's last because the war is far from over, and that's because it will come to this world again in a thousand years. We just need to ensure it's better prepared next time.'

'What are you trying to say?' Dimitar's eyes narrow.

'The three of us escape, and forget about killing Nogoth for now and focus on survival.'

'We can't leave the rest here to die!' Dimitar declares aghast.

Even Kralgen appears shocked.

'Honour demands we die trying to kill the Fey King,' he admonishes, his bushy eyebrows coming together. 'Are you taking even the hope of that away from me?'

I put my head in my hands briefly. I knew this was going to be difficult, but I must make them see sense. With renewed determination, I look them in the eye.

'Have you ever considered that Nogoth might not be here anymore? He could be anywhere by now. But even if he is, we can't defeat his army because all our troops are dead or captured. We can't assassinate him because he's invulnerable to weapons. I don't know if poison would work, but we don't have any, even if he invited us to dinner. He's stronger than us and hasn't even used his magic yet. He's unbelievably powerful in that regard because he's lived so long. We wouldn't stand a chance.

'A thousand years ago, the survivors and their children, and maybe even their children's children, built the wall at Iron Hold, blocked the World Gate at Pine Hold and built a fortress at Midnor, maybe more. They had the right idea and the foresight to prepare, but they didn't know what we do. We know precisely when Nogoth will return and that the ssythlans will pave the way with their machinations and the next generation of Chosen.

'If we survive, we can ensure the world is so well prepared that his armies won't even be able to cross into our world next time. Our bones might be dust when that happens, but the victory will be ours!'

It hurts me to see their disappointment, but they'll come to understand.

'But why just the three of us?' Dimitar demands. 'There are thousands down here, and Kral and I aren't at our best.'

Kral waves his stump at me for emphasis, then pours alcohol over the bandages.

I take Dimitar's hands in my own. It's a cheap way to make him more malleable but needs must.

'What other choice do we have? An uprising will fail and lead to instant death for those who participate. A larger escape will be doomed because it will be spotted immediately. Don't believe for a moment that the fey aren't keeping an eye on us!'

I can see from Dimitar's reaction that he hadn't considered we are being spied upon. As for Kralgen, I don't think he's bothered.

'My magical strength has recovered, so I'm confident I can find and enter the hidden tunnels the ogres use to take our people away. We'll be going in blind, not knowing where they lead or what we'll encounter, but with our skills and some luck, I'm sure we can get out of the city.'

Credit to both Kral and Dimitar; they take their time considering my words, although it's possible Kral is just trying to stay awake. The big man sighs, running the fingers of his remaining hand through his long hair and shrugs indifferently.

'I've never been good at strategy, just fighting. Now, thanks to losing my hand, I'm useless at that too. So, sure, let's run away and lose every shred of honour we have remaining.'

I grip Kralgen's forearm.

'You're wrong, Kral. There's no loss of honour in doing this, far from it!'

'Even if we're not opposed to your plan, the problem is executing it,' Dimitar says.

'Exactly,' Kralgen mutters. 'There won't be a street or house in High Delnor that isn't crawling with fey day and night. You could probably get us out of this place,' he says, gesturing around with his bottle. 'But the city … that's another matter.'

Even drunk, Kralgen has spotted a flaw in my plan. Luck will only get us so far. I could probably walk out in plain sight if it were just me. A Saer Tel on the streets at night wouldn't draw attention, but there'd be no disguising or explaining Kral or Dimitar with me.

Dimitar snaps his stone fingers, a smile spreading across his face.

'Kral's right, and he didn't even mention there are probably gargoyles on every rooftop, nor are the sewers big enough for him or me. So, how about having the fey escort us out of the city. We go as prisoners, and when High Delnor fades from sight, you use your blood magic on our guards.'

'Don't rely on me for too much help. I'm half the man I used to be,' Kral whispers, choking the words out.

'Kral, you're still as strong as an ox.' I reassure him. 'I wasn't feeling good about leaving everyone behind, but if we're in a large group, there's a chance I can free those who travel with us.'

'So, what next, oh mighty King Slayer?' Kral asks, spirit running down his beard as he gulps thirstily from a new bottle.

Dimitar looks at me sideways. It's a habit he's picking up as if self-conscious of his dead eye.

Both of them are physical wrecks.

'First, we need to cauterise that wrist properly. Then, it's eat, sleep and exercise. I need you and Dimitar close to full strength. We'll give it a week, and if we're not taken in the interim, we'll make sure we are after that.'

'I'll start with drinking; that helps me sleep.' Kralgen laughs. 'I won't feel you cauterising my wrist either!'

'Let's do it last thing tonight.' I suggest.

'We'll see,' Kral mutters.

Only the strong survive. We live to kill.

How things have changed,

To survive, we now need to run.

***

As Dimitar and I cross back into the main supply chamber, he pauses at a large timeglass and turns it upside down. Taking a stick of chalk, he draws a line to join six others on the wall.

Seven days.

It's been a whole week since I was dragged from the battlefield, fading in and out of consciousness along with Dimitar and the other wounded. Six days since I began to open my eyes, five days from when I could sit up without a scream being wrenched from my mouth. Four days since I discovered Kral was still alive. Three days since Dimitar led a group of wounded soldiers to wrest the supply room back from a civilian gang that had seized it for themselves. Two days since I could walk again.

Fifteen of the bodies encased in ice resulted from the fight that now sees us overseeing food, water, and medical distribution, the way it was meant to be done, freely but rationed.

I wonder how many days it will be before I have to feed again on more than just food?

Loud, angry voices rising in complaint draw our attention. This is something that can't be ignored.

Dimitar turns toward the front of the chamber, and I follow without a second thought. There's now an unbreakable bond between us. Not the bond that Farsil had alluded to, but I'll always be there for him, especially now.

It was Dimitar's despairing voice that had initially brought me back to consciousness on the battlefield. He hadn't been shouting at me but at the ogres who were considering having me for lunch. Half the words coming out of his mouth hadn't made sense; his mind still scrambled from the blow to the head he'd received. But there he was, crouching over me, stone arm raised in defiance, ready to die so I'd have a chance at living.

I'd seen Nogoth approach, drawn to this shouting madman before I'd passed out. Afterwards, I'd dropped in and out of consciousness as I was hauled back to High Delnor on a makeshift stretcher. During those brief periods of overwhelming pain, I could see the long lines of surrendered, uninjured troops being marched west. The cleansing of this world had begun.

'I want more, damnit!' shouts a man's voice, echoed by several others.

Dimitar glances at me and shakes his head, motioning for me to stay back.

I sigh. My status, which for the civilians has fluctuated from the despicable assassin wanted for killing the High King to a tolerated ally, is now firmly back in the hated category for most of the civilians here. They will forever judge me for the colour of my skin and eyes, which marks me as a fey, not for which side I fought.

At least the soldiers accept me.

Mind you, even that would change if anyone knew what I'd done last night, including Dimitar.

I watch as the Major trudges toward the source of noise, a group of shoving, red-faced braggarts who'd obviously been part of the criminal underbelly of this city. There are about twelve of them, snide and bitter, thinking the world owes them everything for having done nothing but make trouble. I'm sure these loudmouths were part of the gang who'd initially controlled the stores until Dimitar had recovered enough to organise their removal.

Not for them, the battlefield, selflessly fighting to protect other people's lives; these scum serve only their own.

The reason for their displeasure is the meagre rations a group of soldiers hand out. Hardened biscuits, some frozen fish, and a large cup of water. Everyone who comes to the storage chamber is given the same and a coloured wooden token. The token is exchanged for more food in the evening when they're given a different token for the following morning.

It's a fair system, ensuring people only get two helpings a day. Most cram the food into their mouths immediately rather than risk it being stolen as they return to whatever part of the tunnel they've claimed.

How the other levels are faring, we've no idea.

'Who put you in charge? We certainly didn't!' shouts another man.

'None of you lot look hungry. Keeping a lot back for yourselves, are you?' yells another.

The rank hypocrisy makes me want to wring the last speaker's neck.

A shove, and an injured soldier falls to the ground.

'Give us more food!'

I can't see who shouts it, but the vehemence in the voice is ugly.

'Calm down.' Dimitar's strong voice echoes loudly as he steps between the two groups. 'We don't know how long we'll be down here, and the fey took most of the rations, so we're being frugal. Let's save our strength for fighting the fey, not each other.'

A middle-aged man sidles forward. He wears fancy clothes, yet they're filthy, worn and old. Several white scars adorn his cheeks, mementoes of a knife fight, and a tattoo of a sin-hawk's talons appear to draw blood from his neck.

'Fighting the fey! Have you seen yourself, old man?' he says. 'You tried that and lost! Look how the fey messed you all up. You were supposed to be our saviours. Thanks to you, we're doomed, but that doesn't mean we should have to go hungry!'

I spy two other groups easing their way past mothers hugging their wide-eyed children. The way they walk with arms crossed or behind their backs tells me they're concealing weapons. This isn't just a random explosion of anger but a pre-planned attempt to retake the supply chamber with the support of other gangs. Tattoos of talons, daggers, eyes, and more adorn their necks.

Who knows how many more are coming or how many have weapons to our none? They've timed it perfectly, for we're vulnerable, with many of our group dispersed in the tunnels attending to the wounded and basic sanitation.

'Be prepared,' I warn as I stride past a group of injured soldiers to support my friend.

'Please, take your turn in line.' Dimitar raises his hands placatingly.

He's trying to de-escalate things, and the other soldiers do likewise. It's a big mistake. All the soldiers are wounded, weak, and unarmed, and the thugs are emboldened by Dimitar's response.

'You might have been the law on the streets of High Delnor, but far from the glamour of citadel life, you never were,' growls *scar face* opposite him. 'Now you've chosen to feed Tarsians, Hastians, Surians and Rolantrians with our food while we go hungry!'

I'm just about to reach Dimitar's side when the man sees me.

'To make matters worse, YOU ALLY WITH THE FEY!' he screams, pointing.

As Dimitar turns toward me, the man lunges with a knife he'd concealed up his sleeve. Being half-blind, Dimitar doesn't see it coming until it's buried deep in his thigh.

'NO!' I cry, as the gang surges forward with a roar, pulling knives, daggers, and lengths of wood from within their clothing.

Unarmed and injured, the soldiers alongside Dimitar are flattened by the mob who charge into the chamber, intent on attacking everyone, irrespective of whether they're capable of resisting.

I'm desperate to help Dimitar if he's still alive, but first, I'll have to survive this onslaught, and from the numbers stacked against us, it looks unlikely. However, if I do, I'll kill every one of these bastards I can get my hands on.

'TO ME!' I yell, knowing that we stand a better chance together.

A dozen injured soldiers who are close, answer my cry and gather around. Other smaller groups form, but none of them will last long.

'Kill the fey. KILL THE FEY!' the chant goes up, and the main swarm heads toward my group.

I consider using my magic to set one or two on fire, but it will drain me, leaving me physically vulnerable. I pull a dagger from my trousers' drawstring, compliments of my hunt the night before. I'll do this the old-fashioned way. I test my footing, lower my centre of gravity and single out my first victim.

Yet the charge disintegrates as a barrel flies through the air, crunching into the mob, knocking half a dozen men down as it shatters, spilling frozen fish everywhere. The man it hit first will never rise again, and the others twist on the floor, moaning.

The loud shouts of bravado disappear as the eyes of the murdering scum look behind me.

Kralgen staggers unsteadily past, sways to avoid a hastily thrown knife, grabs a pointed chunk of ice from the ground and rams it into the chest of the knife thrower as the remainder back away quickly.

The mob are armed with all manner of weapons, and we had my dagger, but now, we have something else; Kralgen. However drunk he might be, he'd heard my rallying call.

His intervention and now his mere presence have brought this moment to teeter on a knife edge. There are only thirty or so wounded soldiers, Kralgen, and I, against, from what I can see, fifty or so members of different gangs and, without doubt, dozens more in the tunnels. If he can cow the mob, we'll survive. If not ... this won't end well.

'Which one is their leader?' Kralgen growls, ambling forward like a giant, wounded bear. His eyes are bloodshot, his words slurred, and he's swathed in bloodied bandages, but his sheer size is impossible to ignore. He looks half-dead, with his bloodied stump and bruised face, yet somehow it only makes him more foreboding.

'The one in the fancy shirt!'

I point out the man leading the mob who'd stabbed Dimitar. He may or may not be the ringleader, but it doesn't really matter. Muttered words get louder as the shock of Kralgen's attack wears off. It won't be long before the gang members regain their courage and resume their attack.

Kralgen looms over the scar-faced leader.

Credit to the man; there's no hesitation. He's probably killed plenty of people and knows a well-placed knife can end Kralgen's life, and he executes a lightning-fast stab with a stiletto blade for my friend's heart.

It never fails to amaze me how someone so big can move so damned fast, and Kralgen's horrific injuries or inebriated state don't seem to have slowed him. The man squeals in pain as his wrist is trapped in a meaty fist, and the knife drops to the floor as Kralgen squeezes hard.

'You've all made the same mistake,' Kralgen booms. 'You're afraid of the dark, you're afraid of hunger, you're afraid of the fey.' With a yank, he turns the leader around like a puppet, pushing him to his knees. 'But if you come here like this, you need to add another thing to that list.

'ME!'

Kralgen grabs the leader's neck from behind, fingers wrapping around his throat, squeezing tight while he pushes down with his forearm on the man's shoulder. *Scar face* reaches up frantically with both hands, trying to break Kralgen's grip.

Kralgen's roar is bestial as he wrenches hard. There's a horrible cracking noise, and then, Kralgen tears the man's head off. Blood spurts everywhere as he boots the torso forwards, holding his grisly trophy before him. A part of the spine juts downwards from the torn neck.

Face twisting in concentration, Kralgen does something I've rarely witnessed. He summons his magic. The next moment the flaming head bounces out into the tunnel, followed by the panicked, screaming tide of criminal flotsam.

Kralgen wipes his hand on his furs, then nods at me. He's far from being his old self, but it's a start, and I return the gesture.

Then I spring forward, alongside the other soldiers, not to chase the fleeing gang but to assist those who'd fallen.

'Dimitar!' I cry, spying him propped up against the cavern entrance where he'd dragged himself, blood pooling around him.

He smiles weakly at hearing my voice.

'Hey, girl. Come help me up. I'm feeling a little faint,' he moans.

I look at the dagger buried deep in his thigh and the blood pumping from under the hilt. An artery has been severed.

He's not going to make it.

***

# CHAPTER II

Kralgen picks Dimitar up awkwardly, but once in his arms, it's as though the Major weighs little more than a baby. Kral carries him back past the dead gang members.

'I thought I was having a bad day,' Dimitar murmurs, looking at the headless torso. Then despite his fading strength, his eyes open wide. 'Who killed that man with a frozen fish?' he gasps in disbelief.

Kralgen snorts.

'That would be me. Apparently, I'm not that useless. I thought it was a type of swordfish.'

I'm unsure if the tears coming from Dimitar's eyes are from pain or Kralgen's terrible joke.

'Lay him here.'

I point to where I sleep, and Kralgen settles Dimitar down as if he's made of glass. I grab a linen strip and tie it tightly around Dimitar's upper thigh. He grunts with pain, but I need to slow the blood loss. Every second with him is precious now.

'How does it look, Malina?' Dimitar's voice is faint.

'You'll be dead shortly,' Kralgen answers bluntly.

I sigh. Kralgen isn't mean ... he's just direct and drunk, but it's hard to remember that sometimes.

'Damn,' Dimitar mutters. 'I survive a battle against thousands of fey, and some bloody lowlife gets me instead.'

I brush his hair back, feeling his cold skin. Can my magic help? I can't just sear the artery; his leg will become gangrenous due to loss of blood flow. Nor is anyone here skilled or capable enough of amputating his leg.

My magic wriggles as I look at Dimitar's stone arm.

'I'm not ready to die,' he mutters. 'There are things I haven't said that I need to say,' he adds, turning his face away in embarrassment.

I lean forward, taking Dimitar's face in my hand. I don't love him, not the way he wants, but I desperately want him to live. I gently press my lips to his, then lean back with tears flowing down my cheeks as he smiles weakly at me.

'I might be able to save you again, Dimitar,' I say softly, gently rubbing his stone arm. 'I can try the same way as I did last time. I don't know if it will work or how it will turn out.'

Softly spoken words slip from Dimitar's lips, and I lean forward to catch the last few.

'A stone thigh is a small price to pay to walk by your side, my love.'

His words almost move me to tears, but now is the time to act.

I'm vaguely aware of Kralgen waving people away, shouting orders that no one would dare disobey, but that all recedes as I lay my hands on Dimitar's skin. It's already as cold as the stone ground beneath us.

*Do what it takes and take what you need.*

I take the knife hilt, firming my grip, and then slide it free. Blood spurts, but I place my hand over the wound.

The strength I'd regenerated pours out of me as I grip Dimitar's hand and leg. He's fallen unconscious, and it's a good thing too. I'll be joining him soon, for my vision is blurring. The gift of magic is incredible, but to be limited by my own physical strength is beyond frustrating.

The thigh beneath my hand solidifies, but still, the drain continues. I'm too tired to even sit, so I lay down, pressing my hand to Dimitar's thigh while resting my head upon his chest. Surely it's almost finished, for I'm certain I've nothing left to give.

Everything is fading, yet the magic continues to flow like a river. My heart slows, as does the passing of time, yet not the magic. It passes through me faster, a flood, unstoppable, and the noise; it's like a gale, howling past my ears.

Then ... nothing.

***

It's night-time when I awaken.

I'm as weak as a kitten, with barely the strength to open my eyes, yet I can see clearly enough. I'm covered by Kralgen's fur jerkin. It smells indescribably bad, but then everything does down here. It's matted with old and fresh blood, some Kralgen's, but mostly his deceased enemies.

And there sits the giant man, fast asleep, snoring loudly, leaning against the cavern wall. I can see his mighty heart pumping, the red blood rushing around his veins. His immense sinews and muscles might be covered by bandages, but I can see everything as though it's daylight.

My stomach rumbles, hunger pangs rippling through me.

I'm horrified. I can't need to feed yet, and certainly not on my friend.

Why am I so weak and hungry?

Then the memory of what happened earlier hits me like a stone.

I look at Dimitar lying next to me. He's not glowing; there's no beating heart, no blood pumping about his veins, and there's no warmth to his body whatsoever.

'Oh, Dimitar,' I whisper, tears coming to my eyes. 'I'm so sorry.'

Reaching out, I tenderly stroke his face, only to snatch my hand back.

No. I can't have! Yet as I gingerly run my hand over his neck, torso, then legs, the truth is beneath my fingertips. I've turned him entirely to stone.

'Malina!'

I hear my name as if on a gentle breeze rustling autumn leaves through my mind.

Am I imagining this?

'Malina!'

I rise slowly to my feet.

I'd wondered where the Saer Tel were, and here some are.

Six of them twist and twirl, dancing amongst the sleeping wounded on tiptoes, a swirling masterpiece of grace, poise and delight. They're wearing gossamer-thin clothing, which floats around them like a cloud. Yet as they rove, they each hold a slim lance within their hands that could deliver death as soundless and certain as their movement.

'Malina!'

I turn my head to the source of my name. A motionless Saer Tel crouches on a crate, fixing me with those yellow cat's eyes. She's breathtakingly beautiful, yet she serves a monster.

'Nogoth requests your presence. Come with us!'

Again, no words have been uttered from those full lips, but they still caress my mind like a lover's touch. I bristle at the command, anger rising within me.

I want to say no, to defy them, yet those lances persuade me otherwise. Whilst they haven't come near Kralgen, I won't have anyone suffer because of my stubbornness.

Nodding in acquiescence, I step lightly around Dimitar's stone body and make my way after the Saer Tel, who come together like a cloud and move toward the chamber exit.

They leap silently over the crates that act as a barricade, and I can only marvel at their athleticism. I follow suit, running lightly, launching myself; a little magical assistance, and I land softly, rolling, silently to my feet.

I sense their approval, and then we're entering a tunnel where none had been before. It closes silently behind us as a lone ssythlan weaves its hands.

If there's anything to tell my companions apart, I've yet to discern it, but the Saer Tel who'd addressed me is the only one walking. Perfectly poised, she strides with sublime grace whilst the others continue their ethereal dance. To possess such beauty yet be so dark ... it's hard to correlate the two.

'Where are we going?'

I choose my words with care, as *where are you taking me,* would infer I'm their captive. Of course, I am, but I'll not concede anything unless I have to.

'Don't speak. Just focus on me and ask silently.'

The words form in my thoughts like notes from a harp.

'Like this?'

'Exactly. You've not been taught our language, and we try to avoid sullying ourselves by using the common tongue, so this is the best way for us to converse.'

Memories of my youth return. I recall how Karson and I had sometimes understood each other's thoughts. Had he survived, would we eventually have been able to speak like this?

'So, where are we going?' I ask, focussing again on the present.

'You already know the answer to that, Sister.'

'I am not your sister!' The denial comes out harshly, yet it's met with soft laughter.

'Only those with the blood of the Saer Tel can communicate through thought alone. You might wish to discard your heritage, but your heritage will never discard you. We are the same. We are Saer Tel!'

'We are not the same. I am not evil like you!' My rebuttal is angry, instantaneous.

'Yet you kill.' Her reply is calm, a hint of amusement wrapped around the words she projects in my head.

'So do you!'

'No, we don't. No Saer Tel takes a life unless in self-defence. So, tell me, Malina, who is the evil one if my words are true? You or me?'

'The truth is you serve a master who is responsible for the death of millions!'

'Malina. I don't deny your accusation, for we all do what we must to survive, but you consciously avoided answering my question. Perhaps you should reflect on it!'

Her eyebrow arches delicately, and a hint of a smile pulls at the corner of her perfect mouth. However, I'm not ready to let this go.

'In Nogoth's valley, I saw one of your kind feed on a human. She looked demonic!'

'But she didn't kill him. Did she? Our relationship with a paired human is symbiotic and sacred. They share their life force as we protect their life. They give us their body, but we also give ours to them. It's an exchange of pleasure and pain that is highly satisfactory for both parties. As for our feeding sister's appearance, well ... were you ever judged unfairly for yours? I doubt your yellow eyes went unnoticed.'

She's right, and my anger drains away. Like Nogoth, they have all the answers, yet unlike his, I believe theirs aren't deceitful.

'I am sorry that I killed her, your sister.' The words tumble forth with little consideration, but I realise I've spoken the truth.

A shared sadness that makes my heart ache is shortly replaced by the warmth of compassion.

'Life is about balance, Malina. The gods took one sister, but we gained another.'

I'm touched and humbled by their forgiveness and acceptance. But if they're this good ...

'So why are you here if not to feast with the other beasts?'

'We are all beasts, Malina. Yet we're here to heal, not kill. It would make more sense if you understood who we are.'

Silence reigns after that as we journey up passages smoothed by magic. I'm confused by the way my feelings are changing so suddenly. I wonder if there's magic at play here that I don't understand. Yet I'm more interested in her final statement. *If you understood who we are.*

'Tell me about my heritage. Who or what are the Saer Tel?'

Approval resonates in my mind, not just from her but also from the others around me.

'Our history would take years to share, but as we have only minutes, I'll summarise as best I can. Millennia ago, we inhabited a world called Isterzia. It was beautiful, a true paradise. There we lived in symbiosis with nature, living off the land while protecting it. The forests were our home, providing us with everything we needed to thrive. Nature itself blessed us with powers that you've yet to acquire. All was perfect, a utopian life until ...'

The anguish that resonates in my mind almost brings me to tears as I share a sense of loss so acute that I feel it as my own.

'A powerful race calling themselves the Kral appeared on our world through what we now know as a World Gate. They began to destroy our forests and break apart our mountains, searching for an elusive element to feed their own magic. When our entreaties for them to stop failed, it led to war.

'Our people were annihilated. Our magic wasn't enough to defend what we held so dear, for we'd only ever used it to give life, not take it, and we were swept aside. But the torment didn't end there. The Kral killed most males of our race and exiled those of us who remained to another world, a barren and frightening wasteland they'd left behind long ago.'

'It is there that Nogoth, King of the Fey, welcomed us. He offered us protection and the gift of eternal life in return for our unswerving loyalty and service. It seemed an easy choice with our race on the verge of extinction. So, we nurtured his broken world back to health, creating a beautiful new homeland.'

There are so many questions whirring around, begging to be asked, but I know my time is limited, for wherever our destination is, it can't be far now. The power of their magic is breathtaking in its scale. I need to find out more.

'Do you use the four elements to create life?' I ask.

'No. Our magic is completely different.'

'Why? If we share the same blood?'

A gentle laugh fills my thoughts.

'We don't have the answer to everything. The traditional magic of the Saer Tel has historically never been of the brown, blue, red or white. We wield the gold, the power of life itself. You've seen us use the golden Elixir of Life to tend Nogoth's valley, but that power also exists all around us, alongside the other elements. Now we are here to heal this world at Nogoth's bidding.'

The tunnel we're in now shows signs of the citadel's foundations. I don't have much time left. I'm torn between discovering more about the Saer Tel and uncovering any useful information I could use.

'But why am I here? What does Nogoth want with me, and why hasn't he had me killed?'

'Perhaps because you are one of his Chosen or a Saer Tel.'

'No, there's more to it than that. Please tell me, Sister.'

The Saer Tel looks down as if embarrassed.

'None of our males were capable of achieving eternal life, and over the years, they died during these conquests or from old age. Since then, we've all mated with Nogoth, and whilst many have conceived, for some reason, our offspring never survive. Likewise, any human babe he's sired dies shortly after birth.

'It's possible his favour and interest toward you stem from your being a hybrid, a being of two races, two worlds. I believe he has hopes of a relationship and siring an heir with you.'

My head spins. Nogoth had mentioned a child before, but now I understand why, and I'm no less shocked for knowing the reason.

Lotane comes to mind. I had always hoped he and I would have a child one day.

'He is a handsome one. Have you paired?'

'You can see my thoughts?' I ask, aghast.

'No. But you shared his image without realising it. You harbour as much love for this man as the lust you once felt for Nogoth. Does he feel the same way about you?'

I want to hotly deny their accusation, but why lie.

'He did. But I'm not sure he does now.'

'If there's one emotion almost as powerful as love ... it's jealousy. But nothing is as powerful as true love. Let us hope you had the seeds of that!'

Stone steps are ahead, and I know my time is almost up.

'Can you help me in any way?' I ask silently. 'I misjudged you and realise that now. Help put right some of Nogoth's wrongs. Please.'

The Saer Tel gather close around me, a soft melody falling from their perfect lips as they reach out to run fingers through my hair and stroke my skin. Before hearing their story, I'd have shrugged them off in revulsion, but instead, I relax, comforted by their gentle familiarity and a sense of oneness.

'You are our sister, and we always look after our own, but we can't ...'

The sentence remains unfinished, as despairingly, time has run out. We arrive at our destination, and enter somewhere all too familiar. The Throne room.

To my utter amazement, Nogoth stands within, addressing a dozen Delnorians under the light of hundreds of candles. They nod in hurried agreement to every word he says.

As we approach, the Delnorians scurry off, surrounded by ogres. There's no aggressive behaviour from these ruthless creatures; rather, the ogres appear to be escorting them. What the hell is going on?

'Nogoth awaits. Don't endanger yourself by antagonising him.'

The Saer Tel's final words ripple in my head like water, but the feeling they give rise to is like fire.

***

Those violet eyes gaze upon me. I've seen them angry and passionate, and I'd expected to see them full of vengeance, but that's not apparent.

His smile is bright, arms open wide in a warm greeting. The King of Deceit and Misdirection doesn't waste a moment. If I were only feeling stronger, I'd attack him with everything I have, but I'm still weak from attempting to help Dimitar, and as my friend comes to mind, I stagger under the weight of my failure.

Nogoth says something in a musical tongue, and one of the Saer Tel dances off before he returns his attention to me.

'Despite the rags and smell, you're still as lovely as ever, Malina. However, I fear your trials have left you somewhat weakened. Come, sit.'

There he goes again, sitting on the floor, putting himself at my feet. He's as smooth as velvet.

I'm exhausted and have no wish to expose just how weak I am, so I sit cross-legged on the cool, polished tiles. We're not far from where I killed the High King, and I'm sure this is no coincidence.

'There's never been a Chosen like you, Malina. In all my years, none have come close. I admire your strength of spirit despite choosing the wrong side. Have you any idea how boring life can be at times when it's so long?'

I stay quiet despite wanting to say I'll happily end it for him if he's that bored.

'You've surprised me again and again. I can't tell you how grateful I am. I only wish I could have seen you defeat our champion at the World Gate; you got my whole army talking about it. Even getting dumped on my ass by your fellow Chosen, Kralgen, is something I'll remember forever, thanks to you.'

I can't help myself.

'Were you happily surprised when I killed Aigul?'

A flicker of darkness behind Nogoth's eyes and a hint of a frown is all the satisfaction he gives me.

'Tread carefully, Chosen, lest you take a step too far. It might be your friends who suffer for your insolence!' he warns, but it's offset with a smile. 'I do miss her. She could also surprise me in all manner of ways, but it was nothing compared to you!'

A pulse, that damned quickening, and my loins ache.

'I'd suggest you save that for someone who doesn't want to slit your throat!' I growl.

Nogoth smiles sadly.

'I hope you'll see me in a different light again one day.'

At that moment, the Saer Tel he'd sent away returns, and beside me, just out of my reach, places a small goblet. In it sloshes the golden Elixir of Life, and my stomach growls so loudly that Nogoth laughs while my face burns with shame.

'All the comforts of home.' Nogoth chuckles.

My thoughts are spinning. The desire to drink the elixir is overwhelming, and so is the feeling of disgust at myself. I need a distraction to help me ward against such weakness.

'What different light is that? Am I wrong in thinking you a deceitful, genocidal maniac responsible for the death of nations?' I gasp.

'You talk about my deceit, and I'll admit it wounds me, yet I deliver on my every promise. My methods might not be to your liking, but you have to cut deep to remove cancer! The greedy nobles were dealt with the moment the city was taken. Then we have the thieves, rapists, pimps and whores, not forgetting the killers, murderers and kidnappers. They will be taken back to the fey world, where they'll contribute far more than they ever did here.

'Those who remain will build a better world without fear, at least for a while. Those Delnorians you saw me with are bakers, farmers, weavers and woodsmen. Along with some stonemasons, carpenters, healers, and young women with children, they'll be spared and left behind.'

'Why?'

'Because I want the meek and the good to inherit this earth and between them usher in a new golden age of man.'

The words slip smoothly from his tongue, manipulating the truth with ease, but it's been a long time since I was the naïve fool I used to be. Anger stiffens my resolve to speak my mind.

'If only it were about removing the festering heart of civilisation, but that isn't the case. You're taking men who were once farmers, bakers and all the professions you mentioned until they were conscripted as soldiers. There are also plenty of young families with children in the tunnels below. I also fought alongside thieves and killers at Pine Hold, and there was good amongst many of them. Circumstance and manipulation can make killers of us all. You're a prime example of that, as am I, are we not?

'As for your line about the meek and good inheriting this world ... I think it has everything to do with the weaker survivors of this genocide multiplying exponentially so that when you come again in a thousand years, there'll be a bountiful harvest to reap!'

If I thought I would strike a nerve, I was mistaken. Nogoth is enjoying this conquest far too much to be unsettled by my words, and I think he's just playing with me, verbally sparring to make his day more enjoyable. He doesn't see me as a threat, just a distraction from his boredom.

'Brains and beauty, add that to your strength of spirit, the fire in your belly, and a few other things, and it reminds me why I let you live. I want us to be together, Malina!'

'I'd rather kill myself than have that happen,' I hiss.

Nogoth shakes his head.

'Now, who is lying to who? You won't take your life, Malina, because you've already shown that you're willing to do unspeakable things to save it. Have you not recently fed on the people you purport to protect?'

I want to scream it's not true, but who am I lying to.

'You're more fey than human. Why deny it?' Nogoth presses. 'The Saer Tel have sensed this, as have I. Why fight alongside the humans when they're not of your kind anymore? If you stay with them, you'll be cast out or killed sooner or later; your hunger will see to that! Save yourself that pain and come join me now. Help me make this world better, and I'll ensure your friends are safe!'

There it is. Nogoth knows he has leverage, but I mustn't show just how much.

'My friends safe? One is dead, turned entirely to stone by my hand, and the other is a mental and physical broken wreck, a shadow of his former self!'

Nogoth's laugh fills the throne room. It's so infuriatingly genuine that despite feeling weak, my magic rises within me. There's no doubt he can sense it, for he shakes his head.

'You aren't strong enough to challenge me.' This time there's no amused tone, just a statement of fact. 'Nor should you try and bluff me. Your stone friend might well be dead, but I'm sure you wouldn't want Kralgen to join him so soon, even if he isn't the warrior he once was.'

Despite the executioner's axe threatening to fall on Kralgen, I simply can't capitulate so easily.

'I can't serve you again, not now, not ever.'

Nogoth huffs.

'You have no idea, Malina. Ever is a very long time when you live that long, as you'll find out, unless you do something foolish. Anyway, I'm a patient man. While you continue to feed, you'll stay young, and even if I wait a thousand years, it doesn't matter. But until you see the error of your ways, you'll suffer alongside the others who resisted me.'

Something the Saer Tel had said comes to mind. Do I have the key to end this war here and now? Could I save this world by sacrificing my life? I also recall Nogoth offering to leave High Delnor alone in exchange for me. One life for hundreds of thousands. It makes me sick thinking about it, but I can only try.

'If I willingly became yours, would you end this entire conquest now and return through the World Gate with me, never to return?'

Nogoth's gaze is piercing as he looks for signs of duplicity.

'Add selflessness to the list of your qualities. It's a tempting offer, but your price is far too high when I know time will bring you to me without cost. Not forgetting, I enjoy a conquest, and my fey need to be fed. So, no, Malina!'

The musical words of the Saer Tel fall from his lips as he gives them an order, but as he's about to turn away, he stops and fixes me with an inquisitive smile.

'Whatever happened to the one you loved, the one with the green and blue eyes?'

'Lotane.'

'Yes. Lotane. Whatever happened to him?'

This isn't an innocent question, and whilst I don't know where Lotane is, this is an attempt to gain more leverage. I'd learned to lie to Nogoth in the past, and that lesson hasn't been forgotten.

'He couldn't live knowing what happened between you and me.'

Tears come readily to my eyes as I say the terrible words, for the hurt is so raw.

'My condolences.'

Nogoth bows slightly and leaves me in the care of the Saer Tel.

'Drink, Sister,' one urges, pushing the goblet of elixir into my hands.

I'd intended to resist, but the pain, weakness and loss threatens to drag me under.

I drink every drop.

Nogoth will come to regret letting me live, and he's right. I'll come to him in a thousand years, but it won't be for his love. Instead, I'll find a way to take his head.

***

As I leap confidently over the barrier back into the transient safety of the supply chamber, I sigh. The ogres and ssythlans who'd escorted me back, disappear into the blackness, leaving me with the injured and dying. They sleep side by side where I'd left them, sad, lost souls holding on to one another.

Guilt weighs heavily on my shoulders despite my light steps as I head toward my alcove. The elixir might have fully restored me, but many of those around me will never see the light of day again.

I mustn't let their suffering be in vain. I'll use my newly regained strength to ... to what?

Nogoth giving it to me had been more than just a bribe; it also showed he didn't consider me a threat. The Fey King doesn't know fear or doubt, and if one hundred thousand of this world's warriors didn't cause him concern, then why would one angry and rejuvenated Chosen.

I'll make him regret his hubris because I'm the King Slayer!

Even if it's an empty title for now, I'll earn it again; I just have to be patient. A thousand years' patient if I escape. But how many people would die to feed me during that time so I could defeat Nogoth? Would my evil come close to surpassing his if so?

Maybe it doesn't have to be that way.

The Saer Tel, if they're to be believed, never kill. They feed to live, not kill to live, so I could follow their example. Now I know their tale; they no longer seem the outright evil creatures I believed them to be. Instead, they walk a dark path when hunger takes them and a lighter one when it's assuaged. It's a balance my deeds have already made me familiar with, and I'm confident I can follow their example.

Settling cross-legged in my alcove, I wait for the moon globes to brighten.

I feel somewhat alone as I sit beside Dimitar's cold, stone body, holding my emotions in check with rigid discipline. All those years of conditioning are useful at times like this, even if I'm not the machine I once was.

Glowing brightly, a pillar of incredible strength, Kralgen hasn't moved from where I'd left him. To think that once he and I had been enemies of sorts, and now I'd risk my life for him.

The moon globe slowly brightens, heralding a new day above, and thereafter, moans, groans, and cursing breaks the silence.

'Good morning, King Slayer,' Kralgen greets me with a yawn. 'How was your trip?'

'You weren't asleep?' I ask, astonished.

'Hardly,' Kral grimaces, rubbing his temples. 'I have the worst headache ever. I think I might finally have drunk a little too much. Are those the Saer Tel you've talked about?'

'They were.'

'You look and move like them.'

My cheeks burn with shame, but Kralgen just snorts softly.

'You are who you choose to be, Malina. You can be all things; Saer Tel and friend, fey and ally.'

'Thanks, Kral. As you're the only friend I have left, I'll hold onto you a while longer if that's alright.'

'So-what-have-I-done-to-lose-your-friendship-then?'

The voice is barely recognisable and grates slowly as if it's emanating from the bowels of the earth.

I've never seen anything shock Kral or cause him to jump. Nothing has ever fazed him from the early days of the training circle except being unable to beat Nogoth. Yet he jumps backwards and tumbles over a crate with a crash that has everyone turning their heads.

Even I scuttle back on my hands and heels like a crab.

'I-don't-feel-too-well,' grates the voice again. Each word comes out painfully slowly.

'Dimitar?'

'Who-else? Help-me-sit. I-can't-seem-to-move-and-I'm-cold!'

Kral comes around the fallen crate, motioning people to stay back as he and I kneel next to our friend.

I don't know whether to laugh or cry. Dimitar is alive, but as he lies there, his eyes sliding back and forth, I wonder if his condition is a gift or a curse. Leaning forward, I place my hand on his forehead. It's a little warmer than the last time I touched him, and I can see his chest move through his clothes.

'Am-I-going-to-be-alright, Malina? Did-you-save-me?' Dimitar asks, his slate grey eyes locked to mine.

How am I supposed to break this news to him? I could ask Kral, but he's just too blunt an instrument to let loose at a time like this. Sighing, I plunge ahead.

'Remember the last time I saved you, how my magic turned your hand and forearm to stone? It was the only way, and everything turned out alright.'

Dimitar's eyes widen slightly.

'Are-you-trying-to-say-that-I've-got-a-stone-thigh? Things-could-be-worse. Imagine-if-I'd-got-stabbed-in-the-groin.'

The chuckle Dimitar makes sounds like a bag of gravel being churned.

Kralgen leans forward.

'You'd never have to worry about being hard for the women!'

'Exactly.'

I shake my head. The forced levity is just making things worse.

'It's more than that, Dimitar. Much, much more. Don't ask me how or why, but it's not just your thigh or the leg. You'd lost so much blood and were so close to death ...'

I can't continue. I just can't find the words.

'Tell-me, Malina. It-doesn't-matter, really. I-thought-I'd-never-see-you-again-and-that's-worth-the-price, whatever-it-is.'

I don't know whether his words are supposed to make it easier, but they really don't. I breathe deeply, calming myself. I owe him this.

'It's the whole of you, from head to toe. Even your hair, Dimitar. That's why you're so cold and can't move. I don't know if you can live much longer like this or even want to live like this. But that's how you are.'

Those stone eyelids close and open slowly.

'If-that's-the price-so-be-it. I'm-luckier-than-some-I-think. Now-sit-me-up!'

Kralgen grunts and heaves, but Dimitar's body is as solid stone.

'I could lean you upright against a wall, but that's about it.' Kralgen shrugs. 'Best to leave you lying down for a while!'

'Can you still feel and move your left hand, Dimitar?' I take it in mine and squeeze it gently.

To my amazement, a stone tear forms and rolls off the side of Dimitar's cheek. It splashes as it hits the ground and then merges with the rock as if it never was.

'I'll take that as a yes.' I smile, and my tears follow Dimitar's. 'In which case, I might sit and hold your hand for a while, if that's alright with you?'

In response, another stone bead rolls to the ground, and his hand gently squeezes mine in return.

'It's-not-as-bad-as-all-that,' Dimitar assures me quietly, pulling a slow smile.

'I'll get us something to eat,' Kralgen says, rising.

My eyes open wide in surprise.

Kralgen looks a little abashed.

'What can I say. It appears I can still fight, and there's no more alcohol left. Then, we've got some planning to do when I come back. I need some fresh air, and you suggested a run which might clear this hangover.'

'Don't-leave-me-behind-when-you-escape,' Dimitar pleads slowly. 'Promise-me.'

'We won't leave you behind, Dimitar. It's a promise!' I state emphatically.

A faint smile creases those stone lips in response to my words.

Kralgen nods grimly as he looms over us.

'I agree,' he says. 'But that's not only what we need to plan. We can't leave the wounded soldiers here with the supplies until we've dealt with the nearby gangs. They'll come back sooner or later, and we owe them for what happened to Dimitar and the others.

As Kralgen heads off, I know he's right. There's no way what happened to Dimitar and the other soldiers will go unpunished.

The Chosen will hunt again.

***

'I feel utterly useless. I wish I could fight with you,' Dimitar grates.

'Soon, brother,' Kralgen says, patting him on the shoulder with a thud.

At Kral's request, I'd fitted a stone cap at the end of his forearm. With his partially stone limb, Kral claims he and Dimitar must be kin.

'I wasn't talking to you, you gigantic oaf, and I'm not your brother!'

A smile works its way unbidden across my face. I appreciate Kral's efforts. Dimitar's spirits are incredibly low, and he hardly says a word. Thankfully, Kral's humour sometimes reaches through his malaise.

Dimitar still can't stand but has regained movement throughout his body, albeit painfully slow. Regardless of being a little slurred, his speech is more fluid again. Despite his gravelly voice, I can almost pretend he's his old self. Kralgen's jesting with him reminds me of better times and ... Lotane.

My smile fades.

I still hate myself for what I did. I also hate that our love wasn't strong enough to survive my infidelity despite my belief it would last an eternity.

Dimitar looks at me. Is he waiting for me to say something?

Even though I smile, his face drops. His mood rarely rises above depressive, and I often see him crying when he thinks no one is looking. I have to keep his spirits up because I'm sure his stone body will die on him without a will to live driving it.

'I wish you were coming too,' I say, realising what he needs to hear.

How a face that's grey stone can light up, I don't know, but Dimitar's does. A part of me feels guilt, for it transpires a heart of stone can feel love, and maybe as a way to deal with his predicament, Dimitar is letting his grow. He's hearing want he wants to hear. My biggest worry is that when he comes to his senses and realises this love is just one way, that stone heart of his might just break.

'Then wait for me to get better.' Dimitar pleads.

'We can't wait.' Kralgen sighs, saving me the pain of hurting Dimitar's feelings. 'Those tattooed gang bastards have lined up for their food, morning and night these last three days, and they count our numbers every time, seeing how prepared we are. But now we know where they're holed up; we have to act fast.'

'He's right, Dimitar. According to the healers who found their hideout, they've already bolstered their numbers to nearer two hundred,' I say.

'To defend, sometimes you need to attack. I understand,' Dimitar groans, straining to stand. He almost makes it before collapsing with the sound of a small avalanche.

'Patience, Dimitar. You're getting stronger every day.' I rest my hand on his shoulder in sympathy.

'I'm cold. So cold,' he whispers, curling up on the floor.

I cover him in blankets as Kral and I exchange worried looks.

'It's almost time,' Kral rumbles softly. 'We'll leave before the moon globes go out and the barricade goes up.'

I check my weapons. I have three daggers, one of which I'd removed from Dimitar's leg. Two are in their scabbards attached to a belt fashioned from leather, whilst the other I tuck into my boot.

Kralgen, on the other hand, has a short staff I'd made for him out of stone. It's very heavy, but he couldn't be happier and wields it like a stick. Watching him practice to get used to the balance and weight has been something to behold. It smashed heavy empty crates as if they were fragile pottery. Even one-handed, he remains deadly.

I look over Kralgen a final time. He's discarded his fur jerkin. While it gives some decent protection, it is a little too bright for a clandestine operation despite being filthy. Like me, he's wearing just boots, dark trousers and a shirt. I'd gently bound the clothing close to our bodies using leather strips, ensuring no loose material could be grabbed.

Kralgen tries to tie my hair back but fails miserably. He can wield a stone staff but can't tie a knot.

I just give him a knife and pull my own hair taut.

A few ragged cuts later, and that's taken care of.

'Ready?' I ask, the excitement beginning to build.

A nod is all I receive.

I can sense Dimitar is hoping Kralgen will leave us alone briefly so he can say something, but we don't have time, nor do I have the inclination.

'Let's go.'

As we walk toward the chamber entrance, we receive a few salutes. We'd briefed everyone an hour before about our intention, and most wonder if they'll see us again. Two against two hundred are terrible odds, but then again, this isn't a kill operation.

As soon as we're into the tunnels, soldiers start erecting the barricade behind us.

What awaits isn't pleasant. Human misery surrounds us as soon as we're past the safe zone, a marked area extending two dozen paces beyond the barricade.

An endless line of people huddles miserably against the tunnel walls. Despondency and despair are etched upon every face, and it's heart-wrenching to witness. Being unable to see the sun, with nowhere to go and nothing to do, is bad enough. Add foul air, the injured moaning, children crying, and ruthless gangs preying on people, and it's no wonder almost everyone's spirit is broken. All they have to look forward to is being taken away by the ogres or dying to a knife in the dark.

Most families look away, unwilling to meet our gaze, but some sneer at me, and I hear the word *fey* muttered in hatred as we continue. Occasionally groups of bandaged soldiers nod in respect, and it's good to know some realise I'm not all bad.

Here and there, latrine barrels are given a wide berth, not that the smell is any different wherever we go, but perhaps it's to provide a modicum of privacy to those who use them.

At an intersection ahead, two shifty-looking men and women chat quietly in a pool of light beneath a moon globe. When they see us, they turn and run down the tunnel we're going to take.

'That doesn't bode well,' grumbles Kralgen as we pick up our pace.

I break into a jog to keep up with Kralgen's giant stride, following the directions we'd been given. Moon globes are few and far between, and they're already beginning to dim. It doesn't bother me; my eyesight can penetrate the dark, but not Kralgen's.

People grumble, unhappy to see newcomers in their stretch of tunnel so close to lights out. I can't blame them.

'The next turn on the right leads us to the gang's base,' Kralgen mutters, hefting his staff as we move along a long tunnel unusually empty of people. Instead, it's full of old clothes, boots, burned-out torches and all manner of discarded items.

'They've been taking stuff they can't even use,' I mutter softly, motioning for Kral to slow down.

Carefully, we turn the corner, and there before us, about fifty paces away is a large chamber not unlike ours. This one has torches burning, ready for when the moon globe in the ceiling goes out.

Frustratingly, bandaged civilians line the passageway. We hadn't planned for this, nor had we been warned they were here. We have to get them away before we can implement our plan.

'You need to leave, now!' Kralgen says firmly as we move carefully between the lines of civilians. Their bandages are filthy and bloodstained, obviously covering heinous wounds.

'Move!' I hiss.

Slowly and painfully, the injured begin to stir. I want to shout and scream at them to hurry up because the longer they take, the more danger we're in, but they're obviously in terrible distress. I bite my tongue even though, at any moment, two hundred bloodthirsty bastards might charge out of that chamber before we're ready for them.

We're halfway down the entrance tunnel before I realise our mistake.

Since the beginning of our incarceration, gangs have used stolen bandages from the injured to prevent themselves from being taken by ogres. I'd overlooked the obvious; the bloodthirsty bastards are already all around us, and we're entangling ourselves further in their trap with every step.

I'd hoped we could avoid a fight on this mission, even though I'd intended to kill every gang member in the chamber. Now the fight is about to find us.

'Your staff!' I say, lifting my hands toward Kral.

The command in my voice has him hold it out straight away.

A simple thought, a touch of my hands, and elemental fire burns at either end of Kralgen's weapon.

'We do it here and now!'

Shouts erupt around us, deafening in the confines of the tunnel as the bandaged men and women surge to their feet, pulling concealed weapons into the open. We've already passed about forty and can't expect to fight this many and win, let alone two hundred.

'Buy me a minute,' I shout above the noise, crouching on the floor at Kralgen's feet.

With a roar, Kral twirls and spins, protecting me from all sides, the vroom of his staff like a thousand angry bees as it leaves a streaking trail of fire behind it. My life is in his hands, but there are no safer hands to be in. I shut out the crunches, thuds, screams and curses, focusing on my need.

Like in the earthen trench outside of High Delnor's walls, I call upon my magic, sweeping my hands to either side as our closest assailants are flung against the walls, broken and bleeding by Kral's flaming staff.

It's as if I'm lifting a heavy weight as I bring my hands forward in front of me, pressing the palms together, and in response, the sides of the tunnel begin to soften like wet clay. It would be easier if I touched the stone, but I can't move from Kral's sphere of protection.

A thrown dagger flies for my head, and I sway, hearing Kral curse painfully as the weapon takes him instead. The floor rumbles, and I see a wave of vengeful screaming inhumanity pouring from the chamber into the tunnel.

'Bastards,' Kral yells, and I know he's being hurt. He's having to focus more on defending me than attacking them, and so restrained, with just one hand, he's vulnerable.

The horde is almost upon us, and we'll get swept aside irrespective of Kral's strength. Pausing in my efforts, I summon a gust of wind, and in the narrow confines of the passage, it knocks the horde off their feet.

'Come on,' I breathe, visualising the rock moving faster, and just like a spider's web, filaments shoot across the gap, creating a lattice that quickly gets thicker and thicker. Suddenly the horde reaches it, throwing themselves, hacking and smashing with clubs and knives, hatchets and torches, all trying to break down the thickening barrier. Stone fragments sting my face and skitter across the tunnel floor as, for a moment, the horde looks like it will break through.

*Take what you need*, I plead silently, and in response, more filaments shoot from ceiling to floor, and the smashed gaps are filled.

'The passage is sealed,' I yell, although I'm far from finished. I'm going to ensure there's no way out for the scum trapped inside.

'MY TURN!' shouts Kral, and, let off the leash, he goes on the attack. He might be injured, but an injured animal is often the most dangerous, and Kral goes into a berserk frenzy.

I continue pouring my strength into the barrier, ensuring it can never be broken down, at least with what the gangs have inside. Then I turn, leaning against it, feeling the faintest vibration as those beyond hack futilely at its unrelenting rock face.

Kral is nowhere to be seen. However, he's left a trail of destruction, and in the dim light, everything is splashed red as though by some frenzied painter. This macabre artwork changes before my eyes, with blood running, brains oozing and people dying, clawing at horrific wounds.

I'm on the verge of passing out and begin to close my eyes. I hate how my magic drains me, but a better idea comes to mind. I might not be hungry, but I know what gives me strength.

It's time for me to finish what Kral has started, and I lick my lips in anticipation.

***

# CHAPTER III

'They're coming.'

I speak softly so only Dimitar and Kralgen can hear. We're in a tunnel, and I know my words will start a panic that spreads like wildfire if I'm overheard.

Almost everyone wants to escape the festering sewer these tunnels have become, but all that changes whenever the ogres appear. In that instant, the tunnels suddenly become a safe haven again, and people would do anything to be left behind.

I smile at the thought of the gang members sealed in their stone tomb unless they've been found and taken already. It would be unusual for the fey to let so much meat go to waste. I'd gone back the following morning to check on my stone barricade, and all the bodies of Kralgen's victims along the tunnels had disappeared, so I doubt those I'd entombed were left to rot.

My magic enhances the vibration of ogres' footsteps and their conversation through the rock wall, warning me of their impending raid, and I pull my stinking robes close. Nogoth made it clear I'd suffer along with everyone else, so I'm trying to hide my scent in case he plans to keep me here longer. Dimitar is bundled in several robes smelling just as bad as mine to conceal his form. However, there's little point in trying to disguise Kralgen. Even sitting, he's head and shoulders above everyone else.

We're receiving puzzled and somewhat hostile glances. People have got to know one another here, and no one wants a fey, a giant, and a stone-faced man sitting amongst them. They're too afraid to try and move us on, yet nor do they want to give up their space.

'We should have brought the soldiers from the supply chamber with us,' Dimitar grates, struggling to get the words out.

I think he's going to say more, but he falls silent.

These are the first words he's uttered in a while. He mostly observes, listens, and responds to commands but otherwise stays mute and lost in thought. His observation tugs at my conscience.

'These people beside us are just as worthy as those we've left behind,' Kralgen whispers.

I cough loudly to cover their words.

Kralgen is right. Whilst a few soldiers are nearby, most are families. A soldier might seem more valuable in a war, but if this world is to have a chance, we also need families and babies; lots of babies.

Roars suddenly echo along the section of the tunnel we're in, as about thirty paces away to my left, armoured ogres storm into sight, arms wide, jaws gaping.

'Get moving or die!' they roar, their voices thick and cruel.

Screams and shouts from human throats add to the noise as the ogres start propelling everyone before them.

'Let's go.' My voice is calm, but my heart beats like a drum.

Kralgen's muscles bunch as he hauls Dimitar upright. The Major can now move by himself, but unfortunately, he's so slow and heavy. May the gods forgive us, but Kralgen and I had spoken softly about leaving Dimitar behind before friendship and love had won over logic.

People flow around us like rocks in a stream, fleeing ahead, blinded by panic to the fact that more ogres are waiting around the next corner. Sure enough, the front runners are soon flooding back, pushing and shoving, until a little more than a hundred of us are bunched together. Heavily armed ogres hem us in, and behind them are two ssythlans.

A new passage opens under the ssythlans magical coercion, and the stampede starts again.

'Here, let me help,' I say, supporting a woman with a baby who can barely keep her feet. My arm goes around her shoulder, steadying her in the shoving crowd.

She turns with a smile of gratitude, but when she sees the colour of my eyes beneath my hood, she pulls away, screaming. Thankfully, her horror is lost amongst the other screams and shouts of panic as we're almost carried along. Mercifully the gradient is slightly downhill.

I'm getting jostled, so I position myself in front of Kralgen and Dimitar. They're like a breakwater, and I relax, keeping my head down. I'm sure this isn't the same tunnel I'd travelled with the Saer Tel, which is reassuring. I've no wish to face Nogoth again, especially with Kralgen and Dimitar so vulnerable beside me.

Except, is Dimitar really vulnerable anymore?

He moves like an old man, every footstep slow and precise, a massive effort of will and strength. Yet, as Kralgen had said when we'd considered leaving him behind. *How do you kill a man made of stone?*

Not very easily, that's for sure.

Kralgen and his war mallet might smash him to pieces, but most bladed weapons will simply blunt or shatter against him. If Dimitar ever becomes more mobile and regains his spirit, then he might be as unstoppable as Kral.

'Move, human scum!'

We run, stumble, and occasionally the ogres let us walk. But, once we've had a short rest, the beasts roar again, and the journey continues.

'Faster!'

For me, it's no problem, yet Kralgen is flagging a little. He's having to keep Dimitar moving, and I wonder how much longer he can keep it up. What would the repercussions be if Dimitar fell behind and the ogres discovered his true nature?

'Come on, Dimitar. I swear you're slowing down on purpose,' Kralgen grunts. To my astonishment, Kral picks up the Major and carries him awkwardly to near the front of the mob before putting him back down to walk again.

'Sit and rest!'

The order hasn't come soon enough for most, and everyone collapses. I squat, and even Kral does so as not to draw attention, although he still sticks out like a spear amongst swords.

'Use your magic and shape him into a ball so I can roll him along,' Kral groans at me.

'I'm so tired and confused. Leave and go on without me!' Dimitar responds with a rocky grimace, failing to rise to Kral's humour.

I feel so much sadness at his condition. His mind is fragile despite his body being solid.

'Two days ago, you couldn't stand,' I say, laying my hand on his arm. 'Continue for my sake.'

To my relief, Dimitar nods.

It's not long before we're chivvied back to our feet again, the ogres bang swords against their shields to instil fear in the exhausted people around us. I can tell they're frustrated at the lack of pace, and this won't go on for long.

Unfortunately, I'm right. Ogres intermittently line the tunnel walls, and one suddenly reaches out to grab a young man with a bad limp.

'No! Please, no!' the unfortunate victim screams, struggling to break free.

The ogre laughs and rams a serrated dagger into the poor lad's neck. Blood sprays everywhere, and the rush of fear causes everyone to run again in a panicked frenzy, crying and sobbing.

Onwards.

How many years it must have taken the ssythlans to create these hidden tunnels is beyond me. Maybe Nogoth or even the Saer Tel somehow helped, but even so, it's an incredible feat.

Intermittently, the ogres pick off the slowest, the weakest. They don't kill indiscriminately; rather, they just separate the wheat from the chaff ruthlessly, encouraging the pace to be maintained.

Only the strong will survive.

Then, up ahead, a golden glow beckons as sunshine illuminates some worn steps. It promises the illusion of safety if only we can reach its embrace.

I'm not as fearful as those around me, and I know I've dealt with this incarceration better than most, but as I run up, blinking into the blinding sunlight, I fall to my knees amongst my fellow prisoners.

Never in my life have I appreciated the true beauty of the sun until this day. As I bask for a few seconds, feeling its warmth seep through my clothing, I feel a ray of hope. Then my surroundings come into focus, and reality returns in an unpleasant rush.

We're in a walled courtyard, the citadel sitting high on its hill off to the east. We've come a long way and must now be on the city's western outskirts. The paved ground is covered in dried blood, vomit, and faeces, while several dead bodies are piled against the perimeter wall.

It's a sad reminder of those who've come before.

The ogres move away to line the east wall, blocking the steps up which we'd come, not that anyone would consider going back down now we've felt the magic of being above ground again. A dozen gargoyles crouch on walls and rooftops nearby, javelins clutched in their clawed hands. Their wings are stretched open, catching the sun's warmth, and their demonic presence has most people around me cowering in fear.

Slowly the crying and moaning recede as the panic brought about by the run dies away, and people catch their breath.

'Everyone, please listen.'

The voice isn't particularly strong, and it goes mostly unheard. The speaker is an old man standing atop a low podium against the north wall. He has a forced smile and wears fresh white robes cinched at the waist with a golden cord. His feet are bare, and despite looking well-fed, he appears nervous.

'A collaborator,' Kralgen rumbles.

I nod in agreement.

A dozen more, all elderly and trembling, with smiles fixed upon their faces, stand just behind him.

'Everyone, please listen!'

His voice warbles as he raises it, but the buzz of conversation among the people around me gets louder.

'SILENCE, HUMANS!'

The ogre's roar is followed by the clash of its sword against its shield. The creature points its weapon to the podium and steps back as the shocked and obedient crowd turns toward the old man.

With a nod, the robed speaker opens his arms to encompass everyone. Those behind him do the same. It's well-rehearsed, obviously fake, and I can imagine this moment has recently been played out dozens of times already ... historically, maybe hundreds or thousands.

Before speaking, he takes a deep breath and pauses, seeking to establish some self-control. He succeeds in calming his shaking hands, yet his eyes flitter left and right as if unsure where to look.

'Just do as ordered, and a new life awaits. Don't be afraid and come with me.'

***

I stand quietly in the middle of a long row, Kralgen and Dimitar just ahead, maybe fifty people behind me. The old man's words brought back memories of my first hours and days at the Mountain of Souls, let alone my time in the orphanage.

It always amazes me how difficult some people find following simple rules for survival. I could pick out those who'll live or die right now.

Most of the soldiers will survive the days ahead. They understand risk ... when to fight, run, or be quiet. Following orders is second nature to them. The lower class, the downtrodden poor, they'll mostly survive too. Hardship and death are nothing new to them, nor is fighting for survival.

It's the upper class, the wealthy and privileged, who can't keep their mouths shut that will die the quickest. Nothing has prepared them for this; they've rarely, if ever, struggled against adversity.

As those ahead move on, I find myself on some steps, enjoying the shade of a pillared porch at the entrance to a large building.

'This building is a private bathhouse,' Kralgen says quietly, pointing to a plaque on a wall. 'It seems unlikely they'll drown us all, so I think we're going to have a bath. What do you think, Dimitar?'

Dimitar doesn't respond at all.

It seems absurd on the face of it. Yet it's perfect.

How to ensure the cooperation of hundreds of prisoners?

First, incarcerate them in hell, having them fear for their lives night and day, living in filth, starving and desperate. Then ... deliverance.

Just obey, behave, and suddenly life appears worth living again. We'll be marched hundreds of leagues to be thrown into hell, but we'll be cleaned and fed to ensure we're compliant in the interim. Unless I'm wrong.

As I'm finally ushered inside, there's no immediate sign of any fey. I take a moment to use my magic, having it quest out. Sure enough, ogre scent emanates from under a closed wooden door at the end of a blue-plastered and frescoed corridor to my left and behind some heavy, richly embroidered curtains to the right.

They're here, out of sight, but ready if required.

A bell clangs in the background, and shortly after, we shuffle forward again.

'This way, please,' an old lady warbles, indicating along the hallway.

Her comment is unnecessary as everyone is in line, but she's obviously following a script.

I close my eyes briefly, looking through my spirit eye, and sure enough, she's bound by the red thread of blood magic, as is another collaborator nearby.

Maybe they're not entirely guilty of that label if they were bound without their knowledge. Or, perhaps they did whatever it took to keep themselves alive. Whichever, their obedience has certainly been secured. Who knows, maybe when we've all been transported, they'll end up as a tasty morsel for the departing fey.

Slowly but surely, with every clang of the bell, we enter deeper into the building until the corridor opens into the main baths. Piles of rotten, filthy, discarded clothes and bandages fester to our right but are being put into hand carts by elderly assistants. It seems that not only are the old more malleable and unlikely to resist, but any younger prisoner who tries to escape by hiding amongst them will stand out.

Slightly ahead are five large pools, with about fifty people in the first three.

'Relieve yourselves over there!'

To our left are dozens of small cubicles. Considering how bad we all smell as a group, it's impressive that the odour emanating from the toilets is worse than ours. Irrespective, everyone goes.

I squat over a black hole where most of what should have gone inside is splattered where I stand, and try not to breathe. Retching and vomiting from nearby just add to the horror. Those following our group will have an even worse mess to deal with.

We're counted as we return.

'Remove your clothes.'

The instruction is echoed by a dozen elderly men and women who walk up and down our line, smiling.

'Throw them to the side, and when you hear the bell, get into the first pool. Each time you hear it, move on to the next.'

There's a lot of hesitation from everyone, but under the cajoling insistence of our elderly guides, everyone begins to undress.

I'm concerned about disrobing for when I do, my eyes and skin colouring will be immediately apparent, as will the fact that Dimitar is made of stone.

Dimitar looks over his shoulder, perhaps seeking guidance. Kralgen, on the other hand, is tearing off his clothes, unashamed and unworried. He's a little more careful with his bandages, but he's soon standing like a heroic statue of legend. His missing hand just adds to the look. So many sculptures have missing limbs; it's weird.

'Unless there's trouble, I doubt these old folk will report anything untoward to the ogres, and I can't see any fey keeping an eye on things. So just do as they ask,' I murmur and peel off my filthy clothing.

Dimitar looks miserable at the prospect of getting naked. Whispers come from behind, but I can't be bothered to listen closely. As long as they talk quietly, I'll let people have their say.

The bell clangs, and those in the pool ahead clamber out the far side and into the next. As I carefully descend, following the others into the lukewarm liquid, I wonder if I'll come out dirtier than I'm going in.

This experience reminds me of my baths in the orphanage. I'm not sure what's worse, the water with its greasy feel or the unseen bottom of the pool with horrible bits that have me cringing as I step on them.

Nonetheless, everyone gets scrubbing, trying to remove the worst of the filth and stench. We're in there a while before the bell clangs again, and we're straight into the next filthy pool.

This one has blocks of soap sitting on pedestals in the water, which we gather around. The water is covered in brown bubbles, but it smells slightly better, for the soap is fragranced.

'A bastard fey. No wonder the water is so filthy. Get out before I drown your skinny ass!'

The speaker is a heavyset and surly-looking man covered in matted hair. He resembles a wolfen, and I'm inclined to point it out but instead bite my tongue. This isn't the time to have a confrontation and put our plan in jeopardy. Yet my silence doesn't work.

'Didn't you hear me? And what the hell is that thing with you?'

He raises his voice a little, trying to draw peoples' attention to me and Dimitar. Most people keep to themselves, but a few look over, happy to find someone to blame for their ills, and they now have us as a target.

I could deal with him, but my methods might draw too much attention.

'Kral.'

The hirsute man looks at me nonplussed, not understanding what I mean, but not for long.

Kral moves behind him, grabs a fistful of greasy hair, and pushes his face down under the water.

I return to washing and take my time, slathering myself in soap. The fool's thrashing becomes more desperate.

'Enough.'

Kral yanks the man gasping and spluttering back to the surface.

'Say anything more, or even puke, and I'll make you drink the whole bloody pool,' Kral rumbles.

Problem solved.

The water gets progressively clearer in each pool until we're out the other side about an hour later, cleaner than I remember being for way too long.

We're handed damp towels to dry ourselves and then, after a short wait, guided naked along another passage into a chamber.

A half dozen men and women await us. Piles of fresh clothing are stacked around the walls, and after looking at me critically, a woman returns with a pair of light brown trousers, a shirt, socks, a hooded cloak, and boots. To my surprise, they're of high quality and fit almost perfectly.

I remember Nogoth saying he'd spared the artisans, and here they are, fitting into his plan. We're now well-dressed and better able to face the long journey ahead.

Kralgen is guided into a small side room as they don't have clothes to fit him.

A few minutes later and everyone is dressed. Shortly after, Kralgen rejoins us, fully clothed in his newly fitted attire.

'Follow me,' our guide calls, and we're off again.

If only the next room is an armoury.

Unsurprisingly it isn't, yet as I gaze upon the food laid out on tables around the room, I'm not disappointed.

'Eat and drink your fill. You have an hour, so make the most of it.'

After scenting the food, I tuck in, taking note of the faces around me. Almost everyone looks shocked but reborn. Several remain red-eyed, perhaps having lost friends or family during our initial run, and a few look distrustful of this largess.

There's lots of cooked and seasoned fish, vegetables, fruits, and fresh water. I know what's to come, so don't hold back.

Kralgen and Dimitar sit nearby. Kralgen devours enough for three people while Dimitar just stares into nothingness, not attempting to eat anything.

I wonder what's going through Dimitar's mind right now. He worries me. Leaving him behind was never really an option, but bringing him along has its risks. Even his lack of appetite makes him stand out.

I'm not sure I could have dealt with the change he's gone through, even if my life depended on it. I should give him credit, not seek to find fault in him.

The hour passes by all too quickly, and our guide walks back into the room.

It's time.

***

I estimate there are five hundred of us prisoners, sitting and waiting for our journey to begin. No one is manacled or tied up, but there's no thought of escape as the threat of death hangs over us again.

Twenty gargoyles circle overhead while a hundred and fifty heavily equipped ogres watch us closely. Occasionally wolfen appear before disappearing in the blink of an eye. There's no doubt that any sign of disobedience will be met with extreme violence.

Everyone is wide-eyed and fearful, yet at the same time, disbelief is evident on their faces, not at the circumstance they find themselves in but at the landscape surrounding us.

Lush grasses reach to our shoulders, soft, whispering in a gentle breeze. Nearby, to the north side of the road, a copse of young trees reach for the sky, leaves lush, branches heavy with ripe fruit. Flowers grow everywhere, butterflies dancing in between. Surprisingly there's no sign of the defensive fortifications that had scarred the land a few weeks ago, and the trees appear at least two years old.

Everywhere I turn, the landscape has changed, swirling in colours that touch the heart.

I know why. Only magic could have wrought such a transformation, and who but the Saer Tel wield this kind of power. There's no denying the beauty their magic has brought to this land. If only the price for such rebirth wasn't the death of a continent's people.

Wagons hauled by oxen exit the city gates, full of supplies. It appears the siege stores will still serve their purpose of keeping us alive, just to a far different destination than intended. However, if all goes to plan, we'll be bidding farewell to our escort's way before then.

'It seems like yesterday I was outside these walls, confident our preparations were sufficient,' Dimitar grates. 'I failed everyone so terribly and deserved this.' He holds up his hands.

'You need to leave the past behind you, Dimitar,' I whisper. 'We can't change what we've done, but we can choose what we do next. Be strong for me.'

'On your feet!' bellows an ogre. He has a single spike on his shoulder armour denoting low rank.

Obediently we rise, and I keep my head down and hood up. Dimitar does the same, whereas, with Kralgen, there's no point in him attempting a disguise. Our escorts step forward, separating us into smaller groups. Then, we're shoved toward the wagons irrespective of how fast we move.

A metal girdle with a thick loop is fitted around our waists, and it becomes evident why when a long chain is threaded through and padlocked in place. I've been hitched to the last wagon, five to a side, with nine others. I'm at the end, and in addition to the lock, a heavy metal ball slightly smaller than my fist is attached to the final link making it impossible to pull through the loop. Unfortunately, that means I've got additional weight to carry.

Kralgen stands tall near the front of the wagon on the other side. He's too far to communicate with unless I raise my voice, and Dimitar is attached to a wagon further up the line despite us trying to stay close.

The ogres had purposefully split up those they saw together, an obvious precaution against trouble.

*Damnit, Malina. You should have foreseen this.*

I have to hope we'll be released at each day's end and can coordinate our escape then.

Atop each wagon is a single unarmed ogre at the reins. Not that this helps us, these muscle-bound beasts don't need more than their bare hands to kill a human. Four oxen are required to pull the heavy loads, and their tales whip back and forth in a vain attempt to swat away the flies buzzing around their rumps. Knowing how they smell, I'm happy to be at the back of the chain.

From the repositioning of the guards, I can tell we're soon to get underway. That's when my work will begin. Our escape depends on me being able to use blood magic to gain control of some of our captors. Yet how I'll safely lay hands on one of these ogres will be a challenge, especially if they keep their distance the whole time.

A swirl of colour catches my attention as through the gate tunnel, *he* appears. Nogoth, resplendent and regal in purple flowing robes.

My initial instinct is to turn away and hide my face, but his appearance is far from random. I know why he's here.

'Malina, my favourite Chosen. Did you think to leave without saying goodbye?' He laughs, arms outstretched as he strides towards me. 'It matters not. I'll be following you home soon enough, my love.'

My face burns. I'd rather he hate, insult, or curse me, but to label me as his love is infuriating.

With a crash of armour, the entire escort kneels, and all the prisoners quickly follow suit, instinctively knowing that not doing so will invoke the ire of the guards. Only I remain standing.

'It still doesn't have to be this way,' Nogoth says warmly. 'Why don't you stay, and I'll pardon your giant friend too.' He nods toward Kralgen. 'You could both serve me as you were destined to do, as you were trained to do. The days ahead will be beyond your wildest dreams.'

I watch as he pauses, a faraway look in his eyes as he imagines the future.

'Malina. Tomorrow I'm leaving High Delnor, and you can come with me. Imagine riding by my side throughout this conquest. From here, we'll journey to Tars,' he exclaims, sweeping his hand south. 'Despite defeating their main army here, they'll fight tooth and nail as they've always done to protect their homeland. It will be a gloriously vicious fight! Then, when they stand defeated, we can explore their temples, gaze upon the Sea of Sand, climb the highest dunes, and revel in our victory.

'Afterwards, your old home of Hastia beckons. You'll have the opportunity to look down upon those who sold you, who belittled you. I'll give you the power to choose who lives and dies, who stays and who is sent to their fate. The future of Hastia will be yours to decide!

'Then, we'll regroup back here before conquering the forests of Rolantria, the swamps of Suria, and the grasslands of Astoria. Icelandia will give up its people afterwards, and if he desires, Kralgen can stay behind as king once the wheat is separated from the chaff. They'll grow strong again with such a leader, so there'll be no Delnorian empire when we return to this world.

'What do you say?'

Some people are attracted to power, to its indomitable nature. I remember a time when I'd have died for this man. Yet now, as I consider his words, it takes mere moments to reaffirm what I already knew.

'I cannot be complicit in what you're doing here. The simple answer is no.'

I stay silent after that, biting back on the hot words that fight to tumble past my lips. Yet that doesn't stop images of cutting off Nogoth's head and stamping it into a bloody mess running through my mind.

Nogoth stands regarding me, and I feel like an open book under his gaze.

'Even if you have no wish to be near me, you could stay with your fellow Saer Tel. I know you feel their kindred spirit. They could teach you so much about healing this broken world. Look at what they've already done!' Nogoth gestures around with a smile. 'The power they wield could be yours. You could travel this world, making it a paradise!'

Surprisingly, my resolve wavers as I consider this final offer.

'You're right.' I admit. 'I can't deny the unity of their company. But I won't betray or leave my friends and those who've fought alongside me!'

Nogoth sighs, sincere regret mixed with a hint of amusement evident as he receives my answer.

'Stubborn, headstrong, beautiful, and deadly. One day you'll love me again! ... GRULDARN!' he shouts.

I'm distracted from saying anything further as the ground shakes and a shadow passes across the sun. As I look up, people whimper or scream as a giant clambers over the city wall.

I've never seen one of these creatures up close, and its size is awe-inspiring. Whilst not as muscular as the troll I'd defeated through the World Gate, it's half again as tall and carries a club the size of a small tree. It wears no armour, and for clothing, just a loin cloth that does little to disguise its hanging sex. Whereas the ogres and trolls have obviously cruel eyes and features, this goliath has a simpler look. As it observes us drool runs from its mouth, and a tongue the size of a door runs around its thick lips.

'Meet Gruldarn,' Nogoth says, a knowing look in his eye. 'As you're so precious, he'll be accompanying you on your journey home, just in case you were thinking of wandering off. Sadly, he has a voracious appetite, so, thanks to your decision to leave early, some of your fellow travellers won't make it.'

Oh, gods. Why does every path I take lead to someone's death?

Nogoth studies me closely.

'I have one more parting gift.'

His smile does little to reassure me.

'I don't wish to have anything from you. Keep it!'

'You know, Malina, that every action you take has consequences? Even something as simple as sharing a smile with a stranger can lead to marriage and, subsequently, the birth of a new life. On the other hand, constantly denying me, your king, can lead to somewhat less joyous circumstances!'

So saying, he stalks past me, and as I turn to watch, he pulls a dagger and drives it up under the chin of the woman next in line on the chain.

'Gruldarn, breakfast!' Nogoth shouts.

The giant stomps over, wraps one hand around the dead woman's legs, pins the chain to the floor with the other, and pulls.

Whilst loose enough, the metal loop around the woman's waist doesn't fit over her shoulders. So, as Gruldarn yanks his breakfast free, the metal gouges through flesh and tears off her arms at the shoulder.

People scream, some vomit, others cry, whilst a few remain silent, hatred glittering in their eyes. Sadly, not all the hatred is directed at Nogoth or Gruldarn ... some is at me. The poor woman would still be alive if I'd not been argumentative.

Nogoth walks to stand before me as Gruldarn drops the limp corpse into its gaping maw. For once, I'm glad to look into The Once and Future King's face.

'Your hands.'

I raise them, and Nogoth pulls some familiar manacles from inside his robe. They're of the same type I'd been constrained with while briefly incarcerated at his mansion. As he locks them around my wrists, it's like I've lost a child because I can't feel my magic at all.

'Gruldarn will ensure you don't run off, and these will ensure you don't get up to any magical mischief.' Nogoth smiles. 'I'll remove them when I see you again which will be sooner than you think. Remember, once you're through the gate, time passes differently. Two months there equates to nearly two years here, and I'll be back before you know it.'

With a final nod, Nogoth turns away, and I watch his back until he disappears inside High Delnor.

Our ogre driver comes around, first inspecting the wagon, then the chain. He pauses, staring with undisguised contempt at me.

'Traitor,' he growls.

Without warning, he swings his hand at my face. I instinctively duck, causing him to stumble.

'You're pretty fast.'

He chuckles, grabs my shirt and pushes me against the wagon. This time when he drives his fist into my stomach, there's no way I can dodge. The air whooshes from my lungs, and I sink to one knee.

'I'll kill you, you bastard,' I wheeze.

My defiance is answered with a heavy slap and a contemptuous laugh. The ogre leaves me there, gasping for breath as he mounts up.

I feel lost. How I'll escape with my magic imprisoned while being escorted by Gruldarn and the other fey is beyond me.

Nogoth has surely won.

***

# CHAPTER IV

*Malina, THINK!*

I don't want to give up and concede; that's not my way, and that isn't how I've been trained.

But oh, how my spirit is close to being overwhelmed. The temptation to forget the world's terrible fate and simply place one foot in front of the other is huge. If I accept defeat, I could almost enjoy this walk as I take in the magically rejuvenated countryside. Then, in about two months, I'll cross through the World Gate and enjoy a fate far removed from the rest of my fellow travellers.

So why don't I?

Blue and green eyes come to mind alongside the ache of love lost. Yes, it's love that fans the flames of my resistance, and as I look across at Kralgen, I add friendship to the list. Oh, then there's revenge for Lystra, Alyssa and the others.

However, it doesn't matter how much motivation I have; try as I might, I can't reach my magic. After two days of trudging and trying, the only result is a splitting headache. Add to that my sore waist where the girdle chaffs, and I'm in a foul mood.

Contemplating my discomfort brings to mind the woman eaten by Gruldarn at the beginning of our journey. There's now a length of empty chain between me and the next in line, a surly-looking man. He glares over his shoulder at me every so often as if I'm to blame for every wrongdoing he's suffered in his entire life.

If only Kral were walking in line between us.

My inability to communicate with either Kralgen or Dimitar is my biggest frustration other than being unable to reach my magic. Together we'd have a chance to devise a new plan, but instead, the ogres keep us apart every evening and forbid talking.

I grimace as I recall a couple of prisoners who'd decided to test the last rule as we ate our evening meal two nights past. The screams as Gruldarn enforced it has been enough to ensure we've travelled in silence ever since.

*Malina, think!*

As if to punctuate my thoughts, the driver's whip cracks, and a woman on the other side of the wagon cries out. We've all been lashed sporadically, and the ogre laughs happily as he returns his attention to the road ahead.

One problem at a time. I can't fix the world's problems, but maybe I can fix mine. These manacles are my main issue. If I can release them and, consequently my magic too, we'll have a chance.

The sun is briefly obscured by Gruldarn striding around the column, and suddenly the solution is right before my eyes. Nogoth had thought himself cunning by appointing this giant as my guardian, but perhaps I can turn our biggest problem to our advantage.

*Hmmm.*

How can I make physical contact with the giant without getting eaten? Nogoth does want me alive, so maybe I'm off the menu. If I can control him using blood magic, it's unlikely the ogre escort would have much chance if I ordered him to attack.

But first, how to remove these manacles?

If only I had Kral's strength, I could probably break them, but as I strain for the umpteenth time, there's no give or any sign of weakness.

Damn!

I look across at Kral, and it's as if he's heard his name, for he glances back at me and pulls a slight smile before returning to his trudging.

His fire is dimming again, and the weight of responsibility grows. Kral needs me as much as Dimitar. He's undoubtedly been trying to think of a way to break free. Yet, he wouldn't stand a chance even with two good hands and his weapon of choice. No, any escape chance rests entirely on my shoulders.

How else can I free myself?

I study the keyhole, but who am I kidding. Of the many skills I've been taught, lockpicking was not one of them.

Perhaps they don't even need to be removed?

Yes! Maybe breaking the chain that links them might be sufficient to negate their effect.

I can't risk trying to smash the chain with a rock or the metal ball at my waist. I'd only be able to do that at a rest stop or the evening meal, and the noise will immediately attract attention.

How else can I break it? What other force can I apply?

As my thoughts go round and round, a glimmer of an answer forms.

No ogres ever come close because they maintain a perimeter, spread out amongst the tall grasses. Somewhere beyond them, the wolfen are ranging, not that they'll come across any opposition in a conquered land. Discipline is good amongst the fey, but I can use this to my advantage!

Confident I'm not being observed, I slowly turn my right forearm, twisting my wrist within the manacle. The restraints are not overly tight, but I'm careful as I repeat the motion so I don't tear my skin. With every turn, the chain coils around itself until it's bunched up.

My muscles bunch and veins bulge as I twist my forearms, confident the force I'm applying is now focussed on where the final links meet the manacle. I grit my teeth, giving it everything, even as the manacles dig into my flesh.

Break, damnit!

I want to scream my anger to the skies so the gods take heed. There's no give in these restraints at all. Frustrated, I carefully unwind the chain, ensuring my failed attempt at breaking them isn't visible.

After we eat, when it's dark, I'll try again. My eyesight at night is almost as good as during the day, and I'll spot any fey if they approach.

Do the ogres, wolfen and the giant share my gift? I hadn't considered that before. It's possible, so I'll assume the worse.

A loud, exaggerated cough rises above the creaking wagon, then another. It's Kralgen, and this is about as subtle as he gets. He's taking a risk as he's walking only slightly beyond the driver's peripheral vision. Whilst I'm fairly sure no serious harm will befall me on this journey, thanks to Nogoth's interest, that protection is unlikely to extend to Kralgen.

Having caught my attention, he taps the wagon wheel next to him with every step.

What's he trying to communicate?

Maybe he's seen me twisting the chain around and is simply tapping the revolving wheel to show he appreciates the intent. I look quizzical, and Kralgen rolls his eyes.

He dips from view and stands up, waggling a small stick from the road to ensure I've seen it, then hits it against the wheel. He disappears from view again, reappears with both hands empty, and then points to the ground behind us.

As the wagon trundles onwards, the stick appears, mangled in the road.

Kralgen has shown me the answer.

***

We're travelling northwest toward Midnor, but ahead, visible above the long grasses, the wagons and prisoners leading the line turn north.

Interesting.

I assumed we'd go directly to Midnor, covering the same route we'd taken only weeks before, but no. As a fork in the road draws closer, a large sign indicating Eastnor looms above the junction. I'd studied Delnor's geography enough to visualise where it is. It's not much of a detour, and from the carrion birds flying far to the northwest, I wonder if it's to avoid a battlefield. More likely, it's nothing but a dead ox at the roadside.

Onward we tramp, hour after monotonous hour. The pace is slow, as the oxen can't be coaxed into anything more than a steady walk. Even the beautiful countryside can't distract me from the drudgery of our journey; in fact, it darkens my mood. The new growth and lush flora suggest Saer Tel have been here, so it would stand to reason the fey have already conquered Eastnor. Likely, all of Delnor is already under fey control.

Nonetheless, discipline remains strong amongst our escort despite passing through secured territory. The ogre perimeter is well-spaced and alert while gargoyles scout ahead. However, I've happily noted that they focus on the surrounding landscape and not on us well-restrained captives.

Knowing this is the case, I'm more confident my next course of action will go unnoticed.

The chain joining the manacles is about the length of my forearm, and when I bring my wrists together, there's about a hand span's length of loose chain.

It's time.

Moving alongside the wagon, I come abreast of the next prisoner and quickly hunker down, flicking the loose length of chain under the wagon wheel. The wagon is heavily laden with supplies, mostly food and water barrels and exerts more pressure than anything I could ever hope to apply. As it passes over the chain, I flick it under the wheel again. Four times I do this, then drop back to resume my walk.

I resist looking at the chain in case I've been observed by the ogres, yet they're not my problem.

'What are you doing? You'll get us killed!' hisses the surly man in front over his shoulder. 'Do it again, and I'll tell the driver!'

He's taking a risk, but the banging of the wagon along the uneven road shrouds his voice.

I snarl, and he hastily turns away, but this will pose a problem if he carries through with his threat. I've been studying my unwilling companions on my side of the wagon. The two women at the front of the chain are definitely soldiers. They have muscled calves straining against their trousers, broad shoulders, and short hair for fitting under a helm, yet it's even more obvious than that. They have the black skin of Tarsians.

However, the man between us is a civilian. His skin, where it shows, is reddened from the sun, a sure sign he hasn't been in the field on a campaign. His footsteps are short and hurried, with no experienced rhythm from marching in formation. The list of telltale signs go on. If I were to guess, he's some self-important minor noble who escaped Nogoth's initial cull. He has white marks on his fingers where rings have been removed, and only nobles or cutthroats wear such jewellery, and he's certainly not the latter.

He appears cowed by my aggression and looks at his feet as he walks. I expect he'll keep his mouth shut, but I won't risk leaving that to chance. Later on, when the opportunity presents itself, I'll make sure he realises remaining silent is in his best interests.

Shutting him from my mind, I inspect the chain, and a shiver of excitement has me restrain a smile. Several chain links have fine cracks and even seem to have flaked. I'm somewhat surprised but then realise that this material isn't metal. It's similar to the feys' ceramic armour, and

I recall how Kralgen shattered Nogoth's armour with his war mallet. This might be easier than I hoped.

I glance in Kral's direction to find him snatching a glance at me, and I nod. He acknowledges with one of his own, then returns his attention to the road ahead, his posture straighter at the good news.

I'm impatient to try again, but I bide my time, and there's still the issue of the noble.

'Rest stop, humans!'

Coarse ogre voices shout the order down the line, and our wagon grinds to a halt. The perimeter escort closes in, and our wagon driver jumps off his seat to release the chain.

After so many days of travel, we don't need to be told what to do. The four of us hurry into the long grasses to relieve ourselves. We stay spread out, keeping the chain taught. It's not that there's any embarrassment on my behalf, but the ogres don't like us getting closer to one another than we need to.

I sense the noble staring at me and turn toward him.

'You know I'm the King Slayer and what I'm capable of,' I whisper. 'Say a word to the guards, and it'll be your last.'

He flinches and quickly looks away.

I don't feel good threatening him. He's not some evil killer, although I'm sure he or his forebears caused enough misery throughout the years to attain their riches.

I squat down, grateful for the lush undergrowth that affords me privacy and something to wipe myself clean with.

'Back to the wagon,' the ogre wagon master bellows.

Quickly we finish our business and dutifully return. Our reward for obedience are hard biscuits, smoked fish and water. There's enough to keep the hunger pangs at bay and our energy levels up.

Our chain is reattached to the wagon, and Kralgen, with his four companions, emerge from the grass a short time later to receive the same bounty. The ogre munches away on something, and I wonder whether eating human flesh is a delicacy or part of their staple diet. I'm sure they must eat something else, although as screams echo in the distance, I'm not sure Gruldarn does.

Another life snuffed out, thanks to me being here.

*No, Malina!*

I've got to stop thinking this way. So, I killed the High King and countless others, facilitating Nogoth's invasion. Yet even had I failed, the Fey King and his legions would have come to wreak havoc anyway. This has been going on far longer than I've been alive, but if I have my way, it will end during my lifetime, one way or another.

But first, I have to get these damned manacles off.

For once, I'm impatient for the wagons to get moving. Our next stop will be in the evening, and if I can break the chain, I'll bind this annoying noble fool to me so he obeys my every order. Not looking at me and never speaking again will be a good start.

A gargoyle flies down, the grasses waving under its heavy wingbeat. It talks to our ogre wagon master before setting off again. It's the first time this communication has happened.

What's going on?

'Make ready!' the ogre shouts, and we dutifully come to our feet. If we didn't, we'd be dragged through the dirt.

The journey continues. Step after monotonous step. Once the ogre perimeter is set, it's time to test the chain.

Lengthening my stride, I come abreast of the wheel and, stooping down, flick the chain under its heavy metal rim. It makes a satisfying crunch, and I'm just about to repeat my action when a sudden blow to my back sends me sprawling under the wagon.

I twist frantically, a split second from getting crushed to death. I lie flat as the wagon passes over me and roll to my feet before the chain is drawn taut and drags me along.

I'm incandescent with rage.

That sly ignoble bastard had tried to kill me!

From his panicked look, he's now browning his trousers. Revenge is a dish best served cold, but as his gaze flicks back and forth between the driver and me, it's obvious he's considering saying something.

I can't afford to let that happen.

Grabbing the chain that binds us all together, I give it a yank, making him stumble, and as he tries to catch his balance, I close the distance and deliver a vicious kick to the back of his right knee. Crying out, he goes down, and as I shove, he suffers the fate he'd intended for me. The wagon rolls right across his lower back, causing blood to explode from his mouth.

The chain is yanked taught, and the two Tarsians in front are pulled dangerously close to the front wagon wheel, but I pull hard and drag the dying man out to the side, ensuring the women don't get caught up.

The ogre driver looks over his shoulder, aware of the commotion, and pulls the oxen to a halt. With a growl, he leaps off and stalks back to stand over the gurgling, whimpering mess near my feet.

Cold, fey eyes stare at me as its nostrils flare.

I say nothing and look away, not wanting to antagonise him.

'Gruldarn!' the ogre bellows and waves his hand as the shaggy head of the giant slowly turns in response. 'FOOD!'

The driver releases the padlock securing the girdle to the chain and kicks my victim to the side of the road.

A minute later, we're on our way.

I can't believe it, but the noble is still alive. His fingers claw at the dust, and his eyes, so filled with pain and desperation, look at me, pleading for release. Sadly, as the wagon draws me forward, I can't even give him that.

Gruldarn strides past to enjoy this unexpected gift, and I turn away, not wanting to witness the end. The noble might have brought it on himself, but his will be a horrible death. All he'd wanted to do was stay alive on this journey and considered me a danger.

He was right.

Because of me, a wife is without a husband, a son without a father. I feel a moment of sadness, but it doesn't last long as I look down at my manacles. One of the chain links has a chunk missing.

With some tugging, I ought to be able to split the chain in two.

Will it allow me to reach my magic?

I'll soon find out.

***

Whilst I still find the thought of being more fey than human unsettling, there's no denying the advantage of being able to see clearly at night.

My fellow prisoners are fast asleep, as are most of the ogre guards. No gargoyles are aloft, and Gruldarn must be fast asleep somewhere, for he's nowhere to be seen.

However, wolfen roam far and wide, the eyes and ears of the fey when night falls, yet they're far enough away to pose no threat.

Sitting cross-legged, I study the manacles. The break in the link isn't quite big enough to separate the chain, yet I'm confident that where I failed before, I'll now succeed. Twisting my forearm in the manacle, I slowly coil the chain, binding the two cuffs.

I move slowly, conscious of the ogre asleep on the wagon above me. Yet the gentle night breeze rustles the grasses, and their whispering is loud enough to conceal the noises I make. The pressure builds, and the chain fractures as I forcefully twist both forearms in opposite directions.

Several links fall to the ground, and I freeze, listening for any change in the ogre's heavy breathing, but there's none.

My excitement slowly begins to fade. There's no evidence of my magic returning, and the heavy hand of defeat weighs on my soul. I call out to it silently, to no avail, and when I try to use my spirit eye, I fail there too.

Finally, I try to conjure a gust of wind. Nothing.

DAMN.

I was foolish to have pinned my hopes on such a simple solution.

What now?

With so many links shattered, there's no way it will go unnoticed, and who knows what the repercussion of that will be. I might be hogtied and thrown in the back of the wagon, or knowing of my relationship with Kralgen, they might harm or even kill him.

Damn, damn, damn.

Dare I put the manacle cuffs under the wagon wheel to be broken like the chain and free my magic that way? No. At least one of my forearms will be crushed, and I can't get the oxen moving without waking the ogre guard.

There's no going back now.

But without my magic, what options do I have?

Any escape without its assistance is doomed to failure. Freeing us all from the chains that still bind us to the wagons is unlikely without magical help. Not to mention the wolfen will be able to track our scent should we get away. We might all be consummate fighters, but outnumbered, unarmed, and on foot, we just won't survive.

Everything pivots on me using my magic to control the guards and Gruldarn.

There must be a way.

*Think, Malina!*

If only I could slip my hands through the cuffs, but they're too tight.

Unless ...

My pulse begins to rise at what I'm about to do, and I take a moment to bring it back under control, breathing slowly. Then, when I'm ready, I kneel.

I remember both Alyssa and Nestor suffering from an unpleasant injury once.

Laying my forearm on the floor, I rest my knee on the joint of my thumb, then bring my weight forward. There's a small pop, and I want to scream; the pain is excruciating. My jaw aches from clenching my teeth, and tears run down my face as I gingerly slide the manacle over the dislocated digit.

Oh, come on. Please.

Yet there's no familiar wriggle, just a throbbing pain from my hand.

Thinking about dislocating the other thumb sickens me, but there's no going back now. Even if I slide the manacle back on and hope the guard doesn't see the broken chain, the swelling will mean I can't remove it again.

I'll remove the other manacle, use my magic to free Kralgen, and then together find Dimitar. There's no doubt in my mind that the odds are against us escaping, but we've overcome impossible situations before.

With my mind settled, I take my dislocated thumb firmly in the other hand. I'd witnessed Lystra resetting dislocated joints before, and I know it hurts just as bad as the dislocation itself. Breathing deeply to calm myself, I mentally prepare for the next bout of searing pain.

The wagon creaks, and I freeze. A moment later, there's a thump, and the ogre driver lands beside me. I try to roll away but can't as he's landed on the chain attaching me to the wagon. He grabs my shoulder and throws me to my back. I hiss in defiance and am vaguely aware of the two Tarsians scrambling away from the fight. I can't say I blame them. Any interference now would only lead to their deaths. I struggle, twisting, trying to hook the ogre's legs from under him, but he's too heavy and well-balanced. I can't even hit him; his arms are too long.

'Nogoth said you'd try and escape. He's never wrong!' The ogre laughs.

I can't do much other than snarl in defiance as he draws his gnarled fist back and hits me twice on the jaw.

Everything becomes distant, and there's rushing in my ears as if I'm underwater. I'm vaguely aware of being rolled over and my wrists being tied tightly. I'm grateful to be almost unconscious when he slides the discarded manacle over my hand and yanks my thumb back into place.

'You're a slippery one,' he growls as he kicks me onto my back. 'I've got orders not to kill you, but nothing was said about not giving you broken bones. Try anything again, and I'll start snapping fingers!'

Satisfied with himself, he leaps back onto the wagon, snarls at Kralgen and the others, and lies down.

My face hurts, as does my thumb, and now I've got to try and sleep with my arms tied securely behind me. It takes me a while to position myself with my back to the wagon wheel. I curse silently. I'm not used to failure, but one thing is certain, even if escaping isn't.

I'm going to kill that bloody ogre!

***

All I need to do is leap onto the wagon, run along its length, and loop the chain hanging from my waist around the driver's neck. Then, with my knees wedged in his back, I'll count to fifteen while I yank with all my strength. Result. One dead ogre driver.

Revenge would be so sweet ... but sadly short-lived.

There will be no quick getaway on the oxen cart, and it would take no more than a minute or two for the ogre guards, wolfen or Gruldarn to exact a deadly toll for such defiance.

I'm sure everyone around my wagon has thought about this or similar whenever the lash has struck, and our driver is particularly generous this morning. Whilst there's no doubt he enjoys inflicting pain, I think he's being extra sadistic because he keeps turning to keep an eye on me. Once again, my actions are leading to everyone suffering.

The whip cracks again, and the man in front of Kralgen goes down from the shock. Kralgen hoists him up, and I can sense the restrained fury within my friend. It's a positive change, for with such a fiery emotion comes strength, and Kralgen's spirit has been sorely diminished recently. However, if Kralgen vents his anger and kills the driver, we're back to that short-lived sweetness again.

A strong breeze blows my hair back, and the leather cover on the wagon flaps where it's not tied down. It might be summer, but there's a smell of rain in the air. I peer north into the wind; sure enough, distant clouds are darkening the sky and heading our way.

Wonderful. A good soaking to make life even sweeter.

Occasional gusts have us leaning forward, but the oxen don't notice, and we either push on or get dragged along.

Can I use the water to my advantage in any way? If only I was free, then definitely yes. However, with my hands tied behind me, manacled, and under the watchful eye of the driver, I don't see how.

With my disappointment looming large, putting things into perspective is difficult, but we've only been on the road for less than a week and have several more to win freedom. Perhaps an opportunity will arise when we get to Eastnor.

Patience is a virtue, but I'm not sure I've ever been virtuous.

Distant movement catches my attention, and I smile in grim satisfaction. The gargoyles are all over the place, frantically flapping before giving up and dropping to the ground. It would have been amusing to see some hit by lightning. Several fly overhead at speed, and two wolfen run by howling.

Yes, there's the roll of distant thunder, and it's growing louder. But would a mere storm be causing the ogre guards to shout at one another?

Kralgen's head whips around toward me as realisation hits. It's not thunder, but the pounding of hooves and those gargoyles aren't landing; they're falling from the sky injured or dead!

The ogres from both sides of the wagon line run to the head of the column, coming together in a solid line of muscle, arms and armour, heavy shields locked together. Gruldarn stands before them, that tree trunk held in his giant hand like a toothpick.

With a crack of his whip, our driver turns the wagon off-road as others do the same. In mere seconds, the ogres' battle line has its rear protected from a charge by the heavy wagons lined up nose to tail.

Our driver leaps from his seat onto the back of the wagon and throws back the leather covers. I'm tempted to make a move, but Kralgen shakes his head. If we aren't liberated, and we've killed our guard, then Gruldarn will be having a big lunch. The time for action isn't quite yet.

I hate being patient!

After thrusting some stores aside, the driver stands up. He straps a short sword to his waist, then lifts a black, wickedly curved bow and a quiver of arrows that were hidden below.

'Kneel with heads to the ground, or you'll get an arrow in your back!' he roars.

I don't hesitate. Now is not the time to test this ogre's patience.

However, as I drop close to the wagon's side, I make eye contact with Kralgen and the other prisoners. Kralgen curls his good hand into a fist. With my hands behind my back, I can only nod. The Tarsians, understanding our meaning, follow suit, and one of the men on Kralgen's side, who looks Delnorian, does too. We have five willing and ready to fight if the opportunity arises.

It's impossible to see what's happening from so close to the ground, with long grasses waving over us. But the thunder is deafening, the ground shakes, and the war cries of men and women rise loud, joined by the hiss of arrows.

'Hah! Got you,' the ogre crows from atop the wagon.

I'm not going to wait any longer. If whoever the ogre is shooting at is attacking the column despite Gruldarn's presence, it's because they have a chance. Also, as the driver's bow thrums, I know he's distracted by the enemy.

Dropping to my back, I twist and squirm, ignore the cramps, push my wrist bindings past my ass, and then lift my legs and slip the bindings over my feet. Now my hands are in front, I feel like I can function again.

I make a grabbing motion with both fists at Kralgen and the man next to him and point upwards. The other three prisoners on Kralgen's side are curled on the floor, shaking.

I hold my hand steady, listening, waiting.

*Twang.*

'GO!' I mouth, surging to my feet as Kralgen and the Delnorian leap up, grab the ogre's feet, and yank.

As the ogre falls, hands flailing, I loop the chain that had dragged us along all these leagues around its neck. Dropping backwards, I wedge my feet against the underside of the wagon and heave with every ounce of strength I possess.

The ogre's head is bent backwards at an impossible angle, and although it doesn't break, the chain links are deep in its flesh. Kralgen and the Delnorian must still be holding his feet; otherwise, he'd fall off on top of me.

'I told you I'd kill you!' I snarl as it tries to get its fingers under the chain.

Those foul black eyes bulge out of their sockets, then thankfully the ogre goes limp.

One of the Tarsians leaps up and drags the short sword from the driver's scabbard. I hold out my hands, and she cuts through the bindings, only for her eyes to open wide as an arrowhead punches out of her chest.

'Take cover,' I yell, throwing myself under the wagon.

The others join me instantly. An arrow smacks into the head of a cowering prisoner, who dies without a sound. Kralgen unceremoniously drags the remaining two under the wagon with us.

I pass the sword to Kralgen.

'Our escape hasn't gone unnoticed. You provide a distraction, and don't die!' I say.

I look at the Tarsian.

'Osintra.'

'Osintra. Our driver has the key to these padlocks. Drag him off and get us free of these bloody chains.

'Dalyarn,' the Delnorian offers as I look at him.

'Dalyarn. I'm going to kill some of the ogre drivers. It's your job to start freeing the prisoners. Hopefully, enough are soldiers and can help win this battle.

He nods, hope shining in his eyes.

'Ready?'

Unwavering gazes are the only answer I need.

'Kral. GO!'

***

It's strange how sometimes when I move my fastest, time appears to pass in slow motion.

As I step out from cover, the Tarsian following suit, I spy an arrow sailing through the air. It seems to hang momentarily, as if to make me aware of its presence, before speeding up to slam into Osintra's leg. The shock and pain registering on her face, even the cry she utters, seems drawn out, mocking time. Despite the injury, she resolutely grabs the dead ogre's shoulders and hauls him to the ground, continuing with her mission.

Clambering onto the wagon, I hunker down, aware of Kral's blade deflecting an arrow, his face twisted in delight. He finds such happiness in fighting. For him, perfection can be found in the simplistic form of a thrust, the timing of a parry, and the execution of a counter. It reaches him on a level I simply can't comprehend.

I pick up the fallen bow, choose an arrow from the quiver leant against the side of a water barrel, then duck right as I note the driver on the next wagon exhale a split second before he releases.

The eagle feathers caress my cheek as the arrow hisses past, rotating slowly while I pull back on the drawstring of my own bow and release a heartbeat later. Without following its flight, I know that the arrow will punch through the ogre's mouth and out the back of its neck.

I draw another arrow, stepping left, conscious of an arrow parting the air where I'd just been standing. Shoot and move, or shoot and die. I'm grateful the ogre drivers haven't learnt that lesson.

The next driver topples off his bench, an arrow through his eye. It was a lucky shot, I'd been aiming for his chest, but the shaft was warped.

'Dalyarn!' I shout.

At the sound of his name, he's off to the next wagon, searching for the key in the fallen driver's pockets to free the prisoners beneath.

I empty the quiver quickly, six more drivers of the closest wagons falling to my skill. We're now a little safer.

Osintra climbs up painfully and releases my padlock as, for the first time, I take stock of what's going on.

From the black banner bearing the sigil of crossed ball and chains, the attackers are Astorian.

Maybe a hundred of their mounted light horse archers wearing leather armour are peppering the giant and the ogre ranks with arrows from a safe distance. Their shots are mostly ineffective against the giant's thick skin. Likewise, their success against the ceramic plate armour and large shields of the ogres is limited, but perhaps a dozen fey lay dead on the ground. Sadly, a similar number of empty saddles show this hasn't been a one-sided exchange.

Fifty heavy, irregular knights wait patiently off to the side. Their horses are protected by mail, while the riders wear metal plate. They wield an assortment of single-handed weapons, from flails to swords and axes.

This battle is already at an impasse. The heavy cavalry can't charge, or they'll be dashed to pieces by the giant, and the fey are too cumbersome to engage the cavalry unless the latter gets sloppy or foolish.

If the steam runs out of this exchange and the Astorians go their way, things will not end well for us. We need to swing the balance of this fight quickly, yet we hardly have any weapons. Perhaps a dozen prisoners have come to join us, five bearing the bows of the fallen drivers. They huddle in the lee of our wagon awaiting my command. I wonder briefly where Dimitar is and hope he's alright.

I contemplate having the archers open fire on the rear of the ogre line, but when they do, some of the ogres will turn on us with deadly results. We're not armed well enough to withstand even a few of them.

Whilst being on the back of the wagon gives me a good vantage point, I'm also somewhat vulnerable, so I jump off, using it for cover, and pull the chain through the hoop around my waist, freeing myself completely. If only I could rid myself of these damn manacles, we wouldn't need more weapons.

Then the Astorian banner catches my eye, and I sniff at my short-sightedness. I've had a weapon to hand the whole time. The heavy metal ball at the end of this long chain makes a deadly piece of equipment in the right hands. I snatch it up, looping it around my shoulder. The chain is far too long, but I don't have the time to shorten it.

'Kral! We need to break their line before the Astorians give up. Any thoughts beyond a suicidal charge?'

'I like your idea of a charge!' Kralgen grins, gripping his sword.

'You won't survive. Don't even think about it!'

'Not me.' Kralgen shakes his head and rolls his eyes as if talking to a child. 'The oxen!'

Kral never fails to amaze me.

'You archers, keep the other drivers' heads down even if you can't get a kill shot,' Kralgen orders taking over. 'Dalyarn, you're coming with me, and you three,' he says, choosing his herders. 'Malina, this first wagon is yours! Archers, cover us!'

There's no hesitation. I grab the shortsword from Osintra and then run to the front of the wagon. Four heavy oxen are tethered there. They're docile beasts, castrated at an early age and are used to a slow, plodding gait. Not for much longer.

I slash through the harness straps holding them in place, then turn the lead ox toward the line through brute force, cajoling and slapping with the flat of my sword. I feel utterly exposed, but the archers are doing a good job, or someone else is being targeted because no arrows come my way.

When I have them pointing at the back of the ogre line twenty paces distant, I whisper an apology, then jam the sword point into the rump of the closest animal. It jolts forward, bellowing in misery, and the others follow half-heartedly. I work my way around, sword poking until they're all calling out in pain, and with each successive strike, they build up speed.

The others are adopting a similar approach, although I can see one Tarsian manically cracking a whip instead, and a few moments later, the oxen reach the ogre line. It's anticlimactic at first. No ogre bodies are thrown into the air, as this is no stampede by enraged bulls. However, the oxen are relentless in their desire to escape and push into the ogre line, knocking the heavy creatures aside. As the ogres slash out in frustration, the oxen become more enraged, creating bigger gaps, and suddenly, thunder fills the air again.

Twenty Astorian heavy cavalry punch into the milling ogres, breaking through their line, scattering them, axes swinging, flails lashing, swords hacking. They don't pause, not for a moment, and instead ride along the line of wagons, killing the drivers before slamming into the back of the ogre line at the other end, tearing it apart.

'COME ON!' Kralgen yells as he runs back along the line toward me. 'Let's kill the bastards or die trying!'

I fix my eye on the broken line just ahead, allowing the heavy metal ball to hang from a length of chain as I run forward, catching up with Kral. War cries sound behind me as our fellow prisoners surge forward in response to Kral's rallying call.

'I bet I kill more than you,' Kral howls as the rear of the ogre line turns to face our threat, further weakening their cohesion.

'We'll see!'

I swing the heavy ball, enjoying its weight and momentum, while I pick my target. I only hope we're both alive at the end to find out who the winner is.

***

I spin, the metal ball swings wide, and I lengthen the chain a little, grimacing in satisfaction as it smacks into the side of an ogre warrior's helmet. He goes down, an eyeball hanging from its socket.

'Five!' I yell.

'Seven,' Kral shouts back.

'You can't even count to seven,' I grumble, cursing as I quickly back away from a charging ogre.

The ball and chain is a good weapon, but only if the ball is moving. I spin, the slack chain wrapping around my body, the ball picking up speed again as it's whipped up off the ground. The ogre pauses, the ball's ominous vroom, and its blurring passage catching its eye. I can see it judging when to leap forward, but I don't give it a chance. Swinging the ball low, I release the chain, then yank it taut so it wraps around the ogre's legs. As I throw my weight backwards, the creature crashes to the ground. Kralgen jumps in and drives his sword through the ogre's teeth and out the back of its neck.

'Eight!'

I duck under a thrown dagger before letting go of the chain. It's better suited for fighting solo, not in group fighting like this, where I could unintentionally hit an ally if they stray too close. To replace it, I grab my dead opponent's sword and snatch up a heavy shield, only to cast it aside when my thumb complains. I keep my back to Kral's, trying to catch my breath.

Around half the prisoners had joined our attack, recognising this as a last-gasp chance. Sadly, most of them lay dead, hacked to pieces around us. Without armour against the ogres, their ends had been swift and bloody. Yet, just like Kral and I, the survivors now hold enemy weapons and are giving a better account of themselves.

Thankfully, just as many dead ogres litter the ground, and the combat effectiveness of those remaining is diminishing rapidly. Attacked from both sides, the shield wall has fallen apart, and no shield can protect from an arrow to the back if you're facing the wrong way.

Now the fight is turning into a bloody melee between the prisoners and ogres.

Four ogres head toward Kral and I, yet before they become a threat, three horses run them down, flinging them aside. The impact is so savage it breaks bones, killing two before they hit the ground. I run in to make sure they never rise again.

'Seven. I'm catching you!'

Horses whinny, ogres roar, men and women cry out as they fight or die. The ground becomes treacherous as the blood and emptied bowels from the dead and dying soak into the thirsty soil.

A deep roar reverberates in my stomach, and I twist briefly, catching sight of Gruldarn. A contingent of light horse archers is constantly baiting him, firing arrows at his face, causing him to shield his eyes with a hand while swinging blindly with that tree trunk.

One of the archers strays too close, and both horse and rider are flung through the air like toys. Only toys don't scream in agony like they both do.

The next moment I'm facing an ogre with three spikes on her shoulder guard. She's as large as I've seen, and her tusks curl upwards, yellowed with age.

She carries no shield, holding her sword two-handed, bringing her fearsome strength to bear. I'd happily let Kral have this one, but he's fighting off two ogres behind me, and there's no one to come to my aid.

She sidles toward me, confident but not foolishly so. No rash charge, just a steady advance. I sidestep, not knowing what's behind me, and we circle, the tips of our swords questing, touching, awaiting the right moment.

I'm at a huge disadvantage in this fight. She has a longer weapon, a longer reach, and is far stronger. How I wish I had the ball and chain again.

A horse charges in from behind the ogre's right shoulder. The ogre twists the sword in front of her face, and I wait for the rider's axe to take the ogre's head. Yet my opponent ducks and pivots, her sword sweeping out, taking the horse's nearest front leg away, sending both mount and rider crashing to the ground. She's back facing me in guard position as I register that she'd seen the approaching horse in the reflection of her blade.

Incredible.

She attacks; her lunge perfect. I twist away, using my speed, unwilling to meet her blade or commit to my own strike. Then she attacks again, stepping in behind short, powerful sweeps. With her blade swung horizontally, I have to parry, or otherwise, I'll have to step backwards, and I've no wish to do that on uncertain terrain.

The weight of her blows are numbing. My left hand is already weak from my injured thumb, and it won't be long before her blows get through. It's time to go on the attack.

Anticipating the next sweep, I roll under the ogre's blade, my sword flicking out, aiming to slash the thigh muscle, yet the blade glances from her reinforced kilt, and I receive a cut to my shoulder for my troubles.

The sneer I receive just makes me angry and gives me strength.

I flex my shoulder. Not bad, just painful, but any blood loss isn't good. What's taking Kral so bloody long? Another thrust, her blade whispers along mine, and my forearm is bleeding. This time I give better than I got, and black blood flows from a deep cut to her bicep.

We lock blades, and she closes in, not allowing me to disengage, and butts me to the forehead.

I stumble, shaking my head in pain, but it's only a ruse. I twist aside from her finishing overhand strike but yet again fail to land a counter as she dances back.

Damn, but she's good, and I don't think I can win this fight, at least not fairly.

Another ogre with an axe runs in from my left. I pretend not to notice until the last moment, and frantically raise my blade to parry its powerful overhand blow, leaving my side unprotected. The ogress roars in triumph, lunging, knowing she has me.

But I've no intention of parrying the axe. Instead, I spin from its path, sucking in my stomach as the lunge misses me by a hair's breadth. The axe crashes down onto the sword blade of the ogress, smashing it toward the ground, leaving her neck open to a slashing, killing blow from my blade.

Thankfully, Kralgen beheads the axe wielder an instant later.

Chest heaving, I turn my back to Kral, sword extended in exhausted arms.

Another dozen mounted Astorians gallop past, taking advantage of the splintering ranks. Their war cries are joyous despite the carnage, revelling in bloodlust.

'I miss Kralfax,' Kralgen bemoans in the few moments of respite we get. 'He was better than any horse!'

Suddenly the ogres, sensing imminent defeat, decide to kill as many prisoners as possible. As one, they break ranks, charging for the wagons, and we're in their way.

The heavy cavalry whoop, charging down the running ogres, leaving the mounted archers to keep Gruldarn occupied.

I step to meet a running ogre pounding directly toward me, Kralgen at my back. At the last moment, I dodge sideways, but my foe doesn't engage and continues straight on.

'KRAL!' I scream as the ogre swings his sword in a horizontal blow aimed at decapitating my friend.

Kral reacts to my scream and drops to one knee just in time; a small cloud of hair hangs in the air momentarily, a testament to how close the blade had come. Unable to check its momentum, the ogre tumbles over Kral's crouched form and knocks over another of its kin.

Kral just hacks into whatever unprotected flesh presents itself, severing a leg and arm before finishing both creatures off.

Around twenty remaining ogres reach the wagons and begin slaughtering all the prisoners who hadn't participated in the fight.

Then I spy Dimitar.

He's just standing there, stone eyes surveying the carnage, unmoving, like a statue ... oblivious to the half dozen bloodied ogres charging at him.

***

# CHAPTER V

DIMITAR!'

As the words leave my lips, I sprint toward him, Kralgen by my side.

Unlike when I'd warned Kral, there's no instantaneous reflex response. Rather, Dimitar turns slowly toward me as though the ogres between us aren't even there.

The first ogre reaches him, his sword cutting down diagonally in a blow to cut Dimitar in two from neck to hip.

A ringing reaches my ears as the sword bounces off, leaving Dimitar unscathed as if hit by a stick. Enraged, the ogre swings repeatedly, the others joining in, as if it's their final purpose to destroy this stone man in their midst. The musical sound as their blades bounce rhythmically from Dimitar's stone body could be almost harmonic if it didn't presage such violent intent.

Just as we reach Dimitar, one bearing an axe takes an almighty swing, hitting him in the upper arm, which, to my dismay, breaks away. Before the ogres can do any further harm, Kralgen and I fall upon them from behind, wreaking a terrible toll before they can react.

Although armoured, they're not wearing helms, and their arms and legs are bare. My sword, whilst chipped from countless blows, slices through the stout leg of the axe bearer as if it were butter. Its roar of pain is quickly silenced as I reverse the blade and bury it in his neck.

Blood splatters across my face, running into my mouth, sweet and nourishing. I lick it away, forcing back the hunger that washes over me.

I'm shield bashed from the side, and trip on a corpse, falling awkwardly. My right arm is numb; I've dropped my weapon and am badly winded. My attacker rears over me, sword raised, and I frantically kick at his legs, causing him to stumble. But it's not enough.

The ogre roars in victory, and I tense, anticipating the death blow.

A horse flashes past, and the next moment the ogre topples, headless, spurting blood all over me. I heave the corpse to one side, my heart beating like a war drum.

Kralgen leans over me, extending his arm.

'You probably lost.'

He grins, and it takes me a moment to realise he's still keeping count.

I'm pulled to my feet as if I weigh nothing more than a feather. The battle around us is over, but not far away, Gruldarn fights on.

Dimitar kneels next to us. He's holding the broken arm against the stump, looking bewildered.

'Oh, Dimitar,' I sob, sitting beside him. 'Look what they've done to you.'

I put my arm around those stone shoulders, seeking to comfort him, but he doesn't appear perturbed.

'I'll be fine, Malina,' he replies in an emotionless voice and releases his arm. To my amazement, it stays affixed to the stump, with a huge piece missing where the axe blade has broken some stone away. 'I just need to heal by replacing what I lost.'

Kralgen crouches down and gives the reset arm a gentle tug, but it remains solidly attached.

'Maybe I should have tried to stick my hand back together when Nogoth chopped it apart,' he rumbles in amazement.

Dimitar doesn't respond. He just reaches down, pushes his fingers into the gravel lining the roadside, takes a handful, and brings it to his mouth.

Kralgen and I wince at the crunch and exchange horrified looks.

Our friend is changing, becoming less like himself every day. My mother used to tell children's tales of golems, creatures of earth and stone that would rise up and serve the will of their creator. Is that what Dimitar is becoming?

Kralgen beckons.

'Come, let's leave Dimitar to his lunch. Gruldarn fights on. Let's not miss this!'

'Kral. That creature is deadly. Don't do anything foolish!'

'You just don't want me to eclipse you killing a troll!' Kralgen teases.

I don't say a word, in case he takes it as a challenge.

'Dimitar. Will you be alright?' I ask.

I receive a simple nod and head after Kral.

A few survivors stagger toward the final fight. Others drop to the ground, too exhausted to do anything other than bind their wounds. I could help, but like Kral, I need to see the end of this beast. Gruldarn's been responsible for many deaths on this journey and remains too lethal to leave behind, evidenced by the scattered, broken bodies of horses and men who strayed too close.

The horse archers have apparently emptied their quivers, for they're now doing nothing more than bait Gruldarn at a respectful distance. However powerful the bows, very few arrows protrude from its thick hide. They can't do anything other than shoot insults now.

Likewise, as I inspect the remnants of the Astorian irregular cavalry, I have sincere doubts about what they can achieve. They don't have any heavy lances that would be effective, and now only number around thirty.

The riders gather in a circle around two central figures embroiled in a heated discussion. I expect they're thinking the same as me.

Time to move on and not risk any other lives on this behemoth.

I'm wrong.

Moments later, two groups of fourteen riders canter toward Gruldarn, shaking their weapons and shouting war cries. One group looks set to attack from the north, the other south. Two riders remain watching, no doubt the commanders. I'm not impressed for they should lead by example.

Gruldarn roars a challenge, swinging the tree trunk effortlessly.

'This will be painful for the cavalry,' Kralgen says. 'My money is on the giant. Those cavalry are going to get squashed!'

I can only agree with his dire assessment.

'Perhaps we should leave now while Gruldarn is distracted,' I suggest.

'That's interesting!'

Something in Kralgen's tone has me turn back.

The lines of cavalry have approached the giant, but before getting too close, have reined the horses away and streamed past, causing Gruldarn to frantically turn left and right, lashing out unsuccessfully with his weapon. With a roar, Gruldarn spins around to watch this threat closely as both groups form a single line facing him.

'Look!'

Kralgen points to the two riders, who suddenly urge their horses into a gallop toward the giant's back. What they hope to achieve is beyond me. Perhaps if the horses can be made to ride into the giant's legs, it might cause him to stumble, but I'm sure the mounts will veer away, defying the riders' intent.

Then, to my disbelief, the fully armoured riders clamber up to crouch on their saddles. The balance required for such a feat at full gallop is phenomenal, and they each hold a battle axe with a wicked spike on the reverse. As they near Gruldarn, both leap, perfectly timed to coincide with the horses' upward motion.

Their mounts run between Gruldarn's legs as the riders crash against Gruldarn's back. I wince at the impact, but even more so as they slam those spiked weapons home.

Gruldarn's cries of pain are painful to hear, and he casts the tree trunk aside, trying to pluck off the warriors on his back with arms too thick and muscled to reach. I watch in amazement as, using a dagger in one hand and the axe in the other, both warriors climb up Gruldarn's back as if scaling a mountain.

As Gruldarn spins around, the irregular cavalry attack the distracted giant, slashing at its giant legs with swords and stabbing it with spears.

A small part of me feels pity for this creature of legend as both warriors hack at its spine just below the neck. Blow after blow they land, and eventually those mighty legs buckle. Gruldarn falls to his hands and knees, then collapses face down on the plain, fingers digging massive furrows in the ground.

One of the warriors had rolled away with the impact, but the other stands upon that massive back and continues his frenzied assault until Gruldarn twitches a final time.

The second warrior joins the first, and together they raise their axes with a war cry, thrusting them at the sky, the surviving Astorians roaring their approval.

Kralgen does the same, saluting the bravery and skill of the two warriors.

We've escaped, but as I survey the bodies littering the countryside and Dimitar sitting by the wagon, I shudder at the cost.

***

This battle might be over, but as Kralgen and I return to the wounded, the fight for survival begins all over again.

Give me the sound of combat any day over the pitiful cries of those facing death. However brave the man or woman, some wounds are too grievous to cope with, and everyone has their breaking point.

Often the worse wound is one to the gut. If it doesn't kill outright, the victim can stay alive for hours with their entrails spilt on the ground around them. Losing an arm or a leg is also terrible, but most people bleed out quickly, their panicked hearts pumping the lifeblood from their veins, leading to a quick and merciful death in next to no time.

We stop and help everyone, irrespective of the severity.

The first is a heavily scarred soldier, obviously no stranger to pain or combat, who sits in a large pool of blood despite the tourniquet tied around his upper thigh. Iron self-discipline stops him from crying out, but his face is ashen and twisted in pain to match his mangled leg. It's an injury so severe that it renders him beyond hope.

'Can I ease your journey, brother?' Kralgen asks, kneeling next to him.

The man says nothing but lifts a dagger and places the tip against his chest.

Kralgen gently closes his hand around the man's.

'Do you have a wife or child?' Kralgen asks.

A nod and silent tears are the only answer.

'Then close your eyes, brother,' Kralgen says softly. 'Bring their faces to mind and tell them you'll be together soon!'

As Kralgen utters the final word, he thrusts the dagger deep, and with a sigh, the veteran passes away.

Kralgen has brought me to tears, and as we move on to a woman sitting up against a wagon wheel, grimacing in pain as she holds her stomach together, I know many more are to come.

Some wish to be helped to whatever awaits, while others treasure every last breath. An Astorian rider wants to grip his sword as he passes, whilst others just want to hold a hand. Kralgen finds words of kindness for everyone, and I'm touched by his compassion. Is this really the man who once thought a medal should only be given for taking lives?

Thankfully, there are those with less serious injuries that can be treated. There are no medical supplies in the wagons, so we tear strips of clothing from the dead for bindings.

Lost hands or digits, gashes, cuts, and puncture wounds are all survivable if the flesh doesn't fester. Kralgen calls upon his magic to help cauterise wounds where absolutely necessary. However, we leave most of the minor injuries open to allow the bleeding to expel any foreign body and help prevent infection.

'Dalyarn didn't make it,' Kralgen says sadly, pointing to the body of the warrior who'd first helped us. Two arrows protrude from his chest, but next to him is a dead ogre. He'd died fighting.

'Looks like Osintra did though,' I say, spying her hobbling toward us. 'Let's get that arrow out of her thigh!'

As we help the Tarsian, I note the Astorians are busy too. A pile of ogre heads is growing by the minute as a dozen warriors go about the grisly task of hacking them off. Others check bodies and scavenge the battlefield for spent arrows, weapons, and armour. The wagons are also being readied to move. Horse archers are the new drivers for those wagons that still have oxen. Those that don't have their loads redistributed.

The commander is prudent, leaving nothing behind for the enemy.

We finish helping Osintra and return to find Dimitar sitting where we'd left him earlier. He still looks a mess, with cracks and chips all over, but he's stopped eating, and if stone eyes can be more alert, then his appear to be.

'Dimitar. Are you feeling better?'

'Malina. I'm fine. I was just admiring the colours; they're beautiful,' he says, his eyes flicking everywhere.'

I kneel in front of him.

'Why didn't you fight when those ogres attacked you?'

'Because you didn't tell me to,' he answers, tilting his head. 'Should I have?'

'Yes, Dimitar. Fighting to protect yourself and your friends is a good idea.'

Maybe one of the blows Dimitar took to the head has hurt him, but I'm also aware he's become more vacant since he turned to stone.

'Come, let's get the wounded ready to travel,' I suggest.

Kralgen grunts in approval and picks up Osintra. I half smile, wondering if he's drawn to her because she's a Tarsian like Alyssa.

'I can still bloody walk,' she scolds Kralgen in indignation.

'Not as fast as I can,' Kralgen laughs as she thumps him on the chest. 'Want me to drop you?'

'You're so bloody tall, the fall would probably kill me!'

Dimitar looks at me as he stands over an unconscious man with a bandaged head wound, then picks him up effortlessly when I smile in approval. He might be slowly losing his mind, but there's no denying his increasing strength.

Offering my hand to a soldier with a bandaged arm and ankle, I pull him upright, and he leans on my shoulder as we follow Kralgen toward the nearest wagon.

It's laden with supplies, and now the looted fey armour and weapons.

I look along the line, and they're all piled high.

Kralgen puts Osintra down and begins dumping armour off the back to make space for her and Dimitar's patient.

'What do you think you're doing?' shouts an Astorian archer, who leaps down from the driver's bench to confront Kralgen.

'People normally think I'm slow,' Kralgen says, inclining his head toward the Astorian.

I show the wounded man I'm guiding to the archer's mount tethered to the wagon.

'Here. This might be a little more comfortable for you.' I say, helping him onto the gelding.

'Get him off my horse,' the Astorian shouts, unsure whether to deal with Kralgen or me first. He puts his hand to the hilt of a sabre at his waist, and Kralgen steps up to him before he can draw steel.

'If that sword clears that scabbard, I'll rip your arm off and beat you to death with it!'

Kralgen's voice is so full of menace that the man gulps and runs off toward the irregular cavalry, no doubt to report our interference.

'This will lead to no good, mark my words,' I say. 'Let's get as many wounded on board before he stirs up trouble.'

'First things first,' rumbles Kralgen, tossing an ogre sword and a dagger in a weapon belt for me to wear. He shrugs on an ogre's cuirass that barely fits, and I help him buckle it up, then pull on some vambraces and greaves. Likewise, he arms himself with a sword and dagger.

Dimitar has gently placed Osintra and the unconscious man onto the back of the wagon as I finish helping Kralgen. I'm about to suggest Dimitar arms himself with a weapon, but I know there's little point. He's no longer the man he was, and the realisation saddens me immensely.

We manage to load another eight wounded onto the wagon before the pounding of hooves makes us turn. The way the Astorians are charging their horses at us, weapons ready, I don't think they're coming for a friendly talk.

***

'I bet I kill more than you do,' Kral mutters again without conviction as we step away from the wagons toward the thirty irregular cavalry galloping toward us.

Then, to my surprise, Dimitar appears on my left.

'I'm here to protect my friends,' he grates.

It's harrowing, walking toward those charging horses. Despite Kralgen's words, we'll be nothing but smears on the ground if the riders follow through with their charge.

Yet just as it seems we're about to be run down, mailed fists yank back on reins, and the horses come to a sliding stop, no more than two steps away.

Steam rises in plumes from their nostrils before being whisked away by the breeze.

Kralgen steps forward as if nothing untoward has happened and rubs the nose of the lead rider's horse, who, from the armour, is one of those who'd killed Gruldarn.

A golden circlet adorns the top of the closed helm, and I realise this must be the King of Astoria.

'Remove your hands from my mount, peasant!' snaps a metallic voice.

I tense, waiting for Kralgen's angry response, yet, when the need arises, Kralgen intuitively reads the situation and puts aside his baser instincts.

'A peasant I was born,' says Kralgen smiling, 'but I stand before you as a king.'

As he gives the horse a final scratch, it snickers in appreciation.

'I think your horse likes me,' Kralgen grins. 'Now, tell me, has the ruler of Astoria come to offer the King of Icelandia a drink?'

Those mailed hands release the reins and lift to grab the sides of the metal helm, and then, with a push, the helmet is off.

Before me sits the ruler of Astoria. I'd expected a king, but I was wrong. The queen is broad-faced with a cleft chin and high cheekbones and could almost be mistaken for a man, yet there's beauty there too. Her eyes are crystal blue, full lips offset the masculine chin, and sweaty, sable black hair falls around her shoulders as she shakes her head.

Her gaze softens slightly.

'I am Queen Asterz.'

She pauses, a measuring look in her eyes.

'Only a true King of Icelandia would have the balls to stand before a charge without flinching,' she laughs coldly, slapping her mailed thigh. 'Forgive me for testing your metal in such a fashion. Us Astorians value bravery above all else, and in truth, I already knew who you were. Well met, King Kralgen.'

Then those icy eyes focus on me, her nose wrinkling subtly in distaste.

'Unfortunately, you appear to keep poor company,' she continues. 'Malina, King Slayer. Is there anywhere in this world where you're not reviled with a price on your head?' she asks, leaning forward, resting her forearms on the pommel of her saddle.

'I'm not wanted in Delnor, where we're now standing,' I snap back, instantly disliking this woman.

'Sadly, I don't think Delnor has survived,' she sneers. 'Perhaps I'll claim these lands for Astoria!'

She turns back to Kralgen.

'You may be a King, but my soldiers are not your subjects. They have orders that you and this assassin interfered with, and you'll not make that mistake again! Their orders are to gather supplies and leave a bloody message for the fey, not care for the people of Delnor!'

'Many of the injured here are not Delnorian, and even if some are, you can't abandon them!' I exclaim, shocked. 'Have you any idea of the might of the army you're facing? You'll need every man and woman fighting by your side irrespective of nationality.'

'You seek to lecture me, the woman who slew the High King. A half-blood fey rumoured to be responsible for countless other noble deaths!

If it wasn't for the king by your side, your head would join the pile of ogre heads on the trade road. Now, unless you're going to thank me for saving your worthless life, still your black tongue, girl, before I have it removed!'

Kralgen shoots me a warning look, but I'm not ready to give up nor concede to this callous woman, queen or no. I'm also intrigued about how she knows of my heritage and Kralgen's identity.

'Then at least leave some wagons, and I'll ensure the wounded ...'

A large Astorian in black chainmail knees his horse forward, and I'm knocked over hard by its forequarters.

'Didn't you hear the queen, fey scum? Keep your mouth shut, or I'll personally take your head!'

I'm dazed by such an unexpected blow, and as I lie there, looking up in disbelief, Dimitar steps forward.

Till now, every movement he'd made had been slow, deliberate, as if happening at a different speed to the world around him. However, the punch he throws snaps out in a blur to hit the horse on the side of the head. It collapses as if its legs were chopped from under it, pitching the rider forward.

The queen struggles to control her startled mount, as do several others at this sudden violence.

Dimitar lifts the fallen rider up by the neck in one hand.

'Shall I kill him?' he grates as the rider tries uselessly to pry his fingers open.

'No, Dimitar,' I say, hurriedly rising to my feet as weapons are raised and the atmosphere turns even colder. 'He's not our enemy. Put him down.'

Dimitar releases his captive, and the knight, furious at being so handled, steps forward and furiously punches Dimitar hard on the chin. Yet he clutches his hand with a cry of pain and staggers back.

'I demand that thing's head. My honour demands it!' he grimaces, addressing Asterz.

'Let's all just calm down,' Kralgen booms, his arms outspread.

'I am the queen's cousin, and an attack on one of noble blood cannot go unanswered; that's the Astorian way,' the knight growls. 'That thing is an abomination and should be destroyed.'

'That *thing* was Major Conrol of High Delnor, and he was simply following my instructions to protect me!' I protest, intervening.

'From your own mouth, you've just condemned yourself, fey! If the orders are yours, he acts on your will, and it's you who must answer with blood!'

'Lord Fennel.' Queen Asterz addresses the angry knight. 'Whilst that's our way, perhaps given your broken hand and that we're in enemy territory, you should seek to redress your honour another time?'

I stare at Lord Fennel, raise an eyebrow and throw in a small taunting smile for good measure. I'd happily duel this idiot and teach him some good manners. However, apart from personal satisfaction, what would be the point? Even though we're still in Delnor, the enemy could come upon us at any time. It would be prudent to be away before that happens and make camp before the impending storm arrives.

Seemingly in response to this thought, a cold wind blows, and I feel the first gentle raindrop.

'You're right about my hand.' Lord Fennel responds.

He's been given a way out and has taken it. I'm relieved, and Kralgen relaxes too. A catastrophe averted.

Yet my relief is short-lived, as a calculating look appears in Lord Fennel's grey eyes.

'But, I don't care where we are,' he continues. 'As is the law, being injured, I claim the right of replacement. Considering the King Slayer's reputation, I hereby appoint the Queen's consort and champion as my second. Once he's administered justice, we can be on our way!'

Queen Asterz looks to the knight on her left.

Of course, it just had to be.

The big knight that had helped her kill Gruldarn.

***

It's drizzling incessantly, and I'm soaked and shivering. This is definitely not good weather to fight in, let alone die in. But I've trained and fought in worse.

I'm standing with Kralgen and Dimitar next to a flattened circle of grass about fifteen paces across. Weapons have been thrust into the ground around the perimeter. Spears, swords, daggers, and even double axes with curved butterfly heads. This will be a duel the Astorian way, a duel to the death.

Lord Fennel laughs maliciously, a satisfied smirk fixed in place as he looks over at me from the other side of the circle. He's seen me shiver and probably thinks I'm suffering from fear or nerves.

The thought of wiping that smirk away permanently warms me a little. The champion's life is linked to his, so when I spoil his fun by killing the champion ...

I sigh. Effectively killing two of the Astorians responsible for saving me is probably not the best way to ingratiate myself. It will only see me more reviled than I already am.

Great.

I sigh with frustration at the damned magical bracelets that are still around my wrists. Kralgen, with just one hand, hadn't been able to do anything about them, and Dimitar's strength was negated by their magical ability every time he tried.

So, I'm wet and shivering for now.

Kralgen hums cheerfully next to me, indifferent to my plight. In fact, he looks positively happy. No doubt he's nice and warm, thanks to his fire magic. Lucky him!

'He's big, and we've seen his skill when he killed the giant,' Kralgen murmurs as he begins to loosen my shoulder muscles. 'He wielded the axe in his right hand earlier, but I'm sure he's ambidextrous.'

'How do you know I'm fighting a man?' I ask, conscious I'd thought the queen a king.

'He scratched his balls earlier,' Kralgen says seriously. 'He's likely stronger than you, but he's chosen to wear that heavy armour. Keep the fight going, have him wear himself out. That plate will deflect everything but an axe blow, but I don't suggest you choose an axe; it's too heavy for you. Go for a spear instead.'

I ponder Kralgen's words as I watch my opponent limber up. He's moving easily in his armour, obviously not bothered by its weight and familiar with its feel. The full plate is fit for a king and expertly crafted to fit, leaving almost no weak points. The armpits, elbow joints and the back of the legs are the most vulnerable areas but are still protected by chainmail.

'I was going to take a sword and shield,' I mutter softly.

Kralgen shakes his head.

'He'll choose an axe and close the distance. You won't be agile enough to evade for long. You block that axe, and you'll have a broken arm. No, use a spear, and grab a dagger, too, just in case.'

'Kral.'

'Yes.'

'If he kills me, do me a favour and cut his bloody head off!'

Kral smiles at me, pulling a sincere look.

'No way. I want to live!'

I can't help but laugh with Kral. There's no way I'm going to lose this fight. Despite my opponent's size, strength, and reach advantage, I'm supremely confident. All my mortal opponents lie dead behind me, and here I am still standing. Sadly, the same can most likely be said for Fennel's champion.

'I'll kill him if you want,' Dimitar grates, deadly serious.

'No, you won't,' I order. 'You'll look after Kral for me. But I don't intend to die, not today. He's made a mistake wearing that armour in the rain. After a minute or two of fighting, the ground will be a morass, and then he's mine!'

Queen Asterz walks into the circle and beckons me and Fennel's champion inside.

The remaining knights surround the circle, leaving a little space for Dimitar and Kralgen. The horse archers are still out scouting, ensuring this spectacle isn't interrupted. As for the erstwhile captives, some are milling around, and others have taken the opportunity to disappear into the tall grass, although they won't survive long without food or water.

'In the Astorian tradition, this is a duel to the death, allowing the gods to decide the victor, showing us right from wrong ...'

As the queen recites what's obviously a long-standing rite, her voice fades away as I study my opponent. Unfortunately, there's nothing more to garner that I don't already know.

'You will commence fighting on my spoken signal. Do you understand?' Queen Asterz concludes.

The knight and I nod at Asterz. I wonder if water is seeping through the narrow visor slit into that dark helm. Is the man I'm facing young or old? Would I see confidence in his eyes, regret, hatred or anything I could use to understand how he might attack?

As Asterz strides from the circle, I know I'll soon find out.

There are four of each weapon spread evenly around the perimeter. When the queen gives her command, it makes sense that we turn for the weapons behind us. That way, we'll secure our favoured weapon and turn to face one another as we come together in the centre.

A rumble of thunder, and as the rain falls more intensely, I smile. I'd been offered armour but refused. My opponent's weakness is his lack of understanding of subtle battlefield strategies. When fighting, don't just consider the ground you fight upon but the weather too. Fight with the sun at your back wherever possible, or in this instance, fight with no armour when the ground is soft and treacherous.

'DIE WITH HONOUR!'

I spin and run for the spear behind me. Yet I've only gone a few steps when I receive a painful blow to my lower back that sends me skidding face down into the wet grass. The champion has tackled me from behind, and I kick frantically as he tries to hold onto my legs.

Neither Kralgen nor I had foreseen this. The knight hadn't gone for a weapon because he *is* a weapon and had charged straight after me!

This fight will be over if he manages to get on top of me. I won't be able to deal him any damage with my bare hands while his gauntleted fists will break me to pieces.

Wriggling like a snake, I free one leg and, twisting to my back, stamp down at the knight's armoured head. His grip slips with every blow until, with a last desperate effort, I pull my legs, bruised and bleeding from the knight's armoured fists.

I roll sideways as he comes to his knees and launches himself after me, and then I'm stumbling to my feet, running for a spear, as he breaks off and goes for an axe.

My chest is already heaving from exertion, and this isn't good. I can fight for hours if I control myself, so as I grasp the spear shaft, I breathe in through my mouth and out my nose to calm down. Years of conditioning kick in, my heartbeat steadies, and my hands stop shaking.

Damn, that had been close!

I bend to pick up a dagger, then, hearing a grunt of exertion, fling myself to the ground in a desperate manoeuvre to evade the axe spinning sideways toward me. The vroom sends a shiver down my spine as it flies by within a handspan of my head. I've nearly died twice, and we haven't even crossed weapons yet.

Cheers come from the watching Astorians as the fight sways in their countryman's favour.

Leaping to my feet, I watch the champion stalk around the circle toward another axe. His stride is steady, confident, and almost indifferent to the fact I have a spear while he's unarmed. I'm tempted to throw it at him to test his reflexes, but he'll probably just let it glance from his armour.

Instead, I thrust the dagger into my belt and familiarise myself with the spear. It's a little longer than I am tall and has a cord grip to ensure a solid hold for throwing. I twirl it, first left, then right, execute intermittent short and long thrusts, slashing cuts and counters. A minute later, I've ensured that not only is my weapon sound, but I've no additional injuries from being taken down. Even the injuries I'd sustained while fighting the ogres are barely noticeable, and my thumb no longer feels swollen. Swallowing even a small amount of blood during the earlier battle has had a tremendous restorative effect.

My opponent is ready and loosely holds another double-bladed axe, unaffected by its weight. He walks around the circle's perimeter, facing me as I stand in the middle, taking my measure.

My spear would appear a strange weapon of choice to those watching, for only an axe could hope to hurt this iron-clad man. If there had been a hammer pick or a mace, I'd have gone with those instead, but here I am with a spear that can't even scratch him.

But it's one of my favourite weapons.

I shut out the baying Astorians, Kralgen, and the statue that's Dimitar, and allow my subconscious to read my opponent's balance, the shift and tilt of his shoulders, and the placement of his feet. Every movement is a tell, a precursor to an attack, a feint, or simple repositioning.

However, the battle axe isn't a weapon of subtlety but rather of brute, overwhelming force. If that weapon connects, I won't be walking from this circle alive, and thus the champion's attacks will be direct.

Now, as the black-garbed figure attacks, I'm ready.

The giant axe flashes down in a diagonal blow as the knight leaps forward, confident that his armour will protect him. I duck under the whistling weapon and spin away as the knight uses the weapon's momentum to assist his turn and execute a horizontal sweep.

I'm forced to evade each attack, ducking or twisting, swaying or spinning away. I'm waiting, allowing my opponent's heavily booted feet to churn the fighting circle into mud. There's no point in me trying to finish this fight early; I'll simply lose. But the longer I draw this fight out, the easier my victory will be.

The knight recovers from his latest attack, holding the axe at his side whilst my spear is constantly in guard position. I know I can't harm him, but I want to provoke him.

'HAH!' I cry as I stamp forward, executing a perfect short thrust that snaps the champion's head back. My efforts are rewarded by a tilt of the head as he acknowledges the blow, and then he attacks again.

Eight whistling cuts and sweeps of the axe I dodge, each one getting closer as the knight follows me quickly around the circle, giving me no respite. He only needs to land one blow, and I have to evade every single one.

But then, what I was hoping for, happens.

He overextends slightly, and his right foot slides from under him, leaving a muddy churn. The knight recovers quickly but not before the tip of my spear has glanced off his helm a second time.

The rain is getting heavier, the ground softer, and now his heavy suit will become a considerable burden. As I circle him, I grimace a little. My soaking-wet clothing is becoming restrictive for fighting in too. However, at least I'll be cleaner after this fight, with some of the blood I'm caked in washed away.

He attacks again, the axe a blur, his heavy boots sloshing in the puddles. My footing isn't exactly perfect either, but I use the spear butt to provide support, pushing it into the soft ground to ensure my movements are no less swift than before. I pivot out of the way, and then as he stumbles past, I jam the spear between his feet.

I don't follow up, not yet, and it's a good thing, too, as he controls his fall with incredible agility for someone wearing heavy armour. He rolls to his feet smoothly, the axe sweeping out in case I'd strayed too close.

We circle again.

I lunge, the spear tip going for the helm, but it's a feint. As he reflexively brings the axe blade up, I pull back and attempt to spear his foot.

At the last possible moment, he lifts his lead foot so the spear point thrusts into the ground, and before I can withdraw it, he's stamped down, trapping the point beneath his boot. Fast as a swooping sin-hawk, he twists and brings his back leg around, drops his knee onto the angled spear shaft and snaps it.

There's an awful moment as he kneels there, looking up at me, his axe held in both hands by his left hip as he begins a sweeping blow or a throw that will cut me in half.

I can't hesitate.

Stepping forward, I jump, my hands going to the knight's shoulders, and flip over him. The blade whooshes under my feet, and then I hit the ground running. I make it only two steps before the thrown axe blade misses my legs by a hairsbreadth. Unfortunately, the spinning handle thwacks into the back of my legs, and I'm brought to the soggy ground.

I know what's coming and grab two handfuls of mud, rolling onto my back as the knight launches himself at my prone body. I bring my knees up and get my feet under his chest as those gauntleted fists reach for my throat. I slap the mud onto his visor and then, crying with exertion, straighten my legs and launch him through the air to slam onto his back with a splash.

I'm on my feet instantly. The knight has already got to his knees and is attempting to clear or open his visor. Instead of going for another weapon, I run, leap, and slam both feet into the champion's armoured chest, throwing him onto his back again. Regaining my feet, I kick him heavily to the side of the helm until his mailed fists fall limp to the ground.

The broken spear protrudes from the grass, about four handspans of the shaft with the point buried in the mud. As I pull, it comes free with a sucking noise, and I stagger toward the knight, who begins to stir.

I kneel on either side of his metalled chest, raising the spearhead above me in my right hand. With the left, I free his visor latch. I'm going to ram the spear through his eye socket into his brain.

'PLEASE. Don't kill him!' a woman's voice screams, the panic reaching through my anger.

I turn, shocked at what I'm hearing. This is not the Astorian way.

'I'll pardon you and give you whatever you want. Just please, don't kill him!' Asterz pleads.

Lord Fennel adds his voice too, knowing that if I slay the champion, his own death will follow.

Lifting the muddy, grilled visor, I pause.

Will my life forever be cursed?

I firm the grip on the broken spear and drive it down.

***

# CHAPTER VI

I'm in excruciating pain, and even if I could drink my fill of blood, it wouldn't help, even momentarily.

I should feel like celebrating, or if that's a bit crass as the end of the world unfolds, at least happy we've been freed and the wounded taken under the Astorians' protection. Yet instead, I don't believe I've ever been this sad or broken.

The night sky is full of stars now the rain has passed, and the light of the twin moons further adds to nature's canvas. The third moon, which I can now see, sits at the shoulder of the blue moon, black as the darkest night, unseen by human eyes but not mine. If anyone else is awake, they'll probably appreciate the beauty ... but not me.

With my victory, I'd ensured our survival, and by allowing the champion to live, I'd earned the Queen's Favour, which ensured my pleas for the wounded had been granted. The last monarch to bestow me such a gift had died horrifically, and as I look across at Asterz using a wagon for shelter in the darkness, I'm tempted to deliver her the same fate.

She's not asleep either, and from the rhythmic motion under her blankets, she's making the most of her champion's return.

Would my pain be any less if I'd killed him and, instead of driving the speartip into the earth, rammed it into the green or blue eye instead?

Lotane. The Queen's Champion, her consort.

I'm not sure what hurts most. The fact he'd actually tried to kill me, or the vigour with which he's coupling just a dozen steps away.

I've been grateful for my night vision many times, but not this night.

'Can't sleep then?' Kralgen grumbles, sitting up.

'No.'

'I was talking to Dimitar, not you,' he chuckles.

Sure enough, Dimitar just sits there, staring into the distance. He doesn't need to sleep anymore. He just idly crams dirt into his stone maw by the handful. Now he's worked out what to eat; there's no stopping him. Rarely a word leaves his stone lips unless directly spoken to, but I appreciate his solid presence.

'No, you're not,' I whisper back.

Kralgen pushes his hair back, looking confused.

'I wondered where he'd gone, and now we know. I just can't understand why he's coupled with the queen when you and he were inseparable.'

For once, Kralgen thankfully manages to keep his voice low. A few people knew of my infidelity, but not Kralgen. What will he think of me when he finds out? Better it's now, from me, not from Lotane.

'I joined with Nogoth, and Lotane knows.'

The words leave my lips like a sigh, full of regret.

'Gods, Malina.' Kralgen's voice is edged with dismay. 'You and Lotane were like Alyssa and me, perfect for one another. Why?'

'What can I say that justifies my actions. I was seduced by Nogoth as he used his magic on me. But truth be told, I was intoxicated by him at the time. Now I despise him for the lies, for what he's doing to this world, but also for the pain our joining caused Lotane.

'Now Lotane just tried to kill me. I can't help but wonder what's left worth fighting for as you and Dimitar are free.'

'Don't you want children?' Kralgen asks.

'I did, with Lotane.'

'Then that's worth fighting for.' Kralgen spreads his hands as if it's the answer to all my woes.

'Did you miss the bit where Lotane tried to kill me? He hates me and is over there enjoying himself with the queen!'

'He doesn't hate you, Malina. He loves you and would never kill you.'

'What are you talking about, Kralgen. I thought Dimitar was the only one to lose his mind.'

Kralgen shrugs.

'It's time for me to sleep, Malina. Remember, sometimes when you're too close to the fight, you can't see the steel.'

Damn Kral for being so cryptic. Damn Lotane and damn the satisfied moans of Queen Asterz. How the hell am I supposed to sleep with her whining like a wolf.

I wish I could turn back the clock to better times when I lived in ignorant bliss. I was happy living in the mountain, Lotane beside me every night, enjoying his youthful vigour. Even practising and sparring with him was a delight. To witness his supple strength, to know his prowess was only exceeded by Kralgen in the training circle and ... there it is!

Without using my magic, I'd never beaten Lotane. Not once.

Yet he'd tried his best to kill me.

But Kralgen didn't seem to think so.

In such weather, would Lotane choose to fight in heavy armour? Would he choose an axe against an unarmoured opponent? Would he grunt to telegraph a deadly throw or hit my legs with the axe handle, not sever them with the blade?

No.

Lotane is a superlative fighter and would never make such mistakes.

Kralgen is right. Lotane didn't try and kill me and trusted I wouldn't kill him when he gave me a chance. It was all a deception.

I feel better, yet not fully. How can I when his arms are around another woman mere steps away?

But why the deceit?

He hadn't greeted us or revealed himself, which means he doesn't want the queen to know he knew me, the King Slayer, an assassin. This means Asterz is unaware of Lotane's past, which is probably a good thing considering his slaying of Asterz's kin.

I'm sure there's more to it, and hopefully, Lotane will explain when we have a chance to speak on the morrow.

Assuming that Asterz lets him from her clutches.

I lie down, intent on getting some sleep when the soft moans start again.

This is going to be a long, hard night.

***

We've been travelling northeast since before sunrise, heading toward Astoria.

In the distance, the horse archers maintain a disciplined perimeter. Fortunately, no enemy has been spotted, and we're making steady, albeit slow progress. It's possible Nogoth's forces haven't ravaged this far north as the endless sea of grass around us looks healthy without showing signs of the Saer Tel's magically induced growth.

I recall my last conversation with the ethereal fey, and I'm momentarily distracted from the monotony of the journey. I wish I'd had more time to learn about their ways. The sense of belonging I'd once felt at the Mountain of Souls is gone; perhaps I might find that amongst my own kind.

*By the Gods, Malina!*

I look around guiltily, afraid I'd somehow voiced my shocking thoughts. It's the first time I've acknowledged that I'm not just human but fey. Yet, the Saer Tel had once come from another world, not Nogoth's, so perhaps it's incorrect to refer to them in such a way. That thought makes me feel a little better.

I'd initially considered them evil creatures, yet I've maligned them. They feed without killing and use magic to create life rather than take it. It was incredible to witness the beauty of Nogoth's realm and, more recently, the evidence of their power transforming the landscape around High Delnor. Without question, this world will recover from the ravages of humankind's greed with their help. Their power is incredible, but unlike Nogoth and the ssythlans, they claim their power comes from without, not within.

Yet I'm Saer Tel, and my power comes from within, albeit limited by my age and the reservoir of magic my body contains.

Yet perhaps that isn't entirely true.

*You could be powerful beyond imagining.*

Nogoth's words seductively caress my thoughts.

How powerful would I become if I lived a thousand years?

Nogoth has lived longer, so it stands to reason he'll still be more powerful. However, I remember his look of incredulity when he spied Dimitar's stone arm. It would appear I can do things he can't.

I frown at the manacle cuffs on my wrists and determine to get them removed as soon as possible. I need to test Nogoth's honeyed words.

Thinking of magic has me look down at Dimitar striding effortlessly alongside the warhorse I'd inherited from a dead Astorian. My heart aches to see what Dimitar has become. Every day, the man I knew has receded further, and now there's nothing I recognise, not a spark of humour or humanity.

'Dimitar.'

'Yes, Malina.'

The words grate from those stone lips. There's no emotion or inflexion, just an efficient reply.

'Who are you?'

'I'm Dimitar, once referred to as Major Conrol.'

There's no surprise at my question, just an instant response as if someone superior in rank had asked.

'What are you?'

There's a long pause, and that stone head tilts first left, then right, followed by a short nod.

'I am your creation.'

'Do you remember who you were before I created you?'

'I have memories of a different life of flesh and blood before this one. It is that which allows me to exist in this form.'

A tear escapes, running down my cheek as if afraid to be seen. I hadn't managed to save my friend's life. I hope he didn't experience fear or pain and just gently slipped away, unaware.

'Do you love me still?'

Those stone shoulders rise and fall, shrugging off as insignificant, a question that would have once caused a heartbeat to quicken or nervousness to appear.

'I understand the word, but not the feelings.'

I lean to the side, reaching down from my saddle, and gently lay my hand on his cold, stone head.

'What do you feel when I do this?'

'You touching my head. What else is there to feel?'

Not a pause to his stride, nor a hint of the man I used to know, other than his semblance carved in stone.

'So, what is your purpose?'

'To serve my creator.'

'Can you die?'

'Magic cannot die. It is the source of all things, but I can be destroyed.'

'How?'

'By sufficient force, more powerful magic or your simple command.'

Movement catches my attention. Kralgen is looking over his shoulder, waving. I raise my hand in acknowledgement, and he beckons me forward.

'The Astorians fear you, Dimitar. Don't draw attention to yourself or give them a reason to cast us out, yet don't hesitate to come to my aid or Kralgen's if we need you. Do you understand?'

'Yes, Malina.'

So far, I've been riding halfway along the wagon column, way behind the queen and her knights in the lead, staying well away from Lotane.

Having shared my thoughts with Kralgen on awakening, he'd agreed that Lotane had probably hidden our bond, so we'd decided that he'd ride ahead to assess the situation.

'Come on, boy,' I say gently, leaning forward to whisper into my gelding's ear. Like the rest of the Astorians, this horse is unsure about me, but I'm working on building our relationship from scratch, just like I'll have to do with Lotane.

With a gentle nudge of my heels, I coax my horse into a canter and shortly catch up with the slow-moving knights at the column's fore. Several acknowledge my presence with frowns or scowls but no insults, not now they've witnessed me fight.

I wipe some sweat from my forehead with a filthy sleeve, noting the reddened complexions of those around me. The plains offer no protection from the sun, and everyone suffers from the heat. The buzz of flies is met by the constant swish of the horses' tails.

I rein in alongside Kralgen. He looks ridiculous, even on a warhorse. If he took his feet out of the stirrups, I swear they might touch the floor, and he could pick up and carry the horse beneath him. He rides between the queen and I, whilst beyond her is Lotane. The other knights ride behind in ranks of four, in descending order of seniority judged by the sashes on their armour.

'I've just been telling Queen Asterz of the fall of High Delnor,' Kralgen rumbles by way of greeting.

'Haven't I already told you? Just call me Asterz unless we're on ceremony!' she interrupts.

Kralgen smiles subtly and then continues.

'You've already met her champion, but allow me to formally introduce Sir Lotane of Astoria.'

I heel my horse forward to see him better and am rewarded with a curt nod.

'Sir Lotane. You fought well.'

'Not well enough,' he snaps back. 'I'm better in the saddle. The result would have been far different there!'

'He is far better in the saddle. I can attest to that!' Queen Asterz slaps her thigh.

Kralgen applauds the joke, roaring with laughter.

I want to puke but force a smile.

The queen looks at me, a warm look struggling to find its way onto her stern face.

'In truth, you sparing Lotane's life was a righteous act of balance. For weeks, sin-hawks from High Delnor arrived carrying messages of unbelievably dire portent. I'd dismissed them as desperate machinations to buy time for a failing empire, but Lotane argued I give them credence. Because of his insight, we rode to investigate. He really has a perfect mind to match his body.'

I resist a sudden urge to draw my dagger and cut her throat, but if she says just one more suggestive thing ...

Asterz lifts a waterskin from her saddle, takes a gulp, passes it to Lotane, and then continues.

'It turns out he recognised the truth that none of us saw, and our journey has convinced me of the danger we face. Those messages from High Delnor were the truth. Now we have you with first-hand knowledge to help advise our strategy.'

Asterz looks at me expectantly.

'I'm not sure I can tell you more than you've already garnered,' I respond. 'There are overwhelming numbers of the fey, and their king, Nogoth, is a master strategist. As you'll have surmised, your people need to run and hide. Perhaps building a fleet and living on the seas is the best way ...'

Asterz shakes her head.

'We are Astorians, King Slayer,' she growls. 'There will be no running, nor will I allow the fey to invade Astoria. I intend to attack!'

'You mustn't. That's utter madness!'

'Choose your words with more care when you talk to me!' Asterz snaps. 'We've just tested the mettle of these fey, and I've found them wanting. They're too slow to close with our light cavalry. We'll hit and run and have their forces so tied up chasing us that they'll never set foot near Astoria.'

'You have no idea,' Kralgen rumbles. 'I love a fight more than anyone, but this isn't the way to win. I salute your skill and leadership, but Malina is right. You mustn't attack.'

'If I wanted your advice, I'd ask for it!' Asterz doesn't look happy.

'What about you, Sir Lotane?' I enquire, surprised by his silence. 'What do you think?'

'He follows his queen's command, and if you wish to enjoy my protection, you'll continue to do the same. Now enough!' Asterz says. 'We will continue to Astoria, where we'll prepare our forces for battle!'

***

With a final check of my horse's girth strap, I step up into the saddle, noting the Astorian discipline as they prepare to get underway after our brief rest stop.

Overall, it's good. The irregular heavy knights are already astride their warhorses as Asterz mounts last as is customary. The light horse archers on their steppe ponies have set a perimeter, and the wagons are ready to roll.

'Four more wounded died so far this morning.' I sigh. 'These damned wagons move so slowly!'

'At this pace, we'll reach Astoria next year,' Kralgen groans as we nudge our horses into a walk toward the rear of the slow-moving column.

After our earlier disagreement with Asterz, we've kept our distance.

'I found out from a wounded Astorian archer that they field about two hundred armoured nobles, twelve thousand mounted archers and maybe three thousand men-at-arms,' I say. 'It's a considerable force, but against Nogoth's army ...'

'It's utter madness,' Kralgen rumbles, finishing my sentence with a grin. 'Asterz sure is a stubborn one. 'However, I have to admit it's a glorious plan!'

'Don't tell me you agree with Asterz on this?' I groan, knowing Kralgen's love for battle exceeds everything else.

He pauses, looking somewhat puzzled.

'I'm impatient to join Alyssa, wherever her spirit rests, and following Asterz's plan would hasten that ...' Kralgen shakes his head as if confused. 'But it's just not the right thing to do.'

'What did you learn from Lotane?'

'He agrees with us, but it doesn't matter. Yesterday was the first time they engaged the fey, and now Asterz has the taste of victory ...'

'How lucky for us they did.'

'It seems it wasn't luck.' Kralgen smiles, an eyebrow raised like an inquisitive caterpillar.

'What do you mean?'

'Lotane told me they were about to return to Astoria when he dreamt of a beautiful woman with yellow eyes, telling him that everything he sought was a day's journey south. When he awoke, he had two yellow flowers on his chest. So he convinced Asterz to scout south one more day, where they spotted Gruldarn and our convoy. The rest we know.'

We're both silent for a while. Had the gods intervened and given Lotane a sign to rescue us? Then I remember Kralgen's description.

'The woman was a Saer Tel!' I exclaim as the answer dawns on me.

'My thoughts exactly!'

Kralgen looks smug as if he orchestrated the whole thing, and even my horse whinnies as if it had also arrived at that conclusion before me.

'I'd asked for their help when they took me to see Nogoth but never thought for a moment they would. I wonder if ...'

My horse whinnies again, and it's echoed by several others.

Distant shouts sound from the outlying horse archers.

'There!' Kralgen flings his arm out, pointing north.

I turn just in time to see half a dozen horse archers get ripped from their saddles by wolfen.

'There as well!' he shouts, pointing south.

'Dimitar. Stay with us!' I yell, spurring my horse, leaning low over its neck.

'What's going on?' an injured man calls from the back of a wagon, and several others demand the same.

'Arm yourselves,' Kralgen bellows as we hurtle past.

We reach the head of the column to find a horse archer astride a lathered horse reporting to Asterz.

'Hundreds of them. They're everywhere, hiding in the long grass!' he finishes as we approach.

'Sir Lotane, you'll lead half my knights ...'

'You need heavy infantry in formation to have a chance against those things!' I shout over Asterz's command.

'When I need advice on how to fight, I certainly won't ask it of you,' she snaps back.

Panicked shouts and screams rise high, and the horse archers begin pulling back to the column, frantically shooting arrows as they do.

'Wedge formation!' Asterz yells, and the knights begin to form around her.

'They'll melt away before your charge unless there's something to pin them against!' I shout.

'MY QUEEN!' a knight shouts in shock. 'LOOK!'

We all turn, following the knight's outflung arm, toward the column's rear, where a rolling wave of black-furred wolfen engulfs the wagons one after another. Such is the ferocity of their attack that the wagons, the injured inside, even the oxen are flung skyward, blood spraying everywhere.'

'Save the queen! Save the queen!' Fennel shouts in Lotane's face. 'Save her, save Astoria!'

Fennel wheels his horse, and the rest of the knights follow suit. Thirty of them against thousands.

Lotane looks across at me and Kralgen.

Kralgen is preparing to join the knights in their final charge.

'I need you. Kral, with me!' he shouts, then he's off, spurring his horse east, the queen alongside him.

'Don't fight those beasts, Kral!' I call. 'If die you must, die fighting Nogoth!'

'HAH!' Kral yells, having pulled his horse's head around. He digs his heels into its flanks and follows Lotane and Asterz.

*I need you.*

Had Lotane aimed that comment at me? My heart quickens at the possibility.

'Dimitar!'

'I'll follow. The colours will show me the way if I get left behind,' he grates.

I let my horse have its head as Dimitar starts thumping after me.

Looking over my shoulder, I see the final wagon enveloped in that sea of black. The poor survivors, who thought they'd found salvation, scream as they fight for a few more seconds of life before they're torn limb from limb.

I'm slowly leaving Dimitar behind, but he appears oblivious to any peril. As this elemental creature, he knows no fear or pain, just a sense of purpose. His arms and legs pump with perfect rhythm, no sign of fatigue marring those stone features. Could he run forever if I instructed him to?

I watch as the knights' charge hits the wolfen at full gallop.

For a split second, the lead wolfen are flung aside or into the sky, broken and bleeding. But then, horse after horse goes down, spilling their riders, and the charge disintegrates. A heartbeat later, it's as if it never was, and that black tide comes howling after us.

My horse quickly makes up the ground on the others, but we're not outpacing the fey. We need to go faster!

'Dump your armour, or we'll be overtaken!' I shout.

Kralgen and Lotane respond to my instruction immediately. Daggers hack at leather straps and buckles, and soon breastplates, greaves, helmets and other equipment is scattered on the road behind us.

'My queen!' Lotane entreats. 'Your armour. Do as Malina says.'

With a scowl, she follows suit.

'I don't know how long our horses can keep at this pace!' Kralgen yells. 'Especially mine!'

As if to underwrite how winded our horses are becoming, Dimitar catches us, running between our horses.

'Maybe I should jump on his shoulders,' Kralgen quips, but his tone is worried.

The howling gets louder, reaching a fever pitch, and I know, even without looking, that the lead wolfen are gaining. I'm tempted to urge my horse to go faster, but I won't leave my friends.

'We're not going to make it!' Asterz screams, her eyes wide.

Dimitar suddenly runs closer and drags Kral's sword free.

'What do you think you're doing?' Kral roars. 'Give me back my sword!'

Dimitar doesn't answer. He just continues running and reaches out his free hand to me.

I draw mine, reverse it, and pass it to him without saying anything.

'You always tried to save me. Now, it's my turn to protect my friends,' Dimitar says.

We all watch in disbelief as he skids to a halt, then sprints back at the wolfen.

'DIMITAR. COME BACK!' I cry, but he either doesn't hear or chooses to ignore me, and I can't afford to stop and go back after him.

He runs faster and faster, arms outstretched, the swords held horizontally in his hands, and sprints directly at the lead wolves. He disappears under the mass in a heartbeat but reappears moments later, throwing off the beasts that leapt upon him. He turns north, slashing and hacking at the creatures closest, trying to break free.

He doesn't make a scratch in their numbers, but suddenly, the lead creatures forget their pursuit, turning upon Dimitar in their midst, and the chase is over.

I continue to watch as we ride east, but my silent prayers go unanswered. Dimitar doesn't reappear, and the wolfen quickly fade from sight.

'Goodbye, my friend,' I whisper, my words whipped away by the wind along with the tears I cry.

***

# CHAPTER VII

'Hold still, I've almost got it,' Asterz mumbles as she leans close to inspect the damaged manacle on my left wrist.

With daylight fading rapidly, we've made camp, but without a campfire, she's working primarily by touch.

There's a cloth-wrapped dagger in her left hand that she's worked between my forearm and the manacle, and in her right, a heavy rock.

Asterz accurately brings the rock down again. The sharp impact on such a still evening makes us wince and look around nervously.

'Come on,' she mutters.

Her eyes narrow as she smashes the rock down again, and this time the ceramic shatters. As it gives way, the flat metal blade absorbs most of the force, and I'm just bruised as opposed to suffering lacerations or crushed bones.

'That blacksmith's apprentice really taught me a thing or two when I was younger.' Asterz laughs softly as she tosses the rock aside.

I force a smile, flexing my fingers. I'm grateful to be free but irritated that Asterz takes every opportunity to use a sexual innuendo.

Moments later, my smile is genuine as I'm reunited with my magic. It reminds me of some puppies that birthed near our home when I was a child. They'd fall over each other, tumbling, yapping, full of playful energy, driving the mother insane. I'm tempted to laugh as it fights for some attention or release.

*Hush. Soon. Be patient.*

I project my love and happiness, during which my magic twists and turns as if in ecstasy.

'Is it back?' Kralgen asks, leaning forward.

'Yes!'

'Is what back?' Asterz asks, perplexed.

'My magic.'

'You're not serious. Only ssythlans can control magic,' she scoffs. 'That story of you setting the High King on fire was just a myth.'

'Sadly, no. That part of the story is true. In fact, I'm sure most of what you heard is. It's a deed I'd rather forget, yet without it, I'd never have ultimately discovered Nogoth's true intent.'

'What happened to the other assassins in your group?'

I'm irked by Asterz's questions, but I owe her for rescuing Kralgen and me. This last one makes me feel uncomfortable. Lying shouldn't be an issue for me, but nor do I like it. However, this allows me to say something I've wanted to express for a while now.

'They went their own ways. Yet I fervently hope they return, for they mean the world to me.'

I speak a little louder than I should, hoping that Lotane will pick up on their meaning as he returns from caring for the horses.

'So, you knew this war was coming?' Asterz demands.

When will these questions stop? I want to discuss what the future holds, not the past. I sigh to express my irritation but decide to answer a final question.

'In short, yes. I returned to High Delnor to tell my tale, and Commander Farsil, the acting regent, tried to warn everyone else once he came to see the truth. That's why he sent the sin-hawks to your kingdom and the others. No one gave them any credence.'

Kralgen's stomach rumbles loudly.

'Sorry. I'm so hungry,' he apologises, shrugging his shoulders. 'I could eat my horse!'

'It looks like you already did,' Lotane smiles, slapping him on the back. 'Here. I have a few biscuits left. Take them, you greedy oaf.'

I note Asterz's surprise at Lotane's casual attitude toward an Icelandian King, unaware of their long-standing bond. Whilst I want to voice my plans, I know a better way to distract Asterz from her course of questioning, and I have ones of my own.

'So, how did you and Sir Lotane come together?' I ask.

Queen Asterz laughs.

'A perfect choice of words,' she winks. 'In too many positions to count is the answer!'

Kralgen has the good sense not to laugh, and Lotane suddenly finds something to stare at in the distance.

I begin to imagine Asterz bursting into flames but have to stop when my magic stirs in response, ready to carry out my bidding.

'Well, it's a strange story,' Asterz says, sounding wistful. 'He turned up just over two months ago at my castle. It was a judgement day, where I administered justice on disputes or wrongdoing. He waits his turn, and when he stands before me, he goes to one knee and asks to lead my personal bodyguard.

'You should have heard the laughter, and mine was loud than any. There he was, this big, filthy man, wearing rags, with long dishevelled hair, and worse of all, a peasant. I told him to come back when he had a sword. In Astoria, we have an old saying. You keep what you can take. So, he goes up, slaps one of my bodyguards around the face, and challenges him to a duel.

'Honour demanded justice, so empty-handed Lotane faced Sir Quentar. A minute later, Lotane knelt before me again and repeated his request, only this time holding Quentar's sword.

'When I told him he needed a helm, he defeated another bodyguard. A breastplate, yet another. Finally, he defeated my captain, Sir Fennel, and knelt before me, having taken a piece of armour from each in exchange for their lives.

'I told him then that a peasant could never lead my bodyguard and for him to return in three years having trained as a knight. Do you know what he did next?'

'No,' I respond. Despite regretting asking the question, I'm also caught up in the story and want Asterz to continue.

'He reverses his sword, offers me the hilt and says I have but two choices. I either need to kill him or knight him there and then. When I asked him why he was unafraid to die, he said something that made up my mind.'

'What was it?' I ask, leaning forward.

'He told me his heart was broken, and thus he no longer feared death. So, I knighted him, and he has served me since. In return, I've tried to mend his heart with my body every opportunity I get!'

My fingernails dig into my palms as I again control the urge to burn another monarch. It's not her fault, and nor is it Lotane's. The fault is entirely mine.

'He still remains an enigma to me, as he hasn't talked about his past,' Asterz continues, looking over her shoulder at Lotane. 'But I have ways of getting secrets out of men. I just need a little more time to work some magic of my own!'

'We need silence,' Kral rumbles. 'I doubt those wolfen continued their pursuit, but we can't take the risk. Tomorrow, we'll decide on a course of action, but in the meantime, I'll take first watch. Malina, you take second, Lotane the last.'

'Thank you, Kral,' I whisper softly as he hunkers beside me.

A simple nod. He doesn't want me to suffer any more than I already am.

There's no fire, the moon and stars are obscured by thick clouds, and it's soon as dark as can be.

Sadly, with my fey eyesight, Lotane and Asterz are all too plain for me to see. It hurts so much to see them comfortable in the other's arms.

The magic in my stomach twists and turns, eager to assist.

I could wait till Asterz and Lotane are asleep, reach out, touch them softly, and let my blood magic do the rest.

Some gentle suggestion and Asterz would be ecstatic that Lotane and I were reunited again, and as for Lotane, I could ensure his passion rose like never before.

But the knowledge that his love was fake would tear me apart, and I'd be no better than Nogoth.

Damn. Trying to be good is such hard work. No wonder so many people choose to be evil.

***

'I realise my initial faith in the fey losing a skirmish war to Astoria's cavalry was misplaced,' Asterz says with a grimace as we ride east at a gentle pace. 'Seeing my knights and archers destroyed made that clear.'

Kralgen and I quickly exchange a surprised look. Perhaps Asterz is better than I gave her credit for if she can admit to being wrong.

'The problem is, I don't see what else we can do!' She smacks her thigh, causing her horse to snicker. 'If the fey have an army of two hundred thousand, then they almost outnumber Astoria's entire population. We'll have no chance.'

I briefly survey the landscape to the south, but there's no sign of anybody.

'Nogoth told me he'd start by conquering Tars and Hastia, then work his way north through Rolantria and Suria before hitting Astoria and Icelandia.'

'It would make sense,' Lotane says, nodding. 'By not splitting his main force, he'll overwhelm any city defences he encounters and conquer every kingdom individually with minimum loss.'

Kralgen snaps his fingers, a broad smile splitting his craggy features.

'But that means there's time to prepare!'

'Prepare? What, to dig our own graves,' Asterz scoffs. 'It makes me puke to say it, but the best thing everyone can try and do is hide.'

'No!' I smile, my thoughts aligning with Kralgen's. 'You said it yourself; the fey *almost* outnumbers Astoria's people. But if you have till next year to train them ...'

'There still wouldn't be enough!' Asterz snarls.

'How many people of fighting age in Astoria?' I ask.

'Between the ages of fifteen and fifty, we have around one hundred and fifty thousand. As I said, it's not enough against a force superior in numbers and skill!'

'But I can round up maybe another hundred thousand Icelandians of the same age,' Kralgen muses, counting off his fingers.

'Not forgetting Suria and Rolantria will have much the same numbers as Astoria,' Lotane adds. 'Combine them all, and in a year, we can field an army far larger than Nogoth faced outside of High Delnor!'

'You forget Suria and Rolantria are no friends of Astoria. They sided with Delnor in the past to defeat us; more fool them!' Asterz snaps.

'In war, circumstances can make the strangest of allies!' I say. 'Look at us!'

The scowl Asterz gives me shows what she thinks of that remark.

'The people of Suria and Rolantria have no army to defend them. If they're offered a fighting chance instead of annihilation, they'll join us!' Lotane says, putting his hand on Asterz's arm.

Asterz nods slowly, her features softening.

'Let me think. The idea has merit,' she says.

Kralgen, Lotane, and I exchange looks of relief mixed with hope.

I turn in my saddle, studying the landscape south, yet I can't perceive any threat. We're each responsible for keeping a lookout over an assigned bearing. Even this conversation doesn't warrant being less vigilant. However, the further east we head, the more we leave the threat of danger and this war behind. The lure of safety, let alone a semblance of normality, makes me want to heel my horse into a gallop.

'You know, it won't be as easy as just arming half a million people,' Kralgen offers, breaking the silence. 'If we take them from the farms, fishing boats and orchards, we'll soon have no food and starve. If we take them from the mines, tanners, or blacksmiths, we won't have weapons or armour.'

I don't know whose eyes open wider at this insightful comment from Kral, mine or Lotane's, but it all gives us pause for thought. There was a reason why the kingdoms' armies weren't any bigger than they were. Armies cost a fortune in money and resources to support and bring very little return.

'There looks to be a small village to the north,' Lotane points out.

Sure enough, to the northeast, maybe four hundred paces away, some wooden buildings blend perfectly against the backdrop of a heavy forest.

'Let's hope they have some food and water to spare. I'm out of both,' Kralgen bemoans and taps his empty waterskin for emphasis.

'Are we still in Delnor?' I ask.

'We haven't crossed over the River of Tears yet. So, yes, we're still in Delnor,' Asterz replies, then rolls her eyes at Lotane as if I'm some kind of simpleton.

My blood boils.

I reach out to grab a fistful of Asterz's hair to drag her from her saddle when Lotane raises his hand.

'Dismount,' he commands, and Kral and I are out of the saddle in a heartbeat.

'What's the problem?' Asterz complains.

For a warrior queen, she can be painfully slow at times.

'Kral. Catch,' I say, getting his attention.

I grab Asterz's boot and heave, tipping her out of the saddle and straight into Kral's arms.

'How dare you!' she hisses, hand going to the hilt of her sword as Kral sets her down.

I ignore her and, following Lotane's lead, pull softly on my horse's reins.

'Down, boy,' I whisper in my gelding's ear, and being a well-trained war horse, it first kneels, then lays in the grass. Kral does the same with his and Asterz's mount.

Asterz just stands there, fury in her eyes. I'm still seething myself and am contemplating tackling her to the ground when Lotane grabs her hand, and she reluctantly squats down. Seeing how she calms under Lotane's touch makes me wish I'd taken the opportunity to flatten her.

'You two, wait here and guard the horses,' Lotane snaps, all business, gesturing at Kral and Asterz. He's the one who has identified something untoward, so he automatically takes charge.

'Malina, with me!'

'Why her, not me?' Asterz demands.

I can't help but feel satisfaction at the sudden discord, even if now isn't the time.

'She's expendable. You're not!' Lotane says quietly.

That's not the reason why, and my heart flutters. He isn't saying anything I really want to hear, but knowing he still trusts me to have his back is a start.

'I'll need that,' I say with satisfaction, dragging Asterz's sword from her scabbard.

If looks could kill, blood would be flowing.

'If we're not back in thirty minutes ...'

'I know. We'll ride like the wind to Astoria,' Kralgen finishes.

'No bloody way. You come in and rescue us!' Lotane laughs. 'Don't you dare leave me behind to die!'

Again, I note Asterz's gaze flicker between the two men. Lotane and Kral are back to their casual banter, and this is certainly not something that happens between an Icelandian King and an Astorian Queen's consort who've only just met.

Then we're off. Lotane leads the way, crouching so we stay hidden below the tips of the long grass.

'Can you detect anything untoward?' Lotane whispers as we head toward the village.

'It's too far away, and the wind and animals are masking everything,' I reply. Yet I still let my magic have free rein, searching, questing, happily doing what it can to win my praise. Using it again brings the Saer Tel's powerful abilities to mind. How do they call upon the force of life magic beyond their own body's limitations? However, now isn't the time to dwell on that.

'What's got you worried? I couldn't see anything.'

Lotane turns, and it's the first time I've looked into those incredible eyes properly for what seems an eternity. Will he notice my pulse quickening?

'You just said it. I can't detect any movement, yet some doors are open. It's too big a village not to have children running around or people tending crops this time of day. I think they might be hiding in ambush.'

'Let's circle around and approach from the wooded side,' I suggest.

There's no further need for words, and we set off. Normally we'd spread out, but by following in Lotane's footsteps, we're only disturbing one area of grass at a time and can move faster. Speed is of the essence, for it will give any potential assailants less time to coordinate. Even though my magic can't help me discern any telltale noise, I use it to blow the grass in gentle waves, further concealing our passage. This allows us to move faster than we otherwise would, and it doesn't take long to reach the cover of the woods.

The sound of the forest and its wildlife greet us. It's reassuring because a hidden foe would cause the animals to either go silent in fright or loud with indignation at an intrusion.

It's comforting to settle into what we do best. Lotane taps his eye, then points left, and I do the same, pointing right. I'll skirt the edge of the woodland, and he'll be a little deeper in. From shadow to shadow, we glide. No fast movement to draw the eye or startle any wildlife.

My feet unconsciously test the ground before I transfer my weight, ensuring there's nothing to snap and give away my position. I've forgotten how much I've missed this. Being alone with Lotane makes me wonder why we didn't choose to run from this fight and survive in the mountains alone. We could have been happy, I think.

We bisect some hunting trails heading into the woods. We check each one carefully for any signs of recent passage, whether scuffed or disturbed debris, broken stems, or twisted leaves, yet there's nothing.

We've moved swiftly but cautiously, a delicate balance that we manage so well. Then my magic brings a warning, a faint thump that's out of place in the forest. It isn't the sound of a branch falling that disturbs the canopy and takes time to rest. This sounds like a sudden blow, and it's coming from one of the dozen or so wooden cabins.

I raise my clenched fist, and we both freeze.

It could be a door banging or a shutter swinging in the breeze, but no.

*Thump, thump.*

I touch my ear, then point toward the cabins, and we move stealthily to the nearest one.

The shutters are closed, but we carefully look through the cracks, and despite the interior being in shadow, there's no one apparent inside. We sidle around the outside, ensuring no one is about, and then step softly onto the porch. The door has been torn from its leather hinges, and we step silently through the open doorway, weapons ready.

Lotane guards left and I the right.

It's a simple cabin with just one room. The interior is a mess of broken tables and chairs. Chests have been upended, and cupboards tipped over. Lotane moves to the hearth and pushes his fingers into the ashes.

'Cold,' he mouths.

I point out the two beds at the back of the cabin, where the covers are thrown back, unmade.

Yet more interestingly are the scarred marks on the headboard and walls above the beds, made by a dagger in bored hands. The owners of this cabin wouldn't deface their own lodgings, which makes me believe someone has been staying here who doesn't belong. From the depth of the cuts, it's someone strong. I breathe, calling upon my magic for help, and sure enough, the scent of ogre reaches my nostrils.

I know Lotane will have reached the same conclusion without magical assistance, and we cautiously exit the cabin and move to the next one.

*Thump.*

Lotane's head tilts, and I know he's heard it too. Yet we don't allow ourselves to be distracted. We work our way swiftly from cabin to cabin, ensuring all are empty. Each one has been ransacked of supplies, but if someone is left alive here, they've hopefully gathered everything usable together, and this won't be a wasted reconnaissance.

It's obvious where the noise is coming from now. There's a large barn set away from the cabins, back amongst the trees. I curb my impatience as we search a small shack, but our diligence is rewarded, for here are some dried and smoked meats wrapped in greased leather parcels.

With only the barn left to search, we separate to approach from different sides.

There's a moment of vulnerability as Lotane disappears around the far side of the barn, out of sight. We can't see if the other is in trouble with this strategy, but we've scouted thoroughly, thus minimising the risk. This is outweighed by the benefit of seeing into the barn from two different angles and presenting two separate targets to any enemy.

There are no windows to peer through on my side, so I tread silently but purposefully toward the end.

I peer around the corner of the barn to see the doors wide open and Lotane looking back at me.

Thumps and thuds continue to emanate from within, and I can detect the buzz of flies, the rasping of drawn breath, and muffled moans of pure agony. I'm confident there are four people inside, so I hold up four fingers, grasp my sword, and edge toward the opening as Lotane does likewise.

The inside of the barn starts to reveal itself as I near the entrance. Lotane has his back flat against the wall, and on the other side of it, I can see a long bench covered in tools. As he doesn't warn me of anything, I know my side is also absent of any immediate threat.

Reaching the opposite sides of the entrance, we kneel, and both peer around the doorframe.

I draw my head back, and when I look across at Lotane, I recognise the disbelief in his eyes that are no doubt in mine. I wish we'd never come here, never investigated and just carried on past this village. But we hadn't, and we've now witnessed something we can never forget, and if we leave now, it will haunt us forever.

We must do something even if we die trying, for such evil should never go unchallenged. I only wish we had time to go and get Kral and Asterz, but we don't.

Nodding to Lotane, I raise my sword and step into hell.

***

The far end of the barn is outfitted for butchering animals. Under the light of a half dozen lanterns, I can see meat hooks hanging from the roof beams. There's also a broad, varnished wooden bench with drainage grooves perfect for skinning a large forest deer or two.

Unfortunately, there are no deer in sight.

Instead, four tightly bound and gagged villagers are in the far-left corner of the barn. They're curled on the floor, eyes wide with unbridled terror.

To the far-right is another table on which torsos and limbs of men, women and children are piled, all neatly butchered. Blood runs from the channels carved in the wood into precisely placed buckets, and swarms of flies are having the meal of a lifetime.

On the large slaughtering bench are the bodies of two women, and I swallow hard to keep myself from vomiting as I note one is still alive despite having had both arms and legs removed. She's bleeding out fast, but no one should be alive and go through this.

Leaning over the table are four creatures about as tall as Lotane. Garments, like a loose flowing robe, move around them in an unsettling fashion, shimmering from one putrid colour to another. These creatures seem to absorb light as if they're standing in the shade.

Shades. Yes, it's a fitting description.

It's hard to perceive features, for a veil covers their faces, and they're bowed over the table. One lifts a large meat cleaver.

Thump.

A hand is severed at the wrist and tossed into a corner.

We creep forward, silent as the dead. On the table, the woman's eyes flutter at our approach, her disbelieving mind somehow hoping that salvation is at hand.

'Help me,' she moans softly.

One of the creatures whips around, letting out a high-pitched screech as it spies us.

It's tempting to charge, but the barn floor is littered with debris, and it's not as though these things can go anywhere either. There's only one way in, and the way out is past us.

The creatures put down the cleavers and come around the bench to face us. I think they're surrendering, but that thought is quickly discarded as they pull long wavy daggers from their belts.

The plan is simple. We kill these things and free the four survivors.

Strange how plans never quite go as you want them to.

The first thing the creature on the left does is bend down and quickly slit the throats of the four bound people. Blood spurts, bodies strain at their bindings as though there's something to be done, and then, stillness.

Despite there being four of them, I'm confident. We have longer weapons and the skills to use them. In a sword versus dagger fight, there should only ever be one winner.

We close the distance. I feel no fear, just cold dispassion to rid my world of these evil things. Only half a dozen steps separate Lotane and I from the creatures, and we're far enough apart to allow us the freedom to swing without fear of injuring the other.

I sense Lotane preparing to attack, then ...

The creatures disappear.

Lotane hisses with shock and disbelief. We've fought together so often that we don't need to speak to know each other's thoughts. Lotane doesn't lower his guard, and nor do I, not until we know the threat has truly gone.

*Help me.*

I ask, even though the need alone is often enough. Rasping breaths are magnified and brought to me instantly; they're still here.

A whisper and I spin, my sword lashing out, barely deflecting a dagger from a shade that has appeared behind me. I snap out a side kick, sending Lotane falling away from another dagger that would have claimed his life.

He rolls away, comes to his feet, and lashes out with his sword before backing away toward the wall.

The shades disappear again.

We're in a terrible situation. Separated against a foe the like of which we've never faced.

I spin at random, my sword cleaving the air as I make my way toward the barn entrance. The shades appear and then disappear time after time. It seems they can't stay invisible indefinitely, and I breathe a sigh of relief as otherwise, they'd be almost omnipotent in dealing death.

I hope, like me, the longer they use their magic, the more fatigued they become.

Lotane yells, and I see his shirt torn and blood coming from a wound in his arm, and he redoubles his efforts.

If only we could see where they are. A chill runs down my back, and I spin, a dagger slicing my cheek before the shade dances away from my sword and then fades from sight.

I force my breathing to slow, swinging my sword as if I'm going through a warm-up routine, not fighting for my life. I weave it around me, spinning, twisting, changing direction and tempo, ensuring that any attempt on my life will put my attackers in jeopardy too.

To add to our problems, it's stifling in here, and I'm sweating.

There's my solution!

A simple wish and my magic answers my call. As the temperature plummets, not only does it provide instant relief, but my breath plumes, and so does that of the shades.

I lunge, my form perfect, and sense the slightest resistance as my blade flashes a handspan beneath the plume of breath three steps ahead of me. The shade reappears, grasping its throat, black blood spurting betwixt its fingers, and collapses in a heap before me.

Lotane surges toward the plume nearest him, but he doesn't meet with success. Then as we await their next attack, the shades reappear outside of the barn.

Damn.

I can't chill the air outside, not with the sun beating down, and cooling such a large barn has already drained me.

We step outside, the dusty ground providing sound footing beneath our feet. The shades await us calmly, confident that victory will be theirs. Their arms weave, and dagger blades flash as they advance, disappearing a few steps away.

Lotane and I immediately go back-to-back, our swords continually moving.

My blade rings off an invisible dagger, and in that instant, a shade appears, thrusting for my other side. I drive her back with a gust of wind, draining myself again, and see the creature slide across the earth in a cloud of dust before it disappears.

'Get ready,' I forewarn Lotane through gritted teeth. We can read each other's intent in combat, but he won't see this coming.

I'm tiring fast, more from the magic than the combat, and the shades will get us soon.

I visualise what I need, and moments later, the wind picks up, swirling around us like a hurricane, picking up dust and earth, and suddenly, there they are, three forms visible as they're covered in flying debris.

I dart forward, my blade flashing down, smashing through a raised dagger, cleaving into the head of the shade. Moments later, it reappears in the flesh on the ground, its skull split like a ripe fruit.

Spinning, I'm in time to see Lotane's sword eviscerate one shade, slicing through its thin robe and opening its belly before he spins, chopping down diagonally, almost cutting the final shade in two.

The shade whose entrails are flopping from its stomach, screeches hideously. I'm tempted to let it suffer and die a horrific death, but the noise could be heard by any number of other creatures nearby, so I drive my sword down through its gaping mouth.

I stumble, dizziness coming over me in waves. It will pass, but Lotane is there, his hand reaching out for support. I could shrug him off, fight the weakness away; I know I can.

Instead, I sag, allowing myself to fade, so I can feel his arms catch and hold me. Even if it's the last time he ever does this, I'll remember this moment forever.

***

I awaken to find myself propped up against the outside of the barn, my cheek hot from the sun. Kralgen is bent over me, hand raised.

Hmmm, maybe it wasn't the sun that woke me.

'You don't look happy to see me,' Kral says with a wink, looking relieved. 'Now, stop sleeping when the rest of us are working.'

'How long have I been out?'

'Maybe ten minutes. Lotane and Asterz are doing a final sweep for supplies. Let's get you to the horses; we're about ready to go.'

I ignore Kral's outstretched hand, wanting to test my strength. As I clamber upright, I'm relieved to discover I'm pretty steady despite being drained.

'It's a better world without those creatures in. You did a fine job killing them all. Lotane tells me they actually made themselves invisible?'

I nod.

'Gods. As if we haven't got a hard enough fight on our hands,' Kralgen growls.

He's acquired a staff from somewhere to replace the sword Dimitar had taken, which has me looking around for my weapon.

'Asterz took it back. Said it was some family heirloom. Here, I've got you these instead.'

Kral hands me a simple leather harness with three scabbards holding the shades' wavy daggers.

'They're actually well balanced and not bad for throwing,' he says as I take them gratefully. 'There's also a hunting bow and arrows on your horse now.'

I walk across the yard, kneeling down by the bodies of the dead shades. Black blood and flies are everywhere, and the body appears to be moving under the strange fabric that encases it.

Taking a dagger, I lift the veil of one that Lotane had killed and see the flesh sloughing away from the skull, maggots twisting and turning in every bit of visible flesh. The stench is rotten, and I quickly step back, covering my nose and mouth.

'Looks like they've been dead a couple of weeks already,' Kralgen says from behind me. 'There are ogre tracks heading into the forest, so we need to get going quickly before they come back.'

Together we make our way quickly to the horses, reaching them as Asterz and Lotane come jogging over carrying some bulging water skins.

I try to catch Lotane's eye, but he studiously avoids mine. He tosses some skins to Kral, who takes two, then leans over to loop two more from my saddle pommel. Swollen grain bags already hang there, and the bags over the horses' rumps are full to bursting.

Moments later we're mounted, ready to leave.

'We need to move fast along the trade road,' Asterz commands, pulling on her reins. 'If we push hard, we can make the River of Tears by tomorrow night.'

'We should be more cautious!' I counter. 'We didn't anticipate finding Nogoth's creatures this far north, and who is to say that the next village or farmstead we come across won't be swarming with ogres, wolfen or more of those shade things.'

Asterz doesn't look pleased with my interference.

'Wasn't it you who told us that Nogoth is taking his army to conquer the south first? she snaps, then calms herself and continues. 'When we were near High Delnor, we saw little sign of his vast army. The only exceptions were small contingents escorting groups of prisoners.'

'Yet perhaps Malina has a point,' Lotane says respectfully, laying his hand on Asterz's arm. 'We are only four, and even if these are just raiding parties, we're vulnerable until we reach Astoria.'

'Then all the more reason to get there quickly. So, follow your queen's orders and keep me safe!'

She heels her horse into a canter, and Lotane hurries to position himself alongside her.

'Patience, King Slayer,' Kralgen says as we follow after. 'Let's just keep vigilant. We have supplies, so there's no need to approach any villages or towns we encounter.'

I nod, then turn my attention to the countryside, keeping watch to the south, letting my temper cool. Asterz might be a queen, but it frustrates me that my voice isn't heard. However, I'm more upset that Lotane still follows her commands.

Once again, the idea of using blood magic comes to mind, but after a moment's contemplation, I push it from my thoughts. If I use it on Asterz, Lotane will know, so I'll have to use it on him, then Kralgen. I'm not willing to become that kind of person.

Better I focus on other things.

Those hideous shades.

I thought I'd seen all the creatures Nogoth had at his disposal, but apparently not. What if there are monsters even deadlier than giants and shades? It's a worrying thought, but thankfully I have my magic to even the fight.

I project gratitude and warmth at my magic, feeling it squirm with pleasure. Without it at my disposal, I'd have been dead countless times. If there's a way to defeat Nogoth, it must be magical.

But how?

Calling upon my powers drains my strength so quickly. But what if I can call upon the world's magic that exists all around? It's so vast and could never be depleted, and maybe nor would I if I could wield it.

'Kral, watch my sector for a moment.'

There's no questioning why. We don't ask one another to do things through laziness, only through necessity. He nods.

I focus, opening my spirit eye and turn my vision outwards. Magic is evident everywhere, gloriously colourful, and I'm surprised to discern gold alongside the other elements.

Directing my attention toward the colours streaming around me, I project my thoughts, attempting to summon a light breeze as I would with my own magic. There's no noticeable change in their movement, and I don't detect any response to my request.

Of course, it wouldn't be that simple. But if only it was.

I'm already tired from the earlier fight, and this isn't the right time to push myself further. When we break for camp tonight, I'll start exploring this again and can regain my depleted strength when I sleep. I return my focus back to the landscape around me.

'Thanks.'

There's no need to say more to Kralgen and talking above the clatter of hooves isn't easy anyway.

I turn my attention south, watching some birds flutter skyward in distress.

'Birds disturbed to the south,' I call. Any predator could have unsettled them, but there are no taking chances.

I feel unsettled too. Maybe I've been hiding in the shadows so long that riding down a trade road in full view feels careless. Unfortunately, the truth is less palatable. It's because I no longer view myself as the apex predator, but, just like those birds, I consider myself the prey.

***

Unrecognisable but sturdy trees, dense undergrowth, and a rocky overhang provide cover for our evening campsite. It would be perfect, but for the spiders and other insects that call this place home. However, as they've kept their distance, I haven't felt the need to burn them to a crisp, although there's one particular spider that tests my patience.

The horses munch contentedly from their grain bags a few steps away, and I settle down comfortably on a soft bed of ferns covered by my travel blanket.

Despite being in occupied territory, I feel secure and rested enough to experiment with reaching out to the world's magic. I've been impatient to try since failing earlier in the afternoon, and now, this brief moment of tranquillity provides the perfect opportunity.

Lying back, I open my spirit eye and gaze upon my surroundings, then immediately regret doing so. Despite the beauty of the colourful magic swirling around me, I can also make out Asterz holding Lotane's hand a few steps away.

Grrr. Make that two spiders I want to burn.

*Focus, Malina.*

My spirit eye has only ever allowed me to observe, but who knows what I can achieve.

I attempt to stand and touch the colourful ribbons with my spirit, but every time I do, it's my physical body that reacts to my thoughts.

*Just relax, and let your spirit lift free*, I tell myself over and over.

I visualise my spirit standing, leaving my body prone on the ground, and momentarily experience weightlessness. My vision swims, and the feeling disappears.

Damn.

If only things could be easy, just once!

I stand and walk over quietly to Kralgen, who is setting out some food. Every step feels like I'm walking uphill. I'm exhausted.

'Let me do that.'

I kneel beside him but lose my balance and start to topple backwards. I quickly reach out to hold his arm, only to miss.

'What the hell!'

I'm sitting on the ground, and Kralgen continues as if nothing has happened.

'Kral. Something weird is going on,' I say, looking around, then close my mouth with a snap as I see myself lying on the blanket.

I lift my hands before my eyes and realise they're faintly translucent, and when I bring them together, they merge. This is incredible.

Once again, I lose my balance as if the ground is sloping heavily toward my body. Yes, an irresistible urge to return to my physical self is pulling me back.

*Don't give up yet, Malina!*

Gritting my teeth, I strive to reach the edge of our small clearing, but I can't progress more than a couple of steps. The resistance I encounter is beyond my physical or mental strength to overcome.

I return to stand over my body, the force to rejoin lessening now that I'm so close.

It would have been incredible to adventure unseen and unheard while my body rested. But I also know the body cannot survive without the spirit, so it makes sense that I'm unable to wander far or for long.

The colours of magic surround me, and I reach out, my hands passing through their playful flow. Yet I don't feel anything, and nor does my ethereal form interrupt the elements' passage.

I visualise a gust of wind stirring the trees, but there's no response, no sign that my request has been felt.

'Can you feel me?' I whisper, my fingers brushing along a tendril of white, but I know I've gone unheard. Whether I try to grab or embrace the colours, it's like trying to hold onto clouds.

'Can you hear me?' I shout, trying a blunt approach, but unsurprisingly the common tongue doesn't attract the elements' attention any more than an ant's attempts to communicate with me would attract mine.

I shiver, suddenly cold, and the pull on my body increases to such an extent that I lie down, feeling myself merge with my physical self. I keep my eyes closed, enjoying the sound of my heartbeat, the ecstatic tumbling of my magic at my return, and the gentle buzz of voices.

What if I can have my bonded magic communicate with the world's magic, cajoling it, commanding it? I direct my thoughts, confident I've stumbled onto the answer.

*Could you help?*

A sense of regret washes over me, and I sigh softly. Is there any point in pursuing a greater magical power than I already possess? If it were possible to acquire more, surely the ssythlans would have found a way after all their years of working with the elements.

But if there's a way to actually defeat Nogoth, it must lie in my finding a way to harness more power. How else could I defeat an immortal?

Taking a break, I sit up with a yawn, only to frantically catch a packet that Kralgen launches at me.

I roll my eyes but then smile in thanks as I unwrap some hardened trail biscuits. Another packet, this one containing smoked meat, follows. He also tosses four packets at Lotane.

It's simple fayre, but my stomach is already growling in expectation, and it will have to do. As I devour the food, I snort in amusement as Asterz complains softly to Lotane about the cold meat.

Asterz had requested a fire earlier, but fortunately, Lotane had convinced her that it was unnecessary, citing that our food was ready to eat and the weather warm. I wish he'd been stronger in his argument and pointed out it was a damn stupid idea that might draw attention to the fact we're here.

My amusement quickly disappears as Asterz leans her head on Lotane's shoulder.

There's a look in her eyes that I know only too well, and it makes my stomach churn with envy.

'We could do with more water,' Kralgen rumbles.

It's true. It's not only us drinking, but the horses too, and our skins are almost empty as we hadn't come across any water source.

'Lotane and I can find some,' Asterz suggests, her hand squeezing Lotane's.

'No. We stay together as much as possible,' Kralgen rumbles. 'Malina can fill them for us.'

I pull one of the wavy daggers from its sheath and, turning to a tree next to me, carefully bore a hole into its bark. It doesn't take long. Afterwards, I split a thin branch, cut it to the size of my hand, carve a channel along its length, and tap it into the borehole.

Asterz looks on in interest while Lotane and Kralgen gather the water skins.

It's been a long time since I've done something like this, yet it takes little more than my hand on the tree, and a wish, before my magic does the rest. As water pours from the wound in the trunk, my strength is also drained.

This is balance, and whilst I wish my power was unlimited, thus allowing me to defeat Nogoth, no one should be omnipotent.

Kralgen and Lotane work together to fill and stopper the skins, and soon our supply is replenished.

'Why not just have it bubble from the ground?' Asterz asks.

'No one likes drinking muddy water,' I respond with a yawn. 'This might taste a little unpleasant, but it's safe to drink without having to purify it.'

The question had been well meant, but it still rankles. Everything Asterz does or says annoys me. It's unfair to the woman. She might not be someone I'd ever consider a friend, but she doesn't deserve my enmity for sleeping with someone I love when she has no idea of the history between Lotane and me.

I resolve to put my jealousy aside and be more amicable toward her.

'Tell me of Astoria. How did you rise to power, as I thought only kings were allowed to rule there?'

Asterz's face briefly takes on a darker look before she shakes her head as if to clear away some unpleasant thoughts.

'Forgive me if my story is brief, for it brings no joy to retell it. My father held the crown until four years ago when he died in a hunting accident. After that, my brother ruled until he too died last year, this time by an assassin's hand. He had yet to sire a male heir, so I was crowned the interim ruler, being the closest relative alive.'

'Why only interim?' I ask.

'Because, as you say, only a king may sit permanently on the Astorian throne. I may rule for one year, that's our tradition, and I have no qualms abiding by it.'

'But it would be a disaster for Astoria if you were replaced at this time. There must be something you can do!'

Asterz laughs, and this time her eyes brighten in direct contrast to how they'd looked when she'd talked of her family's deaths.

'Oh, I intend to rule for some time yet, for there's indeed a solution to being replaced.'

'And what might that be?' Kralgen asks, leaning forward, interested in our conversation. 'Will you have all your rivals killed?'

Asterz's laughter is pleasantly musical.

'Far from it. The solution is far less deadly and rather more pleasurable.'

Asterz reaches out to clutch Lotane's hand, her eyes shining with happiness.

'Lotane is my solution. He's agreed to marry me, and then Astoria can move forward with both a king and a queen at its head!'

Asterz's voice continues on, her face radiating happiness.

It might be dangerous to leave the camp, but I can't stay.

'Congratulations to you both.'

I somehow manage to say the words without my voice breaking or crying, but I can't hold the tears back for long.

The solitude of the woods beckons, and I make my way into the concealing undergrowth, putting distance between myself and the others. I want to fill the silence surrounding me with screams, yet I hold my despair inside. There's a certain element of justice in what's happened. I'd first broken Lotane's heart by sleeping with a king, and now he's broken mine by sleeping with and then agreeing to marry a queen.

Yet there's only one person to blame for all of this.

Violet eyes come to mind, and anger surges through me.

I want to see him dead, torn apart, utterly destroyed as if he's never been.

Only magic can do this, and I have to find a way to harness more power if I'm to succeed.

Lowering myself to the ground, I close my eyes and focus. The night is still young, and I have work to do.

***

# CHAPTER VIII

I'm so tired.

I'm tired having stayed up till the early hours trying to get the world's magic to respond. I'm tired from crying with a broken heart whenever I think of Lotane and Asterz. I'm also drained having used my magic in a vain attempt to force the world's elements to respond to my will. I'm barely functioning.

I stand, taking stock of my surroundings. The birds are awake, chattering happily in the trees, totally oblivious to the world's fate or my pain. Amongst the undergrowth, a rabbit nibbles contentedly on a new shoot that's fought its way through the mulch. The sun has cleared the horizon, and as I gaze at the canopy, it's streaked with golden light.

Mornings are my favourite time, and this place is so beautiful. If only I could just walk off into the forest and lose myself amongst nature for two years. Then, I could return to a world absent the fey and start my life afresh. Sadly, those I care about will have died, and everyone left won't care to plan for Nogoth's defeat a thousand years hence. They'll be the lucky ones who've inherited the reborn earth. My voice will go ignored, an unpopular reminder of what's happened. I'll be cast out unless I use my blood magic to help me find a place.

Yes. With my blood magic, I could be the queen of this world and ensure no one forgets and everyone works toward Nogoth's demise. This world will be ready in a thousand years, and Nogoth will fall on his return.

Or I can return to the camp, work with the soon-to-be King and Queen of Astoria, help them unite the world, and finish things sooner, not later.

Is it my free will that has me return to camp, or the need to complete a mission?

Soft voices filter through the trees as I approach. The others are breaking their fast, and Kralgen greets me with a knowing smile. He pats the blanket next to him where he's put some food aside.

Asterz is in mid-sentence.

'Upon our return, Astoria's envoys will immediately journey south to Suria and then on to Rolantria to offer sanctuary to their people. Lotane, you'll help me rule Astoria and start preparing our citizens and lands for the war to end all wars.'

Asterz pauses and looks across at me.

'Malina,' she says with a forced smile. 'I don't know your plans or even if you want to fit into all of this, but you're welcome to help train Astoria's people. There's no denying your martial prowess, and every sword arm will strengthen our cause.'

Until last night, I'd have jumped at the chance of being close to Lotane, but now, I can't even look at him.

'You don't need to make your mind up now, King Slayer,' Kralgen says, putting his hand on my shoulder. 'Instead, take Lotane and ensure the road is clear while I speak privately to my fellow monarch on matters of the crown. Go on; we'll bring the horses shortly.'

Great. Kral thinks he's doing me a favour, but the thought of being alone with Lotane brings me close to tears. I swiftly walk from camp before my reaction is noticed.

I pause two dozen steps into the undergrowth and lean against a tree.

Just last night, I was full of strength, dreaming of the vengeance I'd wreak on Nogoth, and now, a few hours later, I've never felt so pathetic in my life. I need to get a grip on myself; this is not me. I'm a Chosen, the King Slayer.

Soft footsteps approach, and I recognise Lotane's tread.

I swallow back the last of my anguish and, without turning, raise my hand and signal for him to take the right. Crouching, I move silently through the woods. It only takes a minute to get to the treeline, and I kneel behind a large bush surveying the road and landscape before me.

There's nothing untoward, and I hope Kralgen doesn't take long. Keeping a lookout while riding will be a welcome distraction. Quiet time is something I definitely don't need right now, and in truth, I've already decided to go to Icelandia with Kral.

Lotane's footsteps come closer.

'Why don't you go hurry the others?' I suggest without turning.

'Alina.'

Why did he have to use that name? Damn him. I swallow hard and visualise entering a fight. Immediately I'm calm, my conditioning kicking in. Yes, this is the way to deal with this situation. Just see it as sparring in the training circle. However hard the blow, just shrug it off and keep fighting without showing weakness.

'We need to talk.'

Turning to face him, our eyes meet for the first time since we parted.

I imagine being struck in the stomach by a staff; that's why it hurts so much. Just carry on.

Raising my eyebrows, I say nothing, allowing the silence to build. I won't beg Lotane not to marry Asterz nor declare my love. These would be signs of weakness to an opponent.

Except that ... Lotane isn't an opponent. He let me live when we duelled; I know that now and we owe each other our lives too many times. Not forgetting, he's been a lover, a friend, and has never wronged me.

I can't take that approach.

A sigh escapes my lips, and I shake my head. He knows me well enough to see through whatever façade I build, so why bother.

'I want to hate you, but I can't,' I say with a wry smile. 'You've chosen wisely. Asterz is a strong woman, fit for a man like you. You'll be a warrior king without peer.'

Lotane looks surprised and emotional.

'I'm sorry you found out the way you did; it must have hurt. I've been meaning to tell you, but there's never been the right time,' Lotane says, genuine regret etched on his features.

'There's never a right time for something like that, Lotane.'

I embrace him warmly, and his arms enfold me a moment later.

'What's important is that it's in the open now, and you're happy,' I whisper.

'Who said anything about being happy?' he whispers back.

My heart beats so hard as his words register that it makes me gasp. I try to step away in surprise, but his arms hold on.

'Do you ever feel you've no control over your destiny?' Lotane says softly, pulling back a little but retaining hold of my hands.

I say nothing, waiting for him to continue as he struggles to articulate his thoughts. After a brief pause, he continues.

'From the moment I was Chosen, I've been following orders, doing what I was told. At the time, it felt so right, and I loved the life, however dangerous it was. Only the strong could survive, but you and I, we were the strongest!'

My heart beats faster, warmth spreading throughout me. Encouraged by my growing smile, Lotane forges ahead.

'With hindsight, I realise all my life's choices were made for me; bound by magic, conditioned in my sleep, made to do what I didn't want to do. I followed a single path, not knowing I could take others. I'd spent my whole life following commands, never my instincts, until this moment.'

Lotane squeezes my hands.

I can barely control my emotions. Just like me, he understands only the two of us can be happy together. When I saw him with Asterz, I knew her love wasn't fully reciprocated. I want to kiss him but hold back, sensing the timing isn't yet perfect.

'Will you help me live my dream, Alina? I know without asking that you want to go with Kral but forgive my actions and stay by my side instead. I believe that together we can ...'

I can't wait. Why have him suffer when I can give an answer he'll never forget.

Stepping forward, I kiss him, enjoying the softness of those full lips, euphoria overwhelming me ... only for Lotane to step back in confusion.

'What ... what are you doing?' he gasps, holding his hands out to keep me at bay.

'What do you mean, what am I doing?' I ask, panicking. 'You're trapped in Asterz's web and need to escape. You said you want me by your side to help you live your dream. Our dream!'

'Oh, gods. That's not what I was saying!' Lotane replies, looking horrified. 'The love you and I had was fabricated using blood magic. Deciding to marry Asterz is the first major decision I've ever made without coercion. I wanted you by my side as a friend, someone I trust implicitly who could help win this war!'

'But, but ...' I think desperately of something to say. 'You said you aren't happy, and I know you don't love her; it's way too soon. You two have nothing like we had, what we still have. You still love me, Lotane. Forgive me, and let's have the life we spoke about!'

My begging sickens me, and I can't believe I've made such a fool of myself, yet I have to try and save our relationship even if it leaves me so vulnerable.

A shake of that tousled blond hair is like a knife to my gut.

'I know this is sudden, and I can't quite explain it, but I need you to accept it. My happiness and love will grow in time. As for forgiveness, I gave you that long ago, Alina. The problem is, I can't forget.'

'Blood magic could make you forget!'

The words fall from my lips before my brain fully registers what I'm saying, and as realisation hits, Lotane grabs me around the throat and slams me back against a tree.

'Don't you ever dare, on me, on Asterz, or ...'

'Shall I tell Asterz it's safe to continue our journey?' Kralgen rumbles from a few steps away.

Lotane releases his hold and steps back, white-faced.

'No. I'll get her!'

As he runs back through the trees, Kral comes over and enfolds me in his massive arms.

'Be strong, King Slayer. Not every war is won at the first battle.'

He means to be kind, but I can't help but think some are lost that way for good.

***

Whenever my gaze is drawn to Lotane and Asterz riding ahead, my heart feels like breaking.

I should be more focused on our surroundings, but Kral's words keep playing over in my head. *Not every war is won at the first battle.*

Do I surrender the battle for Lotane or continue to fight?

Hmmm. That's not the question I should be asking. I smile as the right one comes to mind.

When has a Chosen ever surrendered?

Never!

I haven't conceded in my struggle against Nogoth, an immortal Fey King. So why would I give up fighting for Lotane's heart against Asterz, a mere mortal queen? Lotane hasn't even declared his love for her.

Just like this world is worth fighting for, so is he. My campaign will continue ... so what should my next move be ...

Suddenly my horse whinnies in pain and begins to collapse under me. I leap from the saddle, calling on my magic to help soften my landing, wondering what caused it to fall when I note the other horses going down too.

I don't land well, but I swallow my cry of pain and scurry back to my fallen horse. Two crossbow bolts are buried deep in my mount's side, and whilst it's still breathing, it will never rise again. I snatch my bow from its saddle cover, grab the quiver of arrows, and curse to discover only half a dozen have escaped the fall without damage.

Whistling fills the air, and I fall flat as two more bolts thwack into the horse.

'From the south,' I shout as I stay low, peering over my mount's corpse. That was the sector I should have been watching instead of daydreaming! Whilst the ambush isn't my fault, I should have at least been able to give a warning.

I glance at Kralgen, and he nods back despite the blood flowing down his face.

Lotane is a little further down the road, clothes badly torn, exposing his flesh beneath, which isn't in much better shape. He's crouched over Asterz, whose face is white.

More whistling and hissing and the bolts come from a different angle.

'They're flanking us. We need to move!' Kralgen shouts.

I'm tired and hurt, yet we need cover, so I whip up a wind, causing dust to whirl from the road, and then sprint for the tall grasses to the north. Kralgen runs to help Lotane support Asterz. She's limping badly, and they make slow progress.

Kralgen cries out in pain as one bolt thwacks into his calf, and a heartbeat later, I glimpse another passing through his right bicep, exiting in a spray of red, but then we're into cover and have a brief respite.

Peering toward the south through the waving stems, I make out a dozen ogres with crossbows making their way toward us in a skirmish line. I hadn't appreciated these damned creatures might use ranged weapons.

Crossbows are an evil device in the right hands, and these ogres have already shown their competence. They'd aimed for the horses being the larger target, knowing that killing our mounts would injure us in the fall, leaving us vulnerable and hindering escape.

'She's fine, just winded,' Lotane says as I join them.

I kneel down to inspect Kralgen's wounds. His bicep is bleeding badly, but it's a clean wound, and he can still move his arm. The bolt in his calf is bad, buried deep, with the point almost coming out the other side. We need to be mobile, and if the bolt isn't withdrawn, Kral won't be going far, but he'll bleed like a stuck pig if it is.

'Get ready to seal the wound!' I order Lotane.

Lotane's eyes open wide, silently pleading.

'I'm already drained,' I snap. 'I don't have much strength left. You'll be carrying both Asterz and me if I do it. As for Kral, how can he seal the wound in his right bicep when he has no left hand or fingers! Now's not the time to argue. So, are you ready?'

Lotane nods while Asterz looks on.

Kralgen groans as I grab the bolt and push, forcing the point out the other side of his calf. I work quickly, snapping off the flights, then slide a dagger under the wicked points on the back of the bolt head and pull the shaft through the wound.

'Sorry, Kral,' Lotane mutters, his eyes creasing in concentration and pain as he puts his fingers on the entry and exit wounds. Flesh smoulders as magic cauterises the holes, sealing them shut. Lotane doesn't pause and immediately repeats the process on Kral's bicep.

Asterz looks like she's seen her dead father rise from the grave. Disbelief and incomprehension vie for supremacy on her face while she looks between the three of us with her mouth wide open.

The smell of burning flesh gives me an idea.

'Fire the grasses,' I order, and Lotane doesn't hesitate. Sweat appears on his brow, flames leap from his hands, and thick smoke begins to billow skyward from the burning grass. I conjure a wind, and the flames leap higher and set off toward the road, giving us cover.

Bolts hiss through the smoke, and Lotane staggers as one slices his shoulder.

The ogres aren't stupid and aim for where we're most likely hiding.

'You three head for the tree line to the north,' I order. 'We're in no fit state to fight!'

Kralgen nods grimly. Lotane appears as if he's going to say something, but Asterz grabs his hand, pulling him away, and Kralgen turns and follows.

It's not easy to string a bow while crouched, but I manage it in record time. Notching an arrow, I half-draw, testing the tension. It's never a good idea to engage in combat with an untried weapon, especially a bow, but there's no other choice. Kralgen won't be moving fast, and these ogres will hunt us down unless I give them something else to worry about. I empty the quiver, pick the six arrows that can fly true, and then set off.

I keep low as I run parallel to the road, going around the flames. I let the wind drop as fatigue starts to kick in. No more staying up late practising my magic is one rule I'll definitely follow if I get out of this alive.

The ogres have spread out along the south side of the road by the time I spy them. Six have their bows raised while the others get ready to sprint across the open space. I draw and release from a kneeling position, my bow held horizontally, allowing me to stay low. My target is a ogress standing with a crossbow raised halfway along the line. Despite aiming for the torso, my arrow buries in her neck, and she drops lifeless.

A second arrow follows the first, taking another ogre in the shoulder, and then I'm flinging myself to the ground as crossbow bolts are released in my direction. They've made the mistake of firing at once, and whilst their mighty arms can quickly pull the strings back using a foot stirrup, I'm up and running to the south side of the road before they do.

Lotane and the others are heading north, but this way, the ogres won't pursue them and give me their backs as targets.

I circle quickly, take another shot at an ogre's head, miss, and now only have three arrows remaining.

Damn.

Bolts hiss through the high grass, and one scores my cheek, parting the skin to leave it bleeding as if from a surgeon's perfect incision.

Shoot and move.

Lystra's voice whispers in my mind.

*A badly wounded soldier needs another to care for them.*

I loose three more arrows, aiming low, hitting my targets in the leg and grunt in satisfaction. I hope that saying applies to ogres as it does to humans.

Sure enough, the bellows of pain have the ogres gather protectively around their injured comrades. They've no idea I'm out of arrows, and thankfully no further bolts from their crossbows make their presence felt.

Congratulating myself, I continue my circle, return to the road, and after checking for enemies, run across. I just need to find my friends' trail, and I'll quickly catch them.

Shortly after, I discover a wide path through the lush grass. This is definitely from another group of ogres, and I kick myself for not considering there'd be others involved in the ambush.

Now they're between us.

This day is rapidly going to hell in a handcart.

***

Three daggers, that's all I have.

A wriggle in my stomach reminds me it's three daggers and magic. If only I could have both magic and strength, not one or the other. Forget my previous notions of balance; at this moment, I want to be omnipotent.

A moment's inspection of the trail and bootprints shows maybe a dozen ogres passed this way, trampling the grass flat with no concern for stealth. From the spacing between the deep heel indents, the ogres are running confidently without hesitation, knowing they outnumber us heavily.

My friends are injured and are moving slowly and will be overtaken before they reach the sanctuary of the tree line if I don't intervene. I can't afford to hesitate.

I breathe deeply, filling my lungs. Smoke remains heavy in the air, so my scent will be covered.

Casting my redundant bow to the ground, I take a dagger in each hand and set off. I throw caution to the wind and sprint, the lives of my friends meaning more to me than my own, and it's not long before an ogre straggler appears up ahead. There's always one who isn't as fit as the rest in a squad, or perhaps she's staying behind as a rear guard, although she certainly isn't paying attention behind her.

It's a costly mistake, and I leap upon her back, drawing my dagger across her throat. Her legs collapse a few strides later as she drops a sword to grab at the horrific wound, vainly trying to stem the spurting blood.

I sheath my dagger and sweep up her fallen blade. It's so damned heavy, but I've practised with all types of swords in the past. I prefer shorter weapons, better suited to my frame, strength and speed, but I can wield this two-handed well enough.

I'm off running again a few seconds later. How quickly a long life can be ended and forgotten about.

Another straggler, but this time, I slash my blade across the back of his right leg. With a severed hamstring, he goes down with a crash, roaring in pain and alarm. I want this ... for those ahead to worry about what's behind.

Leaving the trail, I run adjacent to it about five paces to the left. The sound of thumping boots and heavy breathing has me crouch down, and it's a good thing, as four ogres thunder past, unaware of my presence, heading toward their injured comrade.

Once they're out of sight, I'm up and running, trusting that only one group has been sent back. I'm right because I catch sight of another eight ogres up ahead. This is more than I thought there'd be. I close the distance, pushing my luck, but they're intent on catching their quarry. I'm about fifteen paces distant when I hammer the sword into the ground, then cast first one, then another dagger spinning through the air.

The sword is back in my hand before the first dagger takes my first target in the right leg. He yowls in pain and surprise as he collapses to the ground. My second dagger clangs off another ogre's shoulder guard.

Damn!

The group come to a ragged halt and turn to face me.

There's no way I can overcome this many. I could run, but these creatures are quick, and I'm tired of running. Yet nor do I wish to die here, in some field in the middle of bloody nowhere.

Bizarrely, this moment reminds me of my childhood. At the orphanage I often faced down larger opponents and groups of malicious children just by projecting sheer fearlessness and a willingness to fight. It was mostly bluff because I was scared to hell, but they knew I would fight tooth and nail to protect myself and my little brother.

I'm no longer that little girl, but without learning that lesson ...

Drawing my remaining dagger, I run toward them.

*HELP ME,* I ask my magic, visualising my need.

This is all or nothing, do or die, and I don't hold anything back.

I shriek, the sound magnified a hundred times, as fire erupts from my mouth and body and sets the grass ablaze around me as I run at them like fire spewed from a volcano. My weapons glow incandescent, and my clothes fall away in ashes as I descend like a goddess of fire.

For a heart-stopping moment, the ogres stand their ground, but then ... they turn and run.

They scatter in all directions. Two fall over themselves, roaring in a panic. I deliver fearsome blows to injure, maim, and leave them screaming in agony, burning as the elemental fire I've summoned consumes their bodies.

I conjure a fierce wind, sending the flames leaping in all directions, chasing the fleeing creatures, and suddenly find myself alone.

*Enough.*

The flames die away, the air stills, but the fires continue to burn, spewing smoke skywards.

I stumble, drunk from exhaustion. I can't afford to let the darkness take me and can only hope the ogres don't begin the chase again.

The trail lures me onward, mostly north in small zig-zags. Either Lotane or Kralgen is still thinking with a clear head. A straight run for the trees would give any archers a clear shot at their backs.

There's an emptiness in my stomach, a thumping in my head, and the world spins as I continue, yet I won't give up. Had I kept a better lookout, I might have spotted this ambush, so this is my fault, and I want to see my friends again.

The trees loom large, their majestic beauty offering sanctuary. We can disappear amongst the trunks and undergrowth. Even our scent will be disguised by the wisps of smoke should the ogreish sense of smell be refined enough to follow us that way.

My vision is narrowing, and there's no sign of the others. I have but minutes remaining before I pass out. Usually, I'd climb a tree and hide amongst the foliage, but I don't have the strength or anything to tie myself in place to stop me from falling.

There's a thicket of snare bushes, vicious plants with spiny leaves and spiked stems to stop wildlife such as deer from eating them. Low to the ground, though, the stalks are smooth. With my last remaining strength, I wriggle underneath feet first, then gently stir the fallen leaves and mulch with magic to cover my tracks.

I try to stay awake a moment longer to see if I can do anything else, but it's beyond me.

***

I come wide awake as a twig snaps close to my head, setting my heart pounding. Thankfully, years of conditioning kick in, and it slows, allowing me to breathe easily, quelling any panic before it can take hold.

Damn.

A whole day has flown by, for the sun has set. Torchlight flickers, dispelling any hope that it's Kralgen or Lotane; they'd never be so brazen. Guttural voices speaking in the ogreish tongue confirm my fears.

Despite my sword and dagger, my nakedness now bothers me, and I feel strangely vulnerable. Perhaps burning my clothes off wasn't the smartest move. Thankfully, my boots remain mostly intact.

My magic stirs, making me aware I've recovered enough to call upon it if required.

*Not yet, my lovely, but be ready.*

I smile as my magic twists happily in response to my affection, yet it soon fades.

I've been in worse predicaments, but not by much.

Why are they even bothering to search for us?

We were just four random strangers riding through Delnorian lands. I'm sure they must have had plenty of village folk run from them before and given up the chase as not worth the effort. Then again, those villagers probably hadn't killed their comrades, maimed a few others, and turned themselves into walking bonfires.

It's hard to tell how many ogres there are. I'm lying on my back, but the thick foliage that's kept me hidden also prevents me from looking around. The fact that there are ogres even searching the woodland at this time of night means they must have the numbers to do a good job. I'm just relieved they're using torches which tells me they don't have the night sight I enjoy.

I take a moment to consider the situation and my next move.

We'd been foolish travelling so openly. Delnor was the first kingdom to be conquered, and we should have realised that contingents of Nogoth's army would secure the villages and towns in the surrounding countryside.

Being only three days on foot from the River of Tears, I'm sure Kral and the others will have moved on without me, trusting I'll evade capture. With Lotane and Kral injured, it would be foolish for them to stay nearby, and there's nothing they could do to help me anyway.

Yes. They'll strive to reach the sanctuary of Astoria as quickly yet cautiously as possible. Once there, they'll make for the capital, Ast, where Kral will prepare for his journey to Icelandia.

Now I need to find a way to escape this search party, then find and follow my friends' trail. Failing the last, I'll head directly to Astoria and meet them there.

Heavy footfalls and intelligible voices close to my head have me almost afraid to breathe, although they're talking so loudly I could probably sneeze unnoticed. Even Kralgen doesn't talk that loud. I resign myself to staying here throughout the night. If required, I can use a little magic to obtain water from the snare bush, and whilst I'm hungry, lack of food won't kill me.

Carefully, I turn onto my stomach, timing my movement to some coarse guttural speech. It's easier to look around, and I can spy half a dozen ogres in my narrow field of vision. I'm sure there must be many more spread out. It's strange how a human body glows red to my eyes, the blood pumping like lava. Yet the ogres must be cold-blooded, as less heat radiates from them.

A flickering shadow catches my eye, a stealthy movement, one piece of darkness blending into another.

A wolfen.

Now I'm in real trouble. Where there's one, there will undoubtedly be others. Their sense of smell will soon discover me cowering beneath this bush, and then I'll probably be ripped to shreds and eaten.

What the hell can I do?

*Think, Malina.*

Unless I intend to die here, fighting isn't an option. Would my charging inferno trick work again? Probably not. There are just too many ogres, and they're well spread out. Once the fire dies, I'll be weakened and easy prey

What other options are there?

A wind won't cause enough distraction while hiding or sinking myself into the earth will still have me found by the wolfen. There's no way stealth will be enough, and surrendering will see me dead.

Only one idea remains, and with every second bringing me closer to being discovered, I cringe at what I'm about to try. There are so many things that can go wrong, and if the searchers have a good description ...

Summoning a gust of wind, I cause some bushes to rustle two dozen steps away.

The ogres storm toward it, shouting, and I make my move.

Kicking my boots off, I stand smoothly from my hiding place.

I'm naked as the day I was born, surrounded by beasts that would happily feast on my flesh, and I begin to dance. I banish my fear and bring to mind the Saer Tel, how they move, their bodies twisting and swaying like a tree in a breeze.

My footsteps spin me lightly toward the group of ogres who, having speared the bush a dozen times, are looking frustrated at finding nothing within. My movement catches their attention, and they turn, raising their spears. I continue unperturbed, then pause motionless before the wolfen, risking all on this one throw of the dice.

I tilt my head to one side, then the other as if inspecting him and lift my hands to brush his cheek in the softest caress. The creature sniffs loudly, checking my scent. I smile, then continue my dance around the group with wild abandon.

'What are you doing here, Saer Tel, and where are your clothes?' demands an ogre captain in the common tongue. 'Your kind hasn't been sent here!'

I recall the Saer Tel in the tunnels advising that they wouldn't lower themselves to speak in such a fashion, so I ignore him.

His confusion and growing distrust are evident. Here I am, where a Saer Tel isn't supposed to be, whilst they're hunting for some dangerous fugitives. My deception is unravelling with every slightly misplaced footstep and lack of magical growth around me.

I consider running, but those spears or wolfen will get me before I take more than a few steps.

If only I could convince them, but my magic is nothing like that of the Saer Tel, despite my heritage. Nothing I summon can cause saplings to grow or for grass to appear.

Ogre knuckles tighten on spear shafts as suspicion mounts. This is where it ends. Do I set myself and the forest on fire and go out in a blaze of glory?

Yes, it's a good plan. I'll use every last drop of strength to create a firestorm and take most of these bastard fey with me.

My magic rises, but then ... I pause.

The thought of such destruction almost brings me to tears. Some of these trees are ancient, and what right do I have to destroy such a beautiful place if I'm to die anyway.

So, I banish such destructive thoughts, suddenly at peace with my fate, close my eyes and continue to dance, not wanting to see death approach.

What was that?

I hear a song, the words musical, or is it just music? It's haunting yet uplifting, as old as the world yet as young as a newborn. Fresh and invigorating, it's getting louder, and something strange is happening. My dance evolves, and it's nothing to do with me. I'd been somewhat clumsy before, my movements considered and fabricated, but now I'm being pulled around faster as if guided by an external force.

Light filters through my eyelids, and I open them to a world I'd never seen before. I'm not looking through my spirit eye, yet all around me, magic dances, shimmering gold. It's beautiful, and as my movements spiral, the filaments of gold are drawn to me as I create a vortex with my dance.

I perceive my limbs glowing, my body becoming infused with power, unlike anything I'd ever experienced. As my fingertips and feet sweep the forest floor, grasses erupt, and saplings push through.

I'm vaguely aware of the ogres and wolfen turning away from this mad Saer Tel in their midst, continuing their search as I immerse myself in this new gift. Thoughts of my friends whisper in the back of my mind, and my footsteps take me eastward, no longer caring about the fey, for I am Saer Tel, and the power of life magic has found me.

***

Usually, summoning magic leaves me drained, an empty husk devoid of energy, desperate for sustenance and sleep.

Yet as the sun rises and I find myself on the outskirts of the forest, I'm rested and whole. My heartache over Lotane feels almost inconsequential after the highs I'd experienced these last few hours.

I'd experimented, ignoring the search parties, unafraid, hidden in plain sight amongst the searching enemy, continuing my dance long after they'd returned to wherever they came from.

Whilst I danced, giving myself over to the music, the gold was visible, making itself known and available, allowing me to transform the landscape with a touch. If I stop my dance, the song is silent, and how I perceive the world returns to normality.

I can understand now why the Saer Tel always dance even while they're not wielding the magic. Hearing the song, and experiencing the music infuse every fibre of my being, is so addictive. It binds me to the world and nature in a way I'd never thought possible.

It's powerful beyond belief. However, it can't be used as a weapon; that isn't its purpose, nor can it be twisted that way. Elemental magic has that kind of power, yet whilst wielding the gold, there was no sign of the orange, blue, white or brown. If only I could tap into the elemental magic around me, and not just that within.

There's so much to think about, but breathing deeply, I consider my next steps.

Clothing would be a good choice and something to eat and drink. Whilst I'm not uncomfortable being naked, it will undoubtedly cause complications if I encounter someone.

My feet are sore, and as I inspect them, I'm not surprised. A lattice of small cuts ingrained with filth is responsible. Whilst this is a minor inconvenience now, it will become a big problem if they get infected, and walking barefoot will make that more likely.

I cast around, but there's no suitable flora around here to bind them with, so I'll continue as I am.

A large rock catches my eye. Squatting next to it, all it takes is a wish, and it reforms, shaped like a bowl. Nestor comes to mind, and I smile sadly. He'd have been horrified at such a rudimentary design. He always did have an eye for the artistic.

Using a fallen tree limb, I dig a hollow in the ground and place the rock inside. Shortly after, my water problem is solved as water magically rises from the ground below, filling the bowl for me to lift out and drink. It tastes unpleasant, but thirst is now one thing less to worry about.

After a few more minutes of searching, I'm chewing on some roots, feeling much happier.

Picking up the tree limb, I turn it over in my hands and grunt in satisfaction. The rock bowl shortly becomes a sharp-edged stone hatchet, and I trim the wood, smoothing it out, turning it into a useable quarterstaff. It's a simple weapon, which to the unsuspecting adversary doesn't even appear to be one.

Finally, I cut some vines from a nearby tree, choose the thinnest ones and strip away the leaves. Knotting several around my waist, this rudimentary belt now serves to carry my hatchet.

I'm ready.

Funny how, now I know my feet are in bad shape, I wince with every footstep as I walk uncomfortably into the grasslands heading northeast. I'm at my most vulnerable now, but an hour or so away is the next patch of woodland, although, with my feet as they are, I'm happier on the grass.

The trade road is a little to my south, and I consciously keep it in view. I don't know this territory well, but I do know where the road leads. Before the war, it would have been bustling with merchants on their wagons, travellers, envoys, and any number of people. Now, it's empty, and I hope it stays that way until it reaches Astoria.

I become aware of countless semi-circular paths in the grass that emanate from the road before returning, and whilst not anything to be worried about, they get me thinking to pass the time. The amount of disturbance means they're unlikely to be caused by children playing games, and there are so many, in fact, hundreds of these curved paths.

Why would people keep walking off the road?

Hah. Riddle solved.

This must have been when Asterz rode this way with Lotane and her escort, causing people to scurry off the road to avoid them.

Asterz. She could be this world's saviour if she unites the peoples of Icelandia, Suria and Rolantria to fight alongside those of Astoria. However, I can't help but begrudge the power she'll wield if she succeeds and how Lotane is drawn to her.

Whilst saving this world is a priority, so is saving my relationship with Lotane. The sooner I find them, the more time I'll spend with him, and once we're working together again, he'll see the mistake he's made.

*Malina!*

The last time I allowed my attention to wander, we were ambushed.

I banish such distractions from my mind. First things first. I must get to Astoria and find my friends, but not necessarily in that order.

I'll push myself and get to the shaded forest before midday. I've never had sunburn on my breasts, and I don't wish to find out how sore that might be.

This gorgeous weather doesn't seem appropriate. To mark the world's end, it should be grey, with howling winds, snow, and thunder. Unless this glorious morning is a sign from the gods that our plan will work, and Nogoth will be vanquished.

It won't be easy to train so many people, but whereas quality is far better than quantity, there's a lot to be said for an army of the size we're going to amass. Also, in the heat of battle, anything can happen, possibly to an Astorian Queen, if she continues to proves inconvenient ...

No. that must never be me.

Why is it that my thoughts are turning so dark?

I don't want to use blood magic to get my way any more than I want to kill Asterz. If I manage to stay alive, she'll die of old age whilst I remain young. Why kill her when I just need to be patient.

Because, like Asterz, Lotane will die of old age too.

But what if, like me, he could live forever?

***

# CHAPTER IX

It's been a long day, and my feet are a mess, but good fortune is finally shining on me.

Up ahead, a large village sits astride the trade road. A settlement like this will have exactly what I need to resupply. There's no sign of life, and I wonder how long ago the ogres arrived and marched the occupants into captivity. Paddocks that once held livestock are empty, shutters swing, windows gape, and birds sit undisturbed on rooftops.

Yet, despite it being a ghost town, it couldn't feel less threatening. The Saer Tel have been here, and fresh, vibrant growth is everywhere. Once a jarring stain on nature's canvas, this settlement is already returning to mother earth.

I take my time, approaching at a crouch, listening carefully with the aid of my magic. Still, I can't detect anything untoward above the noisy chatter of a hundred birds, at least this far away.

A small cabin sitting slightly apart from the others draws my attention. Thick grass covers its roof, vines pull at its walls, and I can make out a small tree growing inside. One of its branches has pushed through an open window, causing a pink curtain to blow in the breeze like a flag. A well outside, barely visibly amongst a symphony of wildflowers, is a welcome addition. With any luck, looting this one place will be enough. I've no wish to enter deeper into the labyrinth of buildings to encounter any dangers lurking within.

While impatient to find out what's inside, I take my time, moving through the lush undergrowth to observe my target from several angles but discern nothing untoward. I pause, taking a final look around as I hunker outside the property's railed fencing.

Nothing.

Rolling underneath the bottom wooden rail, then staying low, I slip across the yard, quietly lean my quarterstaff against the wooden wall, and pull my stone hatchet free. In confined spaces, the hatchet is a better weapon.

Standing on tiptoes, I snatch a quick glance through the open window, but there's no sign of movement or occupation.

The longer I wait outside, the more chance of being spotted by anything or anyone passing by. Slipping quietly around the edge of the building, I step onto the porch and am relieved no boards creak, even if I'm confident the house is empty.

Sure enough, as I glide into the cool, shaded interior, there's no sign of life or death, which is a relief. Sadly, there are signs of disturbance, with a table and loom overturned. A bucket for the well outside sits by the door, and its wooden inside is dry. As there's no sign of it being used recently, I relax a little further.

Grasses, flowers and the sapling I'd spied from outside have pushed up through the floorboards. I'm sure this had been a lovely home once, but now, despite the broken interior, I couldn't imagine a more beautiful home with nature so present.

Yet there's no time to lose admiring this cabin's recent renovation.

Opening a cupboard reveals brightly dyed clean clothes, all neatly folded. The woman who wore them must have been short and round, for no sleeves or legs are long enough for me, while the waists are enormous. A large bed is neatly made, the sheets and blankets a sky blue, the pillowcase a bright white. The woman who lived here certainly loved colour, making everything unusable. Any bright colours will have me stand out from leagues away.

A small pantry toward the back of the roof smells foul, but just in case, I open it. Flies rise in an angry cloud, and maggots writhe over the spoiled food.

'That's revolting,' I gasp, slamming the door shut.

There must be something here I can use.

Almost hidden by vines, several pairs of shoes are stacked neatly on low shelves. A quick inspection reveals they're too small, and I curse at my luck, for my search has achieved nothing.

Time to search another property.

As I turn to leave, an unopened chest against a wall looks interesting.

'Please be a treasure chest,' I chuckle softly.

Opening the lid, I discover soft rolls of fabric. One is a light green, and lifting it out, I unroll some to find the material thin but fairly sturdy.

It's not ideal, but, like my skin, it will blend well enough with the landscape. Using my hatchet, I cut a length, make a hole in the middle for my head and drape it over my shoulders. A few minutes later, I've tied my vine belt around it, and my skin is now protected from the sun.

Now to take care of my feet.

The well turns out to be deep and the water plentiful, and I return to the house with the bucket full to the brim. My magic makes short work of bringing it to a boil, then I leave it to cool briefly whilst cutting long strips of fabric as wide as my palm.

Sitting on a simple tree stump stool, I soak my feet, letting the dirt soften as I continue my task. The soothing water makes my eyelids droop, and I glance longingly over my shoulder at the bed. The temptation of sleeping somewhere comfortable is almost too much to overcome.

But I have much to do and a lot of ground to cover until I'm safe in Astoria alongside my friends, so I push the thought forcefully aside.

The next fifteen minutes aren't pleasant. I use a strip of cloth to rub the cuts on my feet, vigorously cleaning away the dirt and not stopping until they're either pink or bleeding. I'm tempted to cauterise the worst, but I can't risk infection from sealing something inside.

I summon a gentle breeze to dry my feet and thank my magic for its help. I used to talk to myself a lot as a child, and these small conversations feel as natural now as they did then.

Next, I take the remaining strips of green cloth and tightly bind my feet. I've no doubt if I search enough properties, I'll find suitable boots, but there's something about being in touch with the land. This way, my feet will toughen in time, and soon I'll be able to go barefoot without fear of injury.

I stand, happy with my new outfit, but I need a few more things that this weaver's home hasn't provided me. I either need food or, preferably, the means by which to hunt it. Scavenged roots, fruit and vegetables can supplement whatever I kill.

So, I need to find hunting gear or something with which to make traps. Cord or twine will do, and it shouldn't take me too long to find something suitable.

I cast an appraising eye over the room a final time but spy nothing of interest. Is the owner still alive? If so, she'll probably wish she was dead soon. In a few years, this house will be reclaimed by nature, and it will be as if she was never here.

With that last chilling thought, I step out into the warm sunshine.

***

'What do we have here then?'

The voice is cold, and so is the look the owner of the voice gives me. Filthy-looking and middle-aged, the man has a bloodied bandage over one eye. He's holding an old sword that's seen better days and stands amongst a dozen other bedraggled individuals armed with all manner of weapons. Some appear to have some proficiency in their choice of arms, while others are lucky to be holding the right end.

They're standing spitting distance from the bottom step of the porch I'm on, and I feel like kicking myself for not keeping a better watch.

'I think it's been lootin our village of what little there's left.'

The woman who speaks looks even nastier than the man. She's unarmed, but it's possible the filth under her nails could kill if she ever scratched me. She's leaning against the well, and for a moment, I'm tempted to laugh. If she falls in, the water will be fouled.

'Lootin's a hangable offence,' chimes another.

Damn.

To my left are another group of at least twenty men and women.

A chorus of voices join in, frustrating my attempts to identify a leader.

'I've only taken some fabric for my clothes, nothing else,' I call placatingly, raising my palms and smiling. 'The village was deserted, and I was in sore need, as I'm sure all of you are. I was just leaving unless you have food to spare?'

'You've taken too much already!'

This time a large man angrily shakes a pitchfork.

I don't want this to turn nasty, and I'm sure if I can just get them to talk a little, things will calm down.

'What happened here?' I ask.

'As if yer don't know, you filthy fey!'

'Your lot bloody killed everyone, didn't they!'

'I'm not what you think I am. I'm human, like you,' I call.

'You sure ain't human with those devil eyes and weird skin, you lying bitch!'

My magic wriggles, telling me what I already know. This is an angry mob, and reasoning isn't working; they've suffered too much and need an easy victim to blame. There are too many to fight, and I certainly don't want to run before I have everything I need, but a display of magic should do the trick.

'I stand before you in peace, but to touch me, is to die!' I hiss, thrusting out with open hands, sending a gust of wind that has the crowd stumbling back, shielding their eyes. 'Now leave while you still can!'

Panic ripples through their ranks, and I'm relieved as they edge backwards. A few more steps and they'll break and run. They just require a little more encouragement.

Fire blossoms from my hands as I descend the porch steps, and those at the back of the groups start to break away.

Yet suddenly, I'm stumbling backwards, my vision blurring and ears ringing. The fire and dust storm I'd summoned die away, and for a moment, everything is quiet. I lift my hand to the side of my head, finding it sticky.

A movement to my left has me turning in time to see a young man, no more than sixteen summers old, throw a rock. Time seems to slow as it spins through the air before slamming into my shoulder. My left arm immediately goes numb.

As one, everyone starts advancing toward me.

Time to run, assuming I still can.

I only manage to get two steps before I'm spun full circle by another impact, but at least I manage to keep my feet. My legs weaken, and I see an arrowhead sticking out through my left side.

The shouts and curses of my pursuers are loud as I run around the side of the house, snatching for my quarterstaff where I'd left it leaning against the wall. Unfortunately, my fingertips send it tumbling to the ground, and I can't afford to stop and pick it up.

Another arrow hisses by, and I risk glancing over my shoulder to see the entire mob, faces twisted in malicious glee, charging after me.

Fortunately, they're hindering the archer's aim, and I turn into the village, hoping to lose myself amongst the houses.

Once my head clears, I can use my magic to conceal myself, but the pain of my wounds makes me wonder if I'll ever get the chance. I want to cry out in agony with every step; the pain in my side is excruciating.

I change direction randomly, but the mob maintains its dogged pursuit. The trampled grasses I leave in my wake are a signpost to those following even when they lose sight of me. They're determined to have their vengeance, and my strength is starting to leave me at an ever-increasing rate. My breath comes in gasps as I drive myself onwards, fighting against unconsciousness.

If I don't lose them soon, I'll choose a small house and make my last stand. The doorway of any building will funnel them, leaving me to face one or two at a time before their numbers overwhelm me. I pull my hatchet free, ready to go down fighting.

A large black cat sitting happily on a step looks at me curiously as I stagger past, then resumes washing, oblivious and uncaring of my fate. A few more overgrown streets and I'm almost done. The mob hasn't given up, not one, as far as I can tell.

Another arrow takes me in the right forearm just as I turn a corner into the village square. I stumble a few more steps, my mind refusing to believe there's no escape. The hatchet falls from my grasp into the grass as my right-hand spasms in pain.

The mob runs screaming into the square behind me, and I turn to face them. I might not even have the strength left to kill one, but I'll make sure I leave a mark.

Then, the charging mob comes to a standstill, no more than twenty steps away.

Hairs rise on the back of my neck, and I turn to find three dozen ogres filing into the square behind me. They charge immediately, those wicked swords lifting above their heads, their roars echoed by the mob, who, credit to them, charge as well.

If only I had the magical strength to go out in a final blaze of glory, but I have nothing left.

My last thought is I hope my death is quick.

***

Bells ring, crowds cheer, and the mood is one of celebration.

Coloured ribbons are hung across the street and embellish every window and door. Everyone looks happy, and the air is full of laughter.

The war must be over, for what else could give rise to such a celebration?

'What's happening?' I ask a woman wrapped in a bright red shawl.

She frowns, then turns away.

'Excuse me ...' His smile fading, a man ignores me, unwilling to meet my eye.

'Boy, come here. Where are you going?'

I watch as he scurries off, scared. Gah. I'll find out soon enough.

The crowd carries me along, everyone jostling to get somewhere quickly, although where that is, I don't know. Yet despite the good-natured pushing, no one touches me. It's as if I'm in a bubble, excluded from the festivity even if I'm right in the middle of it.

Nonetheless, the good mood of those around me is contagious, and I find myself dancing along with the crowd. Golden light glows about me, and I spin, my feet and hands tracing intricate patterns, bringing grasses and flowers where once was mud. Yet, despite the beauty, people now frown, and the circle around me gets wider.

'The only good fey is a dead fey!'

I hear this muttered repeatedly, but words can't harm me.

Ahead, on a hill, is a castle. Banners flutter from tall towers standing proudly against a blue sky. The gates are wide open, welcoming the flood of celebrating citizens into its safe embrace.

Laughing children hold hands, dancing in circles, their high voices squealing in delight while bathed in the warm glow of an afternoon sun. I don't think I've ever experienced a day like this where everyone is unified in such happiness.

'You don't belong here. Turn around. Go back to where you belong,' a wizened old lady shrieks, wriggling a crooked finger at me.

Voices rise in agreement, but who here can stop me, for I'm a Chosen, so I continue, head held high.

It's not long before I'm through the gates of the curtain wall, joining the throng who gather at a respectful distance around a tall, polished silver pole that stands the height of three men. Both a long, royal blue and purple ribbon are affixed to the top. Standing opposite one another, two knights grasp the loose end of each ribbon, pulling them taut. Their shining armour is adorned with white strips of fabric tied at the waist, elbows, and knees.

Music starts to play, a bard's soft voice fills the air, and the knights circle in opposite directions. Around they move, skipping and twirling, twisting and dancing, for each other, for the crowd, or just out of sheer happiness. When they pass one another, they bow before continuing on their way. The ribbons wrap around the pole with every rotation, pulling them closer and causing them to move faster and faster.

No!

Beneath the armour, there's no doubt who these two are. I can't let Lotane finish the marriage dance with Asterz.

Pushing my way to the edge of the circle, I await my opportunity. Then as Asterz dances by holding onto the purple ribbon, I throw her to one side, and the earth swallows her up as she crashes to the ground.

The crowd screams in hatred as I take her place, but no one intervenes, for to touch me is to die, and my magic crackles around me. Most importantly, Lotane doesn't seem to care, and as the ribbons wrap around the pole, he and I are drawn closer and closer to one another until, at last, we cannot pass.

Two white-flowered garlands hang from a hook on the pole, and taking one, I drape it around his shoulders, then those mailed hands place one gently on mine.

I struggle to hold back the tears. My heart has never experienced such happiness; it feels set to burst, and my breath comes in short gasps.

His helm comes off easily, and I look into those blue-green eyes, marvelling at their depth, seeing my future within.

Have ever lips looked so soft, so full of promise as his? I doubt it.

'As I am your king, so you are my queen,' he calls out loudly.

'As I am your queen, so you are my king,' I reply, my voice on the verge of breaking.

Our kiss lingers, and the crowd roars.

As our lips part Lotane's strong arms pull me into a warm embrace.

His breath tickles my ear, warm and seductive.

'The problem is,' he whispers, 'the only good fey is a dead fey!'

Pain, unlike anything I've ever known, rips through my side, and I stumble back, noting a bloodied dagger in Lotane's hand with horror and disbelief.

The crowd yells ecstatically as he plunges it into me again.

'I am the Queen Slayer,' he yells as I stumble away, bleeding in disbelief. 'Don't you know the legend of those with blue and green eyes?' He laughs as he tilts his head to one side. 'Now, I bet Nogoth never made you scream like this, did he?'

As the words register, he stabs me again, twisting the blade viciously, and he's right. I've never screamed like this, but I don't know if it's the wound or his betrayal that hurts the most.

***

'Bite on this,' growls a harsh voice, bringing me awake. 'Your screams bring you dishonour!'

I open my eyes to find myself looking up into the broad, ugly tusked face of an ogre as she jams a leather-bound stick into my mouth.

Am I being eaten alive?

My hands and legs are restrained; I can't move them however much I try.

'Lie still, damn you,' she growls as I struggle. The common tongue sounds brutal from those thick fleshy lips. 'There's a piece of arrow shaft broken inside of you, and if we don't get it out, you're dead! Mind you, you've lost enough blood, so you'll likely die anyway. But at least die quietly!'

My head feels as heavy as a rock when I lift it, only to find another ogre digging about with what appear to be pincers in my side; the pain is beyond belief.

'Got it!'

Accompanied by a gross sucking noise, the ogre withdraws a broken piece of wood held firmly in the pincers, and it's followed by a steady flow of black blood.

'You thought that hurt. Now for the fun part!'

The ogre's lips draw back in a smile, exposing pointed yellowed teeth. The restraints are loosened, and I'm rolled to one side.

My eyes widen as a glowing red-hot iron is pulled from a fire. This time I'm ready and bite down on the stick. The waves of pain as it's unceremoniously applied to the entry and exit wound remind me of when I was imbued with magic. Thankfully, just like then, the pain disappears as if it belongs to someone else.

I close my eyes as they begin to work on my arm, a less severe wound but still capable of killing me in this weakened state. Any infection, and I know I'm too weak to fight it.

However, at least I'm still alive to fight, whereas I thought I'd be long dead.

The image of those ogres charging, swords and tusks gleaming, hunger flashing in their eyes, only to part around me like waves around a rock, is something I won't soon forget.

It's now obvious they'd seen one of Nogoth's favoured, a Saer Tel, and had intervened to rip apart the mob behind me. The raw strength, ferocity and training had seen the ogres decimate my pursuers in a one-sided fight that had lasted only a few minutes.

'She's fading.'

The voice is gruff, and my eyelids are pried open by calloused fingers.

'Stay awake or join your ancestors,' the ogress says, her voice slow and drawn out like honey dripping from a spoon.

My head lolls to one side, and through the darkness impinging my vision, I see a couple of other heavily bandaged ogres lying on tables. I'm in a walled garden surrounded by uninjured ogres lounging around on the grass, eating ...

I turn my head the other way to avoid puking as I recognise the human remains they're chomping on with relish, then almost wish I hadn't. Bodies, twisted and rent with horrific wounds, are stacked in a corner, legs and arms sticking out. If only they weren't so neatly piled, then perhaps it wouldn't look so macabre.

I laugh as if it's a funny thought while my heartbeat flutters as it struggles to keep me alive.

Next to the corpses, in a guarded pen, trussed up like pigs awaiting the slaughter, are two survivors, but they aren't the lucky ones.

A shadow falls over me, and I look up to see the towering figure of a troll. Its twisted features are at odds with its superb musculature, and its dark brown skin glistens slightly as if wet. My eyes idly trace its dozens of scars, discerning patterns and runes that hold a beauty of their own.

The distance between my heartbeats is growing, and my eyelids droop shut even though I fight to keep them open.

'She's going to die. We tried our best, but she lost too much blood!'

The ogre medic's words sound muffled, as if she's talking through a blanket.

'WHAT?'

The voice booming in outrage can only come from the troll.

'You were going to let one of Nogoth's favoured die *HERE*, on my watch! Are you stupid or just trying to have us executed?'

I hear heavy footsteps sprinting off, or is it just my heart beating rapidly. The sun must have set because it's suddenly cold, and I start to shiver uncontrollably. Is it so late already?

If only my dream had ended when Lotane kissed me. Maybe if I hold onto that thought, I can rejoin it there, and this time it will have a different ending ... a happy ending.

The table underneath me shakes as those heavy footsteps return.

'Wake up, girl!'

A heavy blow rocks my head.

'Even if you don't deign to speak the common tongue, I know you can understand it. Now OPEN YOUR EYES!' The voice is painfully loud when all I want to do is drift away.

My eyes open a crack, but I don't know if it's me or the ogre medic doing it for me.

Above me is the troll, and in one mighty fist, he grips a prisoner, and despite looking through a mist, I can tell it's the young lad who'd shot me with the arrows.

The terror on his face snaps me back to something approaching consciousness.

'NO!' I want to shout, but nothing other than a croak leaves my lips even if my mouth opens.

The troll, seeing this, draws a taloned finger across his struggling captive's throat and then pushes that gaping, pumping wound onto my mouth.

I swallow reflexively, or perhaps the truth is that I'm not ready to die, and drinking the lad's blood means his death won't be in vain. Warmth returns to my limbs, and my heart slows to something approaching normal.

'Feed her another prisoner's blood in the morning, and she'll be back to her dancing, twirling self the day after the morrow,' the troll commands. 'They might look frail, but these Saer Tel can survive almost anything with some fresh blood!'

'Yes, Chieftain,' the medic responds.

My stomach growls in anticipation as sleep overtakes me, and this time when I dream, Nogoth dances around the marriage pole with me.

***

I open my eyes to the glare of the rising sun.

Pain immediately shoots through my head, and I groan, closing them again. I pull a blanket over my head in protest and wonder if I'll be able to go back to sleep as I'm definitely in no fit state to rise.

I'd briefly regained consciousness several times during the night, vaguely aware of the medic checking my wounds under lamplight. After her final inspection, the straps restraining me were unbuckled.

With arms almost as strong as Kralgen's, she'd gently carried me to a corner of the garden and given me the coarse blanket I'm hiding under.

Sunlight and conditioning win, and I lower the blanket, observing first-hand something I thought never to see; an ogre encampment getting ready for the day ahead. It's strange, but if I just listen, these could just as easily be humans because the coarse jokes and comradeship are one and the same.

My eyes follow the medic as she checks the other wounded before coming to me. She says nothing as she pulls the blanket aside and gently encourages me to turn one way and then another as she inspects my healing wounds.

Her nostrils flare as she tries to detect corruption, although I'm sure all she can smell is scorched skin. Nonetheless, her lips curl back in a terrifying smile that extends to her eyes. Who'd have believed that an ogre could have smile lines?

Despite my fuddled state, I'm amazed at the kindness and care she affords me, believing I'm another fey. I should feel hatred and loathing for this creature and the other ogres. I know I did once, but those feelings are changing.

'It's amazing. I wish my fellow ogres could heal the way you do,' she rumbles. 'Still, you're not to move far; you're still weak. Now, let me get you breakfast.'

I push myself to a sitting position against the wall behind me, grimacing but determined, and turn my attention to the ogre warriors as they line up. I don't know what ranks there are in a fey army, but one, maybe an ogre of a rank similar to a sergeant, is inspecting their equipment and weapons.

He stalks up and down their line, checking armour straps, the condition and edge of their weapons, delivering slaps and curses when he finds something amiss. His targets don't answer back but just grunt in acknowledgement.

Hah, that name fits; the lowliest ogre footsoldier is a grunt. Not that there's anything lowly about them. They're well-muscled, thick of chest and shoulder, and obviously well trained. Their prowess outside of High Delnor was a testament to that.

The grunts fall out, turning to breakfast, and I take a reality check.

How could I possibly begin to judge them less harshly when they begin to eat human body parts with a relish I'd only ever seen on people's faces when they ate cake.

These creatures have no right to live. They could have chosen to be farmers and raised livestock, not butcher humans as an everyday delicacy.

The medic comes to stand before me and drops a bound woman roughly the same age as me to the ground.

'Breakfast,' she growls cheerily.

My eyes must have given away my shock, for the ogre grabs and inspects the prisoner. Twisting the woman's head left and right, she snorts and sniffs, reminding me of a bull.

'She's young and healthy, with no sign of disease. Don't be so picky about your food!' she admonishes, thrusting the woman back toward me. 'Chieftain Orlarn will have my hide if you don't feed, and that's not going to happen. Is it?' The medic snarls to emphasise the importance of me feeding.

My stomach grumbles and an insatiable hunger washes over me. The bound captive is terrified, eyes wide, ashen-faced, and moans of panic make their way around the gag tied firmly in her mouth.

The ogre looks down at me expectantly, and I nod, smiling in thanks, then watch in relief as she turns away, giving me a little more time.

What am I to do?

One moment I'm judging these creatures for their appetites, and the next, my body craves to taste this woman's blood even though my mind wants nothing to do with it. I'm positive I can survive without this woman's blood because, despite the pain, I'm now recovering, whereas yesterday, I was at death's door. I even have enough strength to sense my magic, although I'm too weak to call upon it.

My problem is, if I'm to survive, these fey can't suspect I'm not what they think I am. Then again, I *am* what they think I am. It's just that I fight for humankind.

Then I berate myself for not seeing the obvious. I'm so used to killing that I've overlooked that the Saer Tel don't kill to feed. In fact, they pair with those they feed upon, protecting them.

Relief blossoms as I recognise the way out of this mess.

I drag the captive toward me. It's no easy feat when my right arm is weak, and spasms of pain shoot through my body.

Leaning forward, I bring my mouth close to her ear. She whimpers, tears coursing down her cheek.

'Don't be afraid,' I whisper quietly, tilting my head so none of the ogres sees me talking. 'I won't kill you. I'm not at all like these creatures. Nod if you understand.'

Frantic nods and desperate, pleading eyes show me she's paying attention.

'I can save your life, but it won't be pleasant. Do you want to live?'

Another nod.

'I have to feed. But not like the ogres,' I add quickly, gently pushing her tangled hair back in an attempt to soothe her. 'I will just take some blood, a small amount, to ensure the ogres don't suspect, and then they'll let you live. I'm sorry, but it's the only way.'

The same response, her face filled with fear but also a tinge of hope.

'I'm going to free your hands so you can move. Please don't struggle or try to escape, or they will kill you!'

It doesn't take long to untie the knots, by which time I'm breathing heavily. Even this minor exertion is costing me. I'm weaker than I thought. The wall provides some welcome support as I lean back against it, feeling faint, nauseous even, but knowing I have to go through with this.

'Settle back against me,' I command, opening my arms.

The woman looks over her shoulder and then shuffles between my legs.

I enfold her in my arms, drawing her back.

'Hush,' I whisper, somewhat unnecessarily, as she can't make much noise with the gag on. I brush her long hair to one side, leaving her neck and shoulder bare. Her pulse is beating so fast, and my hunger surges. I lean forward, inhaling, scenting her life's sweetness beneath the sweat and fear. It's extremely arousing, and now I understand why the Saer Tel enjoy pleasure with their paired partner as they're overcome by lust.

I hold the woman tightly, and her hands go to mine, clutching them, and she instinctively leans her head to one side, inviting me to kiss her neck or feast; it matters not which.

I'm only going to take the smallest bite and taste a little sweetness to keep suspicions from arising.

My mouth goes to the meat of her shoulder, my tongue hungrily licking away the sweat. I open my mouth, resisting the urge for as long as I can.

It was the wrong thing to do.

When I finally give in, the fey within me takes over. My teeth sink deep into her shoulder, and I thirstily suck the blood as it runs from the two puncture wounds I've inflicted.

The woman's moans drift between pleasure and pain as she grips my forearms, driving my desire higher. I'd intended to stop after a few drops, but as her hands drop away from mine, I realise I've drunk way more. Even so, it's hard to stop, but I force my mouth away and am struck by the lack of blood left behind.

The woman smiles weakly over her shoulder, her face pale, but the main thing is she's alive.

'I'm sorry,' I whisper, my face buried in her hair. 'I've yet to gain control of my hunger, but next time I'll ensure I do, and I won't need so much anyway.'

I receive a tired nod, for that's all she has the strength for, whereas I'm feeling much better. Now I need to start thinking about escape. My magic squirms, letting me know it's ready to help. I consider the woman leaning back against me. Is there anything I can do to save her even if she was part of the mob who'd tried to kill me?

There's no way I can free her and expect the ogres to just let her go. Why would they do that?

Unless they didn't have a choice!

I smile, thinking about the plan to escape from High Delnor. It had initially revolved around using blood magic to control the guard into letting us go. Yet as I look around the small camp, I realise how short-sighted I'd been. If I can bind these ogres to obey me, I can start stealing

Nogoth's army from under him. What better way to defeat him than to have his army change sides!

The medic approaches, her tusked smile both horrifying and warm.

'I see you've had your fill, favoured one,' she says. 'Are you finished with her?'

I nod.

She reaches down toward the woman.

*'Get ready!'* I tell my magic.

I take the ogre's hand before she can grab the woman's arm.

*Obey me. Love me. Follow me. Be loyal only to me. Protect me.*

I take a deep breath. No Saer Tel sullies herself by speaking the common tongue, but I have no other choice, and this is the ideal opportunity.

'Don't hurt this woman or tell anyone I spoke to you.'

The medic gently pulls her hand free, those huge eyes wide in amazement, and lifts the woman carefully from my lap.

My gamble has paid off!

A second later, she rips the woman's throat out and tosses the twitching body to a nearby group of soldiers.

'The Saer Tel just spoke!' she roars, pointing at me.

Damn.

***

I'm in no fit state to either fight or run, but perhaps I don't need to do either. All I have to do is see out the day, and when night falls, I'll be in good enough shape to slip off into the darkness.

I'd seen birds in cages when I was young, and that's how I feel. The ogres gather around, pointing like I'm some new exotic pet.

Tilting my head from one side to another, I play my part and smile, trying to contain the fear that threatens to overwhelm my conditioning.

My magic had failed, leaving my new exciting plans short-lived and turning to dust before they could form.

'I'm telling you she talks!' roars the medic, getting angry as the grunts start to ridicule her for lying.

'TALK!' she roars, bending down to jab a finger at my face.

To think I'd considered her different, kind and caring a short time ago. Now her clawed fingers are covered in the woman's blood, who has since been ripped to shreds.

'TALK, or I'll rip your head off!'

Now I'm in serious trouble, and her latest statement reignites the grunts' interest. Bloodletting of any kind seems to be their favourite pastime, and they start bellowing encouragement at my former saviour.

She's dicing with death herself. I'm confident the chieftain will have her head if she touches me; he'd alluded to as much should I have died under her care, let alone to her hand. However, I have enough strength to turn her into a bubbling lump of meat before my strength deserts me again. I'll take that option and at least see her demise before I'm killed.

The medic has put herself in an impossible situation. She's looked a fool once by claiming I can talk, followed by the grunts thinking her a liar; now she's made a threat, which, if she doesn't follow through ...

I decide to make the first move.

'WHAT'S GOING ON?' the troll chieftain bellows as he steps over the wall into the camp.

It's as if a god cast a spell of invisibility, for the grunts disappear back to their tasks in a heartbeat, leaving only the medic standing before me.

I get slowly to my feet, testing my strength.

'She spoke, asking me not to hurt a prisoner and to tell no one!' the medic explains, her head bowed.

The troll glances at me. He's heavily armoured, a towering creature of incredible strength. His sword is longer than I am tall, and there's no doubt that he's intelligent, unlike his giant brethren.

Despite my predicament, I smile, shaking my head, laughter in my eyes, and step over to him, tracing my hand down his enormous muscled calf.

*Obey me. Love me. Follow me. Be loyal only to me. Protect me.*

'I've served you for decades. When have I ever lied to you?' the ogre medic protests further, and the troll, after a pause, nods in acknowledgement.

My magic has failed again, and things look bleaker every second.

'Chief!' an ogre grunt calls, but the troll ignores him, totally fixed on me.

'No Saer Tel speaks the common tongue,' growls the troll. 'Yet tales are told of a traitor who killed one of my brothers on the eve of our invasion. A Saer Tel who was born and lived amongst the humans. Prove you're a true Saer Tel; talk to me in their voice!'

I'd faked their dance once, only for the real one to find me, but there's no way I can pull this off; the language of the Saer Tel is pure music. Can I take the troll down with magic? Probably. But even if I did, I'd be weakened and overwhelmed immediately afterwards.

'Chief!'

An ogre runs over, placing himself in the troll's line of vision.

'You have to see this. Something is approaching our camp!'

'Something?'

A finger the size of my forearm prods me.

'We'll continue this conversation shortly!' the troll growls. 'Don't even think of leaving. I've got your scent, and you're not fit enough to run, let alone escape me!'

He turns swiftly, which considering his bulk, is frightening.

Hmmm. *Something* is approaching. Not someone, but something.

Curiosity gets the better of me, and I join a growing crowd of ogres at the west wall of the gardens. The ogres are tall enough to peer over it, and it's only up to the troll's upper thighs. The stones are ill-fitting, so I clamber to the top.

It's the first time I've looked beyond the walls of the garden I'd woken up within, and I can see it's part of a farm. Numerous outbuildings are dotted about, and we're slightly south of the village I'd been chased through.

The chieftain has chosen this position well. The buildings the ogres might have billeted in would have separated his command and being wooden, were vulnerable to fire. Whereas, despite not being covered, the walled garden provides his troops with a ready-made defensive perimeter, ensuring they can't be overrun by cavalry or any other surprise attack. Finally, despite the long grass, there's no cover when approaching the farm; thus, something has attracted the attention of those on watch.

It takes only a moment to see what that something is because it approaches in the distance, halfway between the farm and the village.

It's about an arrow flight away, but I gauge it stands twice as tall as an ogre but still half the size of the troll. The *something* strides purposely toward the walled garden, oblivious or perhaps indifferent to the danger it holds.

'What is that thing, Chief?' an ogre calls out.

I glance at the troll. He's a perfect commander and is looking around, ensuring there aren't other threats to consider. Satisfied, that giant head turns back toward the *something*.

'If it's not with us, it's against us,' growls the troll. 'First and second squads, go fetch us something new to eat!'

A roar of enthusiasm is his only response as two dozen ogres snatch up weapons and shields and clamber over the wall, ignoring the archway to the north. They spread out in a long skirmish line and jog through the grass, conserving energy.

In response, the *thing* picks up speed, and the way it moves is hauntingly familiar.

It reminds me of ... Dimitar.

***

# CHAPTER X

It can't be. I'd seen Dimitar disappear under a thousand black-furred bodies, and this thing is at least twice as large as the man I'd known.

While I consider my friend's possible resurrection and transformation, the ogre line reaches him.

Compared to most humans, the ogres are superior creatures of raw physical power. Yet however sharp their swords or strong the sinews behind their blows, they might as well be wielding sticks.

Dimitar, for who else could this giant stone man be, ignores their weapons, not even thinking of defence, and just grabs for heads, bodies or arms and squeezes them within granite fists. Skulls explode in a bloody spray, limbs are torn off, torsos crushed, and shortly a dozen ogres are retreating at speed, leaving the same number of their brethren behind.

The ogres can move fast when required, and they're shortly jumping over the wall, shaken but unbroken. The troll doesn't berate them, for he's seen what Dimitar can do.

They're all so distracted, I could escape! But what's the point?

Dimitar has come to save me.

I move along the wall to get a better viewpoint from a corner.

'Heavy weapons!' barks the troll, moving back to draw his sword and give himself room.

In response, the ogres cast aside their swords and shields, grabbing axes and maces from a weapon rack in the far corner; it's a wise move.

Dimitar reaches the wall and kicks his way through, sending rubble flying.

Like ants protecting their nest, the ogres throw themselves at Dimitar, their weapons clanging against stone limbs at least twice as thick as my thigh. For a split second, rock chips fly as the grunts cast caution aside, hoping to land a huge decisive blow.

It soon becomes apparent he's impervious to their attacks, so with a short shouted command from a remaining sergeant, Dimitar is suddenly buried under the grunts' bodies as they try to restrain him by sheer weight of numbers. However, he plucks them off one by one, throwing them broken to the ground where his stone feet crush away any remaining life.

Whatever flaws the ogres have, cowardice isn't one of them. I've seen them break and run before, but with their commander looking on, they fight to their last painful and fruitless breath.

I hadn't realised how loud the short battle had been until quietness settles across the courtyard.

Dimitar straightens up, dripping with black blood. His limbs bear fresh scars, chunks gouged away, demonstrating his vulnerability.

The troll doesn't seem perturbed by the loss of his entire command. A smile splits its rugged features. The fey still dwarfs Dimitar, and doubt creeps into my mind. Dimitar is unarmed, and whilst his strength is undisputed, the troll is no mere ogre.

'Come, Stone Man. It's been longer than I can remember since I faced a worthy opponent. Let's see if you're one!' Chieftain Orlarn says, beckoning Dimitar with his left hand while the other holds the hilt of his sword, the blade resting against his shoulder.

Dimitar doesn't hesitate.

He runs forward, arms outstretched. I wonder if he feels confidence or doubt, fear or anger, but then I remember what he'd said about love. He understood what it was, but the actual feeling was beyond him.

Who will prove to be stronger, a man of stone or a creature twice his size made of flesh and bone? I'm about to find out as the troll stands his ground, confident in his size advantage.

But it's a ruse.

I notice the subtle shift in the troll's balance as his weight moves to his right leg, and sure enough, he pivots away from Dimitar's charge. I know what's coming before it happens. That terrible sword, aided by the turn, sweeps down and smashes through Dimitar's outstretched arm near the shoulder, sending it tumbling to the ground.

My heart sinks.

Against any living creature, it would have proved a deadly blow, but Dimitar doesn't flinch, those stone features remain impassive despite the catastrophic injury.

The troll doesn't follow up, obviously intent on enjoying the fight, and cross-steps away, sword in high-guard position.

Dimitar turns, staring at the troll as if only now recognising the threat it presents. Then those stone eyes fix on the stump where his arm was, then to the stone limb on the ground as if trying to piece together what has happened.

Then, those impassive stone lips turn upward, smiling.

Squatting, Dimitar grasps the wrist of his broken arm. I remember how he'd reattached it before when the Astorians had saved us, but to my surprise, it soon becomes apparent this isn't his intent.

It's crude and unbalanced, yet Dimitar now has a weapon.

Once again, he advances on the troll. Unsurprisingly, that sword sweeps down toward Dimitar's unguarded left side, but this time it's Dimitar's turn to pivot. He steps forward, absorbs the sword blow with his makeshift club, ducks underneath the weapon, spins on his right foot, and swings backwards, smashing the club against the troll's knee.

The troll roars, hopping away, shock and pain etched upon its face as Dimitar straightens up.

Discarded weapons catch my eye, leftovers from the decimated ogres. If I help myself to some swords, can I help win this fight?

It's wishful thinking. I'm not close to full strength like when I first faced this creature's brethren, but if I bide my time, then maybe an opportunity will present itself. However, my confidence in Dimitar is growing, and perhaps I won't be needed.

The troll tests its weight, but the knee doesn't seem to have been as badly damaged as I'd first hoped, and now the creature goes on the attack.

A series of lightning-fast overhead cuts that would have hewn a tree in two forces Dimitar to block repeatedly with the broken arm he's using as a club. The ceramic blade chimes like a bell, the sound deeper with every contact, reverberating in the pit of my stomach. Dimitar's head will shatter like an egg if the sword lands.

However, the next cut sees Dimitar feign a block, then sidestep at the last moment. As the blade buries itself in the ground, a ferocious stamp to the flat of the trapped blade sees the sword shatter into a hundred pieces, and that club deliver a crushing blow to the troll's ribs. The troll stumbles backwards, clutching its side ...

The two behemoths circle again.

Dimitar attacks, the club swooshing through the air. The troll evades, hurt but not panicked, yet its breath is starting to come in gasps.

My magic wriggles, making itself known. I could soften the ground and try to bog the troll down, but I resist, knowing it won't be enough, not at this time.

The troll's eyes narrow, and I catch it glancing at the ground as it moves around the garden.

What's it looking for?

The discarded ogre weapons are too small for the troll or Dimitar, and it has no other weapons here. Then the troll's strategy becomes clear. At least a dozen of the ogre bodies lie dead between the two, and as Dimitar attacks, he steps on the bodies, and his foot slips from under him.

There's no hesitation from the troll; it kicks out, catching Dimitar in the shoulder, spinning him to the ground, and then pounces onto his back.

Again and again, I hear that stone head slam into the rocky ground as the troll goes into a frenzy, and as Dimitar's resistance weakens, an enormous arm snakes around Dimitar's neck. The troll has its legs out wide for balance as it brings its entire body weight to bear, keeping Dimitar pinned down.

Giant shoulder muscles bunch as the troll tries to break Dimitar's head off. I don't know if it will be able to, but this is the moment I've been waiting for.

I leap off the wall, cross the garden, and run up the troll's back to push my face close to its ear.

'It was me that killed your brother,' I shout as it glances at me from the corner of a bloodshot eye.

As my words register, I thrust my hand into its hairy ear, unleashing my pent-up magic and anger.

I leap away, rolling as I hit the ground as blood and smoke gush forth, and the troll howls in agony, forgetting all about the fight as it writhes on the floor, clutching at its head. I don't know how long it will take for the elemental fire to consume it, but I'm sure it won't be quick.

Perhaps fortunately for the troll, Dimitar heaves himself off the ground and begins to finish what the fire has started.

***

'How did you find me?'

We're sitting amongst the detritus of the battle, the troll and ogre corpses keeping us company, dead eyes staring accusingly. Flies are already enjoying the fresh meat, and carrion crows are circling overhead, their impatient caws encouraging us to leave.

We won't keep them waiting long.

'I found you from the disturbance you created in the colours,' Dimitar explains, dropping a block of stone from the broken wall into his gaping maw. The sound of stone teeth grinding it to pieces makes me wince.

'The colours of the elements?'

'Yes.'

'Why did it take you so long?'

My question sounds ungrateful even to me.

'The wolfen couldn't destroy me, but they did damage my eyes, leaving me blind. It took a while for them to reform.'

I wait for Dimitar to elucidate, to no avail. I'll have to get used to such concise answers or simply resign myself to asking lots more questions.

He must still be hungry, if that's the proper term, for yet another block follows, which to my count, makes seven so far. It's Dimitar's way of repairing the damage he's suffered, and it's delaying our departure. He's reattached his broken arm, but it looks fragile, with chunks missing and cracks so wide I could put my finger in them. As for his face, I guess having it pounded into the ground is responsible for there being no nose or lips.

He reminds me of a broken statue I'd seen on the docks as a child. It was so old and eroded that people had forgotten who it was supposed to be.

'I've eaten enough. We can go now!'

Thank the gods. I've been impatient to leave the dead behind and find my friends. I'm about to stand when a thought crosses my mind.

'If you eat more, will you grow bigger still?'

'Yes.'

'Is there a limit to how big you'll grow?'

'I don't know.'

'Eat some more. I'll be right back.'

I pick up a ceramic sword from the floor and jog over to investigate the farm buildings, confident there are no other ogres nearby. The recent fight would have raised the dead.

A barn seems like a good place to start, and after scouting and listening with the aid of my magic, I enter. For once, I enjoy the luck of the gods because it's piled full of the ogres' battlefield spoils. They'd collected every piece of equipment from their previous skirmishes and stored it here. It was a prudent move, ensuring it could never be used against them again; until now.

It takes me a while, but I find an assortment of battered, stained leather armour and outfit myself with a cuirass, kilt, greaves and vambraces. The leather is old and soft but better than nothing. I strap a weapon belt around my waist, attaching two dulled shortswords and a dagger. I look at my feet, bound in that green cloth, and try on a few pairs of leather boots but give up in disgust as none fit.

I check the farmhouse and, amongst the destruction wreaked by the looting ogres, discover several loaves of bread so stale that I wonder if they would break Dimitar's stone teeth. I sling a dusty linen bag over my shoulder, pop the bread inside, and cautiously move to the door.

I've had my fill of walking into ambushes of late, so check carefully before exiting and making my way back to the walled garden.

'I can't eat anymore,' Dimitar rumbles, getting to his feet.

'Let's go then. We need to find Kralgen, Lotane and Asterz.

Dimitar looks around slowly, then lifts his good arm, pointing.

'They're a half day northeast.'

'How do you know?'

'Kralgen and Lotane, they create ripples in the colours too.'

'Let's go then. Can you keep a lookout for any fey?'

Dimitar stares at me as if I'm stupid.

'I was blind before, but not now,' he grates, then sets off.

I jog to keep up with Dimitar's enormous strides, enjoying the security of his bulk beside me. Any ogres will think twice before attacking us, although trolls and giants could prove our undoing.

As we travel, I break off some chunks of bread and soften them in my mouth before swallowing.

We pass an untended orchard, and I fill my bag with fruits, enjoying the sweet juices of those I eat. Our only company as the day passes are the insect and animals who go about their business unconcerned. I'd have thought Dimitar would frighten anything and everything away, but a flock of small yellow birds settle on his shoulders, and their song lifts my spirits some more.

Suddenly, something comes to mind, and I can't believe I haven't asked Dimitar about it before.

'Who else can you see that disturbs the colours?'

Dimitar pauses briefly, causing the birds to squawk in indignation. They flap off, leaving small white protests on his head and shoulders.

'I don't know exactly who, as no names attach to the disturbances I can detect. But as Kralgen and Lotane carry the element of fire inside them, I can discern it's them close to our position. A little further, scattered between High Delnor, Eastnor and Midnor, are numerous disturbances to the gold from the Saer Tel. Further south in Tars is the most significant disturbance, creating a maelstrom amongst the colours. This, I believe, must be Nogoth.'

I find myself smiling. The Once and Future King is where he said he'd be, and salvation awaits.

The Astorian kingdom begins just on the other side of the River of Tears. With a year to prepare and train a massive army, Nogoth will have the surprise of his long life when he heads north.

As for the terrifying threat posed by the trolls and giants ...

'Dimitar. Every time you're able to. Eat some more rock,' I command and watch him scoop up a handful from the road. I gaze up at the golem that used to be my friend. When we face the behemoths of Nogoth's army, I hope ours will be the size of a small mountain.

***

I tap the tip of my sword against Kralgen's shoulder as he lies asleep between some tree roots. The oblivious forms of Asterz and Lotane rest under some blankets between the next pair. It's early morning, and a haze of mist adds an ethereal quality to the woods I've found them in.

His eyes open, and he smiles warmly.

'You're getting sloppy in your old age,' I tease quietly.

'So are you, King Slayer!' he whispers in response.

I shrug. There's a presence behind me, but I haven't been caught out, far from it.

'Perhaps I am, or perhaps I'm happy for some people to come up behind me!' I chuckle.

I turn, my smile dazzling for Lotane, only to find Asterz standing there, a sword levelled at my chest.

'Good to see you, Asterz,' I say without losing the smile.

The sword remains, and I note the coldness in her eye. This doesn't bode well.

I ignore the inherent threat, turn my back and reach down toward Kralgen.

'Time to get up, you big lummox!'

He grabs my hand and rises to his feet, gingerly testing his injured calf.

'If Lotane isn't already awake, I'll give him a kick,' he offers.

Lotane, having been woken by the dialogue, stands, letting his blanket fall away.

'With your gammy calf, that might take all day. I'll get myself up.'

'And there it is,' says Asterz, her voice caustic. 'That easy familiarity between a King Slayer, a king, and my consort.'

Silence descends as the spectre of something unpleasant arises.

'My queen!' Lotane pleads, hands pressed together. 'Don't do this!'

'What?' she demands, her eyebrows arching. 'Don't ask the questions that have been tormenting my mind all these nights. Such as how the hell the three of you obviously know one another so well. It isn't just the comfortable talk and banter. It's you choosing *her* over me to fight at your side, and how you so readily obeyed her orders to ... oh, what was it ... use MAGIC to save Kralgen here. What are the odds that three unrelated individuals with this gift should come together? The thing is, you aren't unrelated, are you?'

Her eyes pierce Lotane like an arrow, and he squirms under her gaze.

I knew this would come up, but I hadn't been prepared for it, having been too distracted lately. Do I just grab Asterz, use my magic, assuming it works, and make her compliant?

I look at Lotane. No, he'd never forgive me.

'Your silence says everything your words don't,' Asterz moans in anguish, her sword wavering and falling from her grasp. 'Tell me. Do you love me?'

Lotane looks confused. I hope he tells her the harsh truth, and I want to shout it out for him.

'I do,' he says with sincerity. 'I truly do.'

Why is he lying? Does kingship mean that much to him?

'Then, answer me. How long have you known each other?'

Kralgen clears his throat, looking abashed.

'Since our fourteenth years. We were all bought at auction and ...'

'I'm not talking to you or her, just him!' Asterz interrupts with a hiss and points at Lotane so there can be no misunderstanding.

'Are you, or have you ever been an assassin like her?'

I can tell Lotane is breaking up inside. He might not love this woman, but he certainly cares for her or what she can offer. While a part of me rejoices that this could mean the end of them, another part bleeds for his sorrow.

'Yes.'

A simple answer, yet one that condemns him forever.

'My father was killed by an assassin. Did you three have anything to do with it.'

'Yes.'

'Who killed my father?'

'I did.'

The words spill from my mouth before Lotane has a chance to even frame his answer. Of course, I still remember Lotane's axe throw cutting the old Astorian King down, but my love for Lotane makes me want to protect him too.

'It was me. It was always me who undertook the killings.'

Asterz's eyes glitter with hatred.

'Was it her?' she asks, looking at Lotane.

'Yes.'

'You and I will have a reckoning one day, King Slayer,' she snarls. 'Blood must be repaid with blood!'

Lotane's taken the lifeline I've thrown him. However, this gamble is far from over, and if Asterz asks some searching questions, this could get worse again. We can't afford to have the future of this world in jeopardy.

My stomach flips as I realise what I must do to save the only thing that Lotane and I currently have left. Our friendship.

'Asterz. You and I need to talk. Woman to woman.'

'I have nothing to say to you that I haven't already said. I'd as soon slit your throat than listen to you!'

'But there are things you need to hear whether you want to or not. It's your duty as Astoria's Queen to understand who your friends are.'

'You aren't my friend, and you aren't welcome in Astoria either!'

'Maybe I'm not. But I'm Nogoth's enemy, and as the saying goes, the enemy of thy enemy is your ally until the day you choose to slit their throat. How will you do that to me if you send me on my way?'

Asterz spits on the ground, but her shoulders slump, and she gestures toward the trees.

I nod to Kralgen and smile reassuringly at Lotane before following Asterz from the camp. I'm cautious in case she plans to attack me, but her anger has drained for now.

Taking a deep breath, I decide to get this over with.

'Let me start by telling you something you have to know if you don't already. Lotane loves you.'

'Oh, and how do you know that, exactly?' Asterz asks snidely.

'Because he chose you over me. We were together for years, magically paired against our will. We didn't know better and had no choice, nor did the others this was done to. The magic that bound us was broken, and my love remained, but Lotane, he found you instead and refused to reconcile with me.'

I watch as Asterz's mouth opens and closes as she absorbs the news. I can only imagine how hard all this must be. Then, with a shake of her head, her composure returns.

'If that's all you have to tell me, we can head back.'

'No. It's not all. There's something else. We all served Nogoth, King of the Fey, before we saw the light. It's a story you'll need to hear from start to finish.'

Asterz either sits, or her legs give way. Which doesn't matter.

'It all started in a place called the Mountain of Souls and a woman called Lystra.'

***

'The River of Tears!' Asterz points out as we crest a hill.

Sure enough, there it is. On the west bank of the foaming waters, lit like burnished gold by the setting sun, are the vast fortifications that had, since the last Astorian invasion, housed thousands of vigilant Delnorian troops. A mighty stone bridge spans the raging torrent, and on the east side is surprisingly nothing, just a pass threading through the mountain range leading to the Astorian steppes. What must be Astorian troops are positioned behind a low barricade, with tents and a few horses on picket lines behind them.

I breathe a sigh of relief. I'm sure, like the others, I'd often worried we'd arrive here to find Astoria a smoking ruin already.

'Why is it called the River of Tears?' Kralgen ponders out loud.

'It was named after the first war between Astoria and Delnor. When our armies were defeated, legend tells that the tears of the shamed survivors and the sorrowful families of the fallen turned the small river into the raging torrent it is today.' Asterz explains.

Even from this distance, it's certainly something to behold; a powerful natural barrier that had helped separate the two kingdoms until the Astorian thirst for conquest and revenge had led them to invade. The storybooks of my youth had painted a picture of savage, fur-clad hordes riding small steppe ponies that had flooded across the lands, sowing destruction. Their first conquest had been the seed from which the Delnorian empire had grown. Out of desperation, Delnor had turned to its neighbours, forging an alliance that had ultimately humbled the warlike but undisciplined Astorians three times since records began.

'Except for that low barricade, no fortifications are on your side of the river.' I point out.

'A Delnorian condition to allow trade after my forbears' past misdemeanours.' Asterz frowns, then laughs darkly at the belittling of her nation's historic aggression. 'Strategically, it gives the Delnorians command of the crossing and pass with their siege weapons, ensuring they can contain any large hostile force before it leaves our lands. Those days of conquest are long behind us, but Delnorian suspicion remains. Anyway, it's the only land route in and out of Astoria, and Delnor's trade and harvest helps my people,' she explains, her voice flat.

I consider her words as we continue down the hill.

It's fairly easy to recognise today's Astorians with those in the books. Despite cities replacing the tents of the nomadic culture they'd historically followed, the mounted archers on their steppe ponies that had accompanied Asterz south were much like those I'd read about. Yet, in these terrible times, where only the strong will survive, their culture of martial prowess will offer hope to those seeking their protection.

I catch Asterz looking coldly at me from the corner of her eye and sigh.

She might hate me, but thankfully she hasn't allowed it to outweigh her reason.

Our conversation this morning had not been easy. It would have been if I'd used blood magic, but no ... for too many reasons, no. Yet things had worked out in the end.

Despite who Lotane, Kralgen and me were, Asterz recognises the value of who we now are.

Kralgen is a king, and she wants his Icelandians.

She still loves Lotane even though she feels betrayed, and nothing makes you fight harder than love.

Then there's me.

Keeping me around to take her revenge at some point wasn't enough, especially once she knew of my past relationship with Lotane. However, when she'd seen Dimitar's growth and recognised his potential on the battlefield ...

I glance behind at our rearguard in time to see him devouring a large rock he'd just pulled from the ground. He's taken my order seriously and is consuming as much as possible. Already his wounds, if that's what I can call them, are healing. His smashed nose shows signs of regrowth; the shattered upper arm where he'd reaffixed it to his shoulder is filling out. The regeneration is incredible, and all it takes is stone.

If only stone was what mine took.

Feeling this good only days after recovering from injuries that should have laid me low for months is a heady elixir. The guilt I feel for consuming my victims' blood lessens as my need grows, the end justifying the means.

'Clear?'

It's a simple question, but to relax this close to our destination would be the height of folly.

'Clear!' Kralgen and Lotane confirm, their eyes constantly sweeping for any sign of trouble or movement.

Anything large enough to cause us problems can't be concealed in the open ground between us and the bridge, whilst anything small enough to hide will likely stay that way, considering Dimitar's presence.

It's hard to believe that safety awaits on the other side of that river. How long it remains safe is another matter entirely. The mountains surrounding Astoria provide an unpassable barrier for most of Nogoth's forces, but the pass ahead is the weak link in Astoria's defence.

As if reading my mind, Kralgen speaks up.

'We've talked about training a huge army to fight Nogoth in a pitched battle, but now I wonder if that's necessary. What if we seal the pass with a wall, making it so costly to breach that Nogoth lets us be?'

'But what if he doesn't?' Asterz asks.

'Then we still have our army ready, and his forces will be vastly weakened. We'll have a real chance of victory,' Kralgen responds, raising an eyebrow.

"I've been thinking the same as Kralgen,' Lotane murmurs. 'It needs to be big enough to present an obstacle to his giants and trolls!'

'I've seen a wall designed to defend against them,' I speak up. 'At Iron Hold, an ancient fortification was built for just such a purpose. Something similar could be built here. The terrain is almost identical.'

'That's all well and good,' Asterz interjects, snorting, 'but to build such a wall would take years ...'

She pauses, the corners of her lips turning upward, and for a moment, I see the beauty that must have first attracted Lotane.

'Yet the idea is sound,' she continues, a calculating look in her eyes. 'If the fate of this world rests on Astoria's shoulders, we must all do what it takes to overcome such obstacles, whatever the cost.'

'Well said,' Kralgen rumbles, and Lotane nods in agreement.

'So, if a wall is required, a wall we shall have, and it won't take years!' Asterz states with surety, her face animated. 'Kralgen. You'll accompany Lotane and I on horseback to Ast. It will take us no more than two days. Whilst Lotane and I set the gears of war in motion and organise the labour to build the wall, you'll be escorted to Astwater on the north coast. A fast ship will take you and a sled team as far as the Frozen Sea. If the gods favour you, you'll arrive at Ice Hold in two weeks. Get your people back here as fast as possible to help with the war effort!'

Kralgen grips Asterz's outstretched arm.

'My Icelandians will fight alongside your Astorians!'

'You didn't mention me travelling to Ast,' I point out, my stomach churning like a pit of snakes.

'That's because it's better you stay at the entrance to the pass with the border guard.'

'Better for who?'

I know the answer. Better for her and Lotane if I'm out of the way. Yet she's too shrewd to say it.

'Better for everyone. As you pointed out, you've seen the wall at Iron Hold, so there's none better to help guide its construction. The Delnorian fortifications can provide the materials needed, and of course, there's Dimitar. With your golem helping, progress will be swift. Without you both, I can't see how we can succeed.'

'It's true, King Slayer,' Kralgen adds. 'Only you have the power.'

Damn her. She's manipulated this conversation perfectly, but she's not wrong either.

A gracious smile that I want to wipe off Asterz's face with my fist appears as she recognises her victory in keeping me apart from Lotane.

'I will have cavalry sent to reinforce you in a day and a thousand engineers and labourers within three,' Asterz advises.

I look at Lotane, but he's studiously avoiding my gaze.

My heart sinks.

How's it possible that I'm in such close physical proximity to Lotane, yet I've never felt so far away in my life?

***

# CHAPTER XI

Do you ever need to sleep?' I ask, tilting my head to look up at the night sky, bone-deep weariness slurring my words.

Two hours ago, Asterz had left me in charge of a motley bunch of Astorian border guards before riding off in a hurry with the others on horses commandeered from the picket line. I'm now resting safely, although uncomfortably, on top of a vacant Delnorian barracks, having left the Astorians to their tents. Dimitar sits in the training yard below. Nonetheless, his head is level with the parapet beside me, making conversation easy.

'No,' Dimitar answers, keeping his voice low.

Something soothing about his rumble has my eyelids fluttering as I fight fatigue.

'Do you get tired or feel pain?'

'No.'

'Would you be able to keep watch throughout the night and warn me if anyone or anything comes close?'

'Yes.'

'Then please do so.'

I lie back and close my eyes, expecting sleep to pull me under like a whirlpool. Thinking about that word brings back memories of my father and the tales he'd tell of mythical sea creatures and the terrors of the deep. He'd died alone, and I can't help but wonder if I'll suffer the same fate.

Tears creep from under my eyelids as I recall the comfort of his deep voice and ready smile.

*Gah, don't be so weak, Malina!*

I have a mission, no, several missions, and I must be strong to see them all through.

Ordering them in my mind, I bring clarity to my jumbled thoughts.

There's no escaping that I first need to oversee the building of a wall across this damn pass, rivalling that at Iron Hold to stymy Nogoth's plan to invade Astoria. I don't want to be here, but my misgivings are based on being separated from Lotane, and Asterz manipulating it. Served by Dimitar and my magic, it makes perfect sense for me to take on this pivotal role.

However, once the building work nears completion, I'll leave to focus on my next mission ...

Lotane.

No amount of friends or strangers can ever fill the void my broken heart has left behind. Every day spent at the wall will be a day that brings Asterz and Lotane closer. To win Lotane's affection again, I have to be beside him, showing him that his decision is flawed.

Then there's my magic. If the wall isn't enough to keep Astoria safe, I genuinely believe it's our only hope of defeating Nogoth. I'm sure greater power is mine for the taking, and I must keep pursuing this dream.

Hah.

Just one of these missions is daunting, but all of them together ... Yet if there's one person in this damned world who can complete them, it's me!

'Dimitar. Can you tell me how to command the elemental magic around me?'

'No.'

'Is that because you don't know or won't tell me?'

'I don't know.'

'Have you any thoughts on why I can't command it?'

Dimitar falls silent, and I keep my exasperation in check. If only he could initiate conversation or at least embellish his answers.

'It isn't yours to command,' he eventually answers.

'But the elemental magic trapped inside me is.'

'That's because it's a part of you.'

'Yet I can command the life magic outside of me.'

'No, you can't. You summon its attention, and it uses you as a vessel to redistribute life.'

Hmmm. There's truth in what he says. I can't command a specific tree to grow from nothing; only invigorate what's already there above or below the soil. Life magic is incredible, beautiful, and so powerful that it keeps worlds alive, yet in my fight against Nogoth, it's the weakest of them all.

This line of thought is getting me nowhere. I need to sleep, I really do, but ideas about my magic flash through my head faster than lightning.

'Dimitar. Wake me at sunrise if I'm not already up.'

'Yes.'

I concentrate, visualising as I raise my hands shoulder-width apart and watch as my wish is granted.

Lightning flashes between my palms, and then, as I clench my fists, it flickers over my knuckles like snakes. I imagine choking Nogoth's life away as his body convulses, shocked into submission. The drain on my strength grows as I continue to concentrate, demanding more and more power, knowing it will have to be like nothing I've summoned before to overcome him.

Maybe if I can hold on for long enough, I'll find a reservoir of strength I never knew existed or draw upon the magic around me. Yet despite my efforts, soon, there's nothing left to give.

Blackness encroaches on my vision, and the whirlpool finally pulls me under.

***

Birdsong.

A dozen different competing melodies echo around the vacant fortress. I groan, knuckle my eyes, and sit up with a yawn. The symphony of whistles is beautiful, yet I'm tempted to turn all the little feathered balls of happiness into little balls of flame just to shut them up.

My stomach grumbles.

A roasted bird for breakfast sounds delicious, yet I'm not in the mood for killing, and using my magic while so exhausted will have me sleep throughout the morning too.

It's just before dawn, yet my fey eyesight allows me to see clearly enough. It reminds me of when I used the Soul Gate because everything I see is so grey, devoid of colour and life. I can't wait for the sunrise.

I require more sleep but have learned to function on less than this. I rise and go through a stretching and meditation routine, draw my battered swords, and go through patterns and forms, the blades a blur. It's strange how when I practise dealing death, it makes me feel so alive.

Invigorated, I'm now ready for the day ahead. I'd ordered the Astorians to present themselves at daybreak, but it's still early, and I have time on my hands.

Time to scout this deserted fortress. The Delnorians that occupied it had been ordered to return to High Delnor with all haste. So, it stands to reason much of their equipment and stores will have been left behind.

Sheathing my blades, I leap down from the barrack's roof. It's adjacent to the main trade road that bisects this place and is as good a place to start as any.

Sure enough, each building I enter is full of unmade bunks, discarded personal belongings and cobwebs. Paintings and drawings are pinned to the wooden bed posts. I shake my head sadly as I realise that everyone who'd lived here had likely perished along with the loved ones depicted on the yellowing scraps of paper.

The eerie quietness reminds me of a temple, and I tread softly, respectful of any spirits that might reside here. Occasional rodents squeak in annoyance as I disturb their new empire, my footsteps meandering from building to building.

I exit the barracks into the courtyard and nod toward Dimitar, who, unsurprisingly, doesn't respond.

'Dimitar. If I nod at you, and everything is all right, please nod in return.'

'Yes.'

I nod. That stone head nods back at me. Success!

He might never be human again, but I think I'll enjoy his company more than the Astorians if I can get him to be less of a statue.

There's no point entering the kitchen buildings as I can detect a stomach-churning stench emanating from within. Instead, I cross to the other side, where a barred, locked door leading to a low building with no windows piques my interest.

I'm tempted to have Dimitar smash the door open, but it's too early in the morning for such noise. Instead, I put my hand on the heavy metal padlock and then step away as the elemental fire I summon turns the lock into molten slag.

I grunt as I lift the heavy bar free and lean it against a wall.

The door is made of metal-reinforced wood, but the hinges are well-greased, and it swings open noiselessly with a little effort.

Fire springs from my fingers to provide light as I enter, and I step around the chamber, igniting a brazier in each corner, noting a further closed door in the rear wall as I do so. I can't help but smile as I imagine Kralgen being let loose in here. He'd be like a child in a cake store.

Spare weapons, armour, and all kinds of leather equipment, essential for keeping Delnor's border army at a high state of readiness, line the walls, are piled on shelves or held in racks.

I joyfully rip off my looted and mismatched armour and cast my battered swords aside. The best of what Delnor has to offer is at my fingertips, and it's time for a refit.

Hardened leather armour draws me like a moth to a candle. It's what I've been fighting in my whole life. However, I reconsider when I realise it's highlighted and edged in Delnorian blue because, whilst I don't mind ruffling some feathers, it won't be a good start with my new command.

There must be something else.

I prowl up and down the racks running my fingers over mail-reinforced boots, chainmail shirts and heavy leather garments. I pull some short swords free of their scabbards, testing their balance. They're far better than I'd just discarded, but I'm not overly impressed.

As I pull the door at the back of the chamber open, it creaks ominously, and I summon some light. Immediately it's evident that this room holds equipment for officers.

Armour made of iron shines under the flame in my hand, but just like in the first chamber, braziers are evenly spaced throughout the room and, once lit, are soon shedding their warm glow into every corner.

I run my fingers across a heavily embellished breastplate etched with gold, then rub them together before bringing them to my nostrils. I nod in appreciation, for the armour is heavily oiled, ensuring it remains in good condition even while stored.

This fortress is a treasure trove because the equipment here can be used to equip any new recruits, be they Astorian, Icelandian, Surian or Rolantrian.

The sheen of neatly tied packages peeking through a layer of dust draws my attention to some shelves on the rear wall, and I move closer to investigate.

Sitting cross-legged on the floor, I pull out the first bundle, tug on the strings and blow the dust away. Tooled hunting leathers emerge, and I clap my hands in joy.

The first few packages have sets that are way too big, but I strike lucky as I hold up a pair to the light. I have strong shoulders, a broad upper back, a narrow waist, and the black leather shirt I'm inspecting tapers nicely. I've never cared whether clothing is anything other than functional, but the swirls on the back and short elbow-length sleeves please my eye.

Likewise, the trousers have a drawstring and will suit my narrow waist whilst fitting over my muscled thighs. Dark metal studs are affixed down the outside of each leg, and I nod in approval at this fashionable embellishment.

A few moments later, I ditch my flimsy clothing and torn foot bindings and pull on my new outfit.

Soft, doeskin boots follow from another line of shelves that have my toes wriggling in sheer delight. Walking barefoot close to nature has advantages, but these boots are like pushing your feet into a fluffy cloud.

Everything in this room is of the highest quality. Having rank in the Delnorian army certainly had its privileges.

Two short swords, their edges and points so honed that Kralgen could shave with them, along with two daggers suitable for parrying, throwing, or of course, stabbing, are soon attached to a weapon belt.

Another door, more searching, and I return to the courtyard as the sun edges over the horizon carrying a polished horn bow, several quivers of arrows, and a leather bag slung over my shoulder.

Dimitar looks down at me, so I nod.

He nods back.

This is going to be a good day!

***

Twelve wood-framed tents, five men to a tent. Sixty border guards, all asleep.

In some respects, I understand their indifference. They're at the bottom of the military ladder, low-paid, poorly trained and with the boring task of checking goods coming in and out of Astoria. With the world in flames of late, that hasn't kept them too busy.

I could tell last night that the sergeant in charge, having not seen any hostile forces, was giving no credence to the tale of a fey invasion. Asterz could have done a better job convincing him; after all, she'd returned without the archers and nobles she'd left with, but she was too eager to leave and get to Ast.

Nor is the sergeant happy with his guards being put under my command. Astorians have a rigid social hierarchy based on rank, bloodline and martial prowess, and here I am, an outsider, being put in charge. Maybe if he knew I was part fey, it might shake him up. However, it's too late for that. He's made a bold statement of rebellion by ignoring my command to rally at sunrise. If I let this slide, I'll have no authority again without spilling lots of blood.

I draw a sword, enjoying the feel of its leather-bound hilt in my hand and walk swiftly along the line of tents, appreciating the ease with which the blade cuts through the cords holding them up. By the time the last one has billowed to the ground, a rich chorus of curses and angry voices echoes around the narrow pass.

A small barricade of rocks has been erected across the uneven ground. It couldn't even keep sheep out, let alone an attack, but at least it gives me somewhere to sit as I sheath my sword and then watch with amusement as the writhing, kicking shapes try to extricate themselves.

I don't have to wait too long.

A few minutes later, the red-faced sergeant is stamping toward me, his men in various stages of undress following behind in a group, eager to witness his fury.

He's a squat fellow, with a thick neck and big hands hinting at solid strength, and no doubt he could rip my arm off if he had the chance. I'm glad he hasn't armed himself because otherwise, more blood might be spilt than necessary. His demeanour indicates he intends a brief verbal assault followed by a physical one. He could have chosen contrition, but he's going with violence instead. Big mistake.

Stepping down from the small wall, I meet him with a broad smile, my hands relaxed at my side. He comes toward me, drawing a deep breath to scream some obscenity.

Whatever he's going to say, I'm not interested.

I don't pause; I just walk right up to him and butt him with my forehead square on the bridge of his nose. He staggers back, eyes tearing, blood gushing forth, but I don't leave it there. If I did, he'd gather his senses, and the fight wouldn't finish quickly.

The point of my right elbow finishes the job my head started, crushing what's left of his nose across his face, followed by my boot sinking into his stomach. It's a wicked kick, and he doubles over just in time for my knee to come up onto his nose again.

A little magic, and he's catapulted backwards by a gust of wind to slide across the dusty ground to stop unconscious at the feet of the open-mouthed guards behind him.

Keeping my face impassive, I walk over to his body, lean down, and roll him onto his side, so he doesn't choke to death on his own blood. I doubt he'll be able to see for a week, his eyes are already swollen shut, and as for his nose, I doubt he'll ever breathe properly again. He has a sash of rank attached to his shoulder, and I tear it free.

'You could all be dead. Every single one of you stabbed through the sides of your tents while you slept with no guard to forewarn you.'

Confusion furrows the brows of those watching. It's time to make things clear.

'Astoria is already at WAR. Not with the Delnorians, Surians, Rolantrians or any of the old Delnorian empire, but with an army you've only heard whispers of. Let me tell you, those whispers are true. An army of the fey, comprising of giants, trolls, ogres and far worse, is laying waste to the lands of humankind. The armies of Delnor, Tars, Hastia, Suria and Rolantria have already been slaughtered or captured, leaving Astoria as the last bastion of hope in this dying world.'

Excited voices rise from the back of the watching men and women, and even a few scattered cheers break out as I deliver news of the defeat.

'SILENCE!' I thunder. 'If you think Delnor's defeat is a cause for celebration, you're sorely wrong. An army of around two hundred thousand fey are coming here, not only to crush you but to FEED on you!'

A shocked silence falls over the border guards as the magnitude of my words registers.

'How are we to defeat two hundred thousand of these fey, as you call them?'

I can't see the woman who shouted the question, but it doesn't matter who.

'The plan is simple. We build a wall to the heavens here,' I say, sweeping my hand across the pass. 'It will be a wall as high and strong as the mountains that have protected Astoria since time began. That and the River of Tears will be the first line of defence.'

'Is there a second?' A thin man asks.

'It will be the steel placed in the hands of every Astorian strong enough to wield a sword irrespective of rank or breeding. Also, those you once saw as enemies will soon be your blood brothers. Over the next few days, envoys will go to Rolantria and Suria, inviting their people to take up arms and fight alongside us. The Icelandian people will also come here for sanctuary. Make no mistake, this is a fight for the survival of humankind. Old hatreds must be buried, or this world holds no future for any of us!'

'What about the Tarsians, Hastians or the Delnorians,' the thin man presses.

I shake my head, letting my gaze wander across the watching faces.

'Our enemy currently occupies those lands, and it's unlikely there will be many survivors. Those kingdoms' doom is upon them, but we must use the time their unwilling sacrifice brings to ensure we don't suffer the same fate!'

'Now, who is the longest-serving corporal here?' I demand into the silence.

A tall woman with large cheekbones nervously steps forward.

'Corporal Dundain!'

'That fool,' I shout, pointing to the unconscious man at my feet, 'made the mistake of not heeding his queen, then compounded it by not heeding my command to rally at sunrise. He'll keep his head, but there's a position vacant for a new sergeant who will follow orders.' I toss the sergeant's sash at her. 'That's now you!

'You have ten minutes to ready yourselves. There will be no breaking of fast. I haven't eaten, and nor will you until we've finished the first task of our day.'

'Might I ask what that is?' Dundain asks.

'Yes, Sergeant. We have a fortress to loot!'

***

'Malina.'

Dimitar's grating voice brings me awake immediately.

I press my finger to my lips.

Dimitar nods, points to his ear, and then up the pass toward Astoria.

Two days since we'd arrived, and I've been giving him instructions here and there. Being the size he is, he'll never be subtle or stealthy, but every day I try to give him a semblance of his lost humanity.

A silent wish, and shortly after, I hear what's raised Dimitar's concerns; the clopping of a thousand iron-shod hooves, bumping wagon wheels and shuffling feet. I'm not concerned. Whilst I don't trust Asterz ... when it comes to keeping her kingdom safe, I've no doubts she'll do what it takes. Especially as keeping me busy here keeps me away from her and Lotane.

Nonetheless, I lever myself upright, my body complaining of too little sleep.

I've magicked a smooth sleeping platform high into the side of the pass, and I step off, falling as silent as a shadow, my magic easing my fall to the ground below.

I stride toward the four sentries standing atop a new stone wall constructed across the pass. I'm proud of what we've managed to build so quickly. It's low and rudimentary, but it shows what fifty motivated guards, a golem, and a determined Chosen can achieve. Braziers are placed beyond the wall, their flickering flames lighting the approach from the Delnorian side.

I make myself seen as I approach the first pair, not wishing to frighten anyone unnecessarily.

'Sound the stand to! We have company.' I point back along the pass, so they understand it's not an enemy approaching.

The Delnorian fortress had offered up a trove of useful items beyond just weapons and armour. As a guard slowly bashes one of them, a large bronze gong, I hurry along the wall toward the other two keeping watch, who've drawn their weapons in concern.

'There is nothing to be worried about,' I shout. 'We have visitors.'

I turn back toward the border guards forming outside their tents which are now neatly lined up against the north wall of the pass.

Sergeant Dundain is turning the air blue with curses trying to get them ready.

'Where's your sword, you dried piece of goat dung,' she shouts at one. 'At least tuck your shirt in, if not your belly,' she screams at another.

I can't help but smile. These border guards will never be an elite fighting force, but she's determined to stamp her mark; to impress me or otherwise doesn't matter. Whether too old, slow, weak or passive, these men and women will never climb higher than the lowest military rung. However, they're on it, which means they're significantly above what are considered the common folk, farmers, merchants and similar.

I walk over, nodding in approval despite wanting to shake my head in despair.

'Well done. We'll have company soon, so let's show whoever is coming that you're up to guarding the border. Have every fifth guard holding a torch. I want thirty on the wall and twenty in ranks guarding our stores.'

I turn, my steps taking me back toward Dimitar, where he stands immobile with his back against the sheer mountain face behind him.

'Stay here unless I call for you or need you.'

That huge head nods, and I nod back.

He's getting bigger. When he'd fought the troll, he'd been smaller by a third, yet now he's definitely the same size as one. Incredible.

Light springs up as torches are lit, and order descends as everyone finds their places. It's amazing what respect can do to a unit, and perhaps a little fear.

The sound of the rapidly approaching horses grows, and the narrow pass amplifies the sound of pounding hooves, excited whinnying, and the jingle of mail. Then, around a bend, they appear, a tide of black-garbed Astorians.

I move close to the gate, so I'm highlighted by the torches behind me as the armoured lead rider gallops up.

He makes for an unpleasant sight. Twin horns curve upward from the sides of his open-faced fur-rimmed helmet that frames a face made distinctive by glittering eyes and high cheekbones. Then there's a blade-like nose and a cleft chin that's a common racial trait amongst many Astorians.

He doesn't display a hint of warmth or respect as he rides up to me, but at least he raises his hand, and the column of riders rein in without running me down.

'Who is in charge here?' he demands, his words clipped, spoken fast as if he hasn't the time to waste on them.

'I am.'

'WRONG!' he shouts. 'My name is Captain Rynald, and I'm in charge here.'

He thumps his leather armoured chest for emphasis.

I sigh. Why couldn't this meeting be without confrontation?

As he's sitting astride his charger, I can hardly headbutt him like I had the sergeant earlier, and with so many warriors behind him, they're unlikely to be cowed if I did humble their leader in such a fashion.

Burning him alive or turning him to ice will probably not end well either.

'DIMITAR. Please help the captain from his mount.'

Being just before dawn, the pass is almost entirely in shadow, and the torches only provide localised light. So with Dimitar still against the wall, the Astorian cavalry hadn't noticed him ... until now.

He crosses to Rynald in three giant steps and plucks him from his mount.

Horses whinny in panic while sabres and bows are drawn in their hundreds.

'What should I do with him?' Dimitar grates, holding Rynald high above the ground.

'That's down to Rynald. If he doesn't put himself under my command as he should be by the time I count to five, you can eat him. If any of his warriors try to stop you, harm you, or harm me, you have my permission to kill them all.'

'You can't do this!' screams Rynald, his legs kicking futilely in the air.

'I can, and I am. Your queen put me in charge of this pass, the construction of a wall, and all those who are sent to guard it!' I roar, ensuring those watching warriors can hear. 'You have come here and taken it upon yourself to countermand a royal order.

'ONE.'

'But you're not even Astorian, whereas I'm of royal lineage. I can't take orders from you!'

'TWO.'

'I'll have your bloody head on a pike for his,' he screams, incandescent with rage.

'THREE.'

Dimitar opens his giant maw and lifts the captain closer.

'Are you sure you don't want to change your mind, captain, and do the right thing?

'FOUR!'

'Fine, Damnit,' Rynald yells. 'Just have this thing put me down.'

I nod to Dimitar, who nods back.

Captain Rynald is placed on the ground before me, and Dimitar steps away.

I recognise my mistake immediately.

Rynald flicks his hand at me, and I twist away as a throwing knife spins past, scoring my cheek.

Dimitar steps forward, raising a huge fist.

'NO!' I command, motioning Dimitar away.

Rynald smirks confidently and pulls out a curved sabre and dagger from the scabbards on his belt.

I shake my head. This could have gone so differently. I thought I'd be safe here, at least until Nogoth and his fey turned up. It seems I was wrong. Wherever I go, death follows.

'I am Malina, the King Slayer. As is Astorian custom, I own what I can take. So let it be known I will take this man's life and position as your captain.'

My shout, enhanced by a little magic, reaches everyone.

'I, I didn't know!' Rynald stammers, his sabre point shaking, fear replacing the sadistic menace in his eyes.

'Too late, Rynald. You chose your fate. Now, it's time to meet it!'

***

The sun is at its zenith, and I'm enjoying the shade of a canvas tent, the sides of which have been furled to ensure I can keep an eye on everything. It was erected by the erstwhile Captain Rynald's command. They hadn't seemed too worried about his demise. Apparently, he'd only recently killed the previous captain and wasn't much liked. Now they're out scouting beyond the river to ensure we're not caught unawares by any large force of fey, their orders to report, not engage should they encounter any.

I summon a gentle breeze to whisk away the encroaching heat and project my gratitude for this small but welcome feat. My magic writhes happily like a serpent, and I silently promise to pay it more attention.

Labourers are arriving in a steady stream, and I've appointed Sergeant Dundain to ensure their sleeping and cooking tents don't block the pass for other traffic. I snort in amusement as she waves her hands furiously at a sluggish group, shooing them out of a rider's way.

'No wall needs to be that high or thick. That's madness!' exclaims Arbinger, commander of the Astorian engineers. He looks up from the draft plans he'd asked me to create, then cringes in horror as he realises his outburst has captured my attention.

I can see his eyes flicker to the scorch marks where Captain Rynald had died screaming, flesh sloughing away from his bones. I'd beaten that fool soundly with my swords, making him bleed from a hundred cuts before I'd had my magic finish the job. The scorch marks and tales of his ugly demise have saved me from resorting to any kind of violence since. That my command tent is erected next to what little remains is no coincidence.

Arbinger gulps.

'My apologies. But even the royal castle at Ast has walls a third the size of what you propose.' He presses his hands together, voice and limbs trembling.

I feel a little ashamed. I want to be respected, but the Astorians have only responded to fear so far. However, if it gets the job done ...

'You've seen my companion, Dimitar,' I say, pointing as my friend deposits a huge armful of stone he'd ripped from the Delnorian fortress against the north wall of the pass. 'There are giants in Nogoth's army half his size again. This wall must be indomitable. The mountains surrounding Astoria are too high, and the air too thin for the fey to traverse, so this pass is the only weak point in Astoria's defence. Let's not quibble over a few hundred hands of height.'

'But the amount of stone, wooden scaffolding and ...'

'Calm down, Arbinger. However much stone you need, Dimitar and the sprawling Delnorian fortress will provide, and I'll use my power to strengthen and mould what you create. You've seen what I've done with the existing wall. Consider this your greatest work, something that will have your name on people's lips for centuries to come. Arbinger, the man who helped save Astoria!'

Arbinger's eyes widen, and a faraway look replaces the fear and anxiety.

'As you order, so it shall be,' Arbinger says, bowing out of the command tent.

The rider I'd noted earlier rides his horse over and dismounts. His eyes flicker everywhere, taking in the labourers at work, the discipline of the border guards, and Dimitar, whose presence is impossible to overlook. Like many of the military class I've encountered, he has a hard, unforgiving countenance. He stands confidently, owning the ground he stands upon. Balanced, poised, unconsciously ready for anything. He's without question a warrior to be wary of. I can't see any indication of rank on his scale armour, yet I know he's important or at least wealthy from the quality of his gear. The horse is a fine specimen too, and its saddle, whilst well worn, is expensively tooled.

Once he finishes looking around, those eyes fix on me. Up and down they travel, measuring, considering. I don't feel insulted, for he isn't looking at me as though I'm a piece of meat, and I've already done the same to him.

His lips curve upward a little, and surprisingly his smile appears genuine, although it's not exactly warm. Several scars on his face gleam whitely, at odds against his sun-darkened skin.

One hand grips the hilt of his sword whilst he cautiously extends the other. It's a traditional Astorian greeting to show respect for another warrior.

'I am Jarval, commander of Astoria's military.'

I grip the hilt of my sword and take his hand, noting the calluses.

'Malina.'

'Malina, King Slayer. Yes, your reputation and title are well-earned. But it isn't just kings that you slay, is it?' He raises an eyebrow as he looks at the scorch marks.

Before I can answer, he continues.

'Your work here is progressing well, and I'm duly impressed. However, I didn't come here to inspect your proficiency but to advise that Astoria's army will pass through on the morrow. Please ensure our route is as clear as possible to facilitate an easy passage.'

'Astoria's army? Queen Asterz was going to send envoys to convince Suria and Rolantria to have their people join us?' I point out.

'What are envoys but spies or military men in disguise,' Jarval laughs. 'I convinced the queen that we couldn't risk a small group of envoys being intercepted and killed. She barely made it back alive, having left with several hundred of our best. No. Our army rides, and you and your golem will ensure this wall goes up. Having seen your progress and met you, I feel confident our border is in safe hands until we return with the liberated peoples of Suria and Rolantria.'

'Liberated? Nogoth hasn't conquered their lands yet.'

Jarval smiles, yet this time it's colder than before. It reminds me of a cat eyeing a mouse. Yet I am no mouse, and I meet his gaze unwaveringly. He nods, having obviously made his mind up about something.

'Across the world, the weak will always plot and scheme, hiding behind lies and deceit, whereas in Astoria, being strong, we take what we want and own it,' and he nods at the scorch marks, obviously somehow aware of the story behind them. 'We also have a saying. Know your friends well and know your enemies better. It's been interesting getting to know you, Malina.'

Hmmm. What is he trying to say, that I'm a friend or an enemy? Yet asking will simply show weakness on my part. Jarval turns away, reaching for his horse's reins.

'Where I'm from, we have a saying too.'

Jarval pauses, looking over his shoulder.

'Oh yes, and what is that?'

'Only the strong survive!'

This time Jarval's smile is broad, his teeth shining white against his tanned face, and his laugh booms out.

'That's a saying to rival our own. Let it be so, Malina. Let it be so.'

He mounts smoothly, kicks his heels into his horse's sides, and rides off up the pass in a cloud of dust.

***

# CHAPTER XII

You can rest now, Dimitar,' I say, looking up at my friend towering above me.

His nod is accompanied by a smile showing tombstone teeth as, with a shower of dust, the back of his hand wipes across his forehead in apparent relief.

'I don't need rest, Malina.'

'I know, but everyone else does, and you make a lot of noise. Go have something to eat. You're doing well, but I want you bigger.'

Another nod, and he thumps over to the piles of masonry and rock piled against the north wall. Listening to those teeth grinding rocks sets me on edge, so I make my way to the command tent.

Torches are being lit, their oily smoke an assault on my nostrils, yet the aroma of cooking adds a little balance, and my stomach rumbles in anticipation of the evening meal.

Arbinger looks up briefly from his charts and bits of paper covered in scrawled notes, then returns to his scribbling, muttering under his breath.

I'd never appreciated that building a wall was more than just stacking rocks and bricks on top of one another, but apparently, some formulas need to be followed, and I'm glad he's here.

'Damnit,' he grumbles as a lantern flame gutters, then goes out.

I summon a white ball of fire, and he continues at a faster pace, his quill a blur.

'Done. Thank you,' he says with a brief smile.

I respond in kind. He's a good man, and I'm glad he's become more comfortable in my presence.

Arbinger gestures to a chair and then pulls up one for himself.

'Using your sketches and the notes I took from our briefing, I've completed my calculations and plans for the wall,' he says, turning some of the drawings around. 'In summary, it will house storerooms, barracks, and a hospital whilst the Delnorian war engines and the firing steps for our archers will be protected from any kind of aerial assault by these gargoyle creatures. Once finished, the wall tunnel can be sealed, presenting a deadly obstacle to any that tries to overcome it. I estimated it would take three years by conventional means to complete from scratch. Thankfully, with the Delnorian fortress providing most of our building materials and your indefatigable golem, I'm confident we can do it in three months,' he says triumphantly.

'I hope you're right, and Nogoth's fey allows us the time. Dimitar tells me that the Fey King is now in Hastia, so it would appear we'll be ready for him when he arrives.'

As if to punctuate my statement, another lantern flame dies.

'Gah,' Arbinger complains. 'We're going through supplies at a fearsome rate. I've sent two requests for double the timber, oil, rope and a dozen other things we're not getting enough off. We're making good progress, but it will slow down shortly, and if it wasn't for the supplies we'd looted from the Delnorian fortress, the project would have stalled already. Can you create one of those moon globes I've seen in Ast? I've still got work to do, and one would really help!' Arbinger looks hopeful.

The question catches me out, and I take a moment to answer.

'Sadly, no.'

'Why not?'

'Only the ssythlans can make them.'

'Hah,' Arbinger snorts. 'You're telling me you can create a stone golem but not a moon globe. You just need to figure out how.'

Arbinger's words shake me to my core. He's right. I've created something the ssythlans have never been able to. I've been so focussed on finding a way to command the elements out of my reach that I've overlooked what I might be able to create with what's under my control.

'Looks like I've got you thinking!' Arbinger chortles, noting my introspective look. 'Also, when you reflect on the power of your stone friend, have you ever considered what an army of them might achieve? Each one must be worth a thousand men. Perhaps your time would be better spent creating an army of them to defeat this King of the Fey.'

Momentarily I wonder if Arbinger has stumbled onto the apparent answer to Nogoth's invasion, but then the hope that had started to shine, dims.

'Dimitar's creation was an accident. It took the life of a good friend who loved me dearly for this to come about. It's too high a price to pay, and what would happen if I couldn't control the next one. The havoc just one could wield is unimaginable.'

Arbinger nods soberly.

'From what I've heard and you've told me, we have enough monsters to deal with. A war dog that turns feral is bad enough, but a golem. You're right to disparage my comment. Still, even with just one, you've a powerful magic weapon to hand.'

Arbinger's words are like a breeze clearing away the cobwebs of my brain. I've been walking down the same dead-end with my thoughts of late, yet with a casual encounter, he's shown me a different path that I can't wait to explore.

Something Dimitar has said comes to mind. *You can command your magic because it is trapped within you.* Likewise, the elemental fire magic within the moon globes is trapped and given a purpose. Typically, it would die away without the willpower of the mage continuing to guide it, yet they function for decades. Whilst trying to save Dimitar, magic was trapped inside him and continues to undertake my will, yet it doesn't drain me anymore.

The hair at the back of my neck stands up, for this realisation is the key.

Standing, I hug Arbinger in delight and laugh as he almost falls off his chair in surprise, then nearly skip with excitement as my stomach leads my feet to the kitchen tent. Whilst social hierarchy is rigidly observed in Astoria, this is put aside during meal times, and the atmosphere within is relaxed. Engineers, labourers and even a few guardsmen are taking their evening meal after a long day's work.

'Here you are,' a cook says, passing me a wooden bowl and spoon.

'Thanks.'

Smiling absently, it's only as I'm ducking under the furled sides on my way out that I note I've been served gravel, not food. A deathly silence falls as I retrace my steps.

I stand in front of the cook. She's only a year or two younger than me but has the fresh look of innocence that sadly won't last much longer in this dark world.

Her face turns white with fear as I stare coldly at her, and a wind howls through the tent with merely a thought.

The hilt of my dagger fits snugly into my palm as I pull the blade free, holding her frightened gaze with my own. Then, like a deer surrounded by wolves, her head whips left and right, wondering if there's any chance of escape.

The point of the dagger glints in the lantern light as I lift both hands, and then I stab.

She whimpers in shock.

'It's a little overcooked, don't you think!' I complain with a frown, stirring the gravel with my dagger point before placing the bowl into her hands. 'Even Dimitar would turn his nose up at that!'

Bellows of laughter and the hammering of fists on tables fill the tent, and I smile broadly, sheath my dagger, and nod in satisfaction at the stew and bread I'm promptly offered.

I wave as I leave, politely turning down a few requests to join people at their tables.

Tonight I have food for thought, and as my magic wriggles in my stomach, it's as though we share the same sense of excitement.

***

Dimitar leans back against the pass wall, his head level with my sleeping platform. I enjoy my solitude up here at the end of a busy day and can observe without being observed. As I look down, the figures below are red, their bodies shining with life, and I swallow hard, fighting back a surge of hunger despite having just eaten.

Damn. I don't want to feed again, but it's a lie because I know I do.

Is this what a bird of prey experiences when flying through the skies, seeing rabbits beneath? A deadly killer gifted with flight but cursed to hunt forever, bringing death from above to the innocent below. No, if death I must bring, it must be to the guilty, the evil, or I must follow the way of the Saer Tel and feed to eat, not feed to kill.

With a sigh, I drag my gaze away.

All three moons are bright in the sky, and one of my short swords gleams under their watchful eyes. This is why I'm here, to focus on the death of the evilest of all.

'Do you think this will work?' I ask softly.

Dimitar shrugs, his shoulders grinding against the rock, sending a small avalanche of stone debris down into the pass below. I'm about to berate him, but he's just following my commands to use human mannerisms; thus, the fault is mine.

'The logic appears sound, yet there's nothing logical about magic,' he answers.

A powerful weapon to hand.

Arbinger's words, casually spoken, possibly unlocking a door I never knew existed.

I pick up the sword. It's already deadly with razored edges, a hardened point, suitable for cutting or thrusting, and designed for one purpose, the taking of lives. For some reason, now the moment is upon me; I'm strangely reluctant to see if I can change it.

The fear of failure weighs heavily on me, something I'm not used to, because if creating magic weapons was possible, then surely the ssythlans would have equipped themselves with such potent items. Then there's Nogoth. With the power he's accrued over the millennia, he could fashion something to challenge the gods.

Then again, the symbiotic relationship I enjoy with my elemental powers is far different from everyone else, where magic is commanded through sheer force of will and pain, and I can also reach the gold of life.

Enough.

There's only one way to find out.

Despite being a long day, I've not depleted my magic to any noticeable extent, and it's joyfully awaiting my instruction, enthusiastic about undertaking my bidding. A flaming sword is easy but would drain my strength and extinguish when I grew tired or no longer needed it. No, the sword needs to be a vessel like the moon globes or my giant friend.

Controlling my breathing, I make my wish, projecting what I desire, what would make me happy. Imagining my magic pouring into the sword like wine from a flask into a goblet. I hold onto that vision until the flask is almost empty, the goblet nigh on overflowing.

Nothing.

I try again, visualising, projecting my need, holding on to my wish for longer.

Again, nothing.

My disappointment is overwhelming, the accompanying sadness and frustration sending tears down my cheeks. I hadn't realised how high my hopes had risen in such a short time.

How foolish my reaction. I brush the tears away, taking control of myself; this is not how a Chosen should react. I knew the chances of it working were slim, and in reality, my magic is already a weapon. We have a plan, and my powers will ensure this wall stands firm against Nogoth and his forces, but oh, how having something extra would have eased my residual doubts.

My magic seems subdued, no wriggling in excitement now, as if it shares my despondency.

I turn the sword over in my hand, wondering if my choice of vessel is the issue. It's been heavily fashioned by human hands, making it less malleable to my magical powers. I'll try again on the morrow with something different. I look at my empty dinner bowl and smile to myself. A magical wooden bowl of death might just work and have the fey army running for their lives! However, it can wait, for despite not being drained, I need to sleep.

I lay my sword to one side and yawn, my jaw cracking, exhaustion threatening to overwhelm me.

What's going on?

My head spins, my vision closing in, and as I lie down, I wonder whether my stew has been poisoned. I want to call Dimitar's name, to ask him for help, although what help he can give beyond witnessing my death is beyond me.

The instinct to survive, to protect myself, has me blindly scrabbling for my sword hilt, and as my hand closes over it, the terrible moment passes. There's a loud thumping, and it takes me a moment to realise it's my heart, so I wait for it to calm, then sit up to find Dimitar looking at me impassively.

He nods and smiles in the darkness.

Angry words come to mind over his failure to do anything, but I bite them back. I need to teach him to show concern, so I nod, minus the smile.

I reach over to pick up my discarded bowl, sniff the moist interior, but detect nothing untoward. The odour of the herbs used to spice the previous contents is pleasant to my nostrils ... then I grimace. They must have been used to disguise what was used to drug me! That young cook must be an agent of Nogoth or even Asterz.

This can't go unanswered. I need to send a bloody message.

Dark thoughts enter my mind, my stomach rumbles, and hunger washes over me. Yes. My revenge will serve two purposes, and I salivate in anticipation of tasting her duplicitous blood on my tongue.

Time to climb down and enjoy my just deserts!

Sheathing my sword, I'm about to stand when everything goes black.

I'm vaguely aware of falling backwards, my head hitting the rock, and then ...

***

'Malina.'

My name comes as if from a distance. I'm not ready to open my eyes; I'm too tired.

'Go away,' I mumble.

'Malina.'

This time my name is accompanied by my shoulder receiving a thump from a club or something similar. It doesn't let up, so I open my eyes to be rewarded with a splitting headache.

Dimitar stops prodding me and then nods with a smile.

I'm not sure if nodding will have my head break into a hundred pieces, but I respond with a grimace that Dimitar tries to emulate. I chuckle because if I didn't know better, I'd think he's about to eat me.

As I come to my senses, the noise from below assaults my ears and I note the sun is at least two hours past sunrise. I can't recall the last time I stayed asleep so long.

'Arbinger is asking for you,' Dimitar grates, and I cover my ears.

I feel so fragile, yet the magic in my stomach is dancing around as if impatient to start a good day's work, and even Dimitar appears to have a look of anticipation on his stone brow. Why is everyone so full of enthusiasm but me?

Then I remember.

None of my aches or pains matters any longer, not now I have a mission to complete. A mission of revenge. That cook will rue the day she tried to harm me.

I stand, testing myself. I've felt better, but also a darn sight worse. If anything, I just feel tired, like I need more sleep. The drug I'd been given hasn't had any long-lasting effects, as far as I can tell.

Again my magic wriggles, trying to get my attention, and I realise it must have been responsible for saving my life.

*Thank you.*

My projection is met with the usual happy response, but there's something different, but now isn't the time to wonder what it is.

I yawn, allow myself a good stretch, grab my weapon belt and strap it around my waist. My hands unconsciously go to the sword hilts to familiarise myself with their position, and with a gasp, I snatch my right hand away as I feel ... something strange.

My palm remains unharmed; there's no injury, yet I'd definitely felt something, and my magic is flipping around inside, ecstatic. Then like the clouds parting to reveal the sunshine, the answer becomes clear.

Yet to be doubly sure, looking through my spirit eye, I see the world around me in all its magical glory, and there, at my waist, my sword pulses with trapped magic. This is why I'd passed out last night, not because of a drug or poison, but because I'd visualised emptying a jug, and my magic had complied, leaving me empty and drained.

I'm tired, and the magic within me is recovering its strength, just like I am, whereas the sword at my side resonates with the power from yesterday that I hadn't used.

Now I understand; my gratitude knows no bounds. I mentally fuss my magic, pulling it close, covering it in hugs and kisses, sensing it purr with ecstasy. I haven't felt this excited in a long time, and ... Lotane comes to mind. I wish, I so wish, I could share this moment with him, feel his excitement match mine, and cover him with my affection.

The inability to share my happiness with the one I love makes my heart ache. I need to finish my work here, move on to my next mission, and win him back!

'Malina!'

I look down to see Arbinger below, wave briefly in acknowledgement, then leap from my rocky perch.

The horror on his face shows he thinks I'm going to die splattered against the rocky floor of the pass. He's seen me manifest my magic on the wall before, but not in this fashion. A heartbeat before my plummeting body meets a grisly end, my descent slows, and I land as light as a feather before his astonished face.

'My poor heart,' he huffs. 'It's unlike you not to be up before the rest of us. Are you well?'

His concern appears genuine, and I'm touched.

'Well enough, and a little embarrassed by my lapse,' I laugh, looking around at the organised chaos and nodding in satisfaction. Stone cutters are hard at work, squaring off the giant blocks that Dimitar has brought over. Carpenters prepare scaffolding, and the general labourers are everywhere, moving stone, hauling lumber, or even simply fetching water from the river to keep everyone fresh.

'Two more days, and with the help of your giant friend, the Delnorian fortress will have given us everything we need. Then we get to the fun part; building this monstrosity of a wall,' Arbinger says in a somewhat distracted voice as he looks nervously at his notes. Then, he appears a little fearful.

'I have to ask again. Are you sure you don't want the finished wall to have any gates?'

My hand on his shoulder brings his line of questioning to a halt.

'We've gone over this before; there's no need. Just create the tunnel I asked for.'

'But once it's sealed, there might be no way in, but there'll be no way out either!'

Shaking my head, I laugh to take the sting out of my insistence.

'The risks are simply too great, Arbinger. However strong, no gates will withstand a troll or giant, and if they have enough gargoyles, they could simply fly over and open them from the inside. The answer is a definitive no.'

Arbinger nods in acquiescence.

'As you command.'

'Thank you. Now, As I've overslept, Dimitar needs to make up some lost time.'

Arbinger bows and backs away with his head lowered.

'Come on, Dimitar, you lazy thing, you've got work to do,' I call, watching as the giant head nods. I've got to teach him some new mannerisms, like a wave, but first, I've got other things to do.

My hand rests upon my sword hilt, and I'm excited by the restrained energy beneath my fingertips. It's time to discover whether I can draw upon the power I've stored, but I'm already pretty sure of the answer.

Nogoth's magical strength has grown over a thousand years or more, and should I live so long, I've no doubt mine would expand too. However, if I can store a week's, month's, or half a year's worth of power in this sword, the magic at my command might give us a fighting chance should the worst happen.

Then again, I'm sure he'll give up his plans to conquer Astoria once he sees the wall we'll build, and that being so, when the World Gate opens again in a thousand years, I won't need an army to beat him. By then, I'll have the power to utterly destroy him and his armies on my own.

***

I can tell by Sergeant Dundain's animated walk that something is amiss, let alone by the fact she's on the Astorian side of the ever-growing wall, which now stands as tall as Dimitar.

The border guards take their positions on the far side of the bridge every day. They act as another line of defence and take reports from the mounted scouts when they return. Something untoward must be going on.

'Sergeant,' I call, using my magic to amplify my voice.

A smile splits her face, and I relax. If the enemy were in sight, I can't imagine anything could make her smile.

She snaps a salute, and I tap my forehead with my finger.

'Report, Sergeant.'

'I've been advised that Astorian regular troops are returning, and they've sent a message ahead.'

Dundain pauses, whether to increase the suspense or she's trying to recall the message word for word. Irrespective, I'm too impatient to wait.

'Tell me then!'

Dundain closes her eyes and recites as if she's in a school classroom.

'They'll be passing through after dusk with thousands of refugees and supplies. We're to ensure they have a clear passage and are to let them pass without interference.'

The last bit of the message seems somewhat strange, but I laugh in delight nonetheless, and Dundain's smile grows wider at my good humour. To know that the plan to turn Astoria into a safe haven is coming to fruition fills me with hope for the future.

'Thank you, sergeant. I'll need your guards to maintain a watch on the bridge until the refugees are all through. Can I rely on you to organise that as I need to rest early tonight!'

'Yes, absolutely.'

Dundain salutes and hurries off.

As I watch her pass through the workers swarming like angry ants, my gaze is drawn to the giant figure of Dimitar, who stands like a queen ant amongst them. Everyone is used to his presence now, yet they keep a respectful distance as they should. Dimitar wouldn't even notice if he trod on someone.

He's tireless, and so far, he's negated the need for most of the ropes and pulleys that lie ready further up the pass. For someone so large, he can move with incredible precision, and under Arbinger's guidance, he lifts another heavy rock the size of a horse above the top of the wall.

Arbinger shows utter faith in Dimitar's strength and studies the rock from underneath before directing it to be placed on a readied layer of mortar. Immediately stone masons get to work, feverishly making adjustments with saws, grinders and levers, ensuring the wall is ready for the next delivery.

Soon the wall will be too high for Dimitar to help place these giant jigsaw pieces, yet the progress made with his assistance has been phenomenal. If we were just facing human foes, it would already be suitable for purpose.

I make my way through the throng, entering the coolness of the wall tunnel and feel strangely comforted by the weight of the rock above me.

As I exit into the pass, some scaffolding is erected on the forward face of the wall, and I climb easily, enjoying the exercise, leaping, and swinging, not bothering with the ladders, just pulling myself up by my arms. It brings back memories, some good, some painful.

With a wry smile, I recognise that despite the horror, I miss many things about my time at the Mountain of Souls. I recall learning to use my magic, how I'd experimented and realised I was different from the rest. Now, just like then, it is time to experiment again.

The surface before me is uneven. It hasn't been smoothed nor dressed, and I place my hands against the rocks, appreciating their age and strength as if they're living creatures. Using magic to shape something already in existence has never been as draining as creating something from nothing. As I call for help in binding the giant blocks before me, to merge them into one, to become smooth like polished steel, the cost is minor, a trickle from my reservoir of strength.

I move horizontally across the scaffolding, unbothered by the drop below me or the precarious nature of my perch. My balance is superb, and there's no danger when my magic will lower me softly to the ground.

Like a droplet of water falling into a pond, the rock ripples outward from me in response to my vision, creating a seamless, flawless barrier which offers no chance of a foothold to fingers or claws.

Having traversed the breadth of the wall, I pause, measuring the cost to my strength. Above me, three more levels of scaffolding await, and I need to work along them all to finish the wall as it currently stands. It shouldn't be possible today, as what I've completed has already depleted me by about a third. Unless ...

Time to experiment.

Climbing to the next level is a matter of a simple leap, swing, and pull-up. Forgoing the beckoning ladder is unconscious, my body taking the opportunity to train whenever it's offered.

Touching the hilt of my sword with one hand, I seek to re-energise myself, asking the magic within to return to me, its mother who brought it forth. I sense a willingness to oblige, so I wait a little longer.

The result is nothing.

Disappointment washes over me. Is this how a mother feels when a child rejects them?

Inside, my magic is playful and responsive, like a kitten reminding me that it's my favourite firstborn, whereas that within the sword doesn't seem to have the same level of attachment.

Resting my free hand upon the wall, I visualise myself as a conduit, the magic flowing from the sword through me, to work my will upon the stone. I don't rush, but it's soon apparent that, again, nothing is happening.

Hmmm.

That the magic within the sword is substantial and seeking release is not in doubt, but it appears that having left my body, it can no longer return, at least with what I've tried so far.

I draw the sword, unconsciously shifting my weight on the thin scaffolding poles to compensate, enjoying a gentle thrum through the leather-wrapped grip. I touch the tip of the sword to the undressed stone, then momentarily lose my balance as, without resistance, the blade slides into the stone as if it were water.

My gods!

I release the hilt, staring in awe at the weapon embedded in solid rock. No creature alive, troll, giant, or even Dimitar, could have driven this weapon to its crossguard into the wall. Reaching out, I'm relieved the blade withdraws as easily as it penetrated, although the grating as I do so sets my teeth on edge.

This is incredible.

I touch the flat of the blade against the wall, and the sword makes no imprint, but the blade edge or point, however gently applied, is like a hot knife against butter. Likewise, against a scaffold pole, the blade shaves off a sliver of wood with no resistance.

Imbuing this weapon with power has enhanced its base purposes, to cut, penetrate and kill. If it can do this to solid stone, no troll, giant or ogre, however heavily armoured, will be safe. The question that I wish I knew the answer to is whether Nogoth will still be impervious.

He claims to be invulnerable to all weapons, but something as deadly as this?

I hope this weapon is a thousand times more powerful than it is now by the time I have to find out.

Whilst I want to see what else this weapon is capable of, I can't simply forget my duty in helping to construct the wall. Can the magic within the sword still help, or has its purpose been defined by the vessel it's trapped within?

There's only one way to find out.

Holding the pommel against the stone, I project my vision of a smooth, perfect, polished wall at the sword ... and to my joy, the wall softens before my eyes, shifting even as I watch. Across the scaffolding I move, fulfilling my responsibility, until suddenly, like a goblet being emptied, there's no power left within my sword for it to give.

Once again, it's a regular sword, albeit perfectly crafted. I'm not surprised or disappointed, for I never expected its power to be endless. It gave out as much as I put in.

Now I need to experiment by giving it more power over a number of days to test the limits of what it can hold and what I can do with it.

However, that won't be today. I need to catch up with my work on the wall, and I summon the magic within me again, and it answers as it always does, as I know it always will. Completing the wall takes another half hour, and as I finish, I'm left exhausted but euphoric.

I'm a little less flippant returning to the ground, yet it still takes only a few seconds of swinging and sliding as opposed to minutes traversing the ladders.

When I reach the ground, I step back, shield my eyes, and gaze up at the wall. As long as we have the time to complete it, then this will be enough.

Erratic movement catches my eye. There's a spec high in the sky, yet it doesn't move with the smoothness of a gliding bird, nor hovers motionless like a sin-hawk spying for prey. My blood runs cold as I realise what it is.

A gargoyle.

Even as it heads south, I realise with horror that our plans have been discovered.

What will Nogoth's response be?

An immediate march north with an overwhelming force to reach us before we can complete the wall is likely. In the interim, I'm sure further gargoyles will be sent to harass us from above, impeding our progress.

No!

I'll not allow that to happen. Even if I can't do anything about the gargoyles, whatever losses we suffer will be nothing compared to those that await if this wall isn't finished by the time his main forces arrive.

I'm about to return to deliver the bad news when the hunger I've come to fear washes over me, leaving me faint and dizzy. I've put off feeding for a long time, but with dread, I know I can't any longer. May the gods forgive me because I'm surrounded by allies, and I'll have no choice but to feed on those who trust me to keep them safe.

*You have no choice, Malina. Be strong.*

Yes, I must do what needs dictate.

Then, I tremble, for I recognise that the dread was just a lie because now I've accepted what needs to be done ... I'm full of nothing but excitement.

***

# CHAPTER XIII

The thundering roar of water is painful, reminding me that, however powerful my magic, nothing is more powerful than nature.

I'm humbled as I cross the bridge joining Astoria to Delnor, knowing that the waters below would consume me in a second, continuing oblivious, without pause or issue until the end of days.

I know I should be calling a meeting now that our plans have been discovered, but it can wait a few more hours.

Why did my life have to come to this?

Why couldn't Lotane and I have just run away and stayed hidden through the apocalypse?

Hah. Maybe because I'd slept with Nogoth, thus opening the way for Lotane to join with Asterz.

Momentarily, I'm tempted to cast myself into the torrent below. It would be over so quickly. I'd have no more worries, no heartbreak over Lotane, no confusion over Nogoth, no need to feed on an innocent.

No!

Such a way out is for the weak, and for all my flaws, that's something I'm definitely not.

My boot catches, and I curse at being so distracted.

The once pristine bridge is now scarred, the cobbles fractured, covered in debris from Dimitar's endless trips to the Delnorian fortress, which, as I look up, is now an unpleasant stain on nature's canvas.

Where large buildings and strong walls once stood proud, now only ruins remain like jagged teeth protruding from the earth. It saddens me to witness such a wound in the landscape left untreated, and despite my exhaustion and hunger, something awakens inside.

Sergeant Dundain and a dozen guards are positioned near the end of the bridge, but I walk past them, a faint smile my only acknowledgement of their salutes. Dundain calls something after me, but I can't quite hear her words because a piece of familiar haunting music is beginning to make itself heard in the depths of my mind.

My breathing quickens, and my weapon belt must be too tight because my fingers desperately fumble with the buckle, and it drops away, leaving me unhindered.

Voices, as pure as a mountain stream and as deep as the ocean, call to me in a symphony. They rise and fall like the tide, getting progressively louder, and my heart and body respond.

From one step to the next, I'm dancing.

In the recesses of my mind, I know it's foolish, for there's no doubt that the people here question my heritage due to my skin, hair and eyes, but I've no choice but to dance now, to heal the land when it's within my power to do something about it.

I spin and twirl, my arms and feet sweeping in arcs, and I can see the gold of life magic trailing behind, settling on the ground, reaching through the corruption of human influence to find the seeds of nature, long buried, awaiting their chance.

Grasses spring forth, and saplings push through foundations, breaking free of their imprisonment in frantic explosions of dust and rubble. The fortifications are expansive, and I continue dancing back and forth, leaving no part untouched. By the time the music fades, leaving me standing near the bridge, the sun is approaching the horizon; the day has passed without me even being aware.

I turn slowly, long grasses tickling my fingertips, a sense of fulfilment I'd never experienced before in my entire life pulsing within. I've taken so many lives, ended so many dreams, and revelled in my strength and victories. However, now I recognise true power; to create life where there was none before.

My soul, which I know is dark, has been momentarily cleansed by my actions, and I don't want to return to the wall just yet. In my current state of mind, the temptation to bring it crashing down and replace it with thousands of flowers will be too hard to resist.

Nor do I want to face my returning hunger.

Instead, I follow the riverbank north, exhaustion returning with every step.

Not far ahead, a lush patch of grass where some saplings have created a small copse on the river bank looks enticing. A few weeks ago, a bolt thrower had been positioned there, ready to bring death to any Astorians who crossed the bridge with conquest in their hearts.

Reaching this oasis, I sit down, the only remnants of the siege engine's platform I can find are small pieces of gravel barely noticeable under the blanket of green stems.

Why does humankind destroy the environment, spreading like a disease across the land, instead of finding a symbiotic way to survive? Is Nogoth so wrong to come here and remove us, like a surgeon removing a gangrenous limb?

Violet eyes come to mind, and I recall his velvety tones, soft and seductive.

'Malina.'

I'm shocked from my musing by Dundain's voice and that I'd let my defences drop. Never should anyone be able to approach me without detection, and I berate myself for such a lapse.

The sergeant stands respectfully a few steps away, holding my weapon belt, eyes wide, resembling a started deer, unsure whether to run or approach.

Dismissive words come to my lips, but I swallow them down.

She's a good woman, and in the Astorian military, I fear that might be somewhat unusual.

As I pat the grass next to me, her face is transformed by a bright smile like the rising sun. I reach out to take the weapon belt, and she shyly gives it to me, her fingertips brushing mine as if by accident.

My stomach rumbles.

'The others who saw what you did are unhappy and not a little afraid. But I said to them; if they're alright with you making a stone giant, then a few flowers shouldn't scare them!' She laughs and pushes her fingers through her short hair.

I sigh in resignation.

In my youth, the other children mocked or hated me, and it was unfair, the cruelty of orphaned children in a harsh world. Now in adulthood, people still hate or fear me, yet now I've only myself to blame.

I'm a trained assassin whose reputation has spread across every kingdom, and it doesn't matter what I do to try and redeem myself; death always follows.

'Are you scared of me?'

For some reason, it matters what Dundain thinks.

'Oh, no. What you did was beautiful.'

There's a pause, and Dundain drops her gaze.

'What you are is beautiful too,' she whispers. 'Your eyes and skin give you such an exotic and mystical look.'

Her hand reaches out to take mine.

I can sense her trembling, but it's not her fear of me but of rejection. She's a strange-looking woman, somewhat tall and gangly. There's something disproportionate about her, and I suspect she's been a stranger to genuine affection for much of her life. Being in the border guard can't have helped either, as it would have seriously restricted her romantic options. Being in the lowliest unit in the military meant most other soldiers would have looked down on her, yet neither could she find a relationship with a civilian either.

There's no thrill from her touch; I'm not attracted to her, but my stomach rumbles and that irresistible desire to feed washes over me, and I tremble too.

'You don't need to be afraid of me,' Dundain murmurs, leaning in, finding strength from what she believes to be my vulnerability.

The desire to turn and sink my teeth into her neck, to taste her sweet life, makes my head swim. I recall the girl at the ogre camp. I hadn't killed her even though she'd died, but if I feed on Dundain, she'll know my darkest secret leaving me vulnerable if I leave her alive.

Memories of the Saer Tel, of how they exchanged pleasure for pain, run through my head. A symbiotic relationship where both parties benefit.

Dundain's head rests on my shoulder, and I can detect her heart pounding like galloping hooves.

She'd probably be happy sitting like this, enjoying the moment, hoping in her heart that it leads to something more than rejection.

I turn to her, and watch fear leap up like a flame.

'Dundain. There's something I have to tell you.'

'I know,' she says, interrupting, panicked at losing something she hasn't even found yet. 'Your position far exceeds mine, but I sense a need in you that matches my own. And I can keep a secret, of that, I promise.'

There's a desperation about her. I pity this woman that fate has led her to me and not to someone who can actually love her. I shake my head, trying a final time to resist my urges. I'm not in Nogoth's valley, where our relationship will go unremarked. People will be horrified if they find out, and where that could lead doesn't take much imagination.

'My desires aren't what you might expect.'

'I'm willing to give you anything,' she gasps, her lips parted.

The pulse in her neck mesmerises me, and I gulp back the rising tide of hunger. I can't hold it back much longer, my will to resist crumbling.

'Then you will keep everything that happens between us a secret. You will do as I ask, without question or hesitation, and in exchange, you will feel loved and know happiness like never before.'

I take a moment to look through my spirit eye to ensure my magic hadn't failed, like when I tried to bind the ogre medic and am relieved to find us bound.

Her tears of joy shine in the dying light as I lean in for a kiss.

She will keep our secret and give me everything I need whenever I need it. This is my first pairing as a Saer Tel. Yet as my fingers tug at her clothing, I realise that having used blood magic to secure her service, I've become more like Nogoth than I care to admit.

***

'My people are already working twelve-hour days. It's too dangerous to ask them for more. Mistakes in construction due to tiredness lead to serious injury or death!'

Arbinger stands, hands on his hips, jaw jutting forward, doing his best to stand up for the well-being of his engineers and labourers.

The heat of an angry flush rises but I quell the desire to lash out. Arbinger is overall a good man and just struggles to give credence to the nightmarish stories I've told about Nogoth's fey. Sadly, people only seem to believe when they're finally being eaten alive.

Yet my frustration is growing. I've allowed him way more freedom to argue than I would otherwise, but if I allow that to continue, the five scouts awaiting my address will not respect my authority as they otherwise might.

Grabbing his arm, I pull Arbinger from under the shade of the canvas command tent and point up at the sky. Five distant gargoyles flutter, barely seen, too few and distant to be an immediate threat.

'I don't think you understand the gravity of the situation, Arbinger,' I growl. 'Once Nogoth knows of our plans, we can expect him to dispatch a ground force to overrun us before we complete the wall. In the interim, we might soon have five hundred gargoyles overhead instead of just five. When they start raining javelins down, those who die from accidents will be in the minority! If we lose ten, fifty, a hundred workers or more to complete things faster, it's a price we'll have to pay.'

I lead Arbinger back inside, hoping my point has been made.

'You mean they'll have to pay!' Arbinger growls.

'Yes, that's right!' I hiss, venting. 'They will die, and I won't lose any sleep about it, and neither should you! Why? Because they'll be dying a hero's death for Astoria, and it'll be the closest any stinking civilian will ever get to achieving honour!'

Arbinger's tanned face turns pale as he blanches from my fury.

'As of now, everyone will work a seventeen-hour day,' I continue, my voice rising. 'How you organise the shifts is down to you, but if anyone shirks their duty, they'll receive fifty lashes. Those who knew of it, but didn't report it, will receive the same. There'll be no return to work or Astoria for the guilty, because once that punishment is done, they'll be cast into the River of Tears!'

The scouts nod their approval.

'You, you can't do this ...' Arbinger stutters.

My fist crashes onto the table, shutting him down.

'I can, and I will. This is bigger than any of us, Arbinger! If we fail here because we're afraid of blood, sweat and tears, the world as you know it, ends. Everyone you know will die, and I mean everyone. You're a man of maths, so work it out. Should we lose a few hundred or a few hundred thousand?'

Turning away from the engineer, I note Dundain swaying slightly behind the scouts. Her face looks a little pale despite her summer tan.

'Sergeant!' I snap.

Her eyes focus, and whilst sympathetic, I can't afford it to show.

Your guards are to follow suit with extended shifts. Day and night, I want a fully armoured presence on the wall and bridge. Ensure your guards carry shields at all times. If the gargoyles return in force, those shields will be invaluable.

She salutes, a hint of a smile playing at the corners of her mouth. I don't return it.

The scouts have been standing to attention this whole time, and I hand a written note to the first, a short man who has disproportionately broad shoulders from drawing a bow his entire life.

'Ride to Ast and see that Queen Asterz receives this immediately. In summary, it's a demand for archers to protect the workforce from direct attack and reinforce the pass. You've seen the gargoyles, so I want your words to add weight to mine. Any questions?'

The scout shakes his head.

'Go now and ride fast!'

Turning to the others, I hold their gaze firmly.

'Till now, secrecy has been our best defence, but with our plans discovered, that time is past. As with the workers, no cost is high enough to keep this project from completion. We need early warnings of any enemy forces Nogoth sends our way. Organise as you will, but I want your scouts up to four days' ride from here. As before, kill any fey you come across unless their force is superior to yours, and if it is, keep eyes on them at all times and report back to me. Questions?'

Silence.

These are tough men and women, competent at their job and, despite the danger, revel in being able to ride across Delnorian lands.

'Blood, sweat and tears. We must all give that, for nothing less will be enough. Now go!'

As the scouts leave, I turn my attention back to Arbinger. He's sitting down, hunched over, a quill flashing in his hand. I'm about to say something to soften my earlier words when he pauses with a sigh, looks up and gives me a half smile.

'You're right, of course,' he says, shrugging. 'I lost myself in the challenge of this project and forgot the bigger picture. I know almost all the engineers and labourers personally, having worked with them for more years than I care to remember. But I know they'll rise to the challenge and do everything they can to ensure their families stay safe. Leave it to me.'

'Thank you, Arbinger. I knew I could count on you.'

'Hah. Well, I'll be relying on that stone friend of yours to work even harder, that's for sure. He'll have to shoulder the burden of the most dangerous work.'

'I'll be shouldering it with him, Arbinger. I'll lead by example.'

I extend my hand, and he grips my forearm. Without his expertise, this project could never hope to succeed.

'You know, you had me worried for a moment earlier. At least until I realised that stuff about the flogging and drowning was a bluff to impress the scouts,' Arbinger laughs.

I squeeze his arm harder, pulling him in close, my mouth close to his ear.

'Just ensure that threat is passed on to everyone. Oh, and never call my bluff, Arbinger. Please remember that. It won't end well.'

The horror in his eyes brings me no satisfaction as I step away.

An old mantra comes to mind, and it couldn't be more fitting.

Obey to live.

***

The voices of the joking Astorian cavalry seem utterly at odds with the misery of the refugees they're escorting. The sun has long since set, yet as they pass, there's no chance of sleep for the exhausted labourers who've been working on the wall.

Not that I need sleep, because I'm energised and ready to take on the world. Dundain, on the other hand, is probably the only one who is oblivious to this river of misery, for she hasn't stirred since collapsing onto her bedroll.

The rumble and bump of laden wagons over the uneven rock of the pass, the flickering fire of a hundred torches, and the sobbing and wailing, all magnified and never-ending, have me wondering whether the paths to hell for condemned souls are any different.

The progress of the column is painfully slow. Many of the refugees are wounded, but very few appear to have been given medical attention. None of the wagons are pulled by livestock, but instead of the Astorian cavalry using their horses to help, the refugees push and pull their meagre belongings and supplies along, step by torturous step.

Such inefficiency galls me, and I single out a rider whose armour is embellished with a colourful sash. Like many of the cavalry, he's carrying a flickering torch to provide light for the sad procession.

'Captain,' I call, striding over to him.

He pulls his horse out from the column in response to my address, and his face wrinkles in confusion. I'm not wearing Astorian armour, and there's no sash of rank, yet at my side are two swords and daggers while my expensive leather gear glistens in the night. I can recognise his internal struggle. First, his heart, which I can see almost as plain as day, pumps faster, sending blood surging around his body; second is his hesitancy. That I'm no Astorian is obvious, yet here I am, bearing arms within Astoria's borders, and I stand before him confident and strong.

'Yes,' he acknowledges slowly. 'I don't see your sign of rank ...'

'That's because people like me don't require it, Captain. I need no badge, symbol or title to wield the power I have,' I say sternly, my face dark beneath my hair. 'All you need to know is that I'm here at the bequest of your queen.'

The captain salutes, sitting straighter in his saddle.

'Why haven't you hitched your horses to the wagons to speed up the travel of this column, Captain? Also, why haven't the wounds of the survivors been treated? How can they assist the war effort if they succumb to infection? We need every hand, be they young or old, weak or strong, for all will play a part in our future!'

The captain looks confused and uncomfortable at my line of questioning.

'We have orders ...'

'From whom?'

'From me!'

I recognise the voice and turn to find Commander Jarval observing comfortably from his saddle, scars glistening in the darkness. He leans forward, crossing his forearms over the pommel. Behind him, a half dozen horse archers have arrows notched. This isn't unusual, and they haven't drawn their strings, but the inherent threat is obvious.

'There's some truth in what you've just told the captain. You have power, both vested in you by our queen and also by the swords you're allowed to carry. However, make no mistake, your authority extends only so far as building this wall requires. You've no authority over the military or our actions. It's only through my largess that you have control over the border guards here. So, to ensure there's no misunderstanding or falling out between us, it's better if you leave my soldiers to do their job while you get on with yours!'

I bristle under his tone, let alone his putting me down in front of both his soldiers and the workers listening behind. Yet who am I to question his authority? I hold no official rank, am a guest in their country, and considering the part I played in killing their old king, I should be grateful for that.

'Captain. Rejoin the column.'

'Yes, Commander!'

I can't let this go without further comment.

'Surely these people have suffered enough at the hands of the fey. You're treating them like prisoners of war, not refugees!'

I'm not sure if it's disdain or amusement on Jarval's face because his expression hardly ever changes, yet I've seen more empathy in the black eyes of a shark. He reins his horse around, giving me his back, but doesn't rejoin the column. It's a calculated slight to show he doesn't find me a threat nor trusts me to obey his orders. However, whilst the first is a sign of strength, the second is a sign of weakness, for if he genuinely believed in his authority, he'd have ridden on in confidence.

Interesting.

Gradually, the workers behind me lose interest, returning to their bedrolls or tents to try and snatch some sleep. It won't be easy. Shutting out sounds of misery is no easy thing, and it pulls at my heart to hear the children's tears.

Hah. Maybe I'm not such a monster after all if I actually care.

Yet, that thought doesn't hold much traction when I can see the blood pumping through their veins and feel a stirring of hunger despite having just fed.

My thoughts turn to Dundain, and guilt washes over me.

She'd been so happy to start that I'd almost felt the same. Her eyes had shone with rapture, and she'd tried her hardest to be a considerate lover, putting my pleasure over hers, not that I'd been so selfish as to leave her unsatisfied. Then, when we'd finished joining and she'd laid back into my embrace, her heart beating happily, I couldn't restrain my hunger anymore.

She'd cried afterwards, and despite the blood magic, I'm sure her heart had broken, albeit for a short time.

I look toward her bedroll, and a part of me wants to go and hold her to make up for the betrayal, but I mustn't.

A harsh voice raised in anger pulls me away from my thoughts, and I glance back to see a soldier using the butt of a spear to chivvy along a slow-moving woman holding a child in her arms. My anger begins to rise, and almost as if he senses it, Jarval turns to look at me.

'It will be a long night, Malina. Perhaps you should get some sleep.'

'Let that woman rest. She can have one of our tents.'

'No.'

'Why not? If that were your wife and child, would you want her beaten with a spear butt?'

Jarval growls but controls himself, yet I can see his heart all the while. Its rhythm doesn't increase, and I realise he's feigning anger. He's in perfect control all the time.

'We move at night and rest during the day. That is how we operate. If I pull that woman and child out, what do you think the rest will do when they see that? Cohesion will fall apart instantly, progress will slow, and those who have remained behind might die due to the delay in our return. I thought you'd know better!'

My anger rises, but not at Jarval. He's right. I should know better. These men are risking themselves to save these people, and it's a race against time.

I nod, then turn away. Yet something still bothers me. It's like an insect bite I can't scratch.

Dimitar looms over me.

'Lift me up, my friend.'

He opens the palm of his hand, and I step in and am effortlessly taken to my perch above. I could have used my magic to help me climb, but I'm almost entirely drained, and I want to pour every remaining drop into my swords before I succumb to asleep.

I need to be ready for Nogoth, and who knows, maybe Jarval as well.

***

Panicked shouts of warning followed by screams have me running for the wall where a group of workers converges.

Arbinger stalks past me.

'That's two today already!' he yells.

There's no accusation within his comment, not now, not when a dozen gargoyles pass over us like the hand of death. Without exception, every worker has a sense of urgency to complete the wall now they've witnessed the enemy first-hand. Screeches and shrieks tear at everyone's nerves, and many a fist is shaken skyward.

Stretcher-bearers push through the crowd.

'Back to work, back to work!' I shout, and my call is taken up by others, and as fast as it gathered, the crowd disperses.

A semblance of order returns for a while, but it's not long before the sound of whinnying horses has me turning in concern toward the tunnel. A dozen scouts ride into the sunlight. That they've been in a fight is evident as they're swathed in bloodied bandages. They're in a sorry state, and four have their hands tied to the pommel of their saddles as they sway unsteadily atop their mounts.

For a moment, silence replaces the cacophony of construction. Everyone stops what they're doing as they take in the sight. Then, like a storm front hitting, the noise swells to a roar as work is resumed at a frenetic pace.

A torn sash identifies the leader.

'Corporal!'

The bearded man raises a weary hand in recognition, then gives a brief order to the unit, who continue up the pass. There's nothing our small healing tent here can do for these men.

I make my way through the stream of workers to the scout's side like a swimmer fighting a heavy current.

'Report.'

The corporal takes a drink from a skin that was hanging from his saddle while I wait impatiently.

'It's like someone kicked a wasp nest out there,' he grates. 'Fey are swarming all over, and my unit has been engaged numerous times before we could break free. They've also come at night and taken some of us. The screams are something I'll never forget ...' The corporal shudders, ashen-faced at the memory before composing himself. 'Anyway, my sergeant thinks they're amassing at Eastnor, readying to launch an attack here and wanted to make sure you were forewarned.'

My heart sinks at the news, but I'm not surprised.

'Thank you, Corporal. Go get those wounds seen to.'

As he urges his mount into a walk, more screeches echo around the pass. I shadow my eyes, noting the gargoyles high above, just out of range of the four hundred archers I've been sent as protection that line the walls of the pass.

From such a height, the gargoyles can't throw their javelins accurately, so instead, they're using something more rudimentary.

'INCOMING!'

The shout is taken up, and Dundain's guards run forward, shields at the ready as work temporarily ceases.

Peering upwards, it's easy to discern the gargoyle that's caused the alarm. Its frantic wingbeats as it labours with a heavy rock clasped to its chest give it away.

Twangs announce two arrows shooting into the sky. It's a disciplined test to ensure the gargoyle doesn't get too low. As expected, the arrows begin to drop just before reaching their target, subsequently clattering against the mountainside.

Then, the rock drops downward, and everyone scatters; except the guards. To their credit, they don't hesitate and swiftly form a wide circle around the impact point, plant their shields and kneel behind them. Three seconds later, the rock hits the ground and fragments hiss through the air, many of which bounce off the ring of hardened wood.

No screams, injuries, or panic, and everyone returns to work moments later.

I shake my head in thanks but also in disbelief. I can't understand why the gargoyles don't just pull rocks off the mountainside and drop them by the hundreds. These solo attacks have yet to cause casualties or damage.

Perhaps the gargoyles don't want the bodies of those they slay to spoil in the heat before they can feast and are waiting for the main force before coordinating. If that happens, it will be something to behold. Trolls and giants charging for the walls, followed by hordes of ogres. Bolt throwers and archers trying to stem the tide while gargoyles swoop down, snatching anyone caught unawares and trying to break into the wall from the rear.

Sometimes I wish my imagination was less vivid.

My hands go to my sword hilts, reassured by the power they're holding.

How soon before Nogoth has an army here? I only wish I had more workers so the construction would go quicker.

Hmmm. If the gargoyles aren't attacking in force yet ...

'Corporal!' I shout, heading over to an archer crouched comfortably on a large rock.

'Yes.'

'I want half of your archers to stow their weapons and stand down. They're to report to Arbinger, the lead engineer for assignment and will assist in whatever capacity he requires.'

'What? No! We aren't common labourers!'

Had I just slaughtered his wife and child in front of him, I doubt the look of horror on his face would have been worse. Damn the Astorian military pride. Had I asked him to fight an ogre bare-handed, he'd likely have done so without hesitation, but ask him to pick up a rock or pull a rope, and he's mutinous.

This insubordination can't go unanswered. Do I make his death fast or slow?

Fast will ensure the corporal doesn't suffer unduly. However, slow will ensure that no one else in his unit questions my unpalatable order and save further bloodshed. Yet slow will also have people label me as evil. Hell, that just reinforces the reputation I already have as the King Slayer.

Slow it is.

At that moment, another scout comes riding through the throng, shouting for people to get out of her way. Like the first, she's looking worse for wear. However, I can detect a different demeanour; a hint of excitement surrounds her.

'HERE,' I shout, waving to catch her attention.

Had the crowd of people allowed, I'm sure she'd have galloped right up to me. Scouts are tough, often required to stay in the field for days or weeks, sometimes behind enemy lines. Skilled in foraging and hunting, they're survivors. Despite the filthy hair and face, the broken fingernails and cracked lips, she's still bright-eyed.

'What news?' I ask as she comes closer.

'Icelandians. We've spotted a column two and a half day's march northwest. They appear in good order. We've encountered small units of fey between them and us, but they've been withdrawing these last days.'

It's apparent her unit hasn't suffered too badly, but more importantly, her report corroborates that of the other scout. Nogoth has been notified of the wall's construction and is reacting, rallying his troops for an attack. Now the race is really on!

The scout looks at me expectantly, her eyes intense, awaiting to be dismissed or given orders.

'You're to keep the Icelandian column safe as your main priority. However, advise your sergeant that it appears the enemy is grouping at Eastnor before launching an attack. If you get eyes on the enemy sallying forth, I want daily updates. Understand?'

I receive a firm nod as acknowledgement.

'May the gods give you wings, Scout. Now go!'

She wheels her horse about as I consider these developments.

However fast our progress with building this wall, it needs to be faster still. Yet the bad news has at least been tempered with some good.

Kralgen and his Icelandians are almost here!

It will be so good to see my old friend.

The corporal of archers stands silently, shifting nervously as I turn toward him.

'Luckily for you, I'm now in a relatively good mood,' I say, lowering my voice. 'So, I'll make this easy for you and give you two options, whereas a moment ago, there was just one. First is that you disobey my direct order again, and I take that arrogant head off your shoulders. The other option is to organise your unit in shifts, and at the end of each day, you'll all be archers again.'

The corporal gulps then licks his lips, face pale with anger, fear or just plain disgust; I don't care.

'What if my unit refuses?'

'Then the River of Tears will welcome them, each and every one. Now, GET TO IT!' I roar, sending the corporal tripping over his feet as he hurries off.

I wonder if Lotane had as much trouble getting the Astorian military to train civilians as I just had getting the military to help them.

Then again, it doesn't matter much anymore. We'd hoped for a year to train an unprecedented force to face Nogoth's army in the event they broke through the wall, but all we'll get are a couple of months.

It won't be anywhere near enough.

Finishing this wall quickly and exploring the limits of my magic are now even more critical.

Screeches from above have me looking up at the gargoyles in consternation. A few minutes ago, there'd been a dozen, but now perhaps over fifty circle overhead.

Will they attack in force before the main fey army arrives? If so, the construction of this wall will become a nightmare. But while they don't, I'll demand every ounce of energy from everyone.

Blood, sweat and tears. Whatever it takes, this wall must get built!

***

Arbinger couldn't appear more enrapt if he gazed upon the Love Goddess herself as he looks up at the wall.

'How much longer before it's complete?' I ask.

Two border guards keep watch beside us, newly fashioned tower shields ready to defend against the gargoyle threat. Yet, the fey attacks are sporadic, ill-timed, ill-aimed, and I can't understand why. Those hideous creatures seem strangely indifferent, circling endlessly on the currents, content to simply remind us of our mortality and impending doom without attempting to deliver it.

Arbinger counts off some fingers, and I bite back a snort of amusement. For someone so incredibly intelligent and a mathematician to boot, it's laughable to witness this. Then Kralgen comes to mind, and I remember judging him as slow-minded for doing the same. He'd repeatedly proved me wrong, and I won't make the same mistake here.

'Hmmm,' he ponders. 'Dimitar is becoming less effective now that the wall is twice his height. We are using pulleys and ropes the old-fashioned way now, so the blocks we're hoisting are perforce smaller. I'd say another six weeks at the outside.'

I nod in appreciation. He's overseen an incredible feat of engineering, and whilst Dimitar and I have helped the speed with which the project has progressed, the skill behind its construction is entirely Arbinger's and his fellow engineers. However, we don't have six weeks.

'You have three weeks, maximum!'

'That's impossible!' Arbinger splutters, eyes bulging.

'You will make it possible. From hereon, work continues both night and day. Every archer, cook, medic or guard not on duty will be made available to you. That's another four hundred pairs of hands.'

'Unskilled hands!' Arbinger exclaims in denial.

'It doesn't take skill to haul on a rope or carry a block of stone. Nogoth's army is marching, so you have three weeks. If the wall isn't complete by the time they arrive, every man, woman and child within Astoria will die. That will be on you unless you make the impossible possible.'

It's a harsh thing to say, utterly unfair, but undeniably true.

Arbinger counts on his fingers again, recalculating in a frenzy.

'Stand aside,' a voice shouts, and we hurry to the north wall of the bridge as the latest in the long line of refugees approach. What horrors they've seen, I can well imagine. They're bloodied and broken, yet they still push or pull their meagre belongings in handcarts or wagons, trying to salvage something from their broken lives.

Arbinger looks up from his hands and surveys the stream of misery with indifference before returning to his counting. I'm surprised. He's a warm man who cares passionately for the well-being of his workers and fellow engineers, but apparently not these desperate souls. Strange.

With a frustrated cry, Arbinger shakes his hands as if trying to cast off the figures he's been calculating.

'I don't know how we'll do it,' he states, eyes wild.

Grasping his forearm, I stand before him so he has nowhere else to look.

'If there's anyone who can find a way, it's you! I believe in you, Arbinger. Now believe in yourself!'

I receive half a dozen frantic nods, which doesn't fill me with hope.

Would using blood magic to give him confidence help our cause?

I toy with the idea but discard it. Making him believe he could take on a gargoyle single-handed and win wouldn't make it happen. No, he needs his mind clear of influence.

With a final squeeze, I release him and step back to survey the refugees again.

The accumulated power within my swords thrums as I lightly grip the hilts. How many more people could I have saved had I ridden with the Astorians instead of helping to build this wall? It's galling to have my hands tied here ... and yet I know that's a lie I tell myself to feel better.

I'm here out of choice. No order or blood magic binds me to this task. It's the understanding that I'm best placed here, where my efforts will save hundreds of thousands, not just an extra handful.

However, perhaps it won't be long until the wall is no longer our best defence. An excited wriggling within has me smiling. I'm not the only one who thinks so.

Two weeks have passed since my latest verbal encounter with Commander Jarval, even though he's constantly present, overseeing the refugee crisis. Since that time, other than ensuring the newly placed rocks of the growing wall are bound and smoothed, I've had no further drain on my magic. So, each night I pour every remaining drop into the swords, exhausting myself.

What could I achieve with the release of such accumulated power? It's almost time to find out. I can't afford to go into battle without understanding more of the capabilities of my weapons. Yet however powerful they'll make me, they won't make me invulnerable like Nogoth. The thought cools my enthusiasm because they won't do any good if I'm dead, unless ...

I draw one of my swords.

'Arbinger.'

His eyes widen in consternation, but he then looks confused as I reverse the weapon and offer him the hilt.

'Do you feel anything when you hold this weapon?'

Arbinger hesitantly reaches out to take it.

'I feel a fraud,' he laughs, bringing it up to examine the blade. 'In truth, I feel happy I chose my craft. I might not have status or honour, but the joy I get from designing and building could never be eclipsed.'

I nod.

'Fine words. If everyone shared that sentiment, we'd have a far happier world. However, that's not quite what I meant. Can you sense any underlying power?'

'Perhaps the power to frighten and intimidate,' Arbinger growls, his face twisting into a snarl as he shakes the sword.

'Hah, that's not quite what I meant either. I want you to press the blade edge against the stonework,' I say, indicating the bridge wall, 'and visualise cutting through it.'

It's Arbinger's turn to laugh.

'For what purpose? Shall I visualise the wall across the pass being finished at the same time?'

'Just focus on the sword, please.'

The look Arbinger gives me says more than words; he thinks I'm a little crazy.

But if he can summon the magic, there's nothing to stop me from arming any number of soldiers with magical weapons. How powerful would someone like Kralgen be if he wielded one?

Sadly, despite the concentration on Arbinger's face, the sword remains a sword, and the stonework escapes unscathed.

He passes my weapon back.

'What were you hoping for?' he asks, looking somewhat bemused.

'Perhaps another way to win this war.' I smile while sheathing my blade, unwilling to give him further detail.

We lean back against the wall in companionable silence, watching the steady flow of Rolantrian and Surian survivors stumble past, escorted as ever by Astorian cavalry.

'Every child should see this scene when they dream of growing up to be a warrior, because guaranteed, far less would follow the path if they did,' I say.

With a noncommittal grunt, Arbinger pushes himself away from the wall.

'I've got work to do,' he grumbles. 'I will be seeing you later, for sure.'

I watch him briefly as he walks back toward the wall, kept apart from the desperate souls by the Astorian horsemen. I'm not overly surprised by Arbinger's inability to wield what is essentially my magic. I won't let my hopes get too high that Kralgen or Lotane can either.

Kralgen.

His Icelandians have begun to arrive. There are no young men or women in their prime, just children and youths or the elderly. A whole generation has been wiped out by Nogoth outside of High Delnor, and these are what's left. Nonetheless, they're not bowed or broken. There's a fire in their eyes and determination in their hearts; that much is obvious.

Jarval must have given orders to keep the Icelandians apart from the other refugees, for they're being made to wait, and it's a mistake. Their strength could lift the spirits and straighten the backbones of the other lost souls.

I look at the gathering of furred and feathered Icelandians, yet there's no sign of my old friend. However, I'm not worried, just impatient. He'd be heading the column if there was a fight, yet he's staying with the slowest and most vulnerable at the rear. His transformation from a sullen bully to a caring noble king has been nothing short of astonishing.

Would Lotane make as good a king if he went through with his marriage to Asterz?

He's always at the back of my mind, more recently when I've been joining with Dundain. There's no faking my release with another woman, so I bring Lotane to mind to help me find it, him, or to my shame, Nogoth.

I might hate the Fey King and want to kill him, but there's no denying the memory of his skill in bed arouses me to this very day.

But no, I must think about Lotane. He is where my future lies.

A few more weeks, and with this wall nearing completion, I'll head to Ast and do everything in my power to win his heart back from Asterz before the Fey King arrives.

My hand absently caresses my sword hilts, the power thrumming within them, and for a moment, I dream of cutting Asterz's head from her shoulders.

No! I'll win Lotane's heart without bloodshed, or he'll never forgive me and be lost to me forever.

Dundain approaches, leaving her fellow guards at the end of the bridge.

'Do you want to go for a walk?' she asks.

There's both excitement and trepidation mixed in her eyes.

Will she hate me one day like I hate Nogoth but fantasise about me in the same breath?

My stomach rumbles. I'm not even hungry, but the lure of her sweet blood means I'm happy to share my body for a small taste. Who will I think of today? Green and blue, or violet eyes?

Hmmm.

I smile as a wicked thought comes to mind.

I'll think of them both together.

***

# CHAPTER XIV

I move soundlessly, my footsteps naturally muffled by the old bed of pine needles beneath my feet. Yet, despite this cushion, I test every step, ensuring no hidden twigs will snap to give away my position. My black hunting leathers help me blend seamlessly into this shadow realm; for the most part, I move unnoticed.

It's early morning, and the forest is quiet, as the night-time predators embrace sleep and have yet to be replaced by their daytime equivalents. It doesn't matter that the sun hasn't cleared the horizon, and the shadows are as dark as my soul, for everything is clear as day.

Had I walked these very paths bathed in sunlight, the multitude of animals perched high in the trees or standing frozen at my approach would have been invisible to my eyes. However, against the backdrop of greys, their warm bodies glow red, beacons shining brighter than the fading stars barely visible through the canopy above.

Trails sweep across the canvas of the forest floor, and I kneel down to inspect the signs of a struggle. Yes, a fight occurred here, to the death, and as I carefully lift a leaf to my nostrils, the scent of blood teases at my senses.

I stand, continuing my search.

Many are the signs of combat and death, yet none bother me.

Only animals have met their end at the claws, fangs, and teeth of other animals.

A while later, rays of light filter through the canopy, creating golden shafts that teem with insects vying for space, looking to warm themselves. Their frantic dance absorbs me momentarily. The sun above might not be magic, but it seems the gold always represents life.

Whilst I might not have discovered any signs of the fey, it doesn't mean this forest is entirely safe. Bears and wolves might hunt here, yet I've seen no sign of them, and should they happen upon me, they might soon discover a new animal at the top of the food chain.

I'm only two hours from the bridge. My sense of duty won't let me wander far, yet I'm distant enough not to be overseen. The Astorian scouts are days away, and I passed the Icelandian refugee column an hour back, so I doubt they'll stumble on me. More importantly, I don't want the gargoyles to oversee what I'm doing and spoil any surprises I might have for Nogoth.

My footsteps take me uphill.

Whilst the River of Tears to my east is overshadowed by the mighty Astorian mountains, this side of the border has its own peaks. The gradient I'm climbing becomes steeper, and the trees begin to thin out as the ground becomes rockier.

Yes. This is what I wanted to find.

Ahead, through the trunks, like a small theatre, a rocky bowl comes into view. Surrounded on three sides by craggy slopes, the ground is mostly level, with only a few optimistic saplings trying to find purchase in the sparse soil and some scattered boulders of different sizes.

I run and leap over a dozen rocky pools for fun, landing lightly, sometimes rolling after a particularly long jump, then look around a final time. I imagine a thousand people watching, measuring my entrance, and now awaiting my main performance. The question is, will I give them anything worthwhile to see?

The hilt of my right sword fits perfectly in my hand, and the blade whispers against the scabbard like the souls of the dead as I draw it free. I hold the blade out to catch the morning light, admiring the craftsmanship. I doubt the master blacksmith who had forged this weapon had ever considered their work could be so enhanced.

I'm on a fairly level piece of rock, maybe eight paces square, and I position myself in the centre. I study the ground around me, noting the texture, the undulating surface, and some loose scree, imprinting the most minute detail in my mind. Closing my eyes, I allow my shoulders to relax, the sword to drop to my side and imagine a half dozen opponents slowly closing in, weapons at the ready.

From one heartbeat to the next, I turn and roll, my sword flickering out to take a woman's leg away from above the knee before I rise to my feet, my sword sweeping to high guard. I'm now between two warriors at the perimeter of the circle. Before my neighbouring opponents recover, I'm thrusting and cutting, my second sword unsheathed to join the first as I move like a flame, flickering from one to the next, leaving them scattered in my path.

I open my eyes to find myself back where I started, my breathing slightly elevated, the invisible throng baying my name. I'd not miss-stepped or lost balance once, and a sense of satisfaction washes over me; Lystra would have approved.

Despite this martial display, I'm not here to practice my form and balance. It's time to test the limits of my weapons.

Returning my left sword to its sheath, I take the right and push the point into the rock at my feet. With barely a hint of resistance, it glides into the stone and satisfied, I withdraw the blade. I hold the sword above the ground and drop it, only for fragments of stone to splinter away from the point before the sword topples with a clang.

It needs to be wielded by me for the magic to come alive.

Recovering my sword, I heft it again. Time to up the ante a little, but how?

I stride over to a tall rock. It stands thrice my height and width and might even give Dimitar pause in destroying it. My sword blurs in a figure of eight as I move around the rock, and I return to my starting position just as it collapses in a shower of debris. I twist away, shielding my face from the fragments.

Ye Gods!

I sense the power hasn't diminished. In my hands, this sword can literally slay giants.

Next, I push the sword into the ground and visualise a smooth channel, watching one ripple into existence as if an invisible sculptor was working with clay. Water begins to trickle in from an adjacent pool in the same way my mind is beginning to fill with the knowledge of what I can do.

The magic within me is sentient and fulfils my wishes using its own methods. Despite its strength, it can be subtle, like an artist's hand. However, despite being edged, the sword is more of a blunt instrument, simply following my instructions.

With both sources, my ability to utilise the elements is limited by my imagination and the power required to do so. Still, with the swords able to accumulate so much, I can now think much bigger.

Could I open a chasm to swallow some of Nogoth's army up? The rock and earth I'd need to shift would be the equivalent of a mountain. There's no way I have the time to store the amount of magic required, not for another thousand years. However, if that's what it takes ...

Yet we need to survive the short term, so I need to think of something else.

I've used the power of wind before. Yes, that might do it.

Below me is the forest I've just traversed. It's a place of beauty, and I'm suddenly hesitant to bring destruction down upon it. Yet, it's easy to visualise those thousands of trees as giants, trolls and ogres.

'I'm sorry,' I whisper, knowing that every insect and animal will soon have its world turned upside down. Yet I have to know.

Lifting the sword, I point it toward the forest and channel my thoughts, imagining the howl of storm winds like no other, whipping away from me in a tempest.

*Now.*

I stagger backwards, surprised by the ferocity unleashed directly from the blade tip, watching open-mouthed as small rocks are picked up and carried through the air as if thrown from a catapult. The first three rows of trees are felled instantly, and the ones directly behind thrash as if shaken by an invisible hand. Yet, as the distance increases, like the ripples from a stone dropped into a pool, the force diminishes, and even as I recognise this, the wind fades to nothing.

My sword has been completely drained of magic.

Maybe a hundred trees have been uprooted, whilst hundreds more are missing limbs. Flocks of birds swirl in the air, screeching in indignation and fear, their recriminations assaulting my ears. Guilt washes over me having caused such destruction, simply to understand that whilst powerful, this isn't a viable option.

I curse.

The further the distance, the less effect my magic has, which would also apply to opening a chasm in the ground. I should already have known that would be the case.

What next?

I exchange one sword for the other, contemplating. There's no sea here, no tidal waves to wash away Nogoth's armies, and unless I can convince them to enjoy the sun on a beach, it's unlikely to ever happen.

Could I summon enough rain to wash them away? Unlikely, unless they were in a narrow pass.

Hmmm. That's food for thought. If they break through the wall, I could shower boulders down upon them, although it wouldn't be long before gargoyles or wolfen got to me.

I have to forget Nogoth's army and make this simply about him.

If only the gods could just strike him down for me.

A large rock stands about twenty paces back down the slope, untouched by the wind. What if that were Nogoth?

I lift the sword, thinking how the gods would exact justice, and then as I direct my thoughts, I'm flung from my feet, ears ringing, lights flashing in front of my eyes.

Sitting up, I rub my eyes in disbelief, the imprint of jagged lightning lancing from the now empty blade emblazoned on my vision. Of the rock, there's no sign, and the ground where it stood is scorched and smoking.

Damn! I can control the power of the gods.

This will surely put Nogoth's immortality to the test!

***

Dimitar stands with hands outstretched above his head as a heavy bolt thrower is slowly winched from his palms. It's hard not to hold my breath, despite three other mighty war machines having already been bought safely to the top of the wall without incident. Arbinger is truly a master of his craft. Lines of ropes held by hundreds of men spread out from the wall like a spider web, some to stabilise, others to lift.

Four more machines wait their turn, and once these are in place, the wall can move toward completion with the addition of a roof to keep Nogoth's gargoyles at bay.

But something is already keeping them at bay. A hundred or more fill the skies, urging us by their presence to greater speed. Their rocks have been responsible for maybe twenty deaths, but overall, they've been ineffective in interfering with our work.

Dimitar has continued to grow in size, and I've concluded he keeps them at bay. After all, he can throw rocks further than the archers can shoot their arrows. He'd missed the gargoyles by a hairsbreadth both times I'd ordered him to try bring some down. Unfortunately, the falling rocks he throws are as hazardous as the ones the gargoyles drop, so I'd ordered him to cease.

Labourers are everywhere, forming human chains, passing stone blocks between them into the narrow stairwells at the bottom of the wall that lead to the top, just as they had at Iron Hold. We've lost over eighty workers to accidents. It's a terrible toll, but nothing compared to what we might have suffered had the gods frowned upon us.

I'm impatient for the wall to be finished, so I can hurry to Ast for my next mission.

Dust swirls under the onslaught of a sudden breeze, and a faint image of a lightning bolt hangs before me when I blink. Three days have passed since my experiment with the swords, and I haven't told anyone what I'm able to do; sometimes, it's best to keep such things close to my chest.

However, I'm excited to share what I've achieved with Lotane and Kralgen, and I'm impatient to find out if they'll be able to wield my magic swords.

The sound of hooves and rolling wagons fills the air, and I sigh, standing aside as Astorian cavalry leads the latest band of refugees through. In the beginning, I was moved by their misery, and now, along with everyone else stationed here, I barely even notice them. There are fewer survivors of late, and this rag-tag group made up of young women and children is no exception. By now, the remains of much of the Surian and Rolantrian people have taken refuge in Astoria.

What surprises me is how I've seen no sign of any Surian or Rolantrian nobility; then again, if they're like Kralgen, they'll be the last to leave, just like a captain with a sinking ship.

Ouch.

I swat at a fly that's taken the opportunity to enjoy the taste of my blood. They're everywhere, buzzing incessantly, biting whenever they're given a chance. Initially, I'd summon a gentle wind to blow them away. When that failed, I turned them into little fiery blobs. Now, I just wave at them in frustration. I might have won every battle I fought with them, but they've won this war.

If only there was a king fly I could slay, and as their new queen, they'd leave me alone forever.

I beat a strategic withdrawal into the wall tunnel, which offers some respite from the onslaught. It's crowded with horses and wagons, and I consider turning back. Yet I push on, driven by an urge to see Dundain or, if I'm honest, an urge to feed. My back is against the smooth wall as I sidle along the crowded passage. I've become a little like Nestor, allowing no flaw to exist here. I mentally embrace my magic for helping me accomplish this incredible feat and enjoy its happy response.

The incredible solidity and weight of all this rock around me fill me with hope and confidence. No army will be able to overcome this wall without suffering horrifically.

Despite the dusty ground, I leave barely a trace of my passing as I silently make my way toward the circle of light ahead and the pass leading to the bridge beyond. I can see a group of Icelandians awaiting their turn to pass through, and my spirit soars as I spy a familiar figure looming above those around him.

'Kralgen!'

I whoop with glee and relief, pushing forward at speed, shouting his name.

As I clear the tunnel, I cover the last two dozen paces at a run, and as Kralgen turns at the sound of my voice, I launch myself into his arms to receive a huge bear hug.

'I've missed you. What took you so long?' I laugh as he lets me go after a final squeeze. Those around step back, smiling, giving us a little space, even if not privacy.

'What can I say but that it's a long march from Icelandia, especially for our eldest and youngest.' He smiles, teeth gleaming white against his thick black beard and sun-browned skin. 'I can see you've been busy. What you've achieved here gave me hope for my people when I first saw it.'

Then his eyes turn serious, and he lowers his voice to something approaching a whisper, which for Kralgen is no mean feat.

'We need to talk.'

There's no missing his meaning; something is bothering him.

'Let's cross the bridge!' I suggest.

He takes a few moments to embrace some of the Icelandians and grips the forearms of others, and I hear him asking them to wait. Shortly after, the two of us are walking down the pass.

'Are we safe?' Kralgen asks meaningfully, looking back toward the wall.

'For now, yes. I don't know what Nogoth's orders are, or even if the gargoyles are obeying them, but there have only been ineffective attacks since they arrived.'

Kralgen shakes his head, rolling his eyes.

'That's not what I'm talking about, King Slayer. When did you stop seeing the snakes at your feet for the gargoyles in the sky?'

We briefly stand aside as a larger group of Astorian cavalry pass by.

Dundain and her guards are up ahead, and we walk in silence toward them across the bridge. We'd have to shout to be heard above the roar, and Kralgen obviously wants some privacy. I'm also impatient to share my secret with him about the swords hanging at my waist.

Dundain's smile is wider than the river as we approach, and I note the guards with her exchange knowing looks behind her back.

Damn. Our relationship hasn't gone unnoticed, but as long as the guards just think it's sexual, I can live with that. What annoys me more is that several of them make the sign to avert evil as I approach. Why do they never make those signs for the gargoyles, just me?

I wave in passing as we continue, appearing indifferent to their subtle slights before turning northward.

'What happened here? This reminds me of the magic the Saer Tel worked.'

Kralgen looks across at me as we walk through soft grass and amongst the saplings thriving over the ruins of the Delnorian fortress.

'It was me. I brought about the change.'

Kralgen smiles, shaking his head in wonder.

'You are always full of surprises, King Slayer. However, the biggest one is you seem oblivious to what's happening under your nose. Tell me you see what's going on.'

What is he talking about?

My silence has Kralgen shaking his huge mane again, but this time in mock despair.

'The Astorians,' he prompts.

'I know. They're led by a commander called Jarval. I tried to get them to help the refugees, but he's made it clear I'm not to interfere.'

'It's more than that, much more. Tell me what you see,' he demands, pointing at a bedraggled group of Surians and Rolantrians.

I bite back my frustration. Kralgen could just tell me what's on his mind, but the best way to learn is self-discovery, so ...

'Their morale is broken. Some bear signs of injury, indicating they've fought, whereas all bear signs of despair. They've obviously suffered terribly, and it's mostly women and children making up the refugees. I conclude most men folk died fighting the fey to protect them.'

'I'd agree with you, but for two things. First, Nogoth hadn't planned to invade Rolantria or Suria until after his conquest of Hastia and Tars ...'

'We know he misleads and lies ...'

Kralgen raises his hand.

'Second, even if Nogoth fed you lies, and his fey are causing havoc everywhere, they wouldn't selectively let only women and children live. More damning is that none of the Astorians bear signs of combat, only scratches, despite supposedly riding through occupied lands and liberating these people.

'No, Malina. I'm positive these Surians and Rolantrians aren't refugees; they're prisoners of war!'

***

As we return to the bridge, I'm furious. I'd felt something was amiss, yet had been so engrossed with the wall and my magic that I'd ignored my instincts and let Jarval overrule my concerns when I voiced them.

How could I be so stupid?

The scouts I'd sent out had suffered terribly and sported wounds inflicted by swords, axes, claws and fangs. Those escorting the Surians and Rolantrians bore little more than scratches from fingernails.

Never again.

If Kralgen is correct, and I fear he is, we might have jumped straight from Nogoth's cooking pot into Asterz's cauldron.

'We have to confirm your suspicions. There must be no mistake,' I say, despite knowing the answer already.

Kralgen grunts in acknowledgement.

'The Astorians never let anyone near these wretches to help, let alone speak with them, but that's the only way to be absolutely sure.'

'I'll be the distraction,' Kralgen offers.

We've worked and fought together so often that nothing further needs saying.

'Dundain. Take the guards to the other side of the bridge immediately.' I order as we stride up to her.

There's no hesitation, just immediate, unquestioning action.

'Squad! You heard the order, reform on the other side at the double.'

With a flashing smile, she follows her unit.

'Is she helping you forget Lotane or replacing him?' Kralgen asks with a wink.

Damn his perception, yet without it, I'd still be blind.

'Neither. Now, let's do this.'

Around fifty Astorians are escorting three times the number of Surians and Rolantrians onto the bridge. It's so plain to see what's going on now that I'm aware of it. Yet I have to hear it to dispel any lingering doubts.

Kralgen bides his time, watching as the column moves by; then, just before the last dozen step onto the bridge, he darts forward between two horses toward a woman carrying a child.

'HERE. Let me help,' Kralgen calls, causing the nearest Astorian cavalry to knee their horses forward to intercept.

A mere thought causes dust and gravel to whip up from the bridge. Riders curse and shield their eyes from the stinging, blinding onslaught, and while temporary chaos reigns, I grab a tear-streaked and dishevelled woman by the wrist and yank her off the bridge, pulling her north.

I keep up the dust storm for a few more seconds, then as we reach the long grasses, I throw her roughly to the ground and leap on top, covering her mouth with my hand.

'Stay quiet,' I growl, peering through the grass.

The Astorians are shouting and brandishing their weapons as Kralgen amenably backs away, hands raised, a disarming smile on his face.

'Well done,' I whisper as the column continues, unaware of their loss. Kralgen doesn't even look in my direction but ambles after them before rejoining the group of Icelandians I'd first spotted him with.

The woman underneath me hasn't moved at all. I sit up, carefully withdrawing my hand. Her eyes are screwed shut, tears forcing their way out, and she's biting her lip so hard a bead of blood runs down her cheek.

My hunger soars, threatening to overwhelm me, but the disgust that follows my reaction pushes it firmly away. No, I'll not feed on the innocent, especially one as mistreated as this.

'Don't be afraid.'

My words are softly spoken, and as I sit back, her shaking hands tug at the fastenings of her filthy shirt.

For a moment, I'm confused, then I realise what she's doing and why she's so afraid.

I curse myself.

Taking her hands, I pull them softly away.

'Don't be afraid,' I repeat. 'I'm not Astorian, and I'm not here to ... cause you harm.' I can't even say *rape*, yet I'm sure this poor soul has endured it.

I wait patiently, not forcing the issue, until dark brown eyes appear, drowning beneath a pool of tears as she finally opens her eyes.

'W-what do you want from m-me?' she stammers,

'I want to hear the truth,' I say softly, as my blood magic binds us. 'Start at the beginning, and when you've finished, you'll feel better and forget all the terrible things you've suffered.'

The woman takes a deep breath and nods.

'My name is Yaster, and I'm from a small village in northern Suria ...'

***

I watch as Yaster is given furs and feathers by Kralgen's Icelandians, who have followed their king back across the bridge. The horror and loathing that had leached from her every pore as she'd told her tale are now absent, although a gauntness around her eyes remains.

'What did you learn?' Kralgen asks gruffly.

'You already saw the truth of it,' I sigh. 'The Astorian army has raped and pillaged its way across Suria and, no doubt, across Rolantria. Noble families and village men were slaughtered, and the women beat into submission. The goods in the wagons are whatever the Astorians' deemed worth looting.'

Kralgen's knuckles whiten as he balls his fist.

'I can only imagine what they'll be used for once they're in Astoria,' he growls. 'As for my Icelandians, what fate awaits them? I've led my entire nation to destruction, first against Nogoth and now with that conniving viper, Asterz. Alyssa would be so ashamed of me!'

He hasn't mentioned her in so long, and his eyes redden. I'm so caught up in my heartbreak over Lotane that I often overlook that Kralgen has to deal with the death of his Chosen one.

'No, Kral. You weren't to know. Also, I haven't witnessed your people being maltreated. Perhaps a different fate awaits them.'

'Gah. If that was all that mattered, maybe. But we were supposed to have helped save this world, but instead, we continue to condemn it. I can't sit back and allow the suffering to continue, not while there's breath in my body. Asterz has to pay for what she's done, and anyone else who has helped her ... and I mean anyone!'

Anyone? Is Kral talking about Lotane?

For a moment, words fail me. I can't believe what he's considering. They've been inseparable friends for so long. Could what's going on really break such a bond, and where would that leave me if the two came to blows? I couldn't just sit back!

'Kral, slow down,' I say, raising my hands. 'I can't believe any woman, even a Queen of Astoria, would countenance rape from her soldiery. She understood the importance of training Surian and Rolantrian survivors to keep Astoria safe. There's no way she'd jeopardise her realm like this, and nor would Lotane ever stand back and allow such things to happen!'

Kral stands silently, mulling over my words. Sometimes, he can be as swift as a sin-hawk, but now he mulls over my argument, and every second feels like an hour.

'There's truth in what you say,' Kral finally admits, his forehead furrowed. 'Yet the orders came from someone, and if not Asterz, then who?'

It takes but a few moments for the likely culprit to come to mind.

'Commander Jarval.'

One of Kralgen's shaggy eyebrows lifts inquisitively like a caterpillar going for a walk.

'He's in charge of the Astorian military and has made his presence felt several times,' I explain. 'It was his orders that kept the refugees apart, no doubt to ensure their story was never heard.'

It all makes sense now. Hindsight is such a wonderful and useless thing, showing in detail what I should have seen if only I hadn't been such a blind idiot.

Kralgen bares his teeth.

'We need to find out whether this Jarval acted on his own or others are supporting him,' he growls. 'It could be a coup is about to happen if he's this brazen, but if we just chop off his head, we'll never find out who he's working with.'

'You're right, Kral. We can't act until we know who else is involved. Only then can you chop off some heads,' I laugh mirthlessly.

'But that still leaves fifteen-odd thousand bastard Astorian soldiers who did the deeds for us to deal with!'

There's a hard look behind Kral's eyes … he's deadly serious.

'Gods, Kral. It makes me want to puke to say so, but we need the Astorian army. A few heads can roll, fine, but I'm sure Nogoth's gargoyles now have eyes across Astoria, and we must present a united force against him, not show him a bloodbath.'

Kral glowers, but there's no anger directed at me.

'Damn you for being right.' The words tumble from his mouth like he can't bear their taste. 'We'll have to fight alongside one set of evil bastards against another. I don't even know if ours is the lesser of the two!'

'I don't know either, Kral. Yet once this is over, if we're still alive, we'll make them pay.'

'With blood?'

Yaster and her stories come to mind, and bile rises in my throat.

'The women who've been raped and lost husbands, and the children who've lost parents wouldn't accept anything less.' I state with surety.

'We do this at the first opportunity. Promise me!'

Kral speaks with such intensity, and I'm so sickened by what Yaster has told me that it's an easy promise to make.

'You have my word, Kral.'

'So, what now?'

'You go to Ast. Ensure your Icelandians are well taken care of, and find out who Commander Jarval's cohorts are. Get Lotane to help, as he'll know who can be trusted, but whatever happens, don't tell Asterz. We can't afford to make a move until we know all the perpetrators. I'll join you within the week, and together we'll deliver justice to the guilty.'

'I like the sound of that.' Kralgen's smile as he speaks is full of grim promise.

'Then,' I continue, 'we return here with every able-bodied man or woman, trained or otherwise, who can wield a weapon before Nogoth's army turns up. The Fey King has to understand the futility of attacking Astoria. Once he sees the wall for himself and his gargoyles inform him of our waiting army, he'll hopefully see sense, leave us alone and return to his world.'

'What if he doesn't see sense and decides to rise to our challenge? I have a feeling he'll not give up so easily.'

'Then another surprise awaits him.'

'Let me guess. Dimitar! How big is he now?'

'Easily as big as a troll. But Nogoth will be forewarned of him.'

I draw my sword and reverse it, offering the hilt to Kralgen.

'Pretty sword. I like mine bigger; to make more of a mess. The bigger the pole, the bigger the hole,' he laughs.

'Oh, let me assure you, you haven't seen anything like this sword. Now, I have something to show you that Nogoth will definitely not see coming, and hopefully, it will be the last thing he ever sees!'

***

# CHAPTER XV

The cold goblet of water tastes flat and stale as I wash down the bread, cold meat, and honey. Yet, despite not enjoying the hearty fare that constitutes my breakfast, I'm bursting with energy regardless of the heavy workload and bright-eyed despite the lack of sleep.

In fact, I've never felt healthier or stronger in my life.

It's been nine days since I bid farewell to Kralgen, and I've missed his presence sorely. He'll have arrived at Ast a week ago, and I can't help but wonder how his mission is progressing. A powerhouse of strength and martial skill, he's not best suited to the subtle art of intelligence gathering. But with Lotane helping, I know he'll pull through, as will I, because there's no other choice.

The mountainous horizon burns with the promise of a new dawn as I throw back the tent flap, an invitation to Arbinger, Dundain, and the scouts waiting outside to enter.

I greet each of them warmly, clasping hands, forearms and shoulders, yet I save a warm smile for Dundain. She'll never have a place in my heart, yet there's a bond between us that I cannot deny. She's the font of my energy, frequently offering her own beyond what I actually require.

The scouts form a weary semi-circle facing me, with Dundain a step behind them, whereas Arbinger positions himself at my left side. To my right is a rough wooden table covered in Arbinger's drawings and a large map showing the pass and the Delnorian lands to the west.

'Scouts first.'

'The fey army is on the march. They'll be here in a week, give or take a day,' a dark-haired corporal states with certainty, wiping some sweat from his forehead.

The other three nod in agreement, so there's no need to question them separately.

'What are their numbers?' I press, although had I waited patiently, I'm sure those would have been forthcoming.

'I estimate twenty-five thousand ogres and maybe four thousand wolfen. There were also shades, although it's impossible to tell their numbers.'

No contradiction from the others. Despite being from separate units, it's pleasing to know they're in agreement.

'Are there no trolls or giants amongst them?' I press.

'Eastnor has some tall buildings, so it's possible,' a moustached scout volunteers, curling one end around his finger. 'But I'd wager a year's pay there aren't any. We got closer than I thought they'd allow. It's almost as if they didn't care what we saw.'

He's probably right. A few hundred Astorian cavalry were too insignificant to bother them.

'Arbinger?'

I leave the rest of the question unspoken; he knows what I'm after.

'The reinforced roof will be complete in two days. After that, we only need to seal the wall tunnel, and everything's finished; we've actually done it.'

Genuine hope begins to shine among those assembled in the tent at this incredible news.

'Yes!' Dundain gasps happily, but her cheeks flush as I shake my head.

'No!' I state firmly. 'This isn't the time for celebration, my friends, far from it. Nogoth is a master tactician and mustn't be underestimated. We must expect the unexpected. I've no doubts a large force of trolls and giants is on their way, and whilst we're thoroughly prepared, they'll hit us like a storm.

'Arbinger. Once the wall is finished, I want additional barracks built into the mountainside. The rear of the wall needs defending, and our reinforcements need safe quarters.'

Smiles disappear, and it's a good thing too. Nogoth's victory at High Delnor will never leave me.

'I want every scout back over the bridge within three days. Anyone left on the other side will be on their own.'

'We could use ropes and pulleys to save any stragglers,' Arbinger offers. 'The horses will have to fend for themselves, but the riders ...'

'Three days!' I state firmly, holding the gaze of each scout one by one. 'Ride as if death is but a step behind you because, in truth, it is. After the third day, no ropes will await because the bridge will be destroyed, and you won't be able to get near the wall.

'The River of Tears will be our first line of defence,' I say, wrapping my arm around Arbinger's shoulders. 'Unless the fey army has an amazing engineer like our friend amongst them, it might be an obstacle they'll be unable to overcome. Now, let's move!'

Everyone files out of the tent, whereas Dundain loiters behind. I shake my head, and the disappointment that flashes across her face before she can hide it saddens me. I wish I could give her the love she deserves, but Lotane already has that.

Violet eyes come to mind, and I allow myself a shiver of pleasure before I push the feeling aside. Love and lust can be so confusing at times. Nogoth is as deadly a foe as he's an artful lover, and I mustn't forget that. However well we've prepared, I feel we're overlooking something.

What am I missing?

The unbroken and perennially snow-capped mountains surrounding Astoria are too high for any army to traverse. Likewise, the range is too deep, too cold, and too unstable for the ssythlans to have tunnelled through, which still leaves just two ways into Astoria: this pass and its only port, Astwater, on the north coast.

Nogoth has known about this wall for several weeks now, and an army is on its way to attack it. Does he now have another plan, or, being a master strategist, was there always more than one?

Is the port where Nogoth plans to strike, and if so, how could he do it?

Asterz proudly believes the port is impregnable because of the narrow approach guarded by a chain of forts on the mountainside above, which adds to its impressive natural defences. Unlike Delnor, with its balmy temperature where the trolls and ogres literally walked into the harbour, the north coast of Astoria is renowned for its freezing deep waters, crushing icebergs, and impassable mountain coastline. Nogoth's forces would suffer total losses attacking that way.

Unless we're missing something.

How else could he get a formidable army ashore? Then the mist begins to clear from my foggy mind as I remember how the ssythlans had taken Sea Hold at the beginning of the invasion.

If he uses the combined fleets of Delnor, Hastia and Tars to ferry his army around the coast and manages to get sufficient shades ashore, they'd wreak havoc on the defenders, opening the door for the waiting fleet! Once they established a bridgehead, it would be all over.

My blood runs cold.

This was always going to be a two-pronged attack.

All this time, we've poured resources and time into the wall while ignoring Astwater, believing an attack there was impossible.

We were wrong.

A satisfied smile creases my cheeks. I now have three reasons to go to Ast. To exact revenge on Jarval for the atrocities he's responsible for, to win Lotane back, and now to stymy Nogoth's invasion.

I wish I could see Nogoth's face when he realises his plans have turned to dust.

***

'Do you think they've seen us?' I ask with a laugh.

Dimitar's mighty stone shoulders shrug.

'They've seen me,' he rumbles. 'You, maybe not.'

I sit comfortably astride a black gelding a day's ride east from the wall. Every so often, that long head swings around with a disdainful look and then snorts in disgust when I fail to give it a treat. I have a feeling its previous rider, a scout who'd met a grisly end, must have spoilt it rotten.

My mood had been buoyant till now, with Astoria's western entrance secured. I'd destroyed the bridge, the massive stonework snatched away by the angry waters as if it had been waiting impatiently for the opportunity for decades.

The wall also stood completed. I'd sealed the wall tunnel entrance, so no trace of its existence showed, leaving Arbinger's masons to backfill it. The scouts who'd returned, along with the archers, now man the wall and the war engines, yet I wonder if they'll even be needed the defences are so formidable.

I'd left satisfied with what I'd achieved and exultant at having seen through Nogoth's plans.

Now, I'm on my way to Ast. The pass is behind me, and for a while, it's been liberating to be out from under its perpetual shadow. Yet now, with the plains of Astoria before me, I wonder if this is where the darkness actually begins.

The grasslands stretch for leagues before me, a large trade road heading uninterrupted northeast, yet instead, I turn my horse's head toward two dozen low buildings partially obscured behind a wooden stake wall just off to the south. There's no grass between me and the buildings, just hard-packed earth bearing the scars of wagon wheels and thousands of dragging feet.

It appears the refugees weren't sent straight to Ast, so despite my urgency to get to the capital, I'll take a short detour to find out what's been going on.

'Looks like they're organising a welcome,' I mutter.

The Astorian military seems to like black, and the half dozen gathering at the entrance to this encampment are no exception. Black uniforms are prevalent, with a few coloured sashes visible. From what I can see, there's no sign of armour, but all of them carry shortswords and daggers. As a horn is frantically blown, the half dozen quickly become nearly a hundred who appear unsure of what to do.

I can understand their indecision. A giant stone man, the height of a tree, is likely causing some concern. A discussion is ongoing, and I wonder if they're considering closing and barring the gate in a futile effort to dissuade our approach.

I snort at the thought, and my horse gives me a sidelong glance.

However, the gate remains open, and a captain advances, the perpetual sneer of disdain fixed on his face that so many officers appear to consider an essential part of their training.

'What do you want?' he barks.

I say nothing, my gaze passing over the gathered soldiers. Most military units have a mix of men and women, but at first glance, this is entirely male. I take in the scratched faces, the sneers of disdain, the animal cruelty and lust in their eyes. It was a dark, fateful day that brought such a disgusting bunch of individuals together.

Part of me wants to turn away in case their mere presence somehow infects me, but I owe it to those refugees who've come before me to see this through.

I lift my leg over my mount's neck and slide off its back. I stretch briefly, aware of the growing silence and charged atmosphere. Yet I'm not here to fight, although that might be somewhat rewarding; however, I am playing a risky game of bluff.

'Have you seen Commander Jarval?' I ask, finally deigning to look at the captain.

Name someone important, and the doubt it can put in people's minds is amazing.

'Of course, I've seen him. He was here a week ago with the last of the ... refugees.' He answers hesitantly, the tone of his voice changing dramatically.

I laugh, despite wanting to gut the man there and then.

'Refugees,' I say, tapping the side of my nose. 'Yes, no more will be coming now the wall is finished.'

I step forward, extending my hand.

'You may have heard of me. My name is Malina, although most call me The King Slayer. This is my friend, Dimitar,' I say, nodding over my shoulder. 'He can be quite protective, but he's already eaten today, so you needn't worry.'

The captain looks at my hand, obviously not wanting to shake it.

'Yes. I've heard of you. Who hasn't? Did you really burn the High King of Delnor alive?'

'I did. Astorian gold paid me then as it does now.'

I've told many lies I've regretted, but this one doesn't cause me any misgivings.

'Hah. That was money well spent then!'

The captain hesitantly grips my forearm, looking over my shoulder at Dimitar. It's a good thing as I struggle to contain my disgust at holding this loathsome creature's hand.

Yet this isn't just a pleasantry, for he's bound to me magically within a few heartbeats.

Pulling him close, I whisper in his grimy ear.

'You will obey me and tell me everything I need to know without hesitation, and doing so will bring you great happiness. Do you understand?'

I step away, pulling my hand free, a forced smile on my face.

'What do you want?' he asks, repeating his first question in a reverent tone.

'To be shown around while you tell me how diligently you've done your job.'

The captain's face lights up at being able to do my bidding.

'Back to work, you lazy scum,' he yells. 'They're not a bad bunch,' he adds quietly, leading me through the gates as his men disperse. 'We're getting ready to move out.'

'Are you heading to the wall or back to Ast?'

'Hah. No. We're heading east to the mines, where we sent some of our new guests. We get to look after 'em properly now.'

He chuckles with a wink that makes me want to throw up.

'Was it just the Surians and Rolantrians, or did you look after the Icelandians too when they passed through here?'

'Nah. The Icelandians never did us no wrong, so they went to Ast. But the bloody Surians and Rolantrians allied against us with Delnor all those times. So they had it coming, didn't they,' he says, nodding vehemently.

'They had it coming,' I repeat softly.

'That's where we strip searched 'em,' he says, pointing to an open-sided building with piles of filthy clothing behind it. 'That's where we had fun with the good-looking ones,' he says, pointing out another building. 'We fed 'em, of course, gave 'em good shoes for the march, sturdy clothing too. After all, we ain't animals. As for their gear, all the good stuff went to Ast, n the bad stuff we burned.'

'Did you burn those who didn't comply?' I point to a building with several chimneys crusted with thick, black soot. The smell of burning flesh is impossible to hide, but I need to make sure.

'Don't you know it!' he grins proudly. 'There's always some lippy whore who don't listen or fights back too hard. It's easier to burn 'em than bury 'em, and the noises they make as we chuck 'em in the furnaces is worth a laugh.'

'Did your orders come from Commander Jarval?'

'Who else? He knows how to keep us motivated, letting us do what we do. He's a good un that one. Wouldn't cross him though, cause he's a hard bastard too.'

I've had enough. I want to cut this maggot in two and have Dimitar stomp everyone to death, but it would be hard to conceal the evidence. The news would get out, and whatever their crimes, I'd be seen as a murderer. But ...

'Captain. I want to honour the good work all your men have done. Have them report to me one by one and then stand ready for my address afterwards in the square over there.'

The captain nods enthusiastically.

'Use my office,' he says, leading me to a stone building and opening the door to usher me inside. The interior is grim, like him. It smells of stale sweat, and filthy clothes are piled in a corner. A desk littered with papers, stained with spilt ink and a plate of half-eaten food complete the distasteful picture.

I open the shutters to breathe something a little less foul, then sit on a chair behind his desk that's seen far better days.

'Let's start immediately.'

It takes an hour to shake the hand of every piece of degenerate scum in the camp and to bind them all to me. Now they stand to attention in ragged lines, their faces glowing with expectation as they await my words.

I want to tell them how I loathe them and how any punishment will never be enough to atone for their crimes. I want them to scream, cry, and beg for forgiveness, but it shouldn't be to me. It should be to every woman and child they've forced themselves on.

In the absence of their victims, who am I to pass judgement?

The King Slayer; a drinker of blood who has killed so many and is partly responsible for the tragedy befalling the world.

The men of the Last Hope, who'd journeyed with me to Pine Hold, come to mind. Those murderers had been given a final chance at redemption and had taken it, for the most part, becoming better versions of their former selves.

Now that these men are bound to me, I could change them completely. All I need to do is order them to atone for their crimes for the rest of their lives. To be a force for good, to give everything they have to those they took it from, and more.

I gaze upon them a final time.

'It is time for me to leave. When I do, you will bolt the gates behind me, then lock yourselves securely inside the barracks buildings. Once that's complete, you will take your daggers and mutilate yourselves. Start with your genitals, then your eyes, and if you're still alive at that stage, gut yourselves, pull out and eat your own entrails. This is my final order, and you will carry it out.'

The condemned have sweat pouring down their faces as they struggle to fight against the blood magic and my orders. Moans of fear follow me out of the gates that are slammed behind me.

I wait patiently astride my gelding. About ten minutes later, a symphony of screams pierces the air.

If only it were louder so their victims could hear and know the first bit of justice has been dealt.

***

'Where are Kral and Lotane now?' I shout above the cantering hooves of my mount.

Dimitar tilts his head to one side as he strides along, keeping pace. A small yellow bird flaps away to find another less challenging perch.

'They're still in Ast, one day's ride north.'

His voice carries easily, loud as a rockslide.

'What about Nogoth?'

After a long silence, I'm about to ask again when …

'He's in Ssythla.'

I rein in my horse to a walk, allowing it to catch its breath. Speed is of the essence but managing its stamina will get me to Ast faster.

'Why is he there so far from the frontline?' I muse out loud into the relative silence.

My gelding looks at me as though he has the answer and thinks I'm stupid.

Dimitar just shrugs.

'I wish you could add something to the conversation,' I moan in exasperation. 'Nogoth must be seeking ssythlan help. The ships they build are huge, so if he adds them to the fleet he must be gathering, it will be mighty indeed. Yet even if they left now, it would take them at least a month to navigate along the coast. By the time they arrive, we'll be prepared.'

I snap my fingers, smiling as another answer makes itself known.

'He's going to bring ssythlan mages to ensure favourable winds instead of draining his power.'

'Unless the fleet left already, and he's not gone with them.'

I stare up at Dimitar in horror.

'Did I say something wrong?' he rumbles.

I'm too busy thinking things through to answer.

Of course. A two-pronged attack is at its strongest when coordinated. If the fey army arrives at the wall in a week, give or take a few days, then it's very likely the fleet will arrive at the same time. This is why Nogoth didn't just attack the wall straight away before it was finished. He's too experienced a strategist to lose troops without guaranteeing success.

Familiar screeches and shrieks carried on the wind have me looking skyward; sure enough, gargoyles are scouting over the Astorian prairies. Thankfully Nogoth doesn't have enough of these creatures to cause serious problems behind the frontlines, but these messengers of death are how he'll coordinate the attacks.

'We don't have a moment to lose,' I announce. 'An attack on Astwater and the wall might only be days away.'

There's no further response from Dimitar, and loneliness grips me in its cold hand.

'Yah!' I shout, digging my heels into the gelding's sides, urging him to a gallop.

How have I ended up so alone, with the fate of the world seemingly on my shoulders, and will it ever change?

I don't allow myself to make friends or even socialise. Several times at the pass, I'd been invited to share a table and had turned people down, choosing my own company. Is this a residual part of my conditioning to stay out of sight, or because my eyes are often drawn to the pulse in someone's neck, and I struggle to resist my hunger?

My stomach rumbles as if I'd called its name. Having just fed on Dundain before I'd left, I should be fine for another two weeks, but she'd been so giving, and I'd got used to feeding more frequently.

Her despair when I told her I was leaving continues to tug at my conscience. She'd begged to come with me, and I'd denied her, telling her I'd return, not caring whether my words were true or false. Perhaps she knew it, for only desperation, not hope, swum beneath her tears.

Yes. Once again, I'd chosen my own company. The King Slayer, the assassin, forever walking alone.

Kralgen has his Icelandians and revels in their adulation, and Lotane has found Asterz and Astoria. But now, at long last, I'll be able to remind him of what he's been missing.

I survey the landscape while keeping a wary eye on the sky.

Reassuringly with every passing minute, I see signs of a nation responding to the call of battle.

Military encampments dot the landscape, around which infantry training is being carried out while units of cavalry practice changing formations and direction on the plain. Small towns and tent villages are everywhere, and I'm relieved that Icelandians have found a home amongst many of them. Unfortunately, as the trade road is joined by dozens of other routes, travellers, soldiers, and ladened wagons clog the road ahead.

Dimitar and I move onto the grasslands adjacent to the road to maintain speed. Even from a distance, shouts and screams reach my ears. I can't say I blame them. Dimitar and I hardly represent any force of good I'd have conjured to mind.

'Looks like we have company,' I shout.

A force of perhaps two hundred cavalry are moving to intercept us.

Damn.

They're only doing their duty, challenging what are obviously foreigners to their lands, but any delay could prove disastrous. A single knight in plate armour leads the unit, followed by the mass of irregular archers in their furs and horned helmets.

I pull back on the reins, and Dimitar slows down to match my horse's pace whilst the Astorians halt, spreading out in a line to block our route.

'Wait here,' I command and heel my horse forward till I'm two dozen paces in front of the waiting cavalry. Grimaces, frowns, and feigned indifference, but no smiles are aimed my way. They don't look pleased to see me.

The knight with his bright red sash at odds with his black armour eventually follows suit, coming to meet me halfway. He's removed his helm but otherwise is encased neck to toe in polished steel.

'Malina, King Slayer.'

He knows my name, which isn't good if his troops are blocking my progress. I always resort to violence; maybe I should try a little fun instead.

'Sorry, that's not me. It's my twin sister who is back at the wall.'

'You are ... Wait. Your sister?'

I'm tempted to push the ruse further but decide against it.

'My apologies, Sir Knight. I'm just teasing. You're so handsome, and I'm a little smitten.'

I urge my horse closer, so we're side by side, knees almost touching.

The man coughs and tries to look stern, but I can see I've put him off balance.

'All knights have orders from the Queen and Commander Jarval that you're to remain at the wall, helping to defend Astoria until called upon. Turn around with your stone giant immediately.'

Why am I not surprised? Asterz wants me nowhere near Lotane. As for Jarval, he doesn't like me because I question his ways and don't kiss his boots. If only he knew I was after his head, he'd have given orders for me to be killed on sight instead.

I smile, biting my lip. One word and Dimitar could pound this entire unit to a bloody paste, but there's been enough killing today. Despite the likelihood of these troops being guilty of heinous war crimes, now isn't the time to exact revenge.

'I was unaware of such an order and have urgent news for the queen. She'll need my help and counsel. Would you kindly let me pass?'

'No. Orders are orders. Return to the wall!'

'If I don't turn around. What then?'

'Disobeying an order from the queen or Commander Jarval is punishable by death,' he rasps.

Death. Is that how they'd thank me for all that I've done? Death to the Surians, the Rolantrians, and now me if I don't comply. They deserve everything that's coming their way.

'I see. Such a pity. Having you escort me to Ast would have been very pleasurable.'

Slowly, so as not to startle him, I reach out to caress his cheek. My fingers slide to the back of his neck. It takes but a second to work my magic.

'You should really escort me to Ast. It would be the right thing to do,' I say softly.

'I should escort you to Ast,' the knight responds decisively.

'Then lead on, Sir Knight. I want to be there by nightfall!'

***

It's strange not to have Dimitar's looming presence nearby. Perhaps he's better company than I gave him credit for. Sadly, he's hardly suited to stealth.

As my escort had pointed out, we'd have never got close to Ast with him accompanying me, whereas surrounded by two hundred horsemen,

I passed unseen. A loaned helm ensuring no casual glance from another knight might uncover my identity.

Dimitar is now lying hidden in a barn half a day's ride south. I'd ordered him to wait silently there for me unless the sky was about to fall down. It had taken him a while to understand that I didn't mean it literally, just symbolically. His solemn nod was a welcome relief when he finally understood. As for the shocked farmer who owned the land that the barn sits on, he's now bound by magic to silence.

As water drips from my nose, I think Dimitar is in the better place.

Except for Dundain, I'd resisted using my blood magic for so long, yet I'd bound over a hundred people in the last two days. It would be easy to solve so many of life's problems this way, but robbing people of their free will, will make me more of a monster than I already am.

And whilst I try to fight it, I know I'm a monster because why else would I see the blood pumping through the veins of everyone moving beneath me and feel my stomach rumble with unreasonable hunger?

The sharp tang of wet roof pitch bites at my nose as I crouch upon a shingle roof on the outskirts of Ast. Despite the miserable weather, hundreds of city folk, knights, and soldiers, shout and jostle, testing my patience while I wait for sunset and the streets to quieten.

Has it really been just a year since I was here with the other Chosen to assassinate the King of Ast? I loved my life back then, and whilst the world has changed, I'm still the assassin I used to be, revelling in the hunt to come.

Street lamps begin to throw pools of golden light across the streets below, which is what I've been waiting for. Now, if people look up, they'll be blinded by the lights and the falling rain, unaware of my passing.

'Let's go, Malina,' I whisper.

My sword handles protrude above my shoulders, out of the way so as not to hinder my movement.

*Lend me your help.*

I doubt I even need to project my wish, such is our bond, but I do so nonetheless, along with my love.

The buildings on the city's perimeter are low, poorly built and spread out. Scanning the rooftops, I discern a route which will have me travel parallel to the main thoroughfare I'm overlooking, right up to the killing ground outside the castle walls.

My heart sings with happiness as I run across the rooftop, leap, and sail across a wide gap before hitting the next rooftop at a run. Without my fey sight, I'd never have been able to move so swiftly nor surely, and my only concern is the integrity of the roofs I land on.

The wind hisses past my ears as I run faster, aided by a magical breeze, allowing me to jump distances impossible for someone without my gifts. I land softly, lighter than a feather, a silent shadow, a part of the night's very fabric.

A distant cry of fear, faint but unmistakable.

My mission is urgent, the fate of this world is at stake, but nonetheless, I change direction, my senses thrumming. Away from the main streets, the alleyways below are darker; occasional lanterns, the spillage of light from barred windows, and moonlight provide the only illumination.

For me, it might as well be daytime.

Every rat, roosting bird, scoundrel, thief, pimp, or whore is a glowing red beacon against a backdrop of greys.

There!

The cries of fear and desperation come from a house.

I pause, looking down into the street below. Two ruffians guard the entrance, a splintered door pulled closed between them, evidence of forced entry. Shadows move behind first-floor curtains, crashes of furniture being upended, and items being smashed reach my ears. Finally, a top-floor window almost level with me, allowing me a front-row seat to the horror show that's taking place.

Seven men and three women are torturing a man, taking turns to cut, burn, or puncture his flesh. Yet being gagged, the audible cries aren't his; they're coming from the woman tied naked to a bed who is being forced to watch. Several of the intruders have belted swords, all have daggers, but there might be other weapons to hand I can't see.

This world is so sick and needs to be cleansed.

If I go in through the bedroom window, I'll possibly save the man and woman, but then many of the gang might escape.

The front door it is then.

Drawing my two daggers, I leap off the roof, land lightly before the unsuspecting guards, and drive the blades up under their chins. With a sharp twist, I leave the weapons in place, using my strength to lower the men quietly to the floor as their legs give way.

The street is empty as I glance around. It's hissing down with rain, and no one wants to get involved. Even the neighbours have their curtains drawn tightly and are likely praying to whatever gods they won't be next.

I yank my weapons free and wipe the blood off on my victims' shirts before easing the broken door open and peering into the interior. The furnishings show this isn't a wealthy merchant's house but someone who just gets by with a little extra money on the side. A few paintings adorn the walls, frayed rugs cover the floors, and everywhere the paint is faded, although clean. Two oil lamps create what would have been a homely feel if it wasn't for the bloody corpse of the guard dog that's been kicked into a corner and the muddy bootprints everywhere.

Two open doors lead off the hallway allowing me to see into a kitchen and breakfast room. Both are empty. I open another, but this room is full of coal and wood for the fires, leaving only the stairs up to the next level unexplored. Footsteps are loud overhead, but I don't let them concern me.

I sheath my daggers, extinguish the lamps and swiftly return to the street, heaving the two corpses inside. The door barely closes, but I lean the bodies against it before wedging the splintered locking bar back into place.

This is an old house, and there's not much chance of being stealthy with ill-fitting, warped floorboards underfoot, but with so much noise going on, I'm not worried.

I walk steadily up the stairs, listening to the noise, the voices, and am certain there are three men and a woman doing a thorough job of searching this floor. They're checking for hidden valuables in drawers, cupboards, and from the sound of splintering wood, under the floorboards too. Curses seem to indicate they haven't found much to make them smile.

This isn't going to be their lucky night.

The doors to the rooms are open as my head comes level with the landing. Two men with their backs to me are in the farthest room to my left at the bottom of the next flight of stairs. I turn right, coming face to face with a flat-faced woman with greasy, curly hair and a scar on one cheek that's given her a perpetual grimace.

Her hand grabs for a belted dagger, but my forehead smashes into the bridge of her nose. Arms flailing, she tumbles backwards with a short howl that stops as her head cracks into the corner of a mantelpiece.

I'm turning back into the hallway even as her legs twitch to see a skinny man coming out of the door to my right, perhaps wondering what caused the woman to cry out.

'Are you alright ...?' he starts to ask.

With a lunge, I slam the side of his head into the doorframe with my left hand whilst my right drives my dagger up under his ribcage three times.

Two down, two to go.

One has a heavy cudgel, and the other a long knife. Neither looks particularly competent from their stances.

'We need help down here!' the one with the blade screams in an unusually high-pitched voice.

I sidestep a clumsy lunge, grab his wrist, and pull the man forward just as the cudgel begins its descent. A sickening thud as metal-reinforced wood caves in the back of my adversary's skull, and I'm left facing just the one fool who stands open-mouthed in shock at killing his friend. The cudgel falls from his shaking hand, and I don't think he even blinks as I ram my dagger through his eye.

Loud footsteps and exaggerated whispers give me pause at the bottom of the staircase leading to the next floor, but time is of the essence. I sprint up the stairs two at a time, reaching the landing. There's only one door, and it's closed.

I snuff out two lamps, plunging the landing into darkness, and listen.

The sound of sobbing filters through the thin panelled walls and the scuffing of feet as those behind the door ready themselves. Thick rugs adorn the floor, and I smile appreciatively as I tread softly, keeping close to the wall.

It's time to see what my swords can do.

Drawing them both, I picture the room, the positioning of the cabinets, the bed, dressing table, chairs, and a wardrobe.

Extending my arm, I rattle the door handle with the sword tip.

Wood splinters as two crossbow bolts punch through and bury themselves in the opposite wall. I move immediately, kicking the door hard, shattering it inwards and sending a wind howling through, extinguishing the candles and lamps, plunging the room into darkness as I follow.

My swords sing faintly as they cut through the air, a symphony to which I spin and dance as I move throughout the room.

The blades, which can cut through stone, pass through flesh, bone, leather, and steel with no more effort than parting water. As the last woman falls, I stop, crouched on one knee, looking, and listening.

Only two hearts remain beating. The woman on the bed and mine. Her husband, partner, lover or whoever, has succumbed to his wounds.

I fight a rising tide of hunger as I stand above the bed, looking down at the woman, then cut her bonds without saying a word. She scampers back to crouch in a corner, her eyes like dinner plates, looking at me in the faint moonlight as if I'm a demon, not those who lay slain on the floor.

There's a washing bowl on a table, and I spend the next few minutes sponging myself clean, leaving pristine white towels sullied with gore. Next, I rummage through the wardrobes, finding a hooded cloak. It's dark blue, not black, but it fits and will do. The nearest window opens easily, and I climb out into the rain, afraid that if I stay, I'll give in to my primal urge to feed. Nostalgia washes over me as I make my way to the rooftop, the memories of successful hunts reaping dark souls a heady elixir that fills me with euphoria.

Then, with a sigh, it fades. On this day alone, I'm responsible for the deaths of over a hundred humans, and it's not even over yet. How am I any different from Nogoth?

***

Damn, why couldn't this just be simple?

As I look down from my rooftop, I'm frustrated to see flaming braziers lighting up the killing ground around the castle walls. Despite the rain, discipline is evident as guards are positioned every twenty steps between the crenulations and look neither bored nor sleepy. There's also a dry moat that probably boasts hardened wooden spikes covered in crap, making my final approach riskier than I'd have liked.

After everything I've done, I should be able to stride openly up to the front gate, be met with respectful salutes and welcome smiles and then be escorted directly to the throne room. Sadly, that will lead to an attempted arrest and a possible bloodbath.

Having had one of those already, I'll opt to break in like the assassin I am.

Whilst every hour is precious, I'm rather happy that's the way of it. I'll show them that however safe they think they are, if I can get to them, so can Nogoth. Yet unlike me, he won't take the subtle approach because his giants and trolls will tear these walls down.

A few people are walking the streets despite the weather. This close to Astoria's seat of power, the residences are finely made, the streets well lit, and private militia stroll around in pairs. I take my time, waiting for an opportunity to descend, and then step off the rooftop, landing softly between two men as they pass one another, walking in opposite directions.

I pull my hood up and cross the road, putting some distance between me, the street lamps, the shops and houses. My disguise won't hold up under close scrutiny, and the two sword hilts rising over my shoulders are hardly innocuous either, but most people have their heads down against the rain.

A stone wall rises knee-high on my left, and as I peer over, I can make out the pointed stakes at the bottom of the dry moat. There are several years' worth of rubbish at the bottom too, either blown or thrown there by uncaring people; it doesn't matter. The stakes are fire hardened and will do the ruthless job they were intended for if I attempt an entrance that way.

Ahead is a wooden bridge, one of just two that cross the wide moat to the castle. It's built to be easily destructible, and I'm sure jars of flammable oil are kept ready to douse the timbers, so the whole thing can be burnt to a cinder in minutes.

Foolishly, however, to keep the guard sheltered, it has walls and a roof.

This will be my way in. They won't greet me with smiles, but that's because the fools won't see me as they're not standing out in the rain and have no line of sight in my direction.

I tread carefully, my light footsteps muffled by the rain pattering down, taking note of the other walkers, ensuring no one is paying me any attention. I check behind me, but it's clear, so as I come up to the bridge, I step up onto the wall and, with a silent wish to my magic, step off the other side.

As my fall is halted by an upward surge of wind, I take hold of the wooden struts supporting the bridge. Hand over hand, sometimes swinging and jumping, I nimbly make my way across this weak point in the castle's outer defences, the guards oblivious above.

The path up to the main gates is in the open, leaving anyone crossing it an easy target for an archer. Fortunately, with so much rain falling, it doesn't drain me too much to have the wind howl, sending sheets of rain lashing the walls and the bridge behind me.

As the braziers hiss and let off steam, I move amongst the billowing clouds, reaching the gate unnoticed and stand in the shadows of the adjoining tower, listening.

The pattering rain now has a backdrop of a hundred voices.

Memories of Lystra creating an entrance in the wall of the mage tower come to mind as I make my own. The walls are incredibly thick, but I pass through like a bubble in water.

I'm soon inside the gate tower and look through a doorway into the grounds beyond. It's teeming with soldiers, a few knights, men at arms, stable boys and servants. Blacksmith's hammers ring loud even at this time of night, horses neigh and stamp in their stables, goats and chickens huddle sadly whilst men and women curse the weather loudly.

Torches and braziers flicker and hiss under the onslaught of water, and shadows flicker everywhere. The main gates into the keep are open, but a dozen guards stand under the arch checking anyone going in and out. I can't get in that way, and there's no way I can even pass through this crowd without being seen or bumping into a hundred people.

I chuckle. Having come this far, sometimes the best disguise is no disguise.

My hooded cloak pulled close around me, I step out into the rain, keeping my head down, avoiding eye contact, whilst looking for an entry point. Everyone appears to have a purpose amongst this organised chaos, and I'm happy to see that forging new weapons and armour appears to be a priority. Every time I spy a knight, I give them as much distance as possible, not risking discovery.

It takes almost half an hour to navigate the perimeter of this keep, avoiding contact with everyone and keeping to the shadows wherever possible. There are only two entrances, both well-guarded, and the walls of this keep will be incredibly thick. I could pass through them again if I'm unobserved, but not knowing where I'll exit on the other side is a major concern. The keep will be well-occupied, and the likelihood of bumping into someone is high.

The royal chambers and those for other people of note will be centrally placed, likely high up, affording unparalleled views. If I'm to enter unseen close to Asterz, Lotane or Kralgen, then entering from above is my best option.

A patch of darkness shows itself, and I sigh in relief.

There's what looks to be a tanners shack and a pig pen almost side by side up against the keep wall. The gap between is obviously used as a urinal for those too lazy to find a toilet, as I can see two men relieving themselves. I head straight for them, slowing my stride, thus giving them time to finish.

Despite the rain, the stench is horrible as I step into the gap; it appears this area has been an unofficial toilet for some time, and the pigsty just adds to the flavour. Fortunately, I don't intend to linger.

With no one else coming, I set to work.

The stone blocks here are huge and worn, allowing purchase for my fingers and boots as I ascend. I don't use magic, just my training and skill, scuttling up the wall. I must look like a black beetle, my arms, legs and sword handles poking out from my cloak.

After a minute, as I near the top, I smile. No one will look up into the falling rain, and I'm now safe, at least until my next challenge. The top of the wall extends outwards, so I expend a little magic to ensure my grip as I climb onto the battlements. No guards are present, but I'm not surprised. Security had been tight till now, and no one could have gotten through unless they were trained from an early age to be an assassin and imbued with magic like me.

I smile. Being one of a kind can be rather satisfying.

However, as I scurry over the rooftops toward the proud central tower, I realise how wrong I am because high above, landing on a balcony, is a gargoyle.

***

# CHAPTER XVI

Arms pumping, legs thrusting, I sprint.

Across sloped rooftops slippery with moss and rain, along walls, forever upwards, pushing myself harder than I thought possible. Every building is successively higher, with the keep built on a hill, so I pull on carvings, ledges, in fact, anything to maintain my momentum. My magic constantly helps, softening the stone beneath my feet, ensuring a good grip, understanding the urgency.

Rarely do I ever find myself out of breath, but my lungs heave as I ascend at breakneck speed. There's no one to call for help, nor the time to explain, even if there were.

How many gargoyles have entered, I don't know, although I've spied no others since I began my race. What room the balcony leads to, I've no idea, but there are more balconies above and below its entry point.

Finally, I scramble up a roof and reach the tower's lowest balcony. This one extends all around the square design. Two heavy wooden doors beckon, although I'm sure there are more. I'm tempted to run in and up the stairs, but there's no way I'll remain undetected, and I won't know which room the gargoyle entered, so again, I climb.

I'm proud of my strength and stamina, but I'm flagging. If I arrive too weak to fight, I'll be no good to anybody. Forcing myself to slow down is one of the hardest things I've done, but I slow into a steady climb, the giant ill-fitting blocks assisting my ascent.

My arms tremble and I grimace.

*Use your legs, not your arms, Malina.*

Four levels to go, three ... I slip, and only by balling my fist between two blocks do I stop myself from falling and losing valuable time. Damn this bloody rain; it's like climbing a bloody waterfall with the water pouring off the stonework.

Two levels, and finally, I'm there. I know I've taken far too long.

Will I find a blood bath, the gargoyle and/or its brethren feeding on the queen's corpse? What if Lotane was with her? No, I'd have heard the fight, clashing weapons, screams, the sound of terror.

There's been nothing.

Despite the wind and rain covering any noise I might make, I ease myself over the stone balustrade and pad like a cat to the closed wooden doors. Misty glass panes obscure what's happening inside, but the room's interior becomes clear as I get closer. There's no blood, no signs of a scuffle, let alone a fight. In fact, everything looks perfectly normal. Or it would be if it wasn't for Commander Jarval, reclining in a sumptuous leather chair, drinking red wine from a crystal glass with a gargoyle on one knee before him.

Even before I can formulate the thought, my magic brings the voices to me on a breeze. It's hard to hear above the wind and rain, but I can make out the most of it.

'You have my word,' Jarval says firmly. 'You've kept your side of the bargain, and I will mine. You and yours can have the eastern marshes. There are plenty of reasons no Astorians live there, and it can be your home until this invasion has passed.'

I'm astonished. Then again, there's nothing I'd put past this snake.

The gargoyle places clawed hands and forehead against flagstones in a sign of deference and fealty. Those mighty wings and the thick shoulders bunch up, making it look like some hideous moth.

'I will return later with more news.'

The voice reminds me of Dimitar's, thick and gravelly but colder, like a winter's morn.

The gargoyle rises, reaching for three javelins I'd overlooked leaning against a wall.

'I'll be with the queen until midnight. Return here just after then!'

What do I do?

If I attack now, I could slaughter the gargoyle before it can react, and Jarval too; surely they both deserve it. But then I wouldn't find out what's happening ...

With a silent curse, I vault over the balustrade, my cloak flapping as I plunge to the rooftops below. I land gently, automatically envelop my magic in a projected hug, and then look up, contemplating my next move.

It's time to put my qualms aside and use my magic without a constant moral dilemma stymying my ability to act decisively. I need to find out where Kralgen, Lotane, and Asterz are without stumbling around in the dark, half-blind. With my fellow Chosen behind me, I'll be stronger, Asterz will be forced to listen, and I can expose the traitor in our midst and his heinous deeds.

The dark shape of the gargoyle leaps off the balcony, those mighty wings spread wide. Yet, instead of flapping off, it spirals downward, disappearing around the tower, only to reappear moments later in a whoosh, to land a dozen steps away.

We stand there facing one another, the rain dripping off us, as still as the stone we stand upon. Do I lead with a gust of wind, knocking it off balance or have its feet trapped in the rooftop? Either way, my swords will finish the creature.

The gargoyle makes the first move ... and surprisingly places its javelins on the ground.

Does it really expect me to fight it bare-handed?

'I'm not here to kill you, favoured one,' it grates, bowing its head in deference. 'I detected your scent whilst talking to the commander, so I thought to greet you.'

*Not yet.*

I calm my magic which is coiled, ready for release. The gargoyle has positioned itself too far away to attack and hadn't thrown its javelins whilst flying, so perhaps it's telling the truth. However, that doesn't mean I won't kill it ... but first.

'Why are you here?'

It comes out as a splutter, and I wish this bloody rain would stop running off my nose into my mouth! I doubt it will give me any answers, but if I trap this gargoyle and have it slowly consumed by fire, it might be more talkative. However, I don't think I'll go undiscovered if I try that, and I'll find out anyway from Jarval.

'Telling Commander Jarval everything he needs to know. He's rather amenable and trusting.'

I'm surprised by its forthrightness.

'He's a damn traitor then?'

'No more than I am!' The gargoyle chuckles.

The cryptic answer gives me pause for thought. The gargoyle would never betray Nogoth, for it's bound by blood magic, so is it saying Jarval isn't one either?

'Anyway, Nogoth would be unhappy with me if, having seen you, I didn't extend the hand of friendship and advise you; there's still time to side with your own kind.'

'Hah. My own kind. I'm already fighting alongside them.'

'Once that was true. But now? I can barely detect the taint of a human inside you, yet conversely, despite the rain, I can detect the blood of many upon you!'

My hands go to the swords at my waist, but why? The gargoyle has only spoken the truth, and I'm going to kill it for doing so! I force my hands to let go.

'I don't suppose you'd care to share Nogoth's plans?' I ask. Is it possible this creature will confirm my fears of Nogoth's fleet?

A smile that reveals jagged fangs gives me the answer I expect.

'I'm sure you'll find out soon enough, favoured one. May I leave with my life now?'

Is it wise to let this creature go? As I've killed so many people, maybe this would provide a little balance.

'You may. Yet I'd ask a favour of you.'

I'm not sure who is more surprised by my words, the gargoyle or me.

'Ask it.'

'Tell Nogoth I said that there's no way he'll get into Astoria without his army being bled dry. But in the event he does, I'll have a surprise for him he'll die to see.'

That spiny head nods, those teeth showing in an evil grin. Giant wings extend as the creature prepares to fly before it reaches out a hand to its javelins.

I nod, and it picks them up with a half bow.

'You can tell him yourself. He'll be here within the week, and you can do nothing to stop him.'

Mighty thigh muscles bunch, and then the gargoyle launches itself into the night sky, the downdraft of its wingbeat staggering me. I track it until it disappears, then turn toward one of the wooden doors.

There's no time to waste. My fears about a fleet are well founded, and we must be prepared to repel an attack on two fronts. Then there's Jarval ... The question is, do I deal with him before or after Nogoth?

***

Like never before, I feel the weight of time passing.

Crossing to a wooden door, I try the handle to find it locked from the inside.

Of course, it is.

Thankfully, as the stone door frame peels back, the lock has nothing to engage with, and I open it silently and slip inside.

The tower is well-lit, with wall-mounted oil lanterns shedding a warm glow. Thick rugs are scattered everywhere, tapestries line the walls, and even though I'm in a hallway, chairs are positioned around tables. A mere thought, and moments later, my clothes begin to dry. There will be no holding back with my magic tonight, not now.

Stone steps at the end of the hallway I'm in give access to the next level, whilst doors obviously lead into chambers of one kind or another. However, I don't even know whether this is where I'll find Kralgen and the others, so it's better I find someone who does know.

Until now, I've avoided guards, in fact, anyone at all, but the time for hiding in the shadows is gone. Carpeted stairs muffle my step as I descend. If this tower is guarded, it will most likely be nearer the ground floor.

Therefore, I'm pleasantly surprised to exit the stairwell at the next level to come across a helmeted guard who automatically snaps to attention. As I approach, he finally registers I'm an intruder and grabs for his weapon.

A punch to the throat has him gasping for air; all his thoughts of fighting disappear in his desperate struggle to breathe. I grab his neck, and whereas once I'd have snapped it, I let my blood magic loose, and he's shortly bound to my control tighter than if I'd used steel wire. I wait impatiently for the man to recover, watching for any sign of mischief in his dark brown eyes.

He's entirely mine. Nonetheless, I want to ensure I've covered every possibility, recalling when Dimitar, who was bound to me, tried to kill Lotane after I'd omitted to consider my fellow Chosen in the equation.

'You'll obey me instantly and do everything in your power to protect and help me. You'll also afford that to those I advise are friends. Kralgen, the Icelandian king, is one, and Lotane, the queen's consort, is the other.'

I'd omitted *love me*, knowing the hurt it can cause, and I don't care if he hates me as long as he does what I command.

'Now. I want you to take me to the quarters of King Kralgen.'

The guard nods, then sets off along the carpeted corridor, and I quietly follow. We creep down two more staircases decorated with stone busts of historic Astorian leaders and then turn toward a heavy wooden door reinforced with thick metal strips. As we step through, there are no carpets, just cold flagstones and bare walls. Acrid smoke from lanterns thickens the air, and I bite back a cough. We creep along several passages past closed doors, and twice my guide signals me to wait and even ushers me into a cupboard to avoid detection by three guards who'd otherwise have seen us.

He pauses at a corner, peeks around, and then turns his brown eyes on me.

'There's a guard stationed at the end of this corridor outside the king's chamber. The moment he sees you, he'll raise the alarm. You need to wait here while I deal with him. I'll cough when it's safe for you to approach.'

I glance around the corner and curse softly. He's right, but I just don't like trusting anyone other than myself, Kral or Lotane to get a job done, but what other choice do I have?

'Don't kill him,' I whisper.

A curt nod and my guard saunters around the corner. I restrain myself from looking after him to see what's going on, for the other guard will undoubtedly see my head pop around the corner with his attention this way.

I stand flat against the wall, listening carefully.

'Hey, Danlan,'

'What ya doing 'ere, Jeyob?'

'You won't bloody believe it, but ... hey, what the hell is that ugly insect on your shoulder? Turn around. I better get it off you!'

I cringe at this clumsy attempt to catch someone out, but sure enough, a moment later, there's a cough. A peek around the corner reassures me all is well, and then I'm hurrying down the passage toward the two guards.

Jeyob, as I now know my escort to be called, has his dagger tight against Danlan's throat. Danlan's eyes bulge wide at my approach; no doubt his woeful life is flashing in front of his eyes. I'm tempted to knock Danlan unconscious, but why choose violence when I have far more subtle options? Grabbing his hand is all it takes, and I have another bound and loyal guardian.

'You'll obey me instantly and do everything in your power to protect and help me. You'll also afford that to those I advise are friends. Kralgen is one, and Lotane, the queen's consort, is the other.'

Danlan nods.

'He is with us now, Jeyob. Let him go.'

It doesn't surprise me that Kralgen has a personal guard, as would any royalty, but what does surprise me is that the guard is Astorian, not Icelandian. Also, the door to Kralgen's chamber is as sturdy as a fortress gate.

I turn to my personal bodyguards.

'Keep watch; if you can't keep anyone away without using violence or raising suspicion, warn me!'

The locks are undone, so taking the door handle, I apply my body weight and heave the door inward.

I can't believe what I'm seeing.

'What the hell is going on here?'

***

Hands on hips, a scowl darkening my face, I survey the scene before me, awaiting a response to my demand.

Kral's chamber is split in two by ceiling-to-floor bars thicker than my wrist. On one side of the bars is my friend, Kral, bound securely, sitting on a robust wooden bench, bruised but unbowed. His arms are coiled in chains, which are attached to a sturdy leather belt at his waist. Iron ankle manacles complete the *world's most dangerous prisoner* look.

However, at least his incarceration hasn't been too unpleasant. A large bed in the corner is covered in sumptuous furs, the floor has wall-to-wall rugs, and several impressively large bottles of wine sit unopened on a cupboard beside the bed. Gilt-embellished books, bowls of fruit, and a platter of meats finish this picture of unbridled contrast.

Kral's eyes crease as he smiles in welcome at my entrance.

However, it isn't of him that I've asked my question.

'Well, I'm waiting.'

Lotane couldn't look more horrified than if I'd walked in on him bedding a goat.

'Kral's been ... confined to quarters,' he replies, kicking away a chair as he stands up.

'I'm not bloody blind,' I growl, frustration getting the better of me. 'Why aren't you getting Kral out of there?'

'Cause he's the one who got me locked up,' Kral volunteers, seemingly not too upset with Lotane.

I cuff Lotane around the back of the head. He's fast enough to dodge it, but he accepts the blow.

'Where are the keys to all ... that,' I say, gesturing at the chains and locked door.

'The guard has it, but he won't give it to you without an order from the queen or Commander Jarval.'

'Danlan!' I call. 'Come here and unlock the king.'

'You can't just come in here and do this, Malina!' Lotane warns, lowering his voice, taking my shoulders in his hands. 'This isn't your country, and the laws here aren't made by you. You can't keep playing at the lawless assassin you used to be. You need to move on, like Kral and I have!'

I shake my head in despair, pulling away from Lotane's grasp.

'If this is what happens when you move on, Lotane, I'd rather remain but a lawless assassin. That's our best friend in there!'

'I know that, and if he wasn't, he'd be dead,' Lotane hisses. 'He was talking of killing Commander Jarval and potentially Asterz if she was involved in his terrible crimes. She ordered his execution, but I saved him.'

'She found out because you told her,' Kral adds jovially, looking happy to fill in the gaps.

'Because she's going to be my wife!' Lotane says, looking aghast.

Danlan enters and steps toward the gate with a set of keys in hand.

'Stop, that's an order!' Lotane barks, but Danlan ignores him.

I position myself between them as Lotane's hand goes to the hilt of his sword.

'Have you bound him to you?' Lotane asks, his voice dripping with disgust. 'You can't just take away people's free will.'

'Nor should you just take away a friend's freedom for speaking the truth,' I retort, gesturing at Kral.

Kral nods vigorously in agreement, shaking a finger at Lotane.

'Look, this is not the time for us to fight,' I scold Lotane. 'Nogoth is a few days away from attacking, not months, and we're unprepared. I just witnessed Jarval meeting with a gargoyle. The commander's guilty of more than just the slaughter and rape of the Rolantrian and Surian peoples; he's betrayed Astoria.'

Lotane shakes his head as if trying to clear it.

'The general is a hard man, that I don't deny, but he wouldn't do what you've said. He's Astorian nobility and has been pivotal in mobilising this nation for war and arming Kral's Icelandians.'

'I don't deny he's done what you claim, Lotane; you've always told us the truth. But when have Kral or I ever done any different? If we tell you Jarval is guilty of these things, it's because they're true.'

Lotane's shoulders sag. I've almost got him. He just needs a little more persuasion.

'I have never lied to you, nor has Kral. I was unfaithful, but never have I lied to you.'

Even as the stupid words fall from my lips, I feel like biting my tongue off. Sadly, it's too late.

'Lies on top of lies,' Lotane scowls and, to my disbelief, steps back and draws his weapon. 'I can't let you do this!'

My sword almost sings as it clears its sheath.

'I let you win last time we fought,' Lotane says, frowning. 'Don't make me fight you for real.'

My vision blurs as I blink back tears. To close the gulf that now exists between Lotane and I seems nigh on impossible. Should I give up?

Never!

'You and Kral have always been better than me, Lotane, but not anymore,' I say with a shrug. 'So, let me tell you this, if ever you raise your weapon against Kral or me again, I'll kill you.'

My sword hisses out in a horizontal sweep, returning to its sheath in a heartbeat. With a clang, Lotane's sword blade hits the flagstones, leaving him holding the useless hilt.

The door to the cell squeaks open behind me, and I risk a glance to see Danlan kneeling at Kral's feet, working on the manacles.

'You have two choices, Lotane. Be a fellow Chosen we can trust, and escort us to the queen. She *has* to hear my news. You can help that happen without bloodshed.'

'Oh, and what's my other choice?' Lotane asks, tossing the sword hilt aside.

'You take Kral's place in that cell, and I'll never love you again.'

I can't believe the words that just fell from my lips. My emotions are all over the place. I'm angry at myself, at Lotane, and I can't help but love him so much too, and in this moment of madness, I've laid my soul bare; again.

'You don't love me anymore; you stopped loving me the moment you bedded Nogoth!' Lotane grimaces as though the words taste foul even speaking them.

'Oh no,' Kral mutters. 'Now is *not* the time!'

'I never stopped loving you, even when you took Asterz right in front of me,' I fire back.

I can see uncertainty behind those green-blue eyes, a softening, perhaps the beginning of forgiveness.

'What we had wasn't just about blood magic,' I continue. 'Even now, despite wanting to bash your stupid head in, I also want to ...'

'Malina, Lotane, now isn't the time,' Kral says, stepping between us, free of his chains.

Gah. He's right, but when will I have another opportunity?

'Lotane. Have you made your choice?' Kral asks, resting his stone stump on Lotane's shoulder, his visage dark and brooding.

Lotane snorts ruefully.

'I'm sorry, Kral. Of course, I'm with you. Can you forgive me for having you locked up?'

'I can.'

The next moment Lotane is on the floor, doubled up, gasping like a fish out of water.

Kral grins, flexing his hand, having sucker-punched Lotane in the stomach.

'But I can't forgive you for not opening those bottles of wine for me. I'm one-handed. Damn you for being so cold!'

'We need to go, now!' I growl, exasperated.

I grab Kral's arm and heave him toward the door. Lotane rolls to his feet with a moan, pretending not to notice my outstretched hand.

'The queen will be in the throne room. She's there every night till midnight, dealing with matters of importance,' Lotane wheezes. 'We'll go directly there, and I'll ensure she listens to what you have to say.'

The three of us step into the corridor, and flanked by Danlan and Jeyob, Lotane leads the way, jogging along at a brisk pace. We turn into a corridor to see four heavily armoured guards guarding large wooden doors that, from their size and intricate engraving, might lead to the throne room.

'Open the door,' Lotane orders as we approach.

After a moment's hesitation, and after looking at me and Kral, the guards assume an aggressive stance, glittering spear points lowered. Lotane, Danlan and Jeyob skid to a halt a dozen steps short of the menacing foursome who advance toward us.

'Leave them to me,' I command, and my sword feels like an extension of my will as it sings through the air. However, I'm not going to kill them; they're going to join my bodyguard!

***

Danlan and Jeyob open the throne room doors and step through.

'The queen's consort, Sir Lotane. Kralgen, King of Icelandia. Malina of Hastia,' Jeyob announces loudly as we stride into the heart of Astoria, the four Astorian guards marching behind us. Kral's eyes flicker everywhere, assessing the situation, who's in the room, entrances and exits, and the mood of those we advance upon. I know this implicitly without turning. Why? Because I'm doing the same.

Kral is unarmed, and so am I, having given my swords to Lotane so we don't present an obvious threat. We're here to talk, to avoid bloodshed. Now I wonder if that was such a good idea.

If looks could kill at twenty paces, I'd be dead, and Kral too; Lotane, on the other hand, might just be severely wounded.

Asterz's face is so twisted with malice that even if someone had written it on her forehead in ink, it couldn't be clearer. Next to her, Commander Jarval's features remain somewhat impassive, but his eyes and clenched fists tell me everything I need to know there. A half dozen other men and women stand momentarily transfixed, portraying everything from affront to anger.

'What, by the GODS, is going on here?' Asterz screeches, her finger jabbing like a spear to punctuate her words as she rises threateningly from her stone throne.

The sculpted flames which form the back of her seat of power have the faces of screaming victims amongst them. Lovely.

'Guards!' Jarval calls decisively, drawing his sword. 'Protect the queen!'

A dozen respond to Jarval's summons, running from the other two entrances to position themselves in a line before us. Cold eyes and steady spears show me they're confident and prepared to fight. My magic stirs, ready to respond, and I thank it silently.

'The only person the queen might need protection from in this room, Commander Jarval, is you!' Lotane booms before Jarval can say anything else. 'Return to your posts,' he snaps at the line of men in front of us, but unsurprisingly they don't move a muscle.

'Hah. These aren't the queen's bodyguards that idolised you before they died. They're loyal to me, you fool!' Jarval crows, smiling maliciously.

Lotane looks confused, and I wonder what he's playing at, but then I realise the brilliant subtleness of his play.

'No, Commander Jarval. You've forgotten your place. They are loyal to the Queen of Astoria!'

Lotane bows deeply to Asterz.

'I vouch for both Kralgen and Malina, my love. So if *you* wish the guards to stay because you doubt my loyalty, then I have just one thing to ask. Let it be you who orders the guards to kill me, not Commander Jarval. But whatever you decide, please listen to the news Malina brings.'

Damn, he's good. Going down on one knee, he lowers his head, offering his neck. However, his use of the words *my love* hurt me as keenly as a knife thrust.

My newly acquired Astorian bodyguard shift slightly, awaiting developments. It's a good thing Asterz and Jarval don't realise they're loyal to me, or that could complicate matters tremendously. Kralgen is utterly relaxed, muscles loose, ready to explode into action.

If Asterz orders Lotane's execution, the throne room is going to be redecorated in red very quickly.

'Rise, Sir Lotane. You have it right; the guard *is* loyal to me. How strange, Commander Jarval, for you to forget it!'

Lotane stands and takes a step back, bowing in thanks.

The smile tugging at my mouth doesn't last long.

'However, that doesn't mean I approve of your company, or your actions, *my love*. Your untrustworthy companions are unwelcome in my throne room for obvious reasons.' Asterz sits down but snaps her fingers and shoos the guards back to their positions. My Astorian bodyguards remain behind us without raising suspicion.

'Untrustworthy. Really?' I growl.

I know I should keep my mouth shut, but I'm tired, and this hypocrisy tastes too foul to go unanswered. Also, I've come here to deliver news, so I'll package it how I want to.

'Since you rescued me from the fey, I've done nothing but repay my life by helping to save yours and then overseen the building of a wall to keep Astoria safe. But what do I discover as I race to deliver you important news? Your knights have orders to stop and even kill me if I don't comply!'

Lotane looks from me to Asterz in utter disbelief, which changes to shock as Asterz doesn't argue my point.

'Perhaps I can forgive that considering my history,' I offer, although contrary to my words, I'd like nothing more than to chop her head off. 'But to make matters worse,' I press, 'Commander Jarval betrayed our plans to enrol the help of the Surians and Rolantrians and has been in clandestine meetings with one of Nogoth's gargoyles ... begging the question, which side is he on? So, tell me, who is the untrustworthy one here?'

Silence grows as Asterz leans back on her throne, fingers steepled, deep in thought. Jarval doesn't look bothered at all.

'You knew about this, didn't you,' I sigh as realisation hits home.

'This is my realm, so of course, I know,' Asterz snaps dismissively. 'The commander acted on *my* orders to crush the Surians and Rolantrians. For decades we've plotted our revenge on them for allying with Delnor to defeat us, and we grabbed it with both hands when the opportunity arose. As for the gargoyles, they wanted to change sides and needed a safe haven. We now have over two thousand acting as scouts, ready to fight loyally at our side if required!'

'But why didn't I know?' Lotane asks softly, confused and somewhat dazed.

'Because you're too damned idyllic,' Jarval barks, shaking his head.

Kral glances at me, his eyes full of wrath. Even I'm struggling to control myself. It was Asterz who ordered the slaughter and rape of tens of thousands. She doesn't deserve to live ... but now isn't the time. With Nogoth about to attack, removing the two most powerful figures in Astoria will leave this kingdom in chaos, however many people I bind to me.

'Listen carefully. You can't trust the gargoyles,' I implore, trying to put every ounce of sincerity into my voice, willing Asterz and Jarval to believe. 'All fey are bound to serve Nogoth and will never betray him, ever. Whatever they've told you is lies and misdirection because Nogoth is about to attack on two fronts simultaneously. A fey war fleet is but days away from Astwater, and reinforcements must be sent there immediately!'

A jagged smile works across Jarval's face like a crack in a block of ice.

'Your important news is almost as redundant as you are,' he sneers. 'Lotane has been pressing us for weeks to seal the port. Then, our *untrustworthy* gargoyles gave us warning of the approaching fleet. Astwater was already nigh on impregnable, but thanks to Lotane and our new allies, we blocked the narrow entrance, built fortifications and sent heavy reinforcements. It's now impossible to land a force there. So, you see, King Slayer, we are and always will be prepared for whatever danger appears.'

By some unspoken cue, high on the throne room walls, gallery curtains are pulled back to reveal dozens of archers. Their bows are undrawn, but the message is unmistakable, yet I still want to argue my point further despite the danger.

However, I'm at a loss for words. The gargoyles actually warned of Nogoth's intentions! This could explain why they never pushed their attacks on the wall and only made themselves more of a nuisance. Thanks to them, Astoria is now sealed tight with no way in.

Jarval looks to Asterz for direction, yet her gaze is on Lotane. There's no misinterpreting the look in her eyes. She might be conniving and evil, yet she's in love and doesn't want her decisions to affect their relationship.

With a disappointed sigh, she focuses her full attention on Kral and me again.

'Jarval informs me the wall you helped construct is impossible to overcome if it's well-resourced and defended. Return there with your oversized friend, continue to serve, and as your reward, we'll forgive your impudence and misplaced accusations,' Asterz states firmly.

Lotane turns to look at me. I know he's broken inside. He's just discovered that Asterz planned to kill me, that she's been responsible for rape and slaughter, and that she and Jarval have made alliances, all behind his back. Yet, nonetheless, those amazing eyes beseech me to take the offer.

The alternative will lead to bloodshed, and with the number of adversaries present, it won't end well for anyone.

A creaking as the main throne room doors swing open has everyone turning as an armoured guard pushes in. He hurries forward and bows at the steps to the throne.

'Well, what is it? Out with it, man!' Jarval snaps.

The guard glances around and points at me.

'I have a message for her, my lord. A stone giant at the gates threatened to break the walls down if I didn't deliver it straight away.'

'Well, spit it out then so we can all hear!' Jarval shouts, his eyes narrowing.

The guard gulps as he turns to face me, uncomfortable with the scrutiny.

'The message he gave me doesn't make sense.'

My stomach flips. Dimitar wouldn't have come here unless ...

'He told me to tell you ... The sky has fallen down.'

***

# CHAPTER XVII

We hurry through the corridors; Kral and Lotane are on either side of me, with Asterz, Jarval and a dozen guards a few steps behind. They'd scoffed initially, but they're also intrigued enough to want to hear the supposed apocalyptic news I'd told them Dimitar's message heralded.

The guard who'd delivered the news keeps looking worriedly over his shoulder as he leads the way, probably afraid for his own safety. It wouldn't be the first time an enraged ruler executed a messenger of ill-tidings.

Crossed swords, lances, shields and armour adorn almost every wall space, while cabinets hold maces, daggers, and flails. Dark, foreboding paintings of old battles add to the martial ambience, reminding me a little of Nogoth's mansion.

As we finally exit the keep, I'm not surprised to find the same frenzy of activity as when I entered. Hammers still ring as blacksmiths pound out new weapons while people shout and call because, for all their faults, Asterz and Jarval have Astoria preparing for war.

Guards snap to attention while men at arms salute or bow. Thankfully, it's stopped raining, although we still have to splash through puddles and mud toward the gatehouse. The reinforced gates open as we approach, revealing Dimitar immobile outside. It's the best place for him as he would have struggled to enter unless on hands and knees.

A smile slowly splits the rocky face, and he nods in greeting as we gather around him.

'Malina,' he grates. 'The sky has fallen down!'

'I heard, Dimitar. Tell me what's happened!'

'Nogoth. He left Ssythla.'

'Dimitar can sense Nogoth's location by what he describes as a change in the colours. Essentially, those who command magic create ripples in the world's fabric; thus, he can discern where they are,' I offer, knowing that some of those listening are unaware of his talent. 'Nogoth travelled to Ssythla a few days ago.'

This isn't the type of news I'd expected Dimitar to break cover over. Nevertheless, his presence is a massive reminder to Asterz and Jarval of my importance in defending the realm.

However, Jarval snorts in disgust behind me, determined to undermine me at every turn.

'Apocalyptic news indeed! What a waste of our time. My queen, let's have them escorted to the wall immediately.'

'Where's he heading, Dimitar?' Kralgen asks, his voice booming over Jarval's self-satisfied crowing.

'Here.'

'Of course, he's heading here. It's the last safe haven against his fey horde, and he's going to witness their failure first-hand!' Asterz points out, similarly unimpressed, her foot tapping impatiently.

*It's a safe haven unless you're Surian or Rolantrian!* I want to shout, but I hold my tongue. As soon as the threat from Nogoth is over, Kral and I will finish righting the wrongs they've done.

'So why has the sky fallen down, Dimitar?' Lotane asks loudly.

Dimitar bows his head slightly toward Lotane as if it's the first worthy question he's been asked.

'It's because shortly after Nogoth left Ssythla, he reappeared four days' march southwest of here.'

'What? That's impossible!' Jarval scoffs. 'If he was in Ssythla but a few days ago, it would take weeks to travel that far, plus it would put him plum in the black marshes within our borders!'

'Tell me your giant friend is mistaken!' Asterz demands.

'Dimitar doesn't get these things wrong!' I growl, my stomach churning.

'Are you absolutely sure?' Kralgen asks, looking up at Dimitar. 'Nogoth is within Astoria?'

The stone head nods, no words required.

'If he's here, then he won't have come alone,' Lotane mutters. 'He'll have an army with him.'

'But you can't just magic an army from one place to another!' Asterz splutters nervously.

I put my hand out, grabbing Kral's shoulder for support as my head spins. My legs feel like they've been robbed of all strength as Nogoth's master plan finally becomes clear. It's almost as if I'd seen it before and had simply forgotten it ...

'He's used a World Gate to bring his army in behind us. We just assumed there was one entry point, but we were wrong!' My voice sounds like an echo of words I already knew. 'We've celebrated sealing Astoria so tight, believing there's no way his armies could get in, but in fact, we've ensured there's no way we can get out!'

Silence falls as my words sink in, whilst around us, the rest of the world carries on, unaware its fate has been sealed.

Asterz lets out a scream of frustration that pierces the night.

'But then Nogoth is on the doorstep of Astnor and Astsul, our two western cities,' she says, horrified. 'They've sent us all their troops, and with no walls, they'll fall without a fight! Damn the day I ever met you, King Slayer. Build a wall and secure the port. This is all your fault!'

'That's not fair, my queen!' Lotane says firmly. 'We all thought these were good ideas, and they weren't just Malina's, but mine and Kralgen's too. You and Jarval also endorsed them, so don't seek to apportion blame!'

'How, how dare you support her over me!' Asterz shouts, incandescent with rage.

'It isn't about support; it's about the truth!' Lotane shouts back. 'The truth is we have less than a week before Nogoth's armies sweep over us like a tidal wave, and we need to decide what to do!'

'What's there to decide?' Jarval growls. 'We fight or we surrender, and Astorians don't surrender.'

'We fight!' Asterz states, fists clenched, eyes blazing. 'But we'll bleed that bastard Nogoth and his army for all their worth. We'll recall every man, woman and child here, bottle ourselves up in the castle, and force his armies to fight for our blood room by bloody room!'

'It's a good plan,' rumbles Kral.

'I don't care what you think, Icelandian,' Asterz hisses. 'You're only alive because Lotane pleaded for your life, so best you don't remind me of your presence!

'Commander Jarval!'

'Yes, my queen?'

'I want riders leaving within the hour to gather everyone within two days' march. Those beyond that are on their own. Recall our troops from Astwater and from the wall immediately. I won't have us defeated piecemeal. Then you're in charge of coordinating the defence!'

'Yes, my queen!'

'Lotane. You're responsible for getting supplies into the castle. Take fifty men, sound the city alarm bells, and conscript every person you encounter into forming human chains. If anyone disagrees, they're to be put to the sword!'

I've got to give it to Asterz. When she takes charge, there's no hesitation. The castle will be a tough nut to crack and will help us give Nogoth's forces a bloody nose before falling.

But as javelins suddenly fall from the sky like rain and screams rise to meet them, the plan starts to fall apart before it's even put in motion.

***

Six guards go down in seconds, skewered by the slim but deadly javelins the gargoyles favour.

'Under the gatehouse,' Lotane yells, shoving Asterz unceremoniously ahead.

The rest of us follow right behind, except Dimitar, who remains outside, unbothered by the slim projectiles.

As we take shelter, I'm reminded of a hailstorm I witnessed as a child. The downpour of javelins gets heavier, pinning dozens of unfortunate victims to the muddy ground, where they cry piteously for help. Yet to exit the gatehouse will be suicide, so we have to bear witness to their final moments before further javelins silence them forever.

'We have to get to the keep,' Jarval shouts above the noise.

Asterz's armoured escort nervously heft their shields which can deflect a sword blow or block an arrow, but these javelins will likely punch right through.

It's at least forty steps to the haven of the keep, where guards look toward us across the muddy scene of slaughter, and there'll be no cover once we leave our protective gatehouse. However, as quickly as it began, the rain of javelins cease, leaving the ground between us and the keep like a pincushion.

'Shields at the ready!' Jarval commands, peering out. 'We have to get the queen to safety!'

'NO!' Kral shouts, pulling Jarval back.

'How dare you lay your hand on me!' Jarval shouts, shaking himself free, hand going to his sword hilt.

'Look up there!' Kral commands, pointing. 'You'll take Asterz to her death!'

We all follow Kral's outstretched arm, and sure enough, against the backdrop of broken clouds, thousands of shapes spiral and flutter toward the keep. This isn't just a skirmish; it's an assault.

Jarval snatches his hand away from his weapon as if it's red hot.

'How many soldiers do you have inside the keep?' Kral demands.

'Two, maybe three hundred, and most of our remaining knights. The rest are out in the field training new recruits,' Jarval offers, his voice distant, as he watches in horror, realising too late he's been played by the gargoyles.

'It's not enough, not near enough!' Kral curses.

Like a smothering blanket, the gargoyles settle on the rooftops and walls, entering through doors and windows. The sounds of distant fighting begins to rise on the night air.

'GUARDS!' I shout across at the men and women sheltering in the keep entrance. 'RUN TO US!'

The words barely leave my lips before they spring into action, zigzagging at a sprint through the sea of bodies and spent javelins.

'What are you doing? Asterz hisses, turning toward me. 'How dare you command my troops!'

'Anyone who stays inside is dead; there's nothing we can do but leave, and the sooner, the better!' I say.

It's hard to stay calm while feeling off balance. Every decision we make, Nogoth seems to be ahead of us. Losing the keep, our final bastion ... is a hammer blow we'll never recover from.

'Have your stone giant kill them!' Asterz demands, frantically trying to find a solution to our predicament. 'Those creatures can't harm him!'

'He can't even get inside, let alone catch something that flies. He'd demolish everything and accomplish nothing if he's let loose, nor do we have the troops here to hold it,' Kral argues.

'It doesn't look like the gargoyles are attacking the city, so we should seek shelter there,' Jarval points out. 'We stick with our plan and send riders in every direction to rally our forces. We'll fortify the city and then work on a plan to retake the castle before Nogoth's army gets here!'

'Are there secret passages in and out of the castle? I ask excitedly. 'If we launch a counterattack from the inside, we can force the gargoyles out and retake it without damaging it beyond use!'

Jarval shakes his head in disgust.

'There were several. But after Lotane recounted your tale of how High Delnor was taken from the inside, we sealed them up as a precaution!'

It's unbelievable. Everything we've done has played into Nogoth's hands as if it's preordained.

'TIME TO MOVE!' Kralgen yells, shaking me to get my attention.

He's right; gargoyles are landing on the walls above.

'Dimitar. Cover our retreat!' I order.

We've hesitated enough, but the time for that is over, and the longer we dally, the more dangerous our position. With shields raised up high, the guards form around us as we make for the outer curtain wall. Dimitar follows, his stone form an impenetrable barrier should we be attacked from behind. Thankfully the gargoyles are too busy solidifying their gains to bother our retreat.

By unspoken assent, we pause at the wooden bridge I'd traversed earlier and look back. Our final hope of fighting Nogoth's horde in a glorious last stand from behind those walls disappears as the gates to the keep swing shut. The hundreds of guards, knights, retainers and servants left within will soon be dead … if they're lucky. I shudder when I think of the alternative.

Kralgen moves to my right, and Lotane positions himself on my left, with Dimitar towering above.

Lotane has my swords around his waist, and despite the gloom, I can't help but smile as a dark thought comes to mind. I recall the battle outside High Delnor's walls as defeat loomed and how Kralgen had attempted to slay Nogoth and failed. He'd come so close, but then he'd never had magic weapons like I now possess.

'Till now, we've been fighting to stay alive, and despite our best efforts, that fight is almost lost,' I say, finding it hard to admit defeat. 'So, we have to take another approach.'

The eyes of everyone are upon me, and for once, neither Jarval nor Asterz says anything snide or malicious. No one has the strength anymore.

'Now there's no alternative but to fight and die,' I continue. 'But our final moments have to achieve something more than simply dying with honour; we have to use them to kill Nogoth. If not, this invasion will happen over and again for an eternity.'

We head out into the city, the silence broken only by the sound of our passing. The inhabitants in their beds dream happily, oblivious to what has happened. Sadly for them, they'll awaken to a nightmare.

***

'Your giant can demolish the mansions, here, here and here, then use the rubble to block these streets,' Jarval says, his filthy finger stabbing down at a map of the city laid out on a stone tabletop. 'We lure them down the main thoroughfare with archers attacking from rooftops and balconies. The fey will pay in blood for every single step, and the civilians can fight a guerrilla war from the cellars and sewers under the city. With most of Nogoth's forces so engaged, we can launch a surprise attack with our cavalry, sweeping in from the rear!'

'There's no point,' I growl. 'Nogoth's giants and trolls will smash through any barrier we can make, and he has creatures that will make fighting in the sewers a nightmare. Worst of all, his gargoyles will decimate your archers and forewarn Nogoth of the cavalry wherever we position them. No, it has to be my way!'

'Your way would see this battle over within an hour, and all of us dead with it,' Asterz hisses, her fingers like claws as they grip the arms of her seat.

'At least it will be a glorious death that gives us a chance to kill Nogoth!' Kralgen declares, banging his fist on the table hard enough to rattle its timbers.

'How did that work out for you last time?' Jarval goads, looking at Kral's stone stump pointedly. 'By all accounts, the Fey King is impervious to weapons. Or perhaps, it's just you aren't as fearsome as you look!'

Kral picks up a metal goblet and crumples it like paper.

'Even with one hand, I'm twice the man you are!' he growls.

Lotane puts his hand on Kral's shoulder and says something quietly in his ear. Asterz gives Lotane a hurt glance. It irks her that he's close to Kral despite his words against her. If I'm honest, I'm a little hurt too. After our words by Kral's cell, I thought we'd gotten closer, but he's since kept his distance from me as well.

Whatever Lotane says, Kral chuckles, and the atmosphere eases.

'It won't be Kral that tries to kill him. It will be me!' I announce into the silence that follows. 'I just need to get to him, and I've already outlined how!'

Jarval's mocking laughter goes on and on.

'I've heard it all now. Joking aside, if your Icelandian friend failed, you'll have no chance!'

'You know what I did to the High King of Delnor?'

'I think if you could have done that to Nogoth, you'd have tried it before.'

'Not Nogoth, I'm thinking of doing it to you if you can't control your stupidity!' I hiss, starting to lose control of my temper.

Jarval's face twists in hatred, turning pale at my threat.

'There's still time for you to be executed before the battle!' he says, pushing his chair back from the table.

'Enough of this bickering.' Lotane shouts, his rare outburst having the desired effect. He turns to me, holding my gaze. 'Now is not the time for holding back on anything, Alina. Tell them; they need to believe!'

'Tell us what, exactly?' Asterz demands.

I'm shocked by Lotane addressing me by my affectionate name in front of Asterz, and it reaches through the red mist. I sigh as my anger drains away and receive a warm smile as a reward. I've been reluctant to reveal my hand for fear of raising people's hopes, but Lotane's right. We need unity, and perhaps this can bring it, however short-lived.

I draw my swords, moving away from the table, putting further distance between Asterz, Jarval and myself to ensure they don't panic and call the guards.

'Jarval, you're right,' I say calmly, to the commander's surprise. 'Kralgen is my better in combat, and Nogoth is impervious to weapons. But I still have the best chance to slay Nogoth because he's never faced anything like what I now wield. Watch!'

The stone walls offer no resistance to the blades as I score a deep X, then plunge them in, hilt deep. I step away, leaving them there.

'It doesn't matter what I use them on,' I explain to my silent audience. 'These swords can cut through steel as easily as water, while flesh and blood offer no resistance whatsoever. They can't be parried, no armour can deflect them, and if I can reach Nogoth, I hope to cut him in half before he recognises the danger he's in.

'You can try them if you like,' I offer, gesturing to Asterz and Jarval. 'Unfortunately, the magic they contain only responds to my touch, or I'd have us all wielding such weapons.

Jarval rises from his chair, eyes wide with excitement, which fades when he can't pull them from the wall. Asterz tries too but gives up, similarly defeated.

From their change of demeanour, I can tell I've almost got them. It's time to get them both fully on my side so we can finalise our battle plans. As Lotane had said, they need to believe.

'Nogoth's greatest strengths are also his weaknesses,' I say, raising my voice, commanding the room. 'He has won so many battles, he can never see his army losing, and he believes himself invulnerable, so he's happy to fight for honour, as happened with Kralgen. Jarval, you mocked Kral unfairly. He out-skilled Nogoth in their duel and laid him low. Had Nogoth not been impervious, he would have died at Kral's hands. This time, with these weapons, he will die at mine!'

Asterz rises from her chair and leans forward, putting her palms flat on the table as she fixes me with a determined gaze.

'Tell us what you need from us, King Slayer,' she says. 'It's time for you to earn that damned title again. I just hope the gods let me live long enough to see you do it!'

***

'Why aren't they attacking?' Lotane muses as we take some fresh air outside the house that has become the new command centre.

Kral and I follow Lotane's gaze, looking up at the keep highlighted against a dark sky. It always presented a foreboding sight, but never more so than now. Gargoyles line the walls while others spiral above, their harsh shrieks and cries scraping at everyone's nerves. Two days have passed since it fell, and not once have they even flown over the city.

'I'm sure Nogoth wants as many of us alive as possible. He has a big army to feed,' Kral replies, grimacing.

'Whatever the reason, we can't have the gargoyles occupying the castle and using it as a rallying and resupply point,' I say. 'Lotane, I know Asterz won't agree, but Dimitar needs to drive them out, or they'll wreak havoc on us if Nogoth gives the order.'

Lotane sighs.

'Convincing Asterz that her ancestral home needs to be reduced to rubble before the final battle will be a difficult medicine for her to swallow, but I'll get it done,' he says emphatically.

I kick a pebble, watching it bounce down the street and imagine it's Asterz's head.

'Dimitar will have time to finish the job properly. According to him, Nogoth hasn't changed position much. Asterz was probably right; he's securing Astoria's eastern cities first.'

The city streets are fairly quiet as we stretch our legs, yet no one has been evacuated, and under every roof, a flurry of activity is taking place. Rhythmic sawing and the flat impact of hammers on metal are the backdrops to our conversation.

A team of soldiers driving wagons pulls up on our street outside houses and shops, and they begin banging on doors. I shake my head in sympathy as they run in and out, taking items deemed essential for the final battle. Residents and owners offer little, if any, complaints, under no illusions that life as they know it is coming to an end.

'It's strange,' I say, breathing deeply. 'We have less than a week until Nogoth arrives, and I'm under no illusions that I'll end up dead, yet, I'm impatient for the moment when I face him to come.'

'I don't know about you, Kral,' Lotane says. 'But I don't intend to die, do you?'

'Definitely not!' Kral laughs. 'It's a shame Malina has to, though!'

'You fools,' I laugh, caught up in their humour, and without thought, put my arm around Lotane's waist and pull him in for a hug. It takes a moment to realise what I've done, and I'm about to pull away when his arms wrap around me.

'I'd appreciate you staying alive if you can find a way,' Lotane says softly. 'I'd miss you if you died.'

I flush with warmth at his words.

'If that's the case, I'll try not to,' I reply, struggling to keep my voice from choking up while revelling in the feeling of his arms around me. It's a moment I don't want to end. 'But if I could die right now, I'd die happy,' I whisper.

'Enough talk about dying. Let's try and live!' Kralgen laughs.

Have Asterz's deeds finally made Lotane recognise the poor choice he made, or with the end so near, has he decided there's no point in lying about his feelings anymore? Maybe it's just a moment of nostalgia, the briefest flash of what we once had, never to ignite again.

I don't care which; I'm just glad he brought me close, even if for just this one moment, although it also hurts that he hasn't responded in kind to my final comment.

'Make way!' Distant voices shout.

Kral coughs loudly, and we pull apart, a hint of reluctance evident as Lotane's hands linger on my shoulders before letting go. However, the tale of us hugging might make it back to Asterz and cause all kinds of trouble when we least need it, so Kral's right to gently remind us.

We hastily retreat onto a sidewalk as half a dozen cavalry ride around a corner toward us, their horses lathered.

'Here!' Lotane shouts, raising his hand.

The horses' flanks heave from the exertion as they're brought to a halt before us.

'We have news for the queen and Commander Jarval!' shouts the lead rider. 'Where can they be found?'

'Tell me!' Lotane commands, his voice brooking no disagreement. 'She's taking rest, and I'll be returning to Commander Jarval shortly and can pass on the news. You know who I am?'

'Yes, Sir!' the scout salutes, as do those behind him. 'Even though we didn't see them, the enemy is to the southwest of us! We came across a terrible scene. A hundred guards dead in their barracks. It was horrible. Even though there was no sign of a fight, some creature must have forced them to do the most awful things to themselves ...'

I don't hear the rest of the scout's words as he recounts his discovery.

'This is war. Every death is awful,' I interrupt, realising my dark deed has been discovered and not wishing to hear any more of it.

Lotane flashes a glance at me.

'Be assured I'll pass this news on,' Lotane says. 'Now, take your men back south; I want eyes on this new foe. But whatever you discover, ensure you return by tomorrow night!'

The scouts salute, wheel their horses about, and head off, leaving us in a cloud of dust.

'What new manner of creature have we yet to encounter?' Lotane asks, horrified. 'Or perhaps it's Nogoth, using blood magic on those brave enough to defy him! But it can't be him; he's days to the east of us. We should get back and report this. If Nogoth has forces south, we must reconsider our battle plan!'

'Don't tell them about this,' I say. 'Dimitar destroying their castle is enough bad news for them to swallow in one day.'

'What are you talking about?' Lotane steps back, looking surprised. 'If a new creature can do this, we have to prepare ...'

He stops, eyes searching mine, and I feel stripped naked under his scrutiny, and I drop my gaze, unable to meet his.

'Please don't tell me you know about this, that you had something to do with this?' he asks, his voice hushed, unbelieving.

Kralgen steps forward, palms raised, a welcome peacekeeper.

'Lotane, what Malina ...' he begins to say.

'I'm not talking to you!' Lotane growls, turning his attention back to me.

'They were rapists, all of them.' I explain. 'The things they'd done to the Surian and Rolantrian refugees were unspeakable. They burned alive those who fought back ...'

Lotane steps away, eyes wide, and the warmth we'd briefly enjoyed is torn away by the cold wind of revelation that sweeps between us.

'I thought I knew you,' Lotane says, his voice cracking. 'Guilty or not, your actions were evil. I'll do as you ask and won't tell Asterz or Jarval, but it's only because I'm ashamed of what you did!'

I reach out desperately to bring him close, but he twists away and stumbles down the street.

Kral puts his hand on my shoulders.

'Let him be, King Slayer. He'll come around once he thinks about it. I, for one, am glad they got what they deserved, and I'd see every other bastard Astorian soldier suffer the same fate. Sadly, we need them to give us a chance to kill Nogoth. They'll get what's coming to them then, or in the days after if they're taken back to the fey world!'

Was I right in dealing such harsh justice? I don't know, but if I could bring those Astorians back to life and enjoy Lotane's warmth one more time, I'd do so in an instant.

I feel empty inside, emptier than in a long time, and I want the next few days to pass by in a heartbeat.

***

I stand alone, watching as Dimitar brings down the final tower where I'd first witnessed Jarval meeting the gargoyle. Above, like angry bees, the gargoyles swarm, yet even as I watch, they begin dissipating, fluttering east toward their master.

When Dimitar had first breached the walls, Kralgen had stood beside me, but of Lotane, Asterz or even Jarval, there'd been no sign. Throughout the day, random soldiers and civilians have come and gone, and I realise Kral must have gone with them.

Yes. Kral had said something about spending time with his Icelandians, and I'd turned down an invitation to join him. I wish I'd gone ... I don't want to be alone.

Dimitar's looming form crunches unsteadily toward me over towering mounds of rubble. Hardly anything intact remains behind him. Shattered arches, gaping windows, fragments of walls, and a spiral staircase leading to nowhere are all that remains of the once mighty keep. Destroying it was the right thing. If Dimitar could do this, then so could the giants and trolls.

'I'm finished,' he grates as a rocky smile splits those craggy features.

'Thank you, Dimitar. Are you ... hurt at all?' I ask, noting the small chunks missing from his arms, legs, head and torso. He hadn't been able to avoid all the falling debris and had been partially buried several times.

'Nothing that won't heal by the morrow.'

A handful of stone goes into the gaping maw; all that's necessary to restore his towering frame.

With him by my side, I'd feel confident going into any battle ... except the one that awaits. Dimitar is mightier than a giant, yet we'll face dozens of giants and trolls too. My magic swords are incredibly powerful, but only while the magic lasts, and Nogoth's innate power far exceeds mine.

I just hope he won't see what I've got planned coming. Yet he's fought and won a thousand battles. How will anything be a surprise to him?

'What now, Malina?'

'I think you should go assist with the defensive works.'

That giant head nods.

'Dimitar.'

'Yes, Malina.'

'Thank you for always being here for me.'

'Where else would I be?'

I smile, waving him away, and cast my eye over the devastation he's left behind.

Hopefully, the Saer Tel will work their magic when the battle is over, whether Nogoth lies dead or not.

The streets lay empty, no lights shine from empty windows, no lamps are lit, and there aren't even dogs barking. The city where I walk is as silent as the grave. I turn south toward the massing army of civilians and the Astorian cavalry, missing the sounds of life.

It's incredible, but almost everyone is willing to bear arms, and those who are too young to fight are hidden within cellars throughout Ast, being looked after by the too old. Poison has been distributed, giving those who hide the chance to end things without suffering.

Slowly, as I reach the outskirts, the streets come alive, becoming a hive of activity.

Wagons roll by, filled with thousands of rough-hewn spears and wooden shields. In the distance, hammering and voices shouting orders hang in the air. Everyone moves with a purpose, and yet, despite having orchestrated what's going on, I'm the one who feels out of place.

Hunger washes over me as I see the blood flowing through everyone's veins. The night is always difficult, but it's also a test of my strength and willpower to resist. However, tonight I'm tired, physically and mentally.

'Let's get some sleep, Malina,' I whisper.

I've chosen a top-floor apartment in what used to be a tavern. It's a few doors from the command centre and gives a perfect view over the plains to the south and east of the city. It would be the ideal place to watch the final battle from if only I wasn't going to be on the front line.

The stairs creak as I ascend; another reason I chose my room. Once I'm inside, no one can sneak up to my door without me being aware.

I throw my swords on the bed as I enter. I'll pour what magic I can into them, but first, I need a wash.

The small adjoining bathroom has fresh water in a bowl. There's a scented bar of soap, and I inhale deeply, smiling. Sadly, the accompanying sponge is so rough I feel like the top layer of my skin is being peeled off. I wonder if Asterz chose it for me.

Nonetheless, I persevere and feel better after washing the dust and sweat from my body. Next, I give my leathers some attention, sponging them down.

At least I'll die clean.

I'm rewarded by a fresh breeze coming in through my window as I lay down on the bed. I scent some food that's been left for me, snorting in amusement at a habit I've kept since my first days as a Chosen. Apart from being cold, it's edible, and I wolf it down with relish, drinking some water to leave myself feeling better than I have all day.

I draw my swords and channel my thoughts, draining myself to the point of exhaustion as I imbue them further with magic.

Sleep takes me in its heavy hand, and a part of me wishes I'll never wake up.

***

A delicate odour tugs at my subconscious, while a subtle change of the environment or perhaps even a drop in temperature brings me instantly awake.

*Keep your breathing even, Malina!*

Magic, or perhaps just some primordial instinct, has warned me of danger.

My body tells me I haven't slept for more than a few hours. It's enough to have recovered some strength, although not fully, but it will have to be enough.

I lay there, visualising where I'd tossed my swords. They're two steps from the bed on a chair, but it might as well be two leagues. I won't get there in time. Magic will be my salvation here.

Fire to blind and scorch, wind to slam those in the room back against the walls, by which time my swords will be to hand, and the fight will be over. Unless I'm dead before it gets that far.

Three, two ...

'Nogoth respectfully requests your presence!'

The voice is chilling, promising horror and death, yet the words carry no threat.

As my eyes snap open, a shade appears at the far side of the room. Its cloak shifts around hypnotically, making its form shimmer and disappear even though it's right before me.

It kneels, raising empty hands, putting itself at my mercy.

'Nogoth wants to talk with me?' I ask, slipping out of bed, moving toward the chair, my swords and clothes.

'Yes, and your fellow Chosen.'

'They won't agree to go.'

'They've already agreed and will soon be waiting at the city perimeter.'

'You're lying.'

A shake of the cowled head.

'Nogoth only wishes to talk, to make an offer. He promises you safe passage to the meeting and back again before sunrise.'

'What offer?'

'That I don't know.'

I pull on my leather clothes and boots, then reach for my swords.

'No weapons. There will be no attempt on your life. Were that his intention, you'd be already dead!'

An arm lifts, finger pointing, and as I follow the gesture, I note a wavy dagger lying on the pillow next to where I'd been sleeping but a minute ago.

'Should you decide to bring a weapon, the promise of safe passage will no longer stand.'

Damn!

'Will you join your friends and meet Nogoth in peace?'

If I bring my swords, this battle could be over before it begins. Yet would I, even if I could? Damn the honourable side of me that rails against the thought.

'I will.'

'You friends will be waiting with horses at the city's eastern gatehouse. The guards there are enjoying a long sleep and will be unaware of your passing. Continue east for an hour, and you'll find Nogoth in a farmhouse south of the main trade road.'

'Only an hour away?'

'He has ridden hard in anticipation. Don't worry; the army is still a full day behind.'

'How did you get here before him?'

A further shake of the cowled head as the shade drifts across the room, keeping its distance. Its hand sweeps out, taking its dagger, and then with a subtle bow, it steps out of the window.

By the time I look out, it's already disappeared.

There's no way this creature could have arrived with Nogoth, which means it's been here the whole time. Had it come through the pass before it was sealed, or do the mountains pose no hindrance to its ethereal form?

My real concern now is, have our plans been compromised?

I turn toward the door, reach out for the handle, and pause.

No.

The shade had the right idea.

I run and leap out of the window.

The night is my friend, and the rooftops are the streets I own.

***

# CHAPTER XVIII

My horse gallops powerfully, and I lean forward, exhilarated, not just by the speed I'm travelling but by the prospect of meeting Nogoth again.

What does he want?

The shade had mentioned an offer, but for what; the unconditional surrender of Astoria? Half sacrificing themselves so the other half might live? I wonder how he'll take our refusal.

Despite the promise of safe passage, I focus on the terrain either side of the road, searching for signs of disturbance. As the shade's appearance in my room has reminded me, danger often lurks where you least expect it. Had Nogoth sent it with orders to kill, I'd be dead because I'd thought myself safe. I wonder if the others were similarly caught out.

No words have been spoken since we left the city, the pounding hooves and whistling wind make it nigh-on impossible. Not that Lotane would talk to me even if we slowed. He's purposely avoided my gaze, whereas Kral had given me a warm embrace before we'd mounted up and heeled our horses east.

The moons light up the sky while beside me, Lotane, Kral and their mounts glow red, shining beacons riding across the plain. Then, another light source appears, flickering dimly in the middle distance.

'There!' Kral and Lotane shout, pointing it out.

We continue along the road a little further, then come across a track leading south and slow our horses to a walk on the uneven ground. This has to be Nogoth, as everyone for leagues has been conscripted into the army.

'I wish I had my swords,' I say softly, conscious my words might carry.

'Hah. So you can kill any Astorian soldiers who might be camping here?' Lotane asks sarcastically.

'Lotane, enough. You're being foolish,' Kral snaps. 'If you're angry at Malina, be angry at me too. I'd have chopped all their damned heads off, given the chance! They deserved to die for their crimes.'

'If they deserved to die, then what about us?' Lotane growls. 'We've done nothing but kill for as long as I can remember.'

'We've certainly killed more than our fair share,' Kral sighs. 'But it's really not about that, is it?'

'What's it about then?' Lotane demands, his voice rising.

'It's about you finding any reason to stay angry at Malina instead of admitting you still love her!'

Lotane's mouth opens and closes, but no sound comes out. I wait, my heart hammering, barely able to breathe in anticipation of his next words.

'No, that's rubbish!' he chokes out and urges his horse into a canter.

Kral shakes his head in disappointment.

'We have so little time left in this life,' I sigh.

'Too true. But as I thought mine was already over when that damn shade woke me in my room, every hour I get now seems like a gift,' Kral chuckles. 'Now, let's catch Lotane before he does something stupid.'

Our horses reluctantly pick up the pace, but they're too well trained to disobey, and we draw abreast of Lotane just as he pulls up at the farmstead. It's typical of its kind. A few wooden outbuildings with open doors are on three sides of a central courtyard, whilst a farmhouse occupies the fourth.

Golden light shines warmly from around the back of this low stone structure, and aromatic smoke causes our horses to whinny in concern. Dismounting, we tether them to a water trough by the open front door, then gather close to Kral as he beckons us in.

'Lotane, go up on the roof and make sure he's alone ...' Kral begins.

'He'll just get his hands dirty for no reason,' a velvety voice announces.

We step away from the farmhouse as Nogoth appears from the black interior. Casually attired in boots, dark trousers, and a light shirt, he still manages to look as regal as if he wore a crown and ceremonial robes. There's something about his demeanour, the way he stands, the ageless wisdom he exudes, and then there's the handsome face, intense violet eyes and body that radiates strength and sensuality.

'I'm here alone, of that you have my word. I forgot to bring some herbs, but the previous owner seems to have kindly left some behind,' he says, opening his palm to display some dried leaves.

We don't say a word, and I wonder if Kral or Lotane are contemplating trying to end this here and now despite the parlay.

'Look. Either attack me now and get it over with or let's sit down and eat. I, for one, am famished,' Nogoth says, turning away and offering his back. Then with a shrug, he walks toward the glow of the fire.

'I am hungry,' Kral mumbles, then strolls after Nogoth.

Lotane follows without a word or glance in my direction.

Fine!

As I walk around the corner, I'm met by a campfire burning merrily while a deer carcass roasts on a spit above the flames. A large pot hangs from the skewer, bubbling away. Wooden platters, goblets and what looks like several flasks of wine are on a small table.

Nogoth stands before a seat fashioned from a tree stump and gestures for us to sit on three more laid out in a semi-circle to his right before rubbing the herbs between his palms over the pot.

I'm glad you chose to eat,' he smiles warmly. 'But good food should always be accompanied by good wine, as any Icelandian will tell you!'

I want to ask what the hell is going on, what we're doing here, and why all this damned pretence at civility when we're going to be dead the day after tomorrow. I can see from Kral and Lotane's faces that they're about to vent.

Yet I bite back on the words as Nogoth pours wine into the goblets and then hands them to us with a small bow.

I consciously avoid touching his hand and am grateful to note the others take the same precaution.

'Before you ask or say what's on your minds, I have a small favour to ask,' Nogoth smiles, utterly indifferent to the atmosphere.

'A toast,' Nogoth says loudly, raising his goblet.

'To my Chosen, and to our victory!'

***

Utter silence.

Yes, the fire crackles, the wood pops, and the deer fat hisses as it drips into the flames, but in my mind, there's utter silence. It's the type that can only follow something so unbelievable that it scrambles thoughts and the power of coherent speech.

'What the hell are you talking about?' Lotane snarls, tossing his goblet aside, being the first to recover.

Kral crumples his, throwing it into the fire.

'You might not have noticed because you're a bit old, but we're not your Chosen and aren't on the same side anymore!' he mocks.

Nogoth looks toward me. He smiles, causing the skin around his eyes to crease. There's no disdain I can perceive nor anger at Kral or Lotane's reaction.

'Anything to add?'

My goblet follows the others to the ground, the red wine soaking like blood into the packed earth.

Nogoth sighs.

'That is the best wine you'll ever taste in your lives,' he sighs. 'I have several dozen flasks over a thousand years old in my world. I've shared it with your predecessors many times, often in this very spot; however, this is the first time my toast has been refused!'

'Perhaps you should get used to disappointment.' Lotane leans forward, glaring.

Nogoth nods, his disposition amiable.

'I am not disappointed, far from it. Never have any Chosen freed themselves from the bond of blood magic and fought so hard against their conditioning and training to defeat me. I salute your endeavours and thank you for the challenge you presented.'

'We were told you wanted to make an offer, and I, for one, am not here to make friends!' Kralgen growls, trying to bring the meeting back on track.

'You are right, King Kralgen,' Nogoth acknowledges and rises to his feet. I watch as he expertly cuts meat from the sizzling deer, the slices making an enticing pile on a wooden platter. Turning to the pot, he adds vegetables with a ladle before offering it with a fork to Kralgen. 'We are not friends, but that doesn't mean we can't share food while you listen.'

Nogoth stands there waiting, unperturbed, the platter extended, before, with a grunt of thanks, Kralgen takes the food. The Fey King returns to the fire and prepares food for Lotane and I before sitting back down with some for himself. The aroma from my food is so enticing that I follow Kral's lead and tuck in.

'The first time you saw me, I asked a promise of you,' Nogoth says, pointing a fork in our general direction. 'Can you recall what it was?'

'You said a lot of things because you like to hear your own voice!' Lotane snaps.

Nogoth's laughter rings out merrily into the night before he composes himself with a sip of wine.

'It's true. I do. Now, let's finish our food, shall we? It will give you time to remember.'

Some silences are comfortable, but this one isn't. Lotane bubbles with suppressed anger. Kral is more impatient than anything else and shovels food into his mouth at an insane rate. I, on the other hand, have a feeling of expectation. Something is coming, and I can almost put my finger on it.

As we put our empty platters aside, Nogoth stands, his eyes questioning.

'You made us promise that one day when our mission was over, we'd all sit down and remember the long road we'd travelled,' I offer.

'Thank you, Malina. Today is that day, and I call upon you all to keep that promise. I want you to remember what you've forgotten!' Nogoth's hands and fingers weave strangely as he speaks, and my head spins.

He's drugged the bloody food!

Yet, even as I'm about to lurch to my feet, the spinning stops. Like the sun rising over the horizon, shedding light upon the land, what I've forgotten, or more specifically, what was hidden, is revealed.

No book full of pictures, no page filled with words could make things so utterly clear. Words spoken to me long ago while I slept under the influence of our nightly sleep infusion; maps and charts, timelines and plans all return to me in a rush. It's as if they lay at the bottom of a dark well, and as I fall in, they rush up to meet me until I stare at them right in front of my face.

I'm stuck between horror and awe. The planning that's gone into this campaign has been meticulous, and our role in it stage-managed. Almost every step Lotane, Kral, and I have taken since the invasion has been imprinted on us subliminally for years. There'd been plans for Nestor, Alyssa, and Fianna too, until I'd got them killed.

Kral becoming King of Icelandia, the rallying of the armies at High Delnor, Lotane sealing Astoria's port, me blocking the pass, the remaining

Icelandians, Surians, Rolantrians, and Astorians all brought together. Every idea, every decision, all following instructions given to us that we'd been made to forget.

Even when things didn't quite work out, it hadn't mattered. Lotane was supposed to become King of Astoria but had chosen marriage over assassination, while I was supposed to have become the High Queen of Delnor … or somewhere else, but that memory is still just out of reach.

Had Dimitar stamped on me, I doubt I'd feel as crushed as I do now.

'In the past times, the Chosen were told their roles without subterfuge,' Nogoth speaks softly into the silence. 'Yet despite being bound by blood magic, when my fey armies appeared, most fought consciously against my plans; others took their own lives whilst only one or two fulfilled their duty. Those historic campaigns were prolonged, bloody and fruitless, and sadly those who served me so well rarely survived.

'You were the first Chosen this new approach was tried with. You had many choices throughout this campaign but predominantly chose the path you'd been shown. This invasion has gone nigh on flawlessly, and it's almost complete. As you're now aware, the last of humanity is trapped with no escape. The fate of them all rests with me.'

My hands are shaking, something they haven't done since the first purges. Kral's fists are clenched as he struggles to restrain himself. Lotane seems resigned to the situation, although he slowly shakes his head in denial.

'I admire you all,' Nogoth continues. 'Despite your conditioning, you resisted me, fought against me, and Kralgen even humbled me on the battlefield. It's something I'll never forget. The fact that you served me so well is the reason your lives were always spared.'

Kral raises his eyes briefly as his name is mentioned, but Nogoth's compliment doesn't break through whatever internal struggle he's dealing with.

'You asked what my offer was. It isn't for you to pass on my terms of surrender to Queen Asterz or anyone else.'

'So, what is it then?' Lotane asks bitterly.

'Forgiveness and a future! Be the Chosen you once were, take your place at my side, and be recognised for the greatness you carry inside of you.

'Kralgen. Offer me your fealty again, and you can return to your Icelandians. Keep them from the battlefield, and I swear you can all return to Icelandia unharmed. Your people have lost enough, and they need not suffer further.

'Lotane. You were always destined to be the King of Astoria. Help those I leave behind and set your kingdom on the road to greatness again.'

Finally, those violet eyes turn to me and my stomach flutters. Nogoth doesn't use the quickening, but his sheer animal magnetism has me breathing rapidly.

'Malina. You have two choices before you. Become High Queen of Delnor, or return with me as Queen of the Fey.'

'Don't go with him!' Lotane snaps.

Why did he say that? Is it because he still loves me, or just doesn't want Nogoth to have me?

Nogoth looks back and forth between us.

'Forgive my heartlessness. Another option is that Lotane and even Kralgen can join us. We can enjoy immortality together!'

Nogoth bows deeply.

'Return to Ast, my Chosen. Ensure you keep yourselves and the Icelandians from the battlefield, and when all is over, a future you could only ever have dreamed about awaits.'

Nogoth tosses the half-full wine flask to Kralgen and then walks from the firelight. A few moments later, a horse neighs, followed by the sound of departing hoofbeats.

Kral takes a long pull on the flask and then offers it to me. I've never needed a drink more in my life. It's like liquid gold as it runs down my throat. Nogoth was right. It's the best wine I've ever tasted.

'So, what do you think?' Lotane asks.

'It's really good wine!' Kral winks.

Lotane sighs, shaking his head.

'There's a time for humour, Kral, and I don't think this is it.'

'There's always time for humour, and I've always fancied being immortal.' Kral shrugs.

'Immortality it is then,' I say, taking a slug of wine before throwing the flask at Lotane.

Lotane catches it, tilts his head back, and then downs the contents.

'To immortality!'

***

'So, what are we going to do?'

I gaze across at Lotane, wishing he'd look at me when he talks, as opposed to at Kralgen or an empty space above my head. We're sitting in Kral's room, which is dominated by an oversized bed covered in cushions and surrounded by silken drapes. It hadn't surprised me to discover this building had been a brothel. I can only hope the sheets were changed before he moved in.

'We're going to fight, although truth be told, the promise of eternal life with that incredible wine to hand was quite tempting.' Kral laughs, shaking his head, reclining in an armchair.

It's often said that many a true word is said in jest. Is there some in Kral's? I certainly have my doubts. The chance to live in the beautiful fey world, enjoying Nogoth, Lotane, and the golden elixir.

No! What am I thinking? That's my conditioning talking. It must be.

'Of course, we're going to fight,' I say, pushing those alluring thoughts aside. 'Lotane is asking whether we should stick to the original plan, considering every strategy we've come up with has never been our own. This could be no different.'

'I know what he meant,' Kral sighs. 'By now, I'd hoped you wouldn't always see me as the slow-witted oaf!'

'Sorry. You're faster than all of us, Kral. We're just too slow to keep up with your wit,' I say, reaching over to squeeze his arm.

'And would know when I'm teasing you!'

I snort with amusement. Kral is getting happier the closer this final battle gets. His love for fighting is obvious, but with death certain, he's happy believing that Alyssa is waiting for him.

Kral ponders for a moment, his chin resting on his stone cap.

'Any alternative we consider could have been planted in our thoughts too,' he says, coming to a decision. 'There are but two choices. We attack or defend. Attacking is the only chance we have of facing Nogoth again with weapons in hand, as he won't be in the front line. So we keep with our plan and execute it perfectly!'

'Nogoth anticipates we'll join him, and that will make him complacent. His offer of letting us and the Icelandians live and, of course, Malina spending forever after at his side is something he believes we'll grab with both hands,' Lotane growls bitterly. 'We'll use that against him!'

I'm sad. I know Lotane still has feelings for me, and Nogoth's words must have cut him deeply. I want to shake him out of it, but neither is he entirely wrong, and that guilt would usually keep my recriminations in check.

'If I get close enough to Nogoth, he'll rue the day he made such a stupid assumption,' I fire back pointedly, my temper flaring.

'Enough!' Kralgen growls. 'You two should make up now. You have but one day and night left. If Alyssa was still alive, nothing would be able to pry me from her side if that was all we had!'

I look across at Lotane, reaching out my hand. Those incredible eyes return my gaze, and for the briefest moment, I see the hardness slip, and then, it's gone.

'You're right. If that's all we have left, I'll spend it with someone who loves me,' Lotane says, standing abruptly. 'I need to get back to Asterz. She'll wonder where I've been all night. I'll tell her I was drinking with you, Kral.'

The door slams hard, and it takes all my resolve not to run after Lotane.

'I'm sorry, Malina,' Kral says, getting to his feet. 'I thought he'd see sense, but sometimes it's easier to be angry than to love. Now, my Icelandians need me, and there's still much to be done to prepare for battle. Dimitar will be waiting for your instructions, and without him, we won't be ready.'

'You know, Kral. I envy the home you found amongst your Icelandians. I'm even somewhat envious of Lotane finding a place here in Astoria. I only ever felt at home in the Mountain of Souls. What does that say about me?'

I don't wait for Kral's answer but head down the stairs and into the early morning light.

It's foggy, and people move swiftly through the thick cloud like spirits of the dead. I shiver because, before long, they will be.

*Come on, Malina. Move with a purpose!*

My room, when I return, is as I left it, and I'm relieved to see my swords on the chair.

It's my last day alive, and I'm all alone.

I laugh to myself.

I'd better go find Dimitar then because a stone companion is better than none.

***

'So, there's little left to say ...' Asterz begins.

A captain of scouts walks in, interrupting her mid-flow. He's filthy, unshaven, and smells like he hasn't washed in days. Neither Asterz nor Jarval berates him; everyone is too physically and mentally drained after this last day of desperate preparation to care about salutes. They just waste time.

'The fey army has been spotted.' The scout announces into the expectant silence. 'They're making camp several hours' march to the east. They number over a hundred and seventy thousand, and my troop counted two dozen giants and over thirty trolls amongst the ogres, wolfen and gargoyles.'

'Thank you, Captain. Have your men rest. Ensure they're ready for battle tomorrow,' Asterz says, placing her hand on his shoulder and gently turning him from the room with a nod of thanks.

Only Asterz, Jarval, Lotane, Kral and I are in the command chamber. Only the five of us know the plan we're going to hatch. I just pray that it is only the five of us, or Nogoth will laugh himself to sleep tonight.

'There's little left to say other than I'll see you all at first light tomorrow,' Asterz continues once the scout has gone. 'I can't say it's been a pleasure knowing you all, just some of you,' she says, taking Lotane's hand in hers. 'Goodnight.'

Lotane smiles around the room without actually catching anyone's gaze before following Asterz as she leaves. Guards wait down the corridor and form up to escort them from the building.

Jarval's demeanour is cold, but to my surprise, a smile tugs at his lips.

'King Slayer, Kralgen, we might not be the best of friends ...' he begins.

'We're definitely not friends,' Kralgen corrects him.

'Well, irrespective, tomorrow, we'll ensure Nogoth gets what's coming to him for the sake of Astoria!'

'Tomorrow, everyone will get what's coming to them!' Kralgen growls, leaning forward.

'What the hell do you mean by that?' Jarval shouts.

'Just that I hope you die screaming with your guts around your ankles for what you did to the Surian and Rolantrian people, you sick, twisted bastard!' Kral roars back, sweeping empty food platters and goblets from the table with his hand.

'Enough, Kral,' I say, standing behind him, putting my hands on his shoulders, and applying gentle pressure. 'Enough!'

'You might not like me, but you need me, so watch your bloody mouth!' Jarval hisses, stalking from the room.

It's a wise decision, for Kral is on the verge of doing something rash.

'Sorry. I've kept that bottled inside for way too long, and there's so much more to say!'

'You're right, Kral. He'll get what's coming to him!'

I just hope I get to see it happen. I'm tempted to stick a sword through Jarval's back myself!'

'He'll have a far more horrific death at the hands of the fey. Leave it to them. There's over a hundred and seventy thousand, Kral! By the gods ... whether we achieve our goal or not, there's going to be a slaughter. Anyone who survives will wish they hadn't. Those who take poison in the cellars are the wise ones.'

With a grunt, Kral levers his huge frame from his chair, which creaks in something akin to relief.

'See you at first light, King Slayer!'

I want to ask Kral to keep me company, drink wine, and share old tales, but I can't.

'Goodnight, Kral!'

A few minutes later, I follow Kral out into the night, where a light drizzle does nothing to dampen the noise of hundreds of soldiers and civilians going about some last-minute business. Many walk arm in arm, and Lotane's decision to choose Asterz for his last night cuts deep.

A dark corner creates an opportunity to climb up a drainage pipe unobserved, and I'm shortly on the rooftop of a small stable. It's silent, likely because all the horses have been commandeered for the war effort, but the smell of hay and manure remains powerful. I make myself comfortable for a while, leaning against a wall of the adjoining building.

I relax, feeling cleansed by the rain, high above the bustling streets, and realise that despite feeling lonely, I enjoy my solitude. I breathe easily up here, away from the crowded places, the stench of people and the filth they leave behind.

The rainfall increases, and I climb to my feet. This isn't pleasant anymore, so I head back toward my apartment. I move cautiously, checking behind me, listening carefully, choosing the most waterlogged rooftops so that if I'm being followed, my pursuer will make themselves heard.

I arrive and survey the surrounding rooftops, yet there's no sign of anyone or anything except the giant figure of Dimitar standing motionless in the downpour guarding my quarters. The window to my room I'd locked earlier from the inside is still intact, so I leap down to the street below, landing lightly on the cobblestones.

I pause, but the rhythm of the rainfall isn't disturbed, so I move toward the front door. Dimitar nods at me, and I nod in return. He wouldn't let any threat inside the building, yet that doesn't mean I relax entirely. I let myself in, and stand in the hallway, drenched and dripping. With a silent request, my clothes start to dry, and steam rises off me.

The building is also inhabited by two officers, neither of whom I can hear. The carpet on the stairs is dry, indicating no one has come in from the outside in a while. After the shade caught me unawares, I've no intention of putting myself at risk again, even with my giant guardian outside.

I tread lightly up the stairs and open the door to my room, only to freeze.

Something or someone is inside.

***

Having been so alert throughout my return, rhythmic breathing is brought magically to my ears, forewarning me of the intruder. It's steady and slow, with no hint of anxiety. Whoever Nogoth has sent is supremely confident.

My sword whispers from its scabbard, the voice of death itself, as with the other hand, I ease the door open.

*Get ready.*

My magic squirms as I visualise a flare of light so bright that it will temporarily blind the intruder.

It's dark, but my fey vision has no problem picking out the pulsing red heartbeat and river of blood flowing through the intruder's body ... as it lies curled on my bed.

There's no mistaking the intruder.

Dundain.

With all the Astorian military recalled from the wall and port, there's no surprise she's in Ast. The only surprise is that she's found me.

I shake my head. I'd instructed Dimitar to destroy or warn me of any threat, and as Dundain is anything but, he'd not considered her visit worth mentioning. Damn his lack of initiative ... or perhaps, he's actually taken it for once. Does he know of our pairing?

My stomach rumbles, and I find myself salivating.

The final battle is tomorrow, and here before me is exactly what I need to imbue myself to bursting with strength of body and mind.

So as not to startle her, I close the door quietly behind me.

Dundain doesn't awaken, and I move around the room, lighting candles and an oil lamp by the bed, filling the room with a warm glow.

I look down upon her plain features, cleft chin, the thick eyebrows. I tenderly brush some hair back from her face, surprised to find a warm feeling in my stomach beyond just the need to feed. Here is someone who wants to spend her last night alive with me.

Thanks to her, I won't spend my last night alone.

Suppressing my hunger, I lie beside her, arms pulling her close. She snuggles into my warm embrace, and then, aware of my presence, sleepily opens her eyes.

'Malina!'

I know we're bound by blood magic, but the love in her voice, whether genuine or manufactured, touches me deeply, and I hold her closer still.

'Hey. What's wrong?' She pulls away a little, concern in her eyes. Does she sense my inner turmoil or the fragility of my mind? I don't know, but concern creases her brow.

Then taking my head in her hands, she leans forward and kisses me gently. Her lips brush my forehead, cheeks, closed eyes, and finally, my mouth.

I want to push her away, to tell her that I don't want to go where this is leading. But suddenly, Nogoth comes to mind, violet eyes hypnotically pulsing with an inner light. Memories of his teeth sinking into my neck, my cries of pleasure and pain, and how I'd raked his back with my nails arouse me beyond belief.

Driven by such images, my willpower crumbles, and I pull at the laces and buttons of Dundain's clothes as she does the same to mine.

Time blurs as we join in a frenzied passion of entwined limbs and gasping breaths .., and then it's over. The candles indicate barely a half hour has passed. For a while, I hold Dundain in my arms, my fingers caressing her back, fighting against the upsurge of hunger. It's not just the joining, but the intimate closeness that follows that fulfils her, and I want to give, not just take.

I wish I felt the same, although I know how she feels. I'd enjoyed that intimacy with Lotane, although strangely never with Nogoth. With the Fey King, it was always fire and passion, without any intimacy.

'Sit up,' she tells me, disentangling herself from my embrace.

I groan as if reluctant to move, feigning disappointment, but who am I trying to fool. With cushions supporting me, I recline against the headboard as Dundain sits between my legs and leans back into my embrace. She brushes her hair to one side and tilts her head to the right.

My arms tighten, trapping her as if she were prey. As I bite into her neck, I note with a sense of revulsion the numerous bruised puncture marks where I'd feasted far too many times, but it doesn't stop me from drinking.

Like the golden elixir of life, every drop that passes my lips is a symphony of taste. My nerve-endings tingle as her life force enhances mine, and I savour the ecstasy of the moment. Her soft moans arouse my hunger further but also serve as a warning. I abruptly cease feeding, aware that on the morrow, she needs to be strong too.

'Don't you want more?' Dundain asks, aware I've finished earlier than usual.

'No. You've satiated both my hungers!'

I expect her to settle down, but she sits up and turns around with sorrowful eyes.

'I need to get back to my unit. Forgive me if I don't stay the night?'

Relief floods through me; she's given me what I need.

'I'll just wash before I dress and go?'

I happily smile my assent and close my eyes.

The bed creaks as she stands up, and I hear the bathroom door open and close.

How can I die tomorrow when at this moment, I feel so damned alive?

The door opens and closes softly again.

'Malina.'

I swear my heart misses not just one beat but two before, with a huge thump, it starts again.

'I'm sorry!'

I open my eyes in disbelief to find Lotane standing inside my room. He looks shy, and his eyes are slightly red and puffy. He's obviously upset, and I want to go to him, hold him, ask him if he's ok, but with Dundain in the bathroom ...

'Don't say anything,' he says, holding up his hand, speaking softly but urgently, coming to sit by the bed. 'I've been such a fool, and I now know why! All this time, I just couldn't be with you. I wanted to, but something just kept telling me to push you away. Now I know. It was my mission. To be the King of Astoria, I had to be with Asterz. All these things we did, not knowing why ... this was one of them. It should be us, Alina. I've never stopped loving you, and ...

His eyes finally take in the twisted bed sheets and Dundain's clothes scattered across the floor.

'Who the hell do those belong to?' he shouts, standing up in disbelief.

'It's not what it seems.' I cry, desperately trying to think of a way out of my predicament.

'Did you say something?' Dundain asks, coming out of the bathroom with nothing but a small towel around her mid-drift.

Lotane storms over to her, and she backs away, terrified. My stomach lurches uncontrollably when I note Lotane staring at her neck. Blood is seeping from the fresh puncture wounds, and then there are the scabs and bruises from my previous feeds.

'I could have forgiven you taking a lover whilst I lay with Asterz, but this. THIS!' he shouts, pointing at Dundain's neck. 'What was I thinking? This is why I couldn't be with you; it has nothing to do with conditioning or my mission. You're a monster!'

Lotane storms out of the room, and I'm too in shock to do anything but stare blankly after him as tears pour unchecked down my face.

Dundain gathers her things, gets dressed and gently closes the door behind her.

What have I done?

***

# CHAPTER XIX

The day of death has arrived.

As I sit astride a spirited, armoured warhorse on a mound of earth to the east of Ast, I can't help but think we have the perfect setting. An unseasonally cold wind howls with the bite of winter, and clouds hang low and heavy in the sky, glowing as the city behind us burns. Before me, the red grasslands, blown by the wind, looks like a sea of blood as the fronds ripple and bow before nature's mighty hand.

Nogoth had anticipated us holding the city, fighting for every street, and had sent his gargoyles in with burning brands and flasks of oil before first light. Still, it had mattered little, for, with our army already in the field, only those few non-combatants remaining in the cellars had anything to worry about.

Thanks to the fire at our backs, there will be no retreat today.

Kralgen sits on his warhorse to my right. He's forgone the offer of heavy Astorian plate armour and is dressed in thick Icelandian furs, making him appear even larger than he already is. Somehow, they've found the mother of all horses, a gigantic beast covered in scale armour like mine, and he towers above everyone. His right-hand grasps the shaft of a long lance while a long-handled, double-bladed axe is slung in a harness down his back.

I've also forgone the heavy plate, relying on my speed and skill, complimented by a red kite shield on my left arm for defence. I hold a heavy lance in my right hand while my sword hilts jut over my shoulders, ready and waiting.

Asterz is mounted on my left, encased in steel from head to toe, just like the first time I'd encountered her. Like her own lance, she sits ramrod straight, staring ahead, a haunted look showing beneath her raised visor. She's not said a word to me, and I'm sure she knows Lotane came looking for me last night. Whether she knows what occurred when he found me is immaterial now.

Jarval and Lotane are at opposite ends of our lines, each leading six thousand mounted Astorian light archers who only this morning found out their role in the battle to come.

Glancing over my shoulder, four mounted bodyguards wait, carrying lances with bright red pennants, ready to protect their queen.

Behind them, highlighted against the flames and smoke, the human battle line stretches north to south, made up of two hundred and fifty thousand old men, women, and youths with a few thousand regular men-at-arms and guardsmen in the front rank presenting a disciplined front.

Yet to a distant eye, every one of them looks like a trained soldier because the last few days have seen every bed sheet in the city turned into a bright white tabard and cloak. A forest of spear tips rises above them, although many of the rearmost ranks bear knives bound to staves. Yet, all that matters is that they stand there like an army of the light.

Fifty deep, the line stands, by five thousand long, curving forward at the ends like a bull's horns. These curved points are where Kralgen's Icelandians have been positioned, for even the older men and women were once young warriors, and they won't run.

To the sides and rear of humanity's last hope, an impenetrable thicket of long stakes angle outward, ensuring no enemy can successfully attack from the flank or rear. It is a defensive-looking formation, unwieldy, unmaneuverable, and stands immobile, awaiting and inviting the hammer blow from the enemy arrayed before us.

And what an enemy it is; the scouts had got the numbers right.

It's an overwhelming horde of the most fearsome creatures ever to walk these lands. A hundred and fifty thousand ogres make up the main battle lines, with giants and trolls positioned front, centre and rear.

Directly behind the centre of the line, Nogoth sits like a statue, astride a charger, surrounded by an ogre and troll bodyguard. He makes a commanding figure even at a distance, and I wonder what his thoughts are as he looks across at me.

Beyond Nogoth, along with some trolls and giants, a boiling mass of maybe fifteen thousand wolfen guard the fey rear and flanks, a perfect counter to our light cavalry should they try to encircle.

Shadows pass overhead, and I risk a glance to see gargoyles above the battlefield. These creatures give Nogoth yet another massive advantage. Thanks to his spies in the sky, he knows about our numbers, the defensive stakes, that our cavalry are all light archers, and that Dimitar is nowhere to be seen.

I'm certain Dimitar's notable absence is making Nogoth reticent to engage because gargoyles flutter over the city, no doubt trying to find my stone friend amongst the burning buildings.

'Look!' Kral growls as Nogoth's battle lines reform to match the length of our own.

Asterz's head bobs a little in recognition.

Nogoth has responded like the military genius in charge of a vastly superior force he is, and no doubt finds our crude attempt to lure him into making a costly mistake laughable. Our defensive-looking line is a ruse. A more compact force hoping to attack and break our centre would find our longer line enfold their flanks, the bull's horns closing in on the sides while the cavalry circled and charged the rear. Nogoth knows we still wouldn't win, but he's not willing to risk heavier casualties.

Now, despite Nogoth's formations being only thirty warriors deep to our fifty, he'll still emerge victorious with minimal loss.

'He certainly knows what he's doing!' Kral says admiringly. 'And he's keeping a dozen of his giants and trolls back in reserve to ensure his flanks and rear remain well protected.'

I can only nod in agreement. Nogoth doesn't make mistakes.

Thunder rolls in the distance, but it isn't the weather; Lotane and Jarval have initiated the battle. They know fear is already eating away at the bowels of our pretend army, which could lead to a rout before the enemy even gets close.

From their positions guarding the flanks, the Astorian mounted archers ride towards one another in two long lines, shooting arrows on the move at the front of the enemy ranks. I'd seen how little effect these volleys had on the ogre lines outside of High Delnor. However, twelve thousand arrows raining down every few seconds can't be ignored, and the ogres start taking casualties.

After a solid ten minutes, the arrows eventually sting Nogoth into action. Horns blow, and his army begins a slow advance.

'Don't wait too long,' I murmur, watching as the Astorian archers continue to hold position and shoot.

Clouds of arrows rise from the enemy ranks. Distant horns blare, and suddenly the enemy line surges forward in perfect formation. Before the mounted archers can escape back the way they'd come, the end of the fey line meets the curved ends of our battle lines in a crash that echoes across the field.

Jarval and Lotane have left it too late to lead their commands to safety!

I'm squeezing my lance so tightly that my hand cramps. I look across at Kralgen, taking strength from his calm. If he can look death in the face and remain unfazed, so can I.

Trapped between the centre of the two armies, the archers wheel their ponies about in an undisciplined panic, seeking escape, knowing that, unable to manoeuvre, they'll be decimated. Almost a thousand of their number have already fallen dead and dying on the ground to enemy arrows, and suddenly they arrive at a terrible decision.

Asterz stands in her saddle, eyes wide, and my breathing is shallow and fast.

The mounted archers turn and charge back toward the centre of our lines.

It's a catastrophic decision, and Asterz waves her lance and its Astorian pennant wildly, attempting to rally their retreat.

The ground shakes as they ride by, parting like a river to flow on either side of Kralgen, Asterz and me. Yet behind us, their way is blocked by our lines of infantry, who, seeing this tidal wave of frantic horses bearing down on them, sunder apart in a panic.

The centre of our line has broken before the battle has truly begun!

***

Asterz turns her horse and gallops back after the fleeing archers. Kralgen and I follow, the bodyguard close behind.

I can sense Kralgen's pride and sorrow despite the ends of our battle lines being pushed back. It doesn't matter how brave or determined the older Icelandians are, they're being slaughtered, yet they aren't breaking.

'Hold, my Icelandians. HOLD!' he bellows, even if there's no chance they'll hear his voice, any more than we can hear the scream of the dead and dying at this distance.

'They'll hold,' I shout, trying to reassure him, even though they'll likely die to the last man and woman.

To our west, on the other side of the gaping hole in our lines, the Astorian horse archers are rallying. Sadly, being behind the middle of our lines, there's no chance of them flanking the enemy before the battle is lost.

Horns blare amongst the enemy horde, and an answering roar from thousands of fey throats sends shivers down my back as Nogoth grasps this opportunity to crush us before order can be re-established. He knows his rear and flanks are secure, seeing the horse archers are now redundant to the battle's outcome.

We reach the gap in our lines and wheel our horses about to face the enemy. The rest of the fey line is now charging to engage, led by trolls and giants lumbering ahead of the main ogre force.

'Damn, but that's a scary sight,' Kralgen laughs. 'Are we ready to die?'

I reach over to grasp his forearm, whereas Asterz simply snaps her visor down.

'This is the beginning of the end.' I say. 'I'm glad I'm by your side, Kral!'

The queen and her bodyguard raise their lances high, the red pennants snapping in the breeze. Smoke billows around us, and our warhorses whinny in excitement and fear.

Behind us, thunder rolls as the horse archers led by Jarval and Lotane charge back through the gap.

'Let's see if Nogoth foresaw this one coming!' Kralgen shouts as we heel our mounts forward.

'Yah!' I urge my horse to greater speed, forming with Kralgen and Asterz the tip of the charging wedge that catches up with us.

A glance over my shoulder confirms the mounted archers now bear heavy, iron-tipped lances, and I laugh hysterically. No, Nogoth will not have seen this coming! His gargoyles only saw rows of stakes protecting our rear lines, not lances waiting to be swept up by steady hands that had staged the panicked retreat perfectly.

Directly ahead, the surging sea of ogres halts atop the earth mound we'd occupied earlier, frantically locking shields. On either side, the fey charge loses momentum as their adjoining comrades stop behind, preparing for impact.

Seeing our threat, two nearby giants come together ahead of the ogre line, relying on their cohesive size, strength and hideous studded clubs to block our charge.

It will be like riding face-on into a mountain and will destroy our formation before we hit home.

'DIMITAR!' My voice booms, enhanced by magic.

The mound on which our horses had stood a short while ago erupts in a fountain of dirt. Ogres are thrown into the air screaming as, in response to my call, Dimitar rises from the ground wielding an iron-bound tree trunk as long as he is tall.

He ignores the ogres at his feet and charges the backs of the two behemoths, tackling and throwing them both sideways to the ground, where they begin a struggle for domination.

They disappear behind as the wedge flies toward the ogre line unimpeded.

'Yah!' I shout again, tucking the lance close to my side, lowering the tip, aiming at the neck of a thickly muscled, tusked ogre beating a sword against its body-length shield.

'TROLLS AND GIANTS TO ME!'

Nogoth's voice booms across the battlefield as I catch a glance of him wheeling his horse around, giving frantic orders to gargoyles who flutter furiously into the sky. He flings his arms in our direction, and the wolfen rearguard moves forward to support the ogre line. Without pikes, no formation of infantry thirty deep, however skilled or ferocious, can stop our disciplined charge. The horse archer ponies behind us might be small and light, but the long, heavy lances have temporarily transformed them into shock troops.

Javelins start to rain down from the hastily deployed gargoyles, but it's too little, too late.

'FOR ASTORIA!' Asterz screams, her metallic voice muffled by her helmet. Whether or not they heard her, it's a battle cry echoed by the thousands of following Astorian horsemen.

A heartbeat later, my lance shatters as it catapults my ogre target backwards into his comrades, and my horse leaps into the breach.

'DIE!' Kralgen roars to my right as we urge our mounts onwards into the thick mass of fey; momentum our best weapon. I can feel the shock through my thighs as my warhorse bowls over anything in its way, its padded chest armour absorbing the heavy impacts.

I pull my right sword free, hacking down left and right into the ogreish mass. My blade cuts through everything that gets in its way, leaving my uncomprehending victims dying behind me. Swords ring against my shield and warhorse's armour but bounce off without penetrating.

The clash of steel on ceramic and the screams of dying ogres, men, and horses pierce the air. I laugh from the sheer ecstasy of killing whilst alongside me, Kralgen's blood-splattered face is a picture of joy.

'Come on, we've got the bastard!' Jarval shouts above the cacophony, having come abreast of the queen on my left. As I turn to the right, I'm relieved to see Lotane has made it to Kralgen's side.

I wish I felt the same as Jarval. We've cut through about fifteen ranks of ogres, and it won't be long till we break through the remainder, but beyond them, fresh wolfen await whilst trolls and giants converge on Nogoth. I sense my mount labouring, and it stumbles before righting itself, and if my warhorse is struggling, then the archers' steppe ponies will be in worse straits.

The rain of javelins thickens even as the ogre resistance stiffens. The wedge has flattened to become a broad charge, and as I risk a glance left and right, it appears to be about a hundred horses wide. Behind us, the javelins are taking a terrible toll, emptying saddles at a frightening rate. Thousands are down already, and the ogres are attacking from both flanks, knowing they're safe from the charge taking revenge for their brethren we've slaughtered.

The thrum of restrained power in my right sword is so tempting to unleash, but Nogoth is too far away to guarantee me hitting him. If I miss, which I surely will from this distance, he'll never let me get close for a second attempt ... yet something must be done, or our charge will stall.

Inside, my magic begs to be unleashed, yet if I do so, I'll tire myself terribly ... but what other choice do I have?

What will help us without leaving me exhausted and vulnerable?

Lystra's voice echoes in my mind.

*An enemy who cannot see cannot fight.*

It's already windy, and with a simple thought, a howling cloud of dirt and stones spirals into the massed ranks before us. Unfortunately, unsettled by its appearance, my tired warhorse shies and suddenly wants to turn and run. I tighten my thighs as I seek to control it, and the entire charge falters as other riders struggle with theirs, something I'd never even considered.

'Come on, boy,' I call encouragingly, discarding my shield to thump his armoured neck. 'Keep going!'

Years of training and my voice take effect, and my mount pushes determinedly forward into the partly blinded ranks of ogres. To my dismay, even though we make headway, too many wolfen support the ogres, and I doubt we'll ever get close without using my sword's magic.

I raise my sword, ready to unleash hell. Maybe I'll get lucky.

Then, the giant figure of Dimitar leaps over the line just to Lotane's right, landing amongst the ogre ranks, scattering them with his giant club before rushing at the wolfen beyond. Within moments he's covered in a writhing mass of glossy, black-furred bodies. He stumbles about, plucking them from his face ... but his intervention allows riders with lances and fresher horses to push through and become the new front line.

The charge gains momentum again, and as Kral, Lotane, Asterz, Jarval, and I follow behind, waves of wolfen frantically leap to drag riders from their saddles ... but it's not enough.

We're going to get another crack at the Fey King.

***

'NOGOTH. We're coming for you!' Kralgen roars, and even without any magical aid, his voice carries.

Nogoth's head whips around. I'm too far away to hear what he shouts, but his four troll bodyguards position themselves in our line of charge, leaving only a dozen ogres by his side. However, giants and troll reinforcements are closing in, and if they reach Nogoth before we do, we'll never get the chance we desperately need.

'It's time,' I yell, looking across at Asterz and Jarval.

Asterz flips up her visor, her face pale, eyes full of hatred.

'Just know I want you dead as much as I do that bastard Nogoth,' she hisses.

I hold my tongue, knowing time spent on a conversation is wasting time we don't have. Asterz shouts something at Jarval that I don't make out, and they drop back. It will be their job to rally and lead a group of tired horse archers left and right, to intercept and distract the trolls and giants rallying to their king.

'DIMITAR, CLEAR THE WAY!' I yell, urging my horse onwards. I can feel its mighty heart beating frantically; it hasn't got much more to give.

The horse archers ahead of Kralgen, Lotane and I succumb to the wolfen tide, and once more, Kral's axe glitters, harvesting the fey in glittering arcs. Lotane, whose helm has been knocked clear, lays about him with a longsword. I now have both shortswords drawn and control my horse through knee pressure alone.

Dimitar bellows a challenge and simply kicks his way through the thinning wolfen toward the left-most troll, drawing the other three toward him.

I hack at a wolfen leaping at my horse from behind and am shocked to see less than a few hundred mounted archers following us, sabres drawn. Behind them, the ogre ranks have reformed, cutting us off from any hope of retreat, although that was never our intention. The charge, while successful, has suffered terribly, and the butcher's bill is rising every moment.

Suddenly, my horse dies beneath me. I don't know whether its mighty heart just gave out, or it died to a gargoyle javelin, but in the blink of an eye, I'm landing amidst the claws and fangs of the snarling wolfen pack.

Fire erupts along my sword blades, and I sprint after Kral and Lotane, using them to guard my right flank. Nogoth is but thirty paces away.

I spin and twist, hacking and slashing, sending wolfen limbs flying, setting them on fire, happier now that I'm on foot, able to move freely. My shorter weapons were never that suited to mounted combat, but here, amongst my enemy, they're deadly.

Kralgen's mount goes down, and then we're fighting our way through the flood. We keep our distance, not fighting back to back, just far enough apart to keep out of the arc of the other's weapon. Lotane continues to fight from his warhorse, knowing his heavy armour will hinder him if he ends up dismounted.

An archer on a pony pushes up on my left flank, giving me a little respite, its rider slashing with a sabre. Less than fifty Astorians are left supporting our assault on Nogoth, an ever-diminishing island swamped by the sea. Dimitar continues to fight two trolls, having dispatched two others, but not without cost. One arm is missing from the elbow down, and huge chunks have been smashed from his right leg, while his two opponents remain agile and are baiting him from both sides.

Beyond the titanic struggle, I catch sight of Nogoth. He's still astride his mount, and however much I'm desperate to see if my magical swords can cut him in two, with so few of us left, I'll never make it.

A furred body falls to my magical blades as another leaps at me over its pack mates. I spin, chop off its paws, and elbow it on the muzzle, driving the wolfen to its knees. I kick the dazed creature to the ground, aware of Kral stepping in to finish what I'd started.

The wolfen thin, and suddenly the opportunity presents itself.

I raise my arm and extend a sword, sighting along its length at Nogoth, who is looking directly at me.

'LOOK DOWN!' I shout.

I don't know whether Lotane or Kral hear or even comply, but I lower my eyes a split second before unleashing my sword's magic.

Every hair stands on end, and when I look up, there's no sign of Nogoth. What's left of his horse lies there, surrounded by rings of smoking, charred bodies, neatly laid out in widening circles like black petals on a flower. Even beyond the circle of death, chaos reigns as ogres and wolfen stumble, singed, deafened, and perhaps blinded.

I've just killed Nogoth, King of the Fey.

***

Before me, along the line of the strike, wolfen lay dead or dazed, and those to either side flee, their animal courage pushed beyond limits, hindering others still trying to reach us.

Into the gap, I charge, Kral by my side, stumbling over smoking corpses. Lotane leaps from his exhausted mount that refuses to move and catches up. The three of us, supported by five archers, run forward, dispatching horribly burned and broken wolfen with every step.

I reach the remains of Nogoth's horse, lying blackened and dead on the ground and leap over it.

'There!' shouts Lotane, pointing out Nogoth's black armour-clad body lying twenty paces away.

To our left, three giants close in and run to stand guard over Nogoth's body, having broken past Jarval and Asterz's archers. All I want to do is ensure that Nogoth is dead, and I'll pass from this world satisfied, knowing he'll never invade again.

'We need to get closer, to be sure!' I shout.

Kral and Lotane nod soberly because we surely won't last long on foot against the giants.

Yet even as we advance, Nogoth sits up.

I'm close enough to see his bare chest where his breastplate has been blown apart, but other than smouldering hair, he appears nothing more than somewhat dazed.

'DIE!' I scream, my words lost as forked lightning flashes from my remaining magical sword across the short distance that separates us. It hits Nogoth square in the forehead, then leaps to the three giants, flinging them away with a crash of thunder.

'COME ON!' bellows Kral, leaping forward.

Lotane and I follow him to Nogoth, who struggles to rise.

'For the sake of the gods, die!' Lotane shouts, swinging his sword into Nogoth's cracked helm.

Nogoth is flung to his back, and Kral, Lotane and I stand over him, Kral chopping with his axe, Lotane and I hacking desperately with our swords.

'Don't stop. His magic can't protect him forever,' I shout, gasping for breath.

The five archers who'd followed stand in a circle, their backs toward us, buying us time with their fragile lives as our blows shatter every remaining piece of Nogoth's armour, ripping his clothes, and bouncing off his body beneath.

Violet eyes open, shining, and a vicious smile splits those full lips as Nogoth suddenly grabs Lotane's sword and Kral's axe by the blades. For a moment, my friends strain, vainly trying to pull their weapons free, then ... lightning crackles on Nogoth's fists, and they're flung away empty-handed to crash on the ground.

'I gave you all the chance at life!' Nogoth roars, rolling to his feet, casting the axe and sabre aside. 'I gave you the chance of immortality! Was serving me really too high a price to pay for that? Was it?'

He dismissively waves back the ring of fey who've killed the archers, intent on finishing us off himself.

'No one is to intervene. No one!' Nogoth commands.

I channel what little magic I have left into my swords and lunge with both weapons, hoping the power I've imbued them with pierces Nogoth through. As the points meet his flesh, I gasp in pain as they're jarred from my grasp.

Nogoth steps forward and snaps a punch into my chest, sending me spinning backwards, arms and legs spasming from the lightning impact. The next moment my ribs crack as Nogoth delivers two vicious kicks to my side.

'You could have had everything!' he yells, and suddenly my body is squirming as he channels his power of the quickening.

I groan in pleasure, pain, and despair. The growling, screaming, howling, and clash of weapons grows distant as my senses swim, but then everything roars back in an instant. I open my eyes and spy Lotane and Kral struggling to their feet.

'Leave her alone, you bastard!' Lotane shouts, blood running freely from his nose and ears, as he staggers toward Nogoth, a discarded gargoyle javelin gripped in his hand.

'I'll rip your smug fey head off!' Kral coughs weakly, although he can barely stand. Weaponless, his face twists in concentration, and he summons fire to envelop his hands.

'You call that magic?' Nogoth scoffs. 'Let me show you magic!'

The Once and Future King stretches his arms out, trails of green and purple eldritch energy coursing over his arms like flashing snakes. Thunder rumbles in the sky, and beneath me, the ground begins to shake and convulse. I don't know what he's about to unleash, but it will be the end of us all.

As he stands there, a godlike figure, I summon the strength to attack a final time. Despite everything he's been hit with, his skin is unblemished, with no scratch or mark marring his perfect body, except for ...

*Come on, Malina. Get up and fight.*

I wince as my broken ribs complain.

Lotane and Kral push forward toward an evilly smiling Nogoth. The Fey King raises hands that pulse with such a sickly light that I don't dare consider what it will do when unleashed.

I run toward Nogoth while he's distracted and leap. Sickness washes over me the instant my left arm goes around his neck, my right arm securing it in place as I attempt to strangle him. I wrap my legs around his waist and lock my ankles as he reaches back to throw me off.

I have no weapons other than my hands, feet, and teeth, and as I hold on to him for dear life, I notice two faint scars, puncture wounds from a bite at the base of his muscled neck. With the last of my strength, I clamp my teeth down.

'NO!' Nogoth screams, his magic dissipating as he reaches back, grabbing at my hair, fingers searching for my eyes. I clamp my teeth down harder, ignoring the pain as my hair is ripped out by the roots, and then Nogoth's hands are wrenched away as Lotane and Kralgen grab his arms.

Impervious to weapons, to magic, to disease, to everything, but not the bite of the Saer Tel he turned.

Like someone dying of thirst, I drink.

Nogoth's blood flows into me like a river of pure energy, unlike anything I've ever known, and my body begins to pulse like a star. Nogoth summons lightning to his hands, attempting to free himself, but Kralgen and Lotane refuse to let go despite roaring in pain. Then, it fades, and the struggle with it.

'Please stop,' Nogoth begs, his voice no longer powerful but pleading, just as his legs give way. 'You don't want this!'

But I don't want to stop. I can sense Nogoth's mighty heart beating faster as it struggles to cope with the blood loss, yet I also know I can't take much more. What will happen when I stop? Will he be strong enough to overcome us still?

He must never get the chance.

Instead of opening my mouth, I tear my teeth free, then bite and tear again and again. Against my teeth, Nogoth's skin is as soft as it feels beneath my fingertips. Blood spurts from the horrific wounds, gushing down his chest in black rivers.

Gurgling reaches my ears, and Nogoth goes limp.

Nogoth, The Once and Future King, The King of the Fey, is dead.

Lotane and Kral let go of Nogoth's arms and step back, eyes wide. There's conflict in their stare, for even though we've succeeded in our mission, my true self has been laid bare. I recall the horror of seeing a Saer Tel feed for the first time, and I can't blame them.

In the distance, the battle still rages, and with their king dead, the dozens of giants and trolls who'd stayed back to let him kill us close in. Swarming around their legs, wolfen snap and snarl, saliva dripping to the ground.

I stumble away from Nogoth's body and puke. I've drunk so much, and whilst energised, I'm also nauseated beyond belief. I call upon my magic, but whilst I can sense it within, swamped by Nogoth's power, it's impossible to summon in my current state.

I always knew I'd die in this fight, and now the end is upon me, my legs tremble as my fear of dying alone is realised.

But then a hand takes mine, and I look across to find Lotane holding it, eyes shining with regret. He's cast his gauntlets aside, and his flesh feels warm, banishing the cold of approaching death.

'We might have grown apart of late, but I'm glad I'll die by your side,' he says, taking me in his arms.

Happiness and relief banish my fear.

Kral embraces us both.

'Let's find Alyssa together,' he says.

Six trolls and giants surround us, and we wait for the end.

***

# CHAPTER XX

The trolls' swords are vicious, gigantic things, twice as long as Kralgen is tall, and the giants wield clubs hewn from tree trunks. They're lifted high in unison by creatures that could tear us apart with their hands like pieces of paper.

I close my eyes, feeling Lotane and Kral's arms tighten around me, warm and comforting.

I've inflicted enough death to know it ranges from painful to excruciating, from instantaneous to drawn out. Hopefully, this should be over quickly, as it doesn't appear they intend to eat us alive.

There's a swoosh and then ... impact.

The metallic tang of blood, acrid smoke, and vacated bowels assault my senses alongside the loud chorus of screams and crying. Yet the symphony of death I hear isn't mine, Kral's or Lotane's.

Reluctantly I open my eyes and extricate myself from Lotane and Kralgen's embrace.

Around us, the trolls and giants are on one knee, foreheads pressed against the hilts and handles of their weapons that they've plunged into the ground. Behind them, the wolfen are on their bellies, paws stretched out ahead of them.

'What's going on?' Lotane whispers behind me.

Bloodshot red eyes fix upon us as the trolls and giants lift their heads.

'What are your orders, my queen?' a troll asks, with a voice deeper than rolling thunder.

I gasp.

*My queen.*

Having killed Nogoth, have I somehow assumed his mantle of leadership?

The troll looks at me quizzically.

'Shall we continue with the attack, my queen?' he rumbles, muscles bunching as he shakes his sword for emphasis.

Kral rises up on his toes, peering across the battlefield.

'They're still slaughtering what's left of our army,' he groans.

'Cease the attack, and withdraw. Quickly now!' I say, my legs weak at the enormity of what's happening.

The troll cups its hands to its mouth and bellows so loudly that I cover my ears.

Kral looks again.

'They're still fighting,' he shouts worriedly. 'I don't think they heard the order.'

I breathe deeply, controlling the sickness and trembling. Death isn't coming for me, but hundreds of others die for every second I waste.

'CEASE FIGHTING AND WITHDRAW!'

My voice echoes across the plain, enhanced by magic and emphasised by a roll of thunder. To my relief, with a roar of acknowledgement, the fey tide turns.

Why are they all obeying me? Will some turn on me the moment they discover Nogoth's death?

I focus, looking through my spirit eye, and there's my answer.

A mass of red threads, thousands upon thousands of them.

Blood Magic.

Obey; Worship; Protect; Love; Idolise; Adore; Respect, and so many more commands resonate as I touch them.

How Nogoth had bound himself to every creature doesn't matter. What matters is, having drained his life, his power, each of these creatures is now unequivocally bound to me.

'They're mine to command. The whole fey army is bound to me ... and if they are, then I'm sure the fey back in their world will be too,' I say softly into the relative silence that has now descended as the clash of weapons and war cries die away.

'Have them kill themselves like those Astorians did,' Lotane hisses, grabbing my arm. 'Let's finish this once and for all.'

I look at him, shocked.

'Absolutely not!'

'Why not? These creatures are evil and have no place in this world!'

'Because it is finished. We won. Should I commit genocide for the sake of revenge? All this was Nogoth's doing, and he's now dead.'

'We should hurry back to our lines,' Kral urges, his timing perfect. 'I don't feel comfortable being out here, and my people will need me!'

Lotane huffs, knowing Kral has intervened to silence him, but it's also the right thing to do.

The eyes of the trolls and giants follow our every move, and they're no doubt listening in on our conversation.

'Have the army make camp here, tend to your wounded, and await my further orders on the morrow,' I address the troll who had first spoken to me.

Lotane clenches his fists.

'They should all be put to the sword,' he grumbles but says nothing more.

As we follow the trail of death and destruction we'd created back toward our lines, a mound of rubble catches my eye, surrounded by the corpses of two giants and five trolls.

'Dimitar!'

Ogres bow as they withdraw past us, and in their eyes shines devotion and love. Where are the horrific creatures that we'd been fighting all this time? Nonetheless, Kral and Lotane arm themselves with discarded weapons just in case.

I climb over the body of a headless giant and search amongst the rubble for any sign of life. Dimitar had come back from horrific wounds before, but as I spy a piece of stone eye, a fragment of chiselled broken lip, and a section of rocky skull, I know this is beyond even him.

The fey had recognised the incredible threat he presented and, despite their losses, had destroyed him utterly.

Kneeling, I close my eyes and pray that his soul has finally found peace.

'Without him, we wouldn't have made it,' Kral says, his face grim. 'He was a good ... man.'

'Indeed, he was,' Lotane acknowledges. 'But a lot of good men and women have died today. Now, let's go and see to the ones that are still alive.'

It's strange. But as we walk back to the bloodied human ranks, it feels like I'm heading the wrong way.

***

'How many World Gates are there?'

'Three, my queen. They are here, here, and here.'

I'm sitting amongst the fey army cross-legged opposite a gargoyle whose wings are half extended to catch the first rays of the morning sun. A troll commander kneels to my left, leaning forward to follow the gargoyle's talon with bloodshot eyes.

Pine Hold, Ssythla and Astoria.

Draw a line between the three World Gates, and it makes a perfect triangle. I've a vague recollection of seeing this on a map before and shake my head in disbelief. Such was Nogoth's faith in his blood magic and ssythlan conditioning that we'd been shown all of this to help fulfil his plans.

I look up from the map, gaze back toward Ast's smoking ruins and shake my head in disgust. It's perverse that the lives of so many good people were taken, but the worst somehow managed to survive.

Not long after Kral, Lotane, and I had returned and started organising help for the wounded, Asterz and Jarval had ridden into camp at the head of a dozen bloodied scouts.

Lotane's joy at seeing Asterz alive had been a knife to my gut, and Asterz and Jarval's account of breaking through the rear of the fey line and staying clear of the combat whilst they'd left the army to fight and die behind them had made me want to puke.

Kral had woven the story of Nogoth's demise, telling in detail how my magical swords had almost decapitated Nogoth. Notwithstanding the subsequent toast raised in my honour, I'd felt somehow betrayed by the lie despite its necessity.

But that's not why I'd left before dawn and sit here amongst creatures of nightmare instead of breaking fast in Ast.

I hadn't been too welcome before, and I'd gotten used to the dark looks and whispered curses that followed me everywhere. But having just saved everyone's lives, I'd hoped to be accepted, welcomed even, but that couldn't have been further from the truth. Outspoken curses followed my every step, things were thrown, and I felt like an outcast, a dirty fey that no one wanted near them.

Of course, they were in pain, bitter, and still afraid. The fey army was camped within sight of the city, but what wounded me the most was that even Kral and Lotane seemed slightly wary around me.

'What are your orders, my queen?'

The gargoyle's prompt is respectful, pulling my thoughts and gaze away from Ast and back to the here and now.

'How long till the World Gates close?'

'Thirty of your days.'

Thirty days. I shake my head. Everything Nogoth had said was deceit, lies, and misdirection. I thought the gates would be open for two years, not less than one. All part of his plan of coercion and manipulation. He certainly hadn't needed two years, let alone one, to conquer everything we could throw at him.

'I want all your gargoyle brethren to carry word across the lands that no further humans are to be killed or harmed and that all fey must withdraw through the nearest World Gate immediately. Go now. Fly fast and true.'

'As you command, so it shall be!'

The gargoyle bows, then launches itself skyward, screeching.

The troll waits patiently, hugely muscled arms folded across its chest, breath whooshing in and out like a bellows.

'Today, I want every uninjured fey to dig two graves. One for the human slain and one for our own.'

Our own. Did I really just say that?

'I also want Nogoth's body to be wrapped carefully in cloth. He will not be left here but taken back through the World Gate for burial in his valley.'

To my disbelief, there are tears in the troll commander's eyes as it salutes. Even in death, with the bonds between them severed, the fey still love their old king.

'Thank you, my queen,' it says, choking with emotion on the words, then turns away, bellowing orders.

I'm dumbfounded. A crying troll, whatever next.

Within seconds, the entire fey army is on its feet, getting to work. There are no complaints, just instant obedience. I doubt there's a single shovel or spade among them, but weapons, talons and paws are put to immediate use.

There's hesitant movement behind me, and I breathe deeply, tasting and scenting the air. Two ogres, both injured, await. I discern no threat and turn around.

A large, bandaged ogre stands before me, head bowed, and I'm surprised to see him carrying my two swords across his arms. They've been polished to a sheen, the nocked edges smoothed and sharpened, the blades lightly oiled. He also has two lacquered scabbards attached to a weapon belt looped over a shoulder. Another smaller ogress behind the first carries a simple black leather cuirass similar in style to the type the gargoyles favour.

They both kneel, raising their arms as if in homage, and I step forward to take their gifts.

The cuirass fits surprisingly well, and the swords settle comfortably at my waist.

'Thank you!'

I don't know what else to say, but it's enough. Their tusked faces stretch into huge smiles, and they shuffle away, bowing and clasping their clawed hands together in supplication.

I watch the digging for a while, the fey gouging huge furrows into the plain, piling up the dirt ready to cover the bodies.

What next after this is done?

Should I have the fey help rebuild Ast as reparation for the damage it's caused?

Even if they did, there's hardly anyone left to occupy it unless ...

Movement near Ast catches my eye as a mounted Astorian makes their way toward the fey lines.

Whoever it is must be brave or ... then I recognise the tousled hair and riding style.

Lotane.

I walk out over the trampled grass, stepping over twisted, rent bodies already covered in a blanket of flies. Discarded weapons and broken armour make the footing treacherous, and I know I've seen this before. Yes, the dreams I'd had of Karson when I was first Chosen had foretold all of this, and yet I'd been too blind to see.

'Malina.'

'Lotane.'

I note his awkward posture, the smile that pulls at the eyes but doesn't quite reside there. He's conflicted once again.

'Why are the fey building earthworks? Queen Asterz and all the survivors are frantic with worry that the fey aren't leaving.'

Some wayward hair falls into my eyes, and I brush it back from my face, smiling sadly.

'They're simply digging graves for both sides. Anyway, I think Asterz is more worried that I won't leave.'

'I told her that's what they were doing. Look, this is a time to pull together, not fight. Asterz knows you killed Nogoth, and she'll reward you,' Lotane says, leaning forward to rest his forearms on the saddle's pommel.

'She also believes it was me who killed her father!'

The alarm in Lotane's eyes is quickly contained, and if he's worried about her finding out, it's because he cares what she thinks of him. I might have won the final battle against Nogoth, but the one with Asterz is still in play.

'Don't worry, the secret will stay with me.'

Suddenly, dizziness washes over me, and I stumble. Unfamiliar voices and images flicker through my head and then disappear as quickly as they'd come.

I'm not even aware of Lotane dismounting, but his arms are suddenly around me, concern pushing aside whatever other emotions he might have.

'You don't look so good. Your eyes are so bloodshot, and you're burning up,' Lotane says, palm to my forehead.

I linger in his embrace, savouring every moment, but the dizziness passes, and I can sense he's ready to let go.

'I'll be alright,' I smile, stepping away. 'Tell Asterz the fey army will depart on the morrow, and I'll escort them through the World Gate. I'll return in about two weeks. Tell Kral to have his Icelandians ready. He'll need me to breach the wall and to cross the River of Tears.'

'Two weeks. Why that long?'

I'm about to remind him that the journey to and from the gate will take a week, and one day in the fey world equals ten here, but I decide not to.

'So you realise how much you miss me,' I laugh, then turn away, leaving him standing there, so he doesn't see me blinking away tears that come unbidden to my eyes.

***

The last time I'd stepped through a World Gate, a fey army had been waiting. This time will be no different, except they're not looking to kill me, for I'm their queen.

As I look around, it doesn't surprise me that this gate has gone undiscovered for a thousand years. It sits in the middle of a stinking swamp, with dying trees, foul-smelling mists and voracious swarms of insects. If it wasn't for my magic firming the ground upon which we walked, the army would never have been able to reach it.

I step through, following the last fey into an unfamiliar landscape.

There's no denying it's the fey world. Towering mountains, gigantic forests, rich grasslands, exotic flowers and insects. It's still the paradise I recognise from my first visit. I'd learned on my journey that with three different World Gate locations back in my world, the same applied here.

The other familiar sight are the two temples on either side of the World Gate. These ones are made of polished black rock with thick golden threads.

The troll commander waits for me at the end of the ramp with an ogre entourage while the fey army, excepting the wolfen, form up around the temples. Gargoyles wing their way to the other temples with orders to return the human captives captured in Nogoth's latest conquest through the adjacent World Gates. Having witnessed and suffered the barbarism and feral behaviour of the older human livestock, those would remain incarcerated.

Over four hundred thousand captives would soon be released to make their way home.

I'm sure many won't survive, but at least they'll die free under a familiar sky.

'Take Nogoth's body to his valley. Have him buried by the reflecting pool at the rear of his house.'

'As you command, so shall it be,' the troll rumbles and gives orders to his ogre underlings to head off south bearing the body of their old king.

Not once has a single order been questioned since I earned the title of their queen. It's a heady power, and now I appreciate a little more why Asterz clings to hers so tightly.

'Have all the latest prisoners brought here as quickly as possible. I also want water and suitable food for several days' travel to be sourced and packed.'

Orders are barked, and ogres rush to do my bidding.

I sit on the cold stone of the ramp and enjoy the sun's early embrace. It's not like me to do nothing as time passes, yet I have a headache to end all headaches, and my vision is blurry. Lotane had noted my eyes were badly bloodshot. It's been a long time since I've suffered from an illness, but that must be what it is. I need to get home quickly, but I don't know where that is anymore. Astoria will have to do for the short term, where Kral and perhaps even Lotane will look after me.

I turn my focus inward, noting with relief that the magical turmoil is settling. Whereas before, I had a pool of magic to call upon, there now seems to be an ocean. Despite its vastness, I imagine wrapping my arms around it all, pulling it close, and I'm rewarded with a comforting pulse of light that matches my heartbeat.

Slowly my headache fades away, yet still, I hold on, immersing myself in the colours of magic.

'What now, my queen?'

I blink in surprise and find the troll commander crouching before me, a look of concern on his broad features. I'm about to ask him to let me be when murmuring and crying reaches my ears, and I realise half a day has passed as the sun is now high above me.

Where had the time gone?

As I'd ordered, the remnants of humanity previously taken from Astoria's lands have been brought to the surface. They stand petrified, huddled together with ogres and trolls guarding them.

Nogoth's army had wasted no time when they invaded Astoria to secure their flank and rear by enslaving the population of the two cities north and east of the World Gate. The vast number of people before me are a mix of Astorians alongside the Surians and Rolantrians taken as slaves.

Tear-streaked and filthy faces look about, full of hopelessness and despair. Some have only been incarcerated a few days, but everyone bears scars from what they've seen and endured.

It's time for me to lead them home.

I take a deep breath, ready to order their release when I note the women in the front rank. Some clutch children to their legs or breasts, but the torn clothes many wear catch my attention.

Kralgen's promise to make the Astorian military pay for their actions comes to mind, but the Astorian men in these ranks aren't military, just civilians from the cities and mines. However, the torn clothes and scratches I can see are recent. Obviously, not every Astorian man is evil, but there's no doubt that every evil man here is Astorian. I just don't have the time to work out who is who.

'This is the day of your salvation!' I shout, my amplified voice carrying across the hundreds of thousands cowering before me. 'Soon, you shall return home to Suria, Rolantria, and Astoria!'

I allow the mutterings and hushed whispers to continue a while before raising my hands and catching everyone's attention with a flashing pillar of fire.

'First, noble men of Astoria. Make your way to the right side of the ramp!'

'Commander,' I say, turning to the ever-present troll. 'Hurry this up!'

The troll bounds away, roaring. Ogres leap into action, firmly separating and corralling the mass of those who'd identified as Astorian men to where I'd directed.

The troll soon returns.

I want you and fifteen thousand ogres to help escort the women and children back to Ast.'

'What about the menfolk?' rumbles the troll, looking down at the group.

'Return them to the temples, except for one. The human world is better off without them.'

'And the one?'

'Bring him to me.'

***

'The Astorians hate you for what you did,' Grawn, the troll commander, rumbles, looming over me as we slowly lead the massive column of refugees toward Ast. 'Although as they all look the same, it's hard to tell them apart from the others.'

'I'm used to being hated. It doesn't bother me.'

Grawn nods. I wonder if he can discern my lie because I am actually bothered.

Most Astorians had turned north and east as we'd left the black marshes, heading back to whatever remained of their lives in Astnor and Astsul and the surrounding lands, but several thousand had decided to return to Ast. I'd been glad to be rid of those who'd left, there hadn't been enough supplies anyway, and it had meant more for those journeying west.

Whilst the malice of the Astorian women doesn't surprise me, the Surian and Rolantrians' reactions have. As I've walked alongside them these last four days since we passed through the gate, there's been no gratitude for the revenge I've given them, no recognition of me saving their lives. All they see is a fey, the hated King Slayer, surrounded by ogres whose companion is a troll.

I look up at Grawn. His solid form reminds me of Dimitar, and I'm shocked to realise that his presence is comforting.

'They're not worthy of you, my queen.'

'Perhaps I'm not worthy of them. I'm responsible for so many deaths.'

Grawn huffs and then taps his bulbous nose.

'To rule successfully, you must first be feared before you are loved.'

'Oh, they all fear me, but somehow I doubt they'll ever love me,' I laugh.

'I'm not talking about your human friends. I'm talking about us,' Grawn says, jabbing a thumb at himself before pointing to some ogres. 'We all feared you, and now, we love you!'

I shake my head in amazement. That a creature such as this could fear anything is beyond me. Yet as he is bound to me, he cannot lie, so the truth of his words is undeniable.

'I'm sorry, Grawn. My place is here. In fact, you and your command need to leave now. I can see Ast on the horizon, and your presence will just cause problems.'

'But what are we to do, my queen?' Grawn asks, his taloned hands spread.

'Return through the gate and live your lives. Find a mate, raise your young and know happiness in your family and tribe. Now, have any remaining supplies passed to those strong enough to carry them, and then hurry off.'

For a moment, Grawn looks lost, tears in his giant eyes as if struggling to come to terms with his dismissal and my decision to stay.

'As you command, so shall it be, my queen!'

He kneels and touches his forehead to the ground before bounding off, calling out in the ogreish tongue.

There's no joy visible on the faces of those behind me. The Surians and Rolantrians are fearful of what awaits, and so they should be. But I will lead them safety from these lands. As for the Astorians, they can see the damage wrought upon Ast and still feel the loss of their menfolk.

As we cross the scene of the battle, the ground remains terribly scarred, but at least the bodies have been buried, evidenced by the large mounds of earth that have covered the mass graves dug by the fey.

I'm impatient to press forward, to find Lotane and Kralgen, but despite their ingratitude, I still feel responsible for the column of misery behind me.

I stand to one side, allowing them to pass.

'Ast is less than an hour away. Keep moving,' I shout, walking up and down the line, trying to encourage them all to a final push to reach Ast before sundown.

Murmurs and disquiet spread throughout the column. Those who are Astorian stand out because they're the only ones looking vaguely happy.

'You're leading us back into captivity!' an elderly woman covered in dirt shouts, and suddenly her despairing cry is taken up by a hundred throats.

'No! You have my word. You will return to your homelands,' I shout back. 'We'll stop here just to rest, resupply and get aid for those who need it. I'll lead you safely from Astoria tomorrow, I promise!'

'Liar!'

'Lying bloody fey!'

'Don't trust her!'

The accusations build to a crescendo and wash over me in a wave of such negativity that my patience snaps.

'SILENCE!' I roar, and my voice rolls across the plain, startling everyone into submission. Even the children are too afraid to do anything but whimper.

Damn. Why couldn't I have held my temper in check?

'Here, let me help.' I offer a young woman struggling with two children.

'Stay away from me!' she hisses, thrusting them behind her filthy skirt.

Time and again, any offer of assistance is rebuffed, with every vehement shake of the head or harsh word cutting me deeply.

'Pass the word,' I shout. 'Tonight, all Surians and Rolantrians camp at the city perimeter. I'll ensure food and water are brought to you. Any Astorians are free to do as they wish.'

Hundreds of tents are south of the city, and I direct the column toward them.

I sigh with relief because whether they hate me or not, I've delivered these people.

***

# CHAPTER XXI

Daybreak.

My jaw cracks as I yawn. Standing, I quickly go through a stretching routine, belt my swords around my waist, and put on the leather cuirass over my sweat-stained clothes. I wrinkle my nose, uncomfortable with my own smell.

*Malina. Before we leave on the morrow, you need to clean yourself up!*

From a charred rooftop that had served as my bed, I look down at the refugee camp, noting with satisfaction the lines of women and children being given food and water from the supply tents.

An hour of binding a multitude of Astorian cooks and medics to ensure they helped alleviate the plight of these poor people alongside the wounded had been time well spent.

I turn my gaze over Ast. Much of the poor quarters lie in ruins, the wooden buildings destroyed by the oil-fed fires the gargoyles had started. Typically, the houses of the wealthy, made of stone, remain mostly unscathed.

I wonder where Kral and Lotane are. No doubt, word of the refugees' arrival has reached their ears, so I'll let them come and find me.

Leaping down from the rooftop, I land light as a feather. Some people give me dark looks and cross the road, keeping away from me as I head back toward the refugee camp.

Tomorrow I'll lead them and Kral, with his Icelandians, south. Two days to reach the wall where more supplies wait. Magic will make short work of creating a hole in the wall and bridging the River of Tears. If I can get Lotane to travel with us, there's a good chance the three of us can travel to Icelandia together, leaving Asterz and Astoria behind.

All this time, I've been searching for a home, yet I now know it doesn't matter where I live. It is who I'm with that matters.

Some Astorian archers ride by. There are so few left, but what remain are likely used to keep the peace. If there's one positive from the decimation the human army suffered, it's that there's now an excess of food and shelter for the survivors.

Like a sword penetrating flesh, the crowds before me part as I approach. I walk in a bubble, repelling everyone around me. Yet I feel buoyed because, despite all the souls I've taken, I'll have saved more.

'Will you keep to your word?'

'Do we leave tomorrow?'

I can't see who shouts the questions, but every face holds a mixture of fear, distaste, and hope.

The same questions are asked repeatedly, and my answer remains the same.

'Yes. We leave at first light tomorrow. Spread the word and be ready!'

As the words leave my lips the final time, I sense a shift in the crowds' mood. All hope disappears to be replaced by fear, and the circle around me widens as people push back in a panic.

'No. They'll not leave tomorrow!'

Asterz!

I turn around, hands resting on the hilts of my sword, and freeze.

She's seated on a warhorse, with Jarval beside her. They both wear their usual plate armour and share a look of undisguised hatred as they look down on me. But it's not them that worry me.

Dundain is on her knees before them. She's been beaten black and blue and has her hands tied behind her. A dagger is held to her throat by a guard. Her large eyes shine with love and sorrow, pleading silently for me to save her life.

The bastards. My blood boils with anger, and I struggle to restrain myself.

Twenty Astorian archers with their bows drawn dissuade me from making any move. Spread out in a semi-circle, they're close enough that it's impossible to miss.

My magic wriggles ferociously inside. If I attack first, I'm sure I can knock them off their feet with a blast of wind, have a dust cloud blind them, or the ground swallow them. Yet all it will take is one arrow to find its mark, and I'm dead. Nor will it save Dundain.

I hadn't even known she'd survived the battle till now, but her life matters to me.

Diplomacy is my only safe option. Too many lives are at stake.

'These are Surians and Rolantrians,' I say, extending my arms in a sweeping gesture. 'I saved them so I could take them home.'

Jarval laughs.

'Who are you to decide anything? You're nothing but a common assassin. These vermin are the property of Astoria. Ast needs rebuilding, and they will be the ones to do it! The only person we want gone is you!'

'What does Lotane have to say about this?' I ask, looking at Asterz. 'Do you think he'll love a queen with no heart?'

Asterz's face darkens. Perhaps bringing Lotane's name into this wasn't a good idea. How will I get myself and Dundain out of this dangerous situation whilst saving the refugees around me? I scrabble for something else to say.

'Astoria owes me a debt. I rescued a hundred thousand Astorians from the fey world. Surely, as a reward, you can let me take these people and Dundain south. After that, you'll never have to see me again!'

'A reward?'

Her face twisted in rage, Asterz looks like evil personified.

'You talk about saving Astorians, but I know you left Astoria's men to die and even *feasted* on another! I couldn't believe the last of it, not until I saw the marks on that woman's neck!' she hisses, pointing at Dundain.

I shift subtly, gauging the archers' positions, the wind, and the ground I'm standing on. If this ends up in a fight, I'll be ready. If only I'd thought to replenish my swords' magic. What power could I have invested in them by now?

'But you're right; I do owe you a debt,' Asterz says, calming down, and the sense of danger passes. 'You did what you had to do. You killed the king ...'

Before my astonished eyes, the archer draws his dagger across Dundain's neck.

'No!'

The shout barely escapes my lips before a hail of arrows thunks into me, slamming through my leather armour like paper, driving me to my knees.

'...my father!' Asterz screams, completing her sentence of death.

I look down in disbelief at the arrows protruding from the hardened leather armour; I'm like a pin cushion. My vision blurs, but I can still make out Jarval dismounting, but suddenly the haze drops away.

The commander smiles cordially as he stands over me, then draws his sword and, with a nod from the queen, chops down.

***

Pain.

Heart-wrenching, gut-twisting, bowel-clenching pain.

Dundain's glazed eyes stare back at me as Jarval's blade hacks at my neck, and the pain changes, evolves, and becomes rage.

I don't feel a thing as the razored edge bounces from my skin, chiming like a bell, or when Jarval tries again with both hands as I rise to stand, uninjured before him.

As I grab the blade in my fingers, I don't even receive a scratch, and snapping the blade is nigh on effortless as if it were a twig.

My hand snaps out, grabbing the top of Jarval's breastplate, and I drag him close before slamming the broken sword tip down through his skull.

He staggers away, blood running down his face as his hands claw feebly at the broken shard. He turns to face his queen, then keels over, face down to the ground.

Time seems to have stood still as I step forward to pluck the remains of Jarval's broken sword from his hand, but then, everything roars back to life.

'Kill her,' Asterz yells above the screams of the panicked crowd, yanking on her horse's reins.

A quick step and I send Jarval's broken sword spinning end over end to plunge into the horse's chest. It drops like a stone, trapping Asterz beneath it.

The archers close in on me, drawing sabres and daggers, and I draw my own.

I duck beneath a horizontal sweep, my blade whispering across a bearded archer's stomach, sending his entrails flopping around his ankles. I twist away from a thrust, severing the hand that held the sabre cleanly at the wrist. I dance and twist, inflicting terrible wounds.

I've always been one of the best. Not as fast as Lotane, as strong as Kralgen, nor as multiskilled as Lystra, but I was a Chosen, and only the strongest survive.

Yet now, I'm superb. The best there ever was or ever will be.

I hadn't appreciated what Nogoth had given me with his death till now.

My reflexes are lightning, my strength phenomenal, and my form absolutely perfect. I don't even need to use magic to defeat the Astorians who throw themselves at me in a berserk rage, nor do any of their weapons even touch my impenetrable flesh.

Driven by rage, I leave them screaming in my wake.

Then there are no opponents left, just a trail of the dying. Limbs scatter the ground, blood spurts from between clutching fingers, and whilst not one of the archers has yet died, I've killed them all, for none will survive their injuries.

Frantic movement catches my eye, and I smile grimly as I stalk toward Asterz.

'Stay away from me, you monster!' she yells, trying to free her sword, although her only hope would be to run, and she can't do that with a leg trapped beneath the dead horse.

I crouch before her, lick some blood from one of my swords, and hiss with delight when tears flood down the queen's cheeks.

'Beg me not to kill you!'

'Please. Please don't kill me!'

Snot runs down Asterz's face, and I laugh darkly, shaking my head.

'You need to try harder.'

'Take the Surians and Rolantrians. Take whatever you need. I don't want to die!' she pleads.

'No. Not good enough,' I say, pushing my sword tip under the queen's chin.

'I'll give you anything you want! Just, please don't kill me!'

She's sobbing so loud that the words are barely audible.

'I want just one thing. Give me that, and you can go free,' I muse.

Frantic nods are all Asterz can manage.

'I want my friend back.' I point a sword at Dundain. 'Can you give me that?'

Silence greets my request, and I shrug.

'Then I'll give you what you gave her!'

Asterz's punches glance from my face as if a grain of sand. I push her head to one side, expose her neck, and lower my head. I'm not hungry for once, yet that doesn't stop me.

I bite down on her neck, ripping out a chunk of flesh, then spit it onto the floor in front of her disbelieving eyes. Blood spurts and froths and I watch dispassionately as her fingers attempt to plug the wound. She wants to say something, but all that comes out is a rattling cough.

I leave Asterz behind, and walk listlessly over to Dundain's body, all my fury gone in a heartbeat and slump beside it, cutting the bonds binding her boney wrists.

Brushing her eyelids closed with my fingertips, I stroke her hair, watching fresh tears fall onto her face, aware that they're mine.

Pounding footsteps register in my head, getting closer, and then, around a corner, charges Lotane with Kralgen and dozens of armed Icelandians.

They come to a ragged stop, disbelief and shock evident as they survey the bloody scene.

'Hold this,' Kralgen says, tossing a giant axe to a fur-clad woman at his side, then he jogs forward to kneel at my side.

'Are you alright, Malina?' he asks quietly.

I nod vacantly, my eyes on Lotane as he staggers over to kneel by Asterz's corpse, taking in her horrific wound, head shaking in disbelief. He draws a dagger and finishes what I started.

'They attacked 'er first,' a shrill voice calls.

'She was only trying to keep us free,' shouts another.

'None of this is the fey's fault.'

'Don't blame her.'

Suddenly, all those who'd only seen the evil in me voice their support, and I sob quietly.

Lotane's face is ashen when he stands. He talks to some of Kral's grim Icelandians, who nod and step forward to deal with the corpses.

Kralgen pulls the broken arrow shafts from my armour and tosses the bent heads to Lotane as he joins us.

'She didn't deserve to die like this,' I whisper, cradling Dundain's head in my lap.

'Come, Malina. Kral's Icelandians will take care of her body,' Lotane says gently, taking one of my bloodied hands in his. 'We should get you cleaned up!'

His touch is so gentle, and his voice so concerned that my tears come even faster.

'More importantly,' Kral rumbles as he eases Dundain's body to one side and pulls me carefully to my feet, 'we need to get drunk!'

***

'Remember when Malina brought those two wolf heads back when we thought her dead!' Lotane laughs, leaning back into a sumptuous lounge chair.

It's one of three positioned around a table in a small but cosy room on the ground floor of a noble's house that Kral and Lotane had led me to.

'Owwwww!' Kral howls.

Lotane and I join in and laugh so hard that tears flow.

'Drink!' shouts Kral, and he pushes another goblet into my hand across the low table between us.

Dutifully I gulp it back as Lotane and Kral do the same. The first half dozen goblets hadn't taken effect, but now I've got a good buzz going.

'Or that time you gave me two pieces of toast to replace my eyebrows that Malina singed off,' Kral wheezes, slapping his thighs, his head lolling back briefly onto the cushioned backrest behind him.

'Even Lystra found that funny,' Lotane chokes out, wiping the back of his hand across his eyes.

'Drink!' I shout, and we up-end our goblets again.

Kral is in charge of refills, and he beckons to an Icelandian who brings over some more jugs.

I feel secure here. The city is in an uproar, but with Kral's Icelandians guarding us, we can drink the whole night away in relative peace.

'Then there was Fianna, always blowing her hair around, especially when Lotane didn't have any!' I laugh, but it dies away quickly as I recall how she died.

'To good times!' Kral says, raising his goblet. 'Now drink!'

The wine tastes a little off as I down it, but that's what sadness does; it makes things bitter.

'I miss them all, even Nestor. Remember how dour he was?' Lotane asks.

'I miss Alyssa the most,' Kral adds softly.

'Drink,' the three of us say together.

I put my empty goblet on the table and knock a flask over, the red contents spilling off the side of the table like blood. We all laugh.

Thankfully there's more to replace it.

'Is it just me, or do you miss the early times after we got through the purges?' I ask, unfastening my shirt a little. It seems to be getting hotter by the minute.

Kral nods vehemently.

'I miss the weapons training. I felt invincible then,' he says, shaking his stone stump.

Lotane chuckles.

'You're still invincible, my friend. The man who took that hand is now dead,' Lotane consoles him. 'But do you know what else I miss from those days?'

Kral and I shake our heads.

'I miss the feeling of purpose. We were going to make the world a better place once and look what we did instead.'

'What about you, King Slayer. What do you miss?' Kral asks.

I find it hard to concentrate. I'm not used to drinking so much alcohol, and I pause, trying to focus.

'Out with it,' Kral cajoles.

'I. I miss.' So many things come to mind, but only one thing really matters.

I take a deep breath. Do I really want to say this?

'I miss going to sleep with Lotane's arms around me, knowing they'll still be there when I awake,' I say, choking up with emotion. 'I miss stealing kisses with him when no one was looking or even when they were. I miss saying that I love him and hearing those words back every day and night.'

Silence meets my announcement, and my heart feels like it might break.

'Drink,' Kral huffs shortly.

I down my goblet, my cheeks burning, then miss the table completely when I put it down.

Kral and Lotane laugh, and my half laugh, half sob joins theirs.

'So, what next, Kral?' Lotane asks.

'I owe it to my Icelandians to take them home. There aren't many left, but we'll survive.'

'What would you like to do now?' Lotane asks, his eye filled with tears as he looks at me.

'I promised to see the Surians and Rolantrians safely from Astoria.' My words come out thick, distorted by alcohol. 'But after that, we should all go to Icelandia together.'

'I'd have liked that,' Kral smiles sadly. 'I love you, Malina. Never forget that.'

'Me too,' Lotane sobs.

The room spins ...

I reach out to console Kral and Lotane. They seem so sad, but I'm falling and falling ...

***

The grass is thick beneath my bare feet, comforting, soft, and cool. It's like walking on clouds.

A fresh breeze ripples my loose, flowing robe. It shimmers, changing from white to black as if unsure what colour it wishes to be. I don't recall owning such a garment, but it perfectly fits my mood. One moment I'm smiling, lost in the beauty of the valley I find myself in, and a moment later, full of anger that I'm lost here, miles from anywhere I know.

To my left and right, distant snow-capped mountain ranges rise, straining to reach the sky ... or perhaps they're already holding it up. Alongside my meandering path, a crystal clear stream tinkles merrily along, dancing over small rocks and pebbles, reflecting the uncontested sunshine, its rays soothingly warm like a lover's caress.

Ahead, an apple tree grows along the grassy bank, its branches laden with ripe fruit.

Underneath, a figure sits, munching on an apple, seemingly oblivious to my approach.

Is this person a threat?

My mood darkens along with my robe, and I adjust my approach, moving away from the stream, putting the tree trunk between me and my prey.

Butterflies abound, fluttering amongst the hundreds of small flowers, oblivious or unbothered by the danger I pose. Magic stirs, offering me its help from a reservoir so deep that I could cause mountains to rise and empires to fall.

Quiet as a shadow, I make my way around the trunk, ensuring my adversary has their back to the treacherous sloping stream bank.

I step around, ready to strike ... but there's no one. Had I imagined someone sitting there? After looking around, I study the grass, and there's no sign of it being flattened by being trodden or sat upon.

Breathing easier, I relax, my robe and mood lightening. Plucking an apple, I take a large bite and am rewarded with a sweet juice that has me yearning for more.

'Hello, Alina. I've missed you!'

I almost drop the apple in surprise, but there's no fear, just joy, as I spin around and sweep Karson into my arms.

'Little brother,' I exclaim, pulling him close, enjoying the warmth of his little arms as they hug tightly back. 'I've missed you too. I never thought I'd see you again!'

'Nor I, you,' Karson laughs, his face alight with a broad smile as he wiggles free, taking my empty hand in his, pulling me along the river bank, skipping, laughing and spinning.

I take a final bite of the apple and toss it aside.

Karson frowns up at me and shakes his head.

'Now, more than ever, Alina, you need to listen to me.'

He walks away, picks up the core, brings it back, and places it in my palm.

'Plant it!' He cocks his head to one side, taps his foot, and pulls a lopsided grin that has me laughing as I drop to my knees.

'All right.'

I scoop a hole in the soft ground with my fingertips, empty the seeds inside, and then cover them with the soil. To keep Karson happy, I step down to the stream, carefully cup some water in my hands, bring it back, and moisten the soil.

'There! Are you happy?'

Karson shakes his head sadly.

'It's not about me being happy, Alina; it's about balance. Doesn't it feel good to know you're helping to create life?'

'When did you get so wise, little one?' I tease, chasing him, tickling him. He cries with laughter, and I sweep him up in my arms for another hug.

'Look behind you, Alina,' he says, the happiness in his eyes replaced by sorrow. 'For that is what you have to balance.'

'I don't want to,' I whisper, suddenly afraid.

'Look!'

He points over my shoulder, and I turn around, unable to disobey.

'Those,' he says, 'are all the lives you've taken or whose deaths you're responsible for.'

A mountain of twisted limbs, vacant staring eyes, blood, guts and flies. Lots of flies.

'I don't like these dreams, Karson. Can't it just be you and I?'

A shake of his head and a sad smile give me my answer.

'I show you this out of love, Alina. This might be a dream, but those corpses are a reality. If you look closely, you'll recognise many of them. Now, turn around again.'

Gratefully I turn my back on the grisly monument to my life.

In the distance, the valley we're standing in splits into two. The landscape blurs, flashing by, and we come to an abrupt halt as the path we're on divides.

The left-hand valley is choked with dead, both human and fey, whereas the valley to the right, as far as the eye can see, is full of demonic creatures, winged and violet-eyed.

'We should turn back, Karson,' I say, keeping an eye on the demons.

To my surprise and horror, one of them approaches, its leathery wings creating a vicious downdraft, and I make ready to fight. Yet rather than attack, it wheels away, but not before I've seen that it bears my face.

'What the hell is this?' I whisper.

'When you awaken, Alina, these will be the two possible futures that eventually await you.'

'There must be an alternative,' I gasp. 'Surely my life can't be this cursed.'

'Life is about balance. I've told you that already. Yet you can't escape the fate that's been chosen for you. Nogoth tried to warn you before he died, but by then, it was too late.'

I collapse to the ground, despair washing over me.

'I'm tired of fighting, Karson. I just want to enjoy the company of my friends. I'm going to Icelandia with Kral and Lotane, and ...'

'You won't see Icelandia again in Kral's lifetime, Alina.' Karson's arms hold me tight. 'Now it's time for me to go. I no longer fear we'll never see one another again, for being Saer Tel, our spirits will always be joined and being immortal, you'll have plenty of time to dream.'

'Wait!'

But it's too late, and everything goes dark ...

***

I open my eyes to find myself in a luxurious, four-poster bed with silk sheets and thick fur blankets.

Gossamer thin drapes hang between the posts, creating a small oasis of tranquillity.

Lotane or Kral must have put me here, and despite the vast amount of alcohol I'd drunk, I'm relieved to feel clear-headed. Today will be a long day, and there's much to be done. Getting the Surians and Rolantrians home is a promise I intend to keep, but with Asterz dead, perhaps leaving today won't be so important.

I recall my dream and Karson showing me my possible futures. Neither of them are acceptable to me, and I'm determined to prove him wrong. From this very day, I'll forge my own fate. Kral loves me dearly, and he'd already said he'd have loved me to join him.

I stretch out across the bed, wondering at the luxury of the room I'm in. It's so opulent that I wonder whose house Lotane and Kralgen have commandeered.

My lips are dry, and as I lick them, a subtle but familiar taste sets alarm bells ringing.

I've been drugged!

A cold shiver runs down my back as I sit up. My stomach rumbles painfully, and my feeling of well-being disappears instantly as the craving to feed leaves me gasping. It's been but a couple of days since I last fed on poor Dundain ... I shouldn't be this hungry, but if I've been given sleep weed, I could have been under for days. Looking down at myself, I realise I'm wearing soft night garments of a material I don't recognise.

I rise from bed, forcing my hunger aside through sheer willpower while worry and rising anger fuel my strength.

What the hell is going on?

The sun dazzles through a window as I pad around the room on rugs so thick that my feet disappear with every step. Beneath the window stands a writing desk, so beautifully carved and polished that it draws me like a moth to a candle flame.

As I approach, I look out the window at the city of Ast ... but it's not there.

On unsteady legs, I grasp for the back of the chair by the desk and lean against it for support as I look out upon the fey world. In the gardens and valley beyond, Saer Tel dance, their human pairings working dutifully at their feet.

'No, no, no. This can't be,' I whisper, lowering myself into the chair, the room blurring as tears well up in my eyes.

How could this be? How could I have gotten here?

Kralgen and Lotane.

Now I remember.

The wine had tasted strange, and they'd been so sad at the end, with them both saying they loved me. Yet they'd also been horrified by what I'd done and what I'd become.

I'd become too monstrous even for them.

As my head slumps into my hands, an envelope catches my attention with my name written on it in a beautiful flowing script. With shaking hands, I open it with a silvered blade, then replace it next to a quill and a bottle of ink on a red velvet pad.

*Dear Malina,*

*Welcome to your new home.*

*If you're reading this, it's because I'm dead by your hand.*

*My death has been so long coming, and I've feared and hoped for it for longer than you'll believe.*

*You weren't just chosen to serve, but to replace me if you were strong enough, and from the moment I saw you, I wanted it to be you, prayed it would be you.*

*It was you, so thank you.*

*One day you'll write a letter such as this, as my predecessor did for me.*

*Rule wisely, Nogotha, Queen of the Fey. Conquer your inner demons if you can, which I was never strong enough to do.*

*With love eternal.*
*Nogoth.*

I sit, staring at the letter, reading it again and again, feeling darkness rising inside me. I'm exiled here with thousands of years of conquest ahead of me unless I fight my inner demons to stop that from happening. At least my dream now makes sense. Thousands of years imprisoned in a world of monsters ... but at least they love me.

Those I thought once did, Lotane, and Kral, have betrayed me. Why stay here, keeping the human world safe, when I've been hated since my birth, right up to my death? I can understand why Nogoth chose his path, for he wanted to wipe out the world's injustice ... or perhaps he wanted revenge?

Was he once a Chosen, a human?

I'm sure I know the answer.

My gods. How long has this cycle been going on for?

I wipe a final tear away. I won't cry again, not now, not ever!

A wardrobe stands tall in the corner of the room, and I stride over and open the door. A mirror reflects my image, and I pause briefly, taking in the violet eyes staring back at me.

I dress, unsurprised that the clothes within fit me like a glove. Artfully tooled leather trousers, tight shirt, belt, and boots. An exquisitely slim silver circlet keeps my unruly hair back from my face.

Nogotha, Queen of the Fey. I certainly look the part ... now to act it!

If I hurry, maybe the World Gate is open, and I can return and bring about an empire of equality that will last an eternity, one where I am loved and cherished.

I pull open the door to my room to find a ssythlan on one knee outside, a platter held at arm's length bearing a goblet.

Never has the elixir of life tasted so good, and my hunger disappears as if it never was.

'The World Gate?' I ask, beckoning the ssythlan to stand, returning the empty goblet.

'Closed, my queen,' it hisses. 'It will reopen again in one hundred of our years.'

I stagger briefly at the news as loss briefly pushes back the darkness. I will never see Lotane or Kralgen again. But then the darkness comes rushing back ... they'd betrayed me, so what matter!

'Damn! Summon the leaders of the various races. I want to know my generals and the hearts of those that follow me.'

'They are already here, my queen, in the gardens. Your inauguration will be the day after the morrow, and they have arrived early to present you with gifts.'

I stride down the corridor, toward the spiral staircase, past the suits of armour and weapon cases while the ssythlan hurries to catch up. Guards at the bottom salute and open the enormous mansion doors.

I step into the daylight to see a semicircle of kneeling figures.

A stone throne before which a stone table has been placed sit upon the immaculate lawn. The ssythlan ushers me toward them, and I take my seat, looking at the creatures before me.

To my right, a giant steps forward and bends down to place a tiny statue of a tree made from red-veined stone on the table. The sculpture is so delicate and detailed, and it's beyond me how such a large and clumsy creature could craft something of such beauty.

The troll approaches next, leaving behind a polished, finely wrought silver cloak pin. A gargoyle places a folded cloak of shimmering feathers beside it. Creature after creature gives something beautiful made with love.

I am in awe at such gifts, yet my mood remains grim.

The creatures all depart until finally only a Saer Tel remains.

'Sister,' she sings, her voice resonating in my mind, dancing over to embrace me with such warmth that, for a moment, my anger diminishes. 'I have a gift for you!'

I look at the table beside me, full of treasures, yet they're meaningless to me.

'I need nothing more, sister,' I smile sadly.

'We all need something more,' she says, speaking loudly in the common tongue. 'For a Saer Tel, one of the most important things we need is to be paired. Your soul is dark, and a pairing will re-establish balance by bringing light to your life. It will help you fight your inner demons.'

'How will pairing create that?' I ask bitterly, unable to contemplate the thought.

'Perhaps we could find out together,' a voice I know so well asks.

'Lotane!' I cry, jumping to my feet, turning to find his strong arms enfolding me, crushing me to his chest. Shadows suddenly impinge on my vision, but they don't bother me because somehow, I begin to shine, my skin glowing, radiating light as happiness banishes the darkness.

Lotane's mouth presses close to my ear.

'Marry me, Alina, and let's be gods together!'

'Forever,' I whisper, and as our lips meet, I know I've finally made it.

I'm home.

# THE END

Dear Reader and fellow fantasy lover.
PLEASE REVIEW THIS BOOK
If you enjoyed this tale, then please take a moment to rate or review it on Amazon. It would mean SO much to me.
Thank you.
Marcus Lee

***

Are you looking for a new magical adventure?

**THE GIFTED AND THE CURSED TRILOGY**

A dark fantasy trilogy set in a dystopian land, with heroes that are at times more demonic than the evil they face. The bloody battles, quests for revenge and fights for survival are artfully balanced with light romance, tales of redemption, and breathtaking magical gifts.

Book 1 - KINGS AND DAEMONS

Book 2 - TRISTAN'S FOLLY

Book 3 - THE END OF DREAMS